A COOL BREEZE ON THE UNDERGROUND

BOOKS BY DON WINSLOW

NEAL CAREY:

A Cool Breeze on the Underground (1991)
The Trail to Buddha's Mirror (1992)
Way Down on the High Lonely (1993)
A Long Walk Up the Water Slide (1994)
While Drowning in the Desert (1996)

SAVAGES:

The Kings of Cool (2012)
Savages (2010)

POWER OF THE DOG:

The Power of the Dog (2005)
The Cartel (2015)
The Border (2018)

CITY:

City on Fire (2022)
City of Dreams (2023)

STANDALONE NOVELS:

Isle of Joy (1996)
The Death and Life of Bobby Z (1997)
California Fire and Life (1999)
The Winter of Frankie Machine (2006)
The Dawn Patrol (2008)
The Gentlemen's Hour (2009)
Satori (2011)
The Force (2017)

NONFICTION

*Looking for a Hero: Staff Sergeant Joe Ronnie Hooper
and the Vietnam War* (with Peter Maslowski, 2009)

DON
WINSLOW
A COOL BREEZE ON THE UNDERGROUND

**BLACK
STONE**
PUBLISHING

Printed in the United States of America

ISBN 978-1-5047-6319-6
Fiction / Mystery & Detective / Hard-Boiled

Version 1
s
Blackstone Publishing
31 Mistletoe Rd.
Ashland, OR 97520

www.BlackstonePublishing.com

For Jean and Thomas, the how and the why

| INTRODUCTION |

IT WAS THE HOTTEST SUMMER in recorded English history, and I was standing on a platform in London's sweltering Leicester Square tube stop. The heat was impenetrable. Suddenly, inexplicably, a cool breeze wafted down the underground tunnel.

Flash forward ten years—I was squatting by a predawn fire in Kenya's Masai Mara game reserve, thinking about a broadcast I'd heard the night before on a crackly radio, in which Joseph Wambaugh said that when he was trying to write his first novel, he wrote ten pages a day, no matter what. I'd been wanting to write a novel for a long time, never got around to it, but now I thought, *If I don't do it now, I never will.* I knew I couldn't do ten pages a day, but I thought I could do five. I went back to my tent, grabbed a yellow manuscript pad, and started writing.

The phrase "a cool breeze on the underground" had been stuck in my head for a decade, and now I asked myself, *What about it? Who was standing in the underground to feel that breeze? What was he doing there?* I came up with the character of Neal Carey, a graduate student who, much like me, was too busy making a living as a private detective to finish his degree.

I had no idea what I was doing. I only knew that I loved the crime fiction that I'd been reading for years (sometimes on stakeouts)—Elmore Leonard, Lawrence Block, Charles Willeford, John D. Macdonald, James Ellroy, Joseph Wambaugh, and others—so I decided to try that, to write a book about a young man, trained in childhood to become a street operative, sent to London to find a runaway teenage girl.

I wrote my five pages a day, no matter what. In African tents, Oxford college rooms (a long story for another time), Buddhist monasteries precariously perched on Chinese mountainsides (ditto), hotel rooms, rented apartments, rented houses, and literally on planes, trains, and automobiles.

Three years later I had a book.

The first fourteen publishers disagreed.

But while I was getting rejection letters (it was remarkable how many people's "current needs" I didn't meet), I was stubbornly writing the second Neal Carey novel. You see, I had no choice but to decide that I was right and the rest of the world was wrong. It takes a certain kind of insanity to do this thing.

When the fifteenth publisher offered me a contract, based on the first two chapters of *Cool Breeze*, I was back in Africa working on a safari, and my wife went through the scattered collection of pages left on desks and in briefcases, backpacks, and coat pockets, and she put the manuscript together and sent it in.

I never did find out where the cool breeze came from.

I only know that it started me writing a book for which I still have a genuine fondness, and launched me on a career that I love and am so grateful to have.

I hope you enjoy reading these books as much as I enjoyed writing them.

DAD'S CALL

NEAL KNEW HE SHOULDN'T HAVE answered the phone. Sometimes they just ring with that certain rotten jangle that can mean only bad news. He listened to it ring for a full thirty seconds before it stopped, and then he looked at his watch. Exactly thirty seconds later it rang again, and he knew he had to answer it. So he set his book down on the bed and picked up the receiver.

"Hello," he said sourly.

"Hello, son!" a cheerfully mocking voice answered.

"Dad, it's been a long time."

"Meet me." It was an order.

Neal hung up the phone.

"What's up?" Diane asked.

Neal pulled on his sneakers. "I have to go out. A friend of the family."

"You have an exam in the morning," she protested.

"I won't be long."

"It's eleven o'clock at night!"

"Gotta go."

She was puzzled. One of the few things Neal had ever told her about himself was that he'd never known his father.

NEAL PULLED ON A BLACK NYLON WINDBREAKER for the cool May night and hit the streets. Broadway was still busy this time of night. It was one reason he loved living on the Upper West Side. He was a New Yorker, born and bred, and for all of his twenty-three years had never lived anywhere but on the Upper West Side. He bought a *Times* at the newsstand on Seventy-ninth in case Graham was late, as he often was. He hadn't seen or heard from Graham in eight months and he wondered what was so goddamn urgent that he had to meet him right away.

Whatever it is, he thought, please let it be in town. A quick trip down to the Village to pick up some kid and bring him back to Mama, or maybe a couple of quick sneaky snapshots of somebody's old lady dining out with a saxophone player.

He and Graham always met at the Burger Joint. This had been Neal's idea. For a hamburger lover, it was mecca. A narrow little place, jammed in on the first floor of the Hotel Belleclaire, it catered to everyone from junkies who had scraped together a few bucks to movie stars who had scraped together a lot of bucks. Nick made the best burgers in town, if not the civilized world, and it was a terrific place to pick up a fast meal and a tip about a ball game. The Yankees would be in it this summer for sure—the Pennant and Series, too, just for the Bicentennial.

Neal went in and waved at Stavros behind the counter, then took an empty booth in the corner. Sure enough, Graham wasn't there yet, but Neal was early. He ordered a cheeseburger with Swiss cheese, fries, and an iced coffee. He settled into the *Times* and waited comfortably for things to happen. In his line of work, waiting well was an acquired talent and a necessity. Neal was a newspaper addict. He read the three major dailies religiously and absorbed the variety of weeklies that New York served up like a heavy dessert. Tonight it was the sports news that interested him, convinced as he was of the Yankees' destiny.

He started right in when the food came. Although "Meet me" always meant in one half hour at the last designated spot, Neal knew that he could double the time and still be waiting on Graham. He figured that Graham did it on purpose to annoy him. So he did his best to cover his embarrassment when he looked up from his paper to see the smiling face of Joe Graham looking across the table at him. Neal was glad to see him, but he didn't want to show that, either.

"You look like a bum," Graham said.

So Graham wasn't being followed or in any immediate trouble.

"Been working hard," Neal answered. "How are you?"

"Ah." He shrugged.

"So . . . what's up?"

"You in a hurry? You mind if I eat? I see you waited for me."

Graham signaled the waiter.

"I'll have what he's having on a clean plate."

"Tell me this isn't an all-nighter," Neal said. "I have a test at eight-thirty in the morning."

Graham chuckled. "You don't know the half. Why do we always have to meet in this toilet?"

"I want you to feel at home."

The waiter came with Graham's food. Graham examined it carefully before pouring half a bottle of catsup all over it. He sipped at his coffee.

"When are you guys going to break down and make a fresh pot of coffee?"

"When you change your shorts," the waiter answered happily, and walked away. He'd put in his time on Broadway.

Graham sat silently for a minute. Neal recognized the

technique. Graham wanted him to ask the questions. Screw him, he thought. *He hasn't called me in eight months.*

"You're going out of town tomorrow," Graham said finally, wiping a smear of catsup from his mouth.

"The hell I am."

"To Providence. Rhode Island."

"I know where it is. I'm not going, though."

Graham smirked. "What? You got hurt feelings we haven't called? Your rent gets paid, college kid."

"How's your hamburger?"

"Maybe they'd cook it next time. The man wants to see you."

"Levine?"

"Levine lives in Providence?"

"For all I see of Levine, he could be living in Afghanistan."

"Let me tell you something. Levine would rather never see you again. Levine would like to see you pumping gas in Butte, Wyoming. I'm talking about The Man. At the bank. In Providence, Rhode Island."

"Montana, and I have a test tomorrow."

"Not anymore."

"I can't screw around this semester, Graham."

"Your professor understands. Turns out he's a friend of the family."

Graham was grinning at him. Graham was an evil leprechaun, Neal decided. A short, round-faced, middle-aged little harp with thinning hair, beady blue eyes, and the nastiest smile in the whole history of smiles.

"Whatever you say, Dad."

"You're a good son, son."

PART ONE

THE SOUND OF ONE HAND CLAPPING

1

NEAL CAREY WAS ELEVEN YEARS OLD AND BROKE. That wasn't a big deal for most eleven-year-olds, but Neal was basically self-supporting, as his father had never put in an appearance and his mother had an expensive habit that more than ate up whatever money she brought home when she was capable of leaving the apartment. So when Neal snuck into Meg's one slow summer afternoon, he was looking for a contribution. He was a skinny, dirty kid like a lot of others on the West Side. There was nothing unusual about Neal and he liked it that way. The ability to blend into a crowd is an important trait for a pickpocket.

There was nothing unusual about Meg's, either. It was just another bar that served beer, whiskey, and the occasional gin and tonic to the remnants of the neighborhood's Irish population. McKeegan, the bartender, felt he'd landed in a pretty soft bog when he'd married Meg.

"There is nothing more fortuitous than wedding an Irish broad with her own bar," he was telling Graham that afternoon. "She'll keep you in food, whiskey, and you know what, and all you have to do is stand behind the bar and make conversation with other drunks, no offense to yourself, you'll be under-standing."

Graham also felt lucky. He had an afternoon to kill, *he* was making a living, and he was parked on a bar stool in front of a cold glass of beer. A child of Delancey Street knew things didn't get much better.

Young Neal slid up and crouched under the bar next to Graham, listening to the sounds of the baseball game with which the man seemed involved. He waited until he heard the crack of a bat and the cheer of the crowd. Experience had taught him that men sitting in saloons lean forward when home runs are hit. Sure enough, this sucker did, and Neal placed his index and forefingers in a gentle pinch on the now-exposed top of the man's wallet. When the man sat back again, the wallet popped into the kid's hand as if it was saying "Take me home." Neal, who didn't have a set at home, nevertheless thought that tele-vision was a wonderful thing.

Stealing something is relatively easy; getting out with it is something else again. A thief is basically confronted with two choices: bluff or run. He needs to know himself and his gifts, his strengths and his weaknesses. A successful thief must possess an unusual amount of self-knowledge. Neal had some infor-mation, readily available from the swift observation that is part and parcel to a poor city kid. He knew that he was in an Irish bar with two more or less sober micks, that he was eleven years old, and that there was no way in hell that he was going to bluff these two guys. He also knew that there was no way on God's good earth that either of these middle-aged guzzlers could ever catch him in a flat-out race. Baseball might be a spectator sport; theft is strictly participatory. He analyzed this data in the space of about a second and a half, and headed full speed for the door.

Graham hadn't felt his wallet being lifted, but he sure felt it was gone. Joe Graham never had much money, so he tended to know where it was and where it wasn't, and even a Roger Maris shot over the left-field fence couldn't mask the fact that his money wasn't in its right and proper place in his pocket. He turned around, to see the back of a little kid running out the door.

Graham didn't pause to comment. Those who take the time to say something like, "That little bastard just took my wallet!" are acknowledging a fait accompli. He shot out the door after the kid, intent on the recovery of his property and the punishment of the perpetrator.

Neal took a hard right out of the door and headed up Amsterdam, then jagged a left on Eighty-first Street. Halfway down the block, he decked right, spun left, and plunged into the alley, where a chain-link fence and an unlocked basement door promised haven. He hit the fence at full stride, digging in with the toe of his sneaker and pulling up with his arms. Neal knew from his childhood days of ringalevio that he could take a fence faster than any kid in the neighborhood. He knew he was being chased, but he also knew that by the time this jerk got over that fence, he would be separating fives from tens in the cool of the basement. He was in the middle of this pleasant thought when something hard and heavy hit him about kidney height in the back and dropped him off the fence. He was sucking for air for just a moment before he blacked out.

Graham had seen as soon as he turned into the alley that this kid was a sprinter and that he wasn't going to catch him. His clean shirt was soaked with sweat now and four beers were bouncing around in his belly and threatening worse. He knew that if this kid got over that fence, his wallet was history. So he grabbed his artificial right arm, a heavy hard-rubber affair, and jerked it out. Then, with his overdeveloped left arm, threw it at the thief.

When Neal came to, he saw a mean little leprechaun leering down at him—a one-armed leprechaun.

"Life stinks, doesn't it?" observed the man. "You think you've picked yourself up a couple of bucks, you just about got it made, and some guy takes his arm off, for Chrissakes, and flattens you with it."

He grabbed Neal by the shirt and hauled him to his feet.

"C'mon, let's go see McKeegan. My beer's getting warm."

He frog-marched Neal back to Meg's. Nobody on the street took any notice. Graham slammed Neal down on a bar stool. Neal watched with fascinated horror as Graham put his arm back on and rolled his sleeve down over it.

"Neal, you little fuck," said McKeegan.

"You know him?" Graham asked.

"He lives in the neighborhood. His mother's on the needle."

"Lucky for you you didn't have time to spend any of this," Graham said to Neal. Then he slapped him hard across the face.

"You want the cops?" asked McKeegan, reaching for the phone.

"What for?"

Neal knew enough to keep his mouth shut. There wasn't any use trying to deny the obvious. Besides, he was a little demoralized, having just been cornered and beaten up by a guy with one arm. Life sure does stink, he thought.

"You do this a lot? Pick pockets?" Graham asked.

"Only since last Friday."

"What happened last Friday?"

"I took a bath in the market."

"You got a smart mouth for a pick who gets caught so *easy*. I were you, I'd work on my technique, *let* Jackie Gleason do the jokes."

Graham looked *real* hard at this child. He was just pissed off enough to call the cops and make the kid take the trip to juvenile hall. But a younger *Joe* Graham had found *more* than one meal in someone *else's* pocket. And you never knew when a smart kid could be useful.

"What's your name?"

"Neal."

"You a rock-and-roll star, or you got a last name, Neal?"

"Carey."

"McKeegan, how about making a *cheeseburger* for Neal Carey?"

McKeegan gestured behind him. "Do you know what this is?"

"A grill."

"A clean grill, and it's going to stay a clean grill until five o'clock. I'll not be dirtying it up for a sneaky thief who's after robbing my customers. I rob my customers."

"How about a turkey sandwich?"

"That, I'll make."

McKeegan turned to the counter to make the sandwich. Graham turned to Neal.

"Your mother takes dope?"

"Yeah."

"Do you take dope?"

"I take wallets."

Neal was confused. Generally speaking, people whose pockets have been rifled don't buy lunch for the rifler. This was the first time in a two-year *career* that he'd *ever* been caught. He knew from neighborhood *wise* guys what to expect from the cops, but this was another thing altogether. He contemplated another run for it, but his back still hurt from the last attempt, and from the corner of his eye he could *see* a thick turkey sandwich on rye with mayonnaise. Knowing that a full stomach beat an empty one, he decided to play along for a while.

"Your mother get money from you?"

"When she can."

"You eat regular?"

"I get by."

"Right."

McKeegan delivered the food and Neal wolfed it down.

"You eat like an animal," said Graham. "You'll get sick."

Neal barely heard him. The sandwich was wonderful. When McKeegan, unbidden, served up a Coke, Neal thought he might like to get caught more often.

When he was finished, Graham said, "Now get out of here."

"Thanks. Thanks a lot. And if there's ever anything I can do for you—"

"You can get out of my sight."

Neal headed for the door. He wasn't one to push his luck.

"And Neal Carey . . ."

Neal turned around.

"If I ever catch you in my pocket again . . . I'll cut your balls off."

This time, Neal ran.

A week later, Neal was hiding in an alley. It was pretty late at night, but his mother was entertaining a customer and Neal didn't feel like going home. People in the neighborhood lived on the streets on summer nights like this one, a sticky New York City night, the air as hot and black as tar. The multicolored carnival of a West Side night went on around him, but he was only dimly aware of the decadent beauty that made up this world. He was savoring a Hershey bar filched from a local bodega on Eighty-fifth Street. He was in a quiet mood, wanting to be alone, and that was why he was sitting in an alley, resting, in a position to see a very large man in his underwear come pounding down a fire escape in pursuit of a fleeing Joe Graham.

"I'll kill you, you bastid." The fat man huffed, his sweaty gut bouncing over his Jockey shorts.

Neal heard a woman's voice and looked up to see a naked blond lady screaming out the window: "The film! Get the film!"

Joe Graham didn't pause a second when he glimpsed Neal Carey. With a quick backhand toss, he flipped the camera down to the boy and kept running. Neal didn't have to be told what to do. When you are holding an item urgently desired by a furious three-hundred-pound man in his underwear, there is only one thing to do. Neal took off down the alley and into the street, where he soon lost himself in the crowd.

The camera was one of those new small jobs, designed to fit—or more exactly to be concealed—in the palm of the hand. It was clearly not a device Uncle Dave carried to get a shot of Aunt Edna on top of the Empire State Building.

Neal hung around the streets for a while, keeping a wary eye out for angry-looking gargantuans, then he made his way over to Meg's. Joe Graham was at the bar nursing a whiskey and holding a piece of hamburger over his left eye.

"I'm thinking you have to use a steak," McKeegan was saying.

"You have one?"

"No."

"Then I'll take another whiskey."

The bar was crowded. Neal squeezed his way over to Graham.

"Did you lose something?" Neal asked him.

"Did you find something?"

Neal handed him the camera. Graham opened it up.

"Where's the film?"

"I'd like a hamburger. Rare. Not the one you have on your face, either. Some french fries and a beer."

"I could just take it from you, child."

"Unless I stashed it somewhere."

"Get the little bastard what he wants," Graham said to McKeegan.

Neal reached into his pocket and handed him the film. "Dirty pictures?"

"Valuable dirty pictures."

"That's what I figured. Where's the gorilla?"

"Soaking his balls in ice, and they should fall off."

"Looks like he caught you a good one."

"Comes with the job."

"Couldn't you get your arm off quick enough?"

"I was scared he'd eat it."

"I didn't think you'd get out of that alley."

"I notice you didn't stick around long enough to find out."

"I thought the film was more important."

"You were right."

"I know it."

"You want a job?"

"Yeah."

"When can you start?"

"Now."

"Okay, hustle down to the Carnegie Deli. Find a guy named Ed Levine, big, tall guy, curly black hair. Tell him you're from *me*. Give him the film. He asks why I didn't come, tell him I'm wounded and getting drunk. You got that?"

"Easy."

"Yeah, also easy to find the fat guy and sell the film back to him, but don't do it, because I'll find you and—"

"I know."

"Meet me back here two o'clock tomorrow afternoon."

"What for?"

"For your education, my son."

So Neal Carey went to work for Friends of the Family. Not full-time, of course, and not even very often. But an agency like Friends often had a need to get quietly into small places and quickly out of them.

2

ANYONE WHO GREW UP IN or near Providence, Rhode Island, knew the old bank building. Its gray stones had held in safety the treasure of piggy banks, the birthday presents from fond uncles, the weekly paychecks and stock dividends of the thrifty working-class New Englanders since rum, slaves, and guns had made the town more than just a farm market. Later, the bank housed the profits from the textile mills of southern New England, from the slate quarries of Pawtucket, and from the fishing fleets of Galilee and Jerusalem, at the mouth of Narragansett Bay.

Everyone knew that the bank was solid. It offered no toasters, electric blankets, or water tumblers to lure prospective savers. It had a reputation: trustworthy, solid, and steady, which brought people to its mahogany counters, where the tellers' windows resembled the gun ports of the old frigates that had brought the city wealth, to deposit their nickels, dimes, and dollars. No deposit was too small or too large.

Something different brought the wealthy customers: privacy. The bank was the Kitteredge family, and the Kitteredge family was the bank. The Kitteredges had been counting, saving, invest-ing, and hiding the money of the rich from the days when British tax collectors sought the Crown's share of the lucra-tive molasses trade to the present era of the slick and merciless IRS computers. The Kitteredges were private people, private in the way that can be found only in New England and the Deep South. For the Kitteredges, a new customer was merely a third-generation saver at the bank. Their steady clientele were those who had hoarded their money during the Revolution until they were sure just how things would turn out. Money from the bank fought the Revolution in the form of uniforms, muskets, and powder, although one Kitteredge, Samuel Joshua, displeased his grandfather by donning one of those uniforms and dying at the head of his platoon on the ramparts of Yorktown. Far more sensible in the old man's eyes were the Kitteredge-financed priva-teers who raided British shipping on the high Atlantic, thereby serving their country by crippling British sea power, while at the same time bringing home nice profits to the bank.

The Kitteredges were fortunate—some say provident—in producing the right numbers of male and female offspring. Kitteredge followed Kitteredge in direct line as presidents of the bank, with few enough descendants to avoid destructive squabbling and just enough to keep the business in the family.

The nineteenth century was a golden era for the family and its bank, an age when patrician attitudes went hand in hand with the growth of the republic. The Civil War brought a financial boom, and another son, Joshua Samuel, marched off to help destroy the evil institution of slavery that his forefathers had done so much to establish. Young Joshua did not march back; a grave was chipped out on the frozen slopes of Fredericksburg, where a Rhode Island general had ordered him to his death. ("A foolish charge," Joshua's father had grumbled at the memorial service, "like someone from Massachusetts might do"—that state having a reputation for fanaticism akin to Rhode Island's legacy of unprovoked orneriness.)

In the halcyon years between Appomattox and the sinking of the *Lusitania,* the bank thrived. The gaslight gave way to the electric light, furnaces took the place of potbellied stoves, but the old stone building itself never changed. (And never would. "A bank isn't plastic, glass, and steel," one Kitteredge had thundered during an infamous 1962 board meeting when a foolish member had proposed a "new look." "A bank is stone, brass, and hardwood. People bring their money here.")

The Kitteredge lifestyle was as conservative as the building itself. "Keep the business in the office and out of the newspapers" was the honored family motto. No Newport mansions or debutante balls for the Kitteredges. Their large houses were tucked away in Narragansett or in the woods of Lincoln, and, of course, the old family home on College Hill remained occupied and freshly painted. The Kitteredge youths attended Brown (Yale, too progressive; Harvard, too flashy; Princeton, in New Jersey), berthed their sailboats in a small cove in Wickford, married girls from New Hampshire and Vermont, and drank their whiskey in their dens at night.

July 8, 1913, stands out as a significant date in terms of the lives of Neal Carey and Joe Graham. On that day, one William Kitteredge, in roughly the middle of the standard twenty-to-thirty-year apprenticeship as vice president of something, beat the scion of another family rather too easily in their weekly tennis match at the club. This gentleman, whose family maintained reserves of at least two sets of books at the bank, confessed to Bill that the light of his life, his young daughter, had run away with an Italian. This disturbing revelation provoked sympathy in Bill, who thought something should be done—quietly.

That evening, Bill had a word with Jack Quinn, a janitor at the bank, whose son, Jack Junior, was a promising young prizefighter and youth about town. Could young Jack perhaps lend a hand? Jack was delighted and located the couple, had a few friendly words of counsel with the now-less-than-ardent husband, and delivered the girl to Bill at his house in town. Bill, in turn, had a drink with his friend the judge, and the marriage never happened. Bill returned the daughter, received copious thanks, and thought no more about it until he was summoned into the office promptly at seven o'clock Monday morning.

"Hear you've been rescuing damsels in distress from the clutches of recent Mediterranean arrivals," his father said.

"That's right."

"Plan to continue this sort of thing?"

"Might."

"Then you had better get organized."

Actually, the old man said, it made sense. The world had changed, and could be a more troublesome sort of place than it should. The bank despised a scandal, he said, and more and more of its old customers seemed to be getting in the newspapers these days. "We're old friends of these families, and moreover, it's in our interest to keep them safe and happy. Cheaper in the long run to take care of some of these little problems ourselves."

So Bill got a raise and a budget and orders to put together an agency within the bank to be at the service of old friends whose private problems might not be best ameliorated by the public arm of the law and the grimy hands of the press. The agency never existed on paper, and the door of Room 211 never proclaimed FRIENDS OF THE FAMILY, but that's what the agency came to be called, and the word passed quickly around the locker rooms and boardrooms of southern New England. The word was that if you needed something done quietly, go visit Bill or drop a word at the bank. That old stone building housed Friends.

Of course, the needs of Friends' clients changed with the century. Prohibition brought in its wake waves of arrests, which, in turn, brought showers of envelopes cheerfully dropped on enterprising police and judiciary. And a wave of a different sort—the immigrant wave—changed New England forever. But the bank held its ground, and Friends, with both fists and favors, carved out a modus vivendi with other tight-knit ethnic organizations. The Depression winnowed the bank's customers and forced the bank to burrow deeply into its reserves to survive until Hitler and Tojo filled the shipyard with contracts and workers again, and people remarked over dinner how provident the Kitteredges had been to invest in the arms industry way back in the Thirties.

New England was already on its way to becoming a backwater, however. The textile mills packed up and went south to the cheap labor, and the business talent caught the train to New York City, whose glass and steel monoliths began to buy up more and more New England businesses. Friends' clients were increasingly finding the worms in the Big Apple, so in 1960, a quiet branch office was opened in Manhattan. Not long after that, Friends hired a foulmouthed, one-armed, too-clever-by-half private dick named Joe Graham. Not long after that, on one of his early cases, Graham was sitting in a quiet West Side bar when some kid tried to pick his pocket.

3

THE 3:40 A.M. TRAIN FROM NEW YORK to Providence said AMTRAK on it, but actually it was something Dante had designed for collection agents to spend eternity in—which is about how long the train took to get to Providence.

The seats were as comfortable as a tax audit, featured torn upholstery, and could have served as the focus for a rousing game of Name That Stain. Old newspapers, paper coffee cups, and beer cans festooned the aisles and the seats. The smell of stale everything perfumed what passed for air.

Neal returned from the snack car with a cup of coffee that was already semi-solid, and a Danish older than Hamlet. Graham had brought his own food, sealed in little Tupperware containers. Graham had ridden the train before.

"Why couldn't we fly?" Neal asked.

"Because I didn't want to."

"You're afraid."

"I don't like to fly," Graham said, munching on a carrot stick.

"Why don't you like to fly?"

"Because I'm afraid."

Graham twisted open a thermos and poured hot coffee into his cup. He smiled at Neal and said, "'Failing to prepare is preparing to fail.'"

Neal huddled up in his sport coat and tried to look out the gunged-up window. They were somewhere in Connecticut, stopped dead in their tracks, as it were, for no discernible reason. Nor did this seem to cause undue concern to the conductor, who was sleeping the sleep of the innocent in the backseat of the car. Neal thought the guy must have the metabolism of a polar bear to sleep in this cold. There was no heat on the train and it was cold for a May morning.

"You want to get drunk?" he asked Graham.

Graham opened the thermos again and held it up to Neal's nose. "Yes."

Neal smelled it and gave Graham his best lost-puppy look. Graham sighed and shook his head and pulled an extra plastic cup out of his bag. He removed it from its plastic wrapping and poured Neal a heavy tot.

"Love you, Dad."

"How could you help it, son?"

The nice thing about Irish coffee, Neal thought, was that it kept your body awake but put your mind to sleep. He sat back and let the warmth spread through him. Eight or ten more of these might make the trip almost bearable. The train lurched forward.

"Wakey, wakey."

"We there already?"

"Not quite. You have to get cleaned up."

Graham was leaning over him. Clean-shaven, straight tie, eyes clear, and breath fresh. Neal hated Graham.

"I brought you an extra razor."

Sure enough, Graham had brought two cordless electric

shavers with him; also a lint brush, Visine, and Cēpacol. Neal hauled himself and his kit into the rest room and got himself into shape. He felt like shit and was surprised to feel butterflies in his stomach. In almost twelve years of working for Friends, this would be the first time he would meet The Man. And The Man had more or less run his life so far.

"Why," he asked Graham when he returned to his seat, "is this the first time I meet The Man?"

"No need."

"And there's a need now?"

"You look good, son. Straighten your tie."

Levine waited for them at the platform. Levine was six-three and at thirty-one beginning to thicken around the middle. He had curly black hair, blue eyes, and a face that was just a couple of six-packs this side of fat. His heavily muscled body didn't begin to hint at his speed. Levine was cat-quick, and that, with his size, made a very ugly package for anybody on the wrong side of his fists. He was a black belt who thought that breaking boards was a waste of time and good wood.

He had come into Friends strictly as muscle, someone to help out a short, one-armed guy when things got out of hand. But Levine had a brain and was very, very hip. Brainy enough and hip enough to know he didn't want to stay on the street all his life. So he'd put himself through night classes at City and came out with a management degree, and now he headed up the New York office of Friends, passing by his old friend and partner Joe Graham.

"Levine hates you," Graham told Neal.

"I know."

This wasn't exactly news to Neal. He knew Levine hated him and he was tired of it. Really tired of it.

"He figures you got a free ride. Fancy private school. Ivy

League. Now graduass school. All paid for. Doesn't think you're worth it."

"He's probably right."

"Probably."

"I don't want his job, Dad."

That was the problem, Neal thought. Levine knew that Neal was being groomed. Neal knew it; Graham knew it. The Man was paying for his master's degree, for the upscale clothing, for the speech teacher who had taken away Neal's street dialect. But groomed for what? Neal didn't want to run Friends. He wanted to be an English professor. Honest to God.

"I know. You want to teach poetry to fags."

Well, not exactly. Eighteenth-century English novels . . . Fielding, Richardson, Smollett.

"How many times do I have to say it?" Neal asked. He had told Ed. He had told everybody. He had written The Man. Don't put me through any more college, because I'm not going to stay with you forever. It was all right, they said. "Work for us when you can, part-time, case by case. No strings attached." Then they jerk you out of classes two weeks before finals. You don't get to be an English professor by flunking your graduate English seminars. Even getting a B could be death.

"Maybe if you hadn't pronged his wife," Graham said.

The train was pulling into the grimy Providence suburbs.

"She wasn't his wife then," Neal said. He'd been over this ground so many times. "Christ, I introduced them."

"Maybe Ed just figures you got everything he should have had. First." Neal shrugged. Maybe that was true. But he hadn't asked for any of it.

PROVIDENCE IS THE KIND OF CITY where all the men still wear hats. The soul of the city was stuck back in the good old Forties, when you kept a lid on things and rooted against the Japs, the Germans, and the Yankees, not necessarily in that order. A hat was a symbol of respectability, a nod to the order of things, to a city run by Irish politicians, Sicilian gangs, and French priests, all of whom came together for Knights of Columbus breakfasts and Providence College basketball games and otherwise stayed in their respective realms.

Union Station was a perfect representative of the city. Sad, drab, dirty, and hopeless, it was the right place to enter Providence. You didn't get your hopes up.

Levine greeted them as they got off the train.

"Laurel and Hardy," he said.

"Hello, Ed," said Graham.

Levine ignored Neal. He said to Graham, "Anybody follow you?"

Graham and Neal exchanged an amused glance.

"I think we're clean, Ed."

"You better be."

"Well, there was that guy with dark glasses, a fake mustache, and a trench coat. You don't suppose . . .?"

Ed didn't laugh. "C'mon."

He led them downstairs into the old terminal, where a few old winos held some ragged newspapers down on the old wooden benches. A couple of them were watching the dust filtered through the dirty, yellow windows.

As they walked past a stand of metal lockers, Ed grabbed Neal by the neck and pushed him none too gently against a locker. He lifted Neal until only his toes touched the floor. Graham started to move in but was stopped by a straight-arm and an ice-cold look.

Neal tried to slide out of the hold, but Ed's big arms held him tight. He managed to get his own arms inside Ed's and grab him by the collar. It was merely a symbolic hold.

"Now listen to me, you little bastard," Ed whispered. "This job is important. Got it? Important. You're going to do just what you're told, just the way you're told to do it. None of your smart mouth or your smart ideas.

"You are the last person in the world I'd pick for this job, but The Man wants you, so it's you. So you don't fuck around and you don't fuck up. Because if you do, I'm going to bust you up. I'm going to hurt you real bad. Got it?"

"Jesus, Ed," said Graham.

"Got it?"

"You're going to do this to me sometime, Ed, and I'm . . ."

Ed tightened his grip and laughed. "You're going to do what, Neal? Huh? What are you going to do?"

Neal could barely breathe. He needed air—even Providence air. Levine could break him into little bits without breaking a sweat. The book said to hit Ed in the nose with the heel of his palm. The book wasn't going to get killed.

So Neal did the best thing he could under the circumstances. He kept his mouth shut. After a few long seconds, Ed let him go and walked away. Graham rolled his eyes at Neal and hurried after Ed.

Neal slouched against the lockers and caught his breath. Then he shouted after Levine, "So, Ed! How's the little woman?"

He watched as Graham nudged Levine through the door. Neal was getting tired of this shit—very tired.

4

AT FORTY, ETHAN KITTEREDGE LOOKED younger than Neal thought he would. A lock of ash blond hair fell over his forehead and the pale blue eyes that peered from behind his wire-rim glasses. He was about five ten, Neal guessed, and weighed maybe one seventy, one seventy-five. The body under the gray banker's suit was trim: tennis or handball.

Then Neal quit playing Sherlock Holmes, because The Man was reaching out his hand and smiling.

"You must be Mr. Carey," he said. His handshake was firm and quick: nothing to prove.

"And you're Mr. Kitteredge." Witty, Neal, he thought. Great first impression.

"I've heard a lot about you," Kitteredge said. "How is your graduate work coming?"

"I'm missing an exam as we speak. Otherwise, it's going great, thanks."

Graham found something fascinating on the floor to stare at. Levine stared at Neal and shook his head.

"Yes, I chatted with Professor Boskin about it," Kitteredge

said. If he was bugged, he didn't show it. "He mumbled something about giving you an Incomplete."

"That was nice of you to do, Mr. Kitteredge, but I like to finish what I start."

"Just so. Gentlemen, please sit down. Coffee, tea?"

Three wooden chairs had been placed in an arc facing Kitteredge's desk. Levine sat down on the right, Graham on the left. Neal plunked himself down in the remaining chair. The center of attention.

Kitteredge stepped to a silver coffee service. Neal noticed he moved in the awkward manner produced by generations of New England breeding—stops and starts which imply that any choice of motion is merely a necessary evil, that the real virtue is to remain still. Nevertheless, he managed to pour four cups of coffee and serve them around.

This took a while, and Neal used the quiet moments to study the office, which was pure bank, pure Kitteredge. The twentieth century had yet to intrude its vulgarities. Sunlight shone a soft, filtered amber on a room ruled by mahogany and oak. Glass-enclosed bookshelves lining the walls housed leather-bound sets of Dickens, Emerson, Thoreau, and, of course, Melville. Bowditch's *Navigation* held a prominent spot, flanked by various obscure whaling memoirs and sailing treatises. Wooden models of old China clippers completed the decor. These were the vessels that had carried Kitteredge tea, Kitteredge guns, Kitteredge opium, and Kitteredge slaves across the oceans, and Neal imagined that the profits from these voyages still rested beneath his feet in Kitteredge vaults.

One modern memento held the pride of place. An exquisite scale model of the sloop *Haridan* sat on the glossy polished oak of Ethan's desk. Some skilled craftsman had faithfully rendered the boat's sleek structure and clean lines. Ethan spent every free moment on *Haridan*, sailing Narragansett Bay, Long Island Sound, and the open Atlantic. He often docked on Block Island, where he kept a summer home. For Ethan Kitteredge, responsible banker, responsible husband, responsible father, *Haridan* meant rare and precious moments of heady freedom.

The coffee successfully served, Kitteredge took his seat behind his desk and pulled a file from the top center drawer. He looked at the file for a moment, shook his head, and handed it across the desk to Neal. Then he sat back in his chair and pressed his fingers together in "This is the church, this is the steeple" fashion.

Kitteredge talked like he walked. "Some . . . uh . . . old family friends have a bit of a . . . problem, and we have offered our . . . services . . . to assist them in finding a . . . resolution."

He smiled, as if to suggest that disorderly people were amusing, weren't they, and a bit of a bother, but they are our friends, and we must do our best. He paused for a moment to allow Neal to open the file.

"Senator John Chase comes from a prominent Rhode Island family," said Kitteredge. "The family name has undoubtedly been an asset . . . in his political progress, but I hasten to add that the Senator is a talented, intelligent, and . . . ah . . . energetic man."

Okay.

Kitteredge continued: "The Senator sits on several important committees, where his performance has attracted . . . national attention, from the press as well as party professionals. Despite the somewhat distasteful fact that John is a Democrat . . . we support him in his ambitions."

Money in the bank.

"The probable Democratic nominee will need to look northward for a running mate. Ah . . . emissaries have already been sent."

Kitteredge paused to allow the import of this last statement to sink in.

It didn't.

So what? Neal thought. Despite the somewhat distasteful fact that I'm going to vote for whatever Democrat is running, what's all this have to do with me?

"There is, however, a problem."

Which is where I come in.

"The problem is Allie."

Neal turned a few pages of the file and saw a picture of a teenaged girl. She had shiny blond hair and blue eyes and looked as if she belonged on a magazine cover.

Kitteredge stared at the model of *Haridan* as he said, "Actually, Alison always has been the problem."

He seemed lost in his thoughts, or in some more happy memory on board his boat.

Neal said, "But specifically now?"

"Allie has run away."

Yeah, okay, so we'll go get her. But there was something else going on here, Neal sensed. Things were a little too tense. He looked at Graham and didn't see a clue. He looked at Ed, but Ed wouldn't look back.

"Any idea where?" Neal finally asked.

"She was last seen in London," Ed said. "A former school-mate saw her there over a spring-break trip. He tried to speak to her, but she ran away from him. It's all there in your file."

Neal looked it over. This schoolmate, a Scott Mackensen, had seen her about three weeks ago. "What do the British cops say?"

Kitteredge stared harder at the boat. "No police, Mr. Carey."

This time, Ed did look at Neal—hard. Neal buried his face in the file, then asked, "Alison is seventeen years old?"

Nobody answered.

Neal looked through the file some more. "A seventeen-year-old girl has been gone for over three months and nobody has called the police?"

Another few seconds of silence and Kitteredge would actually will himself onto the model boat: a tiny model captain on a toy boat.

Levine said, "The Senator was reluctant to risk publicity." Less reluctant to risk his daughter.

"Does the Senator like his daughter?" Neal asked.

"Not particularly."

This came from Kitteredge, who continued: "Nevertheless, he wants her back. By August."

He wants her back. Not right away, not tomorrow morning, but by August. Let me see, what happens in August? It gets hot and muggy, the Yankee pitching falls apart . . . oh, yeah. The Democrats have a convention.

"I trust you will not be offended, Mr. Carey, when I say that sometimes a . . . situation . . . arises that requires a blend of the . . . common . . . and the sophisticated. When someone is needed whose education has occurred as much . . . in the street . . . as well as in the classroom. This is just such a case. You are just such a person."

Except I don't want to do it. God, how much I don't want to do it. Not after the Halperin kid. Please, no more teenage runaways. Never again after the Halperin kid.

Levine frowned as he said, "You're going to go to London, find Alison Chase, and bring her back in time for the Democratic convention."

No I'm not.

"What happens if Chase doesn't get nominated, Ed? You want me to throw the kid back?"

"Your fine sense of moral indignation will not be required, Mr. Carey."

"I'm not the man for this job, Mr. Kitteredge."

"The Halperin . . . tragedy . . . was an aberration, Mr. Carey. It could have happened to anyone."

"But it happened to me."

"It wasn't your fault, son."

"Then why have I been on the shelf since it happened?"

Kitteredge's hand traced the sleek bow of *Haridan*. "The . . . hiatus . . . was for your benefit, not Friends'."

Well, then, it worked. After the drinking, and the insomnia, and the nightmares had gone on for a while, I found Diane. And school again. And now I don't want to come back.

"For once, I agree with Carey, Mr. Kitteredge," said Ed. "He's wrong for this one."

"I'm sorry to pull you out of your classes, but your adviser understands," Kitteredge said. "He's a friend of the family."

So that's it, Neal thought. You bought me; you own me.

"I'm sorry, Neal, but this assignment is important . . . vital."

Neal closed the file and put it in his lap. He knew a dismissal line when he heard one. "I'll need to talk to the Senator and Mrs. Chase as soon as possible."

Because the first place to start looking for a runaway, he knew, is at home.

"THIS IS A CASE FOR THE NEW YORK RANGERS," Neal said to Graham out on the sidewalk.

"It stinks on ice, all right. But there it is, son. You gotta pay rent."

They were following Levine they knew not where, and he was pacing out in front of them.

"Just because she was in London three goddamn weeks ago doesn't mean she's there now. A kid with her money could be anywhere in the world. And even if she is in London, there are what, twelve, thirteen million people there with her? The odds on finding her are—"

"Shitty. I know."

Levine led them into a parking garage.

Neal kept at it. "So what's the point?"

"The point is . . . it's your job. You do your best, you take the money, you forget about it."

"Cold."

"Hey."

They were walking up the ramps. What does Ed have against elevators? Graham asked himself.

"And why do they all of a sudden want their kid back? Why now, why not three months ago when she first took off?"

"Talk to them."

They were on the third level, the orange one, when Ed turned around.

"White Porsche. Guy's name is Rich Lombardi," he said to Neal. "He's Chase's aide. He'll brief you, take you to the Chases'."

Graham tried to look serious. Neal didn't bother. "What's all this *Mission: Impossible* crap, Ed?"

"Professionalism."

"Right."

"Everything you need to know is in the file."

"Got Allie's London address in it?"

"Fuck you."

"I'll need some prep time in the States."

"For what?"

"For trying to find out a little about this kid. For talking to the boy who saw her. Little shit like that."

"Read the file. I already talked to him."

"So go get her then."

"You don't have a lot of time on this thing."

"No kidding."

"So get going."

Graham put his heavy rubber arm around Neal's neck and pulled him a few feet away. "You know Billy Connor, the alderman? You know how much he takes in under the table? Think about how much a vice president hauls in. Don't fuck around with this one, son. See you back in the city."

"Take it easy, Dad."

Neal had taken about five steps away from them when he heard Ed's cheerful voice.

"Hey, Neal, try to bring this one back alive, okay?!"

THE GUY IN THE DRIVER'S SEAT of the white Porsche was reading the Providence *Journal* when Neal tapped on the window. He looked about thirty. Thick, wavy black hair tamed by cutting it short. Brown eyes. Pressed jeans, red sweater, and running shoes. White socks. He seemed confident and comfortable and was probably the kind of a guy who looked in the mirror and said, "Confident and comfortable."

The guy smiled broadly as he rolled the window down. "You're Neal Carey, right?"

"And if you know I'm Neal Carey, that makes you Rich Lombardi."

"Hey, we're both right."

Neal stepped away from the door so Lombardi could get out. Lombardi shook Neal's hand as if he could pump money out of it.

"I have to tell you we're really glad you're on board, Neal."

Have to tell me?

He took Neal's shoulder bag and slung it into the backseat. "Hop in."

Neal hopped in. In fact, he sunk into the deep upholstery of the bucket seat. If Chase's gofer drives a Porsche . . .

"We hear you're the best."

"Hey, Rich?"

"Yeah, Neal?"

"Want to do me a favor?"

"Hey, you're doing us one, right?"

"Quit stroking me."

"You got it." He started the car, took a perfunctory glance in the rearview mirror, and backed out of the slot. "I mean, the way we hear it, if you'd been at the Watergate, Nixon would still be President."

"Good thing I wasn't there, then."

"Hey, you got that right."

Hey.

"Where are we going, Rich?"

"Newport. You ever been?"

"No."

Lombardi wheeled the car in to the light traffic. He made a few semi-legal maneuvers through the narrow downtown streets and then hit the entrance ramp onto I-95. If he was worried about cops, his foot sure wasn't.

"We'll take the scenic route," he said.

THE SCENIC ROUTE TOOK THEM across two bridges that spanned Narragansett Bay. Sailboats danced on the blue water.

"Welcome to Newport," Lombardi said. He turned down Farewell Street, which ran alongside a cemetery, and drove on past the quaint houses that had stood since before the Revolution. The island town of Newport had seen many lives, having been a pirate haven, a fishing port, and a home for whalers and sea traders. Widows' walks and carved wooden pineapples attested to the maritime tradition. The captains' wives would stroll the widows' walks, scanning the horizon for the sight of a sail that might be bearing their husbands home. These stalwarts, once home, and not having been with their mates in maybe two years, would place a pineapple on the front steps when they were ready to leave the bedroom and receive visitors. Eventually, the carved pineapple became a symbol of hospitality. Or fertility. Or sexual satiation.

There was actually zoning in certain parts of old Newport that would demand the houses be painted only in colors available in Colonial times. The BMWs could be any color, though.

Around the turn of the twentieth century, Newport became a playground for the old and new rich, whose mansions lined Bellevue Avenue and the Cliff Walk and were just "summer homes." These cottages, each about the size of Versailles, were inhabited by their owners for about seven weeks in the short Rhode Island summer. They survived the bitter, windswept winters, the corrosive salt air, and the autumn hurricanes, only to succumb to the mundane but lethal assault of the graduated income tax. Most of the larger places had become museums or junior colleges. Few survived intact. One of the few was the Chase home.

Lombardi entertained Neal on the drive with a description of Allie.

"Allie Chase," he had begun, "is one messed-up kid."

"I sort of figured that out."

"Alcohol, drugs, whatever. Allie has done it. Last time I searched her room in D.C., I found enough stuff to stock a Grateful Dead concert. Allie doesn't care if she goes up or down, just as long as she goes."

"When did this start?" When did this start? Christ, I sound like the family physician. Neal Welby, M.D.

"Allie's what, seventeen? Around thirteen, I guess. Call her an early bloomer."

If they noticed it at thirteen, it means she really started at eleven or twelve, Neal thought.

"Make a list of the best boarding schools in the country," Lombardi continued, "and title it 'Places Allie Chase Has Been Thrown Out Of.' She's had at least one abortion we know about—"

"When?"

"A year ago last March, and affairs with at least two of her teachers and one of her shrinks. Title their book *Men Who Will Never Work Again,* by the way."

"Are you telling me all this so Mom and Dad won't have to?"

Lombardi laughed. "A big part of my job is to spare the Senator any embarrassments."

"And Allie's a big one."

"The biggest. *Cops and Reporters I Have Bullied or Bribed,* by Rich Lombardi. Drugs, minor in possession, shoplifting . . . all gone without a trace."

"Congratulations."

"A lot of work, my friend. Still and all, I like the kid."

"Yeah?"

Lombardi look startled for a second, then laughed. "Oh, no, babe. Not me. I like my job. You have a suspicious mind, Neal."

"Yeah, well . . ."

"Comes with the territory, I'm into it. So here's the problem, Neal. We think we have a real shot at the VP thing, and after that, who knows? The Senator is of that stature, Neal. Trust me on that, okay?"

"Okay."

"Right. Call our movie *Remember the Eagleton.* Conceptually speaking. You remember the Eagleton thing, Neal. McGovern's people tab this senator from the Show-me State, turns out his brain runs on batteries. The Party is a little touchy on the subject. Now they check these things out a little more closely. Like a proctoscope."

"So a drugged-out, boozing teenage thief stands out."

"There we go."

"I'd think, then, you'd want her to stay disappeared."

Lombardi stopped the car at a gate. pulled one of those garage-door gadgets out of his pocket and hit a combination of numbers. The gate swung open.

"Ali Baba," he said. "It's this post-Watergate ethics thing, Neal. Everybody's talking values. Family. You have a front-runner who's been 'born again,' although you'd think once was enough, right? Everybody looking for *Mr. Smith Goes to Washington*. Shit, we'd probably run Jimmy Stewart, except he's a buddy of Ronald Reagan's."

Lombardi pulled the car slowly down a long, crushed-stone driveway flanked by willows.

"The front-runner," Lombardi went on, "dresses like Robert What's-his-name in *Father Knows Best*, and drags his daughter around all over the place. We have more kids in this campaign than in the Our Gang comedies."

"Maybe Chase should just buy a dog, with a cute little ring around the eye."

"I'll make a note. But seriously, Neal, we have to have Allie back by convention time."

"Looking like Elinor Donahue."

"Yeah. And quietly, Neal. The press and the Party people are going to be all over us."

He parked the car on the side of the circular driveway in front of the house, or in front of part of the house. The house was endless, like *The Ancient Mariner*. A broad expanse of mani-cured lawn led down to the ocean and a private dock and boat house. Neal saw a fence he assumed screened a pool, and a double tennis court. Grass.

"Where's the helicopter pad?" Neal asked.

"Other side."

Lombardi handed Neal's bag to your basic liveried servant, who disappeared with it.

"Hey, Rich, I have an idea. Maybe you could make like Allie never existed—airbrush her from photos, steal her birth records, kill anyone who remembers her . . . ."

"Pretty good, Neal. But don't joke like that in the house, okay?"

Okay.

Senator John Chase was one of those rare people who resemble their photographs. He was tall, craggy, and muscled, with an Adam's apple and a set of shoulders that competed for attention. He looked like an Ichabod Crane who had bumped into Charles Atlas on the road someplace. He stalked into the room and headed straight for the bar. "I'm John Chase and I'm having a scotch. What are you having?"

"Scotch is fine, thank you."

"Scotch is fine, and you're welcome. Soda or water?"

"Neither."

"Ice?"

"Mr. Campbell in fifth-grade science told me ice melts and becomes water."

"Mr. Campbell wasn't drinking fast enough. Here you are."

Just because the room was exactly what you'd expect doesn't mean it didn't impress, Neal thought. Three walls were glassed in, and all the furniture was casual and expensive. Each seat offered an ocean view. Neal took the proffered drink, perched himself on the edge of the sofa, and took a sip. The whiskey was older than he was. A point that Chase picked up on right away.

"Are you as young as you look, Neal?"

"Younger."

Chase turned a chair around and sat down, leaning over the back. It was a campaign photo of the no-nonsense legislator getting down to some serious turkey talking. "I thought the bank would send somebody a little more mature."

"You can probably still trade me in for the toaster or the luggage."

"How old are you, Neal?"

"Senator Chase, how old do I have to be to find her? How old did you have to be to lose her?"

Chase smiled with all the joy of a dog eating grass. "Rich, get Mr. Kitteredge on the phone. This isn't going to work out."

Neal finished off his scotch and stood up. "Yeah, Rich, get Mr. Kitteredge on the phone. Tell him the Senator wants Strom Thurmond or somebody."

"Let's just everybody sit down, shall we?"

Neal looked at the woman who had just spoken, and couldn't believe he hadn't noticed her standing in the doorway. She was a lovely woman and she stood framed in the doorway just a second longer than necessary to let Neal realize that she was a lovely woman. She's made such entrances into this room before, Neal thought. She used the door frame like Bacall used a movie screen, but she was small. Her long blond hair was pulled tightly back, almost prim. Brown eyes flecked with green smiled at him. She wore a black jersey and jeans. She was barefoot. She walked over to her husband, took a sip of his drink, made a face, and moved behind the bar, where she poured grapefruit juice over crushed ice. Then she sat down on the opposite end of the sofa from Neal and pulled her legs up under her. Nobody said a word during all this. Nobody was expected to.

"Neal Carey is twenty-three," she said to the room at large in a voice that whistled "Dixie."

"How do you know?" Chase asked.

"I inquired."

"And you don't think he's too young?"

"Of course I do, John. I think they're all too young. But what you and I think hasn't worked out all that well, has it?"

She fixed her husband with those brown eyes. The issue was settled.

Then she turned them on Neal. "I'll bet you have some questions for us."

IT WAS ALL PRETTY MUCH as Rich Lombardi had described. Alison Chase was a brat of the first order, a spoiled baby turned spoiled kid, turned spoiled teenager, and on the fast track toward turning ruined adult. Bored by age ten, jaded by thirteen, hopeless by the time she celebrated sweet sixteen, Alison was the classic case of too much too soon and too little too late.

Child Allie had garnered all kinds of attention from the doting parents who hauled her out to perform for dinner guests and hauled her back in when the evening's supply of cute had been played out. She made the usual adolescent progression from ballet to horses to tennis, and had littered New England and Washington with the tattered detritus of dance teachers, horse masters, and court coaches. The proud parents made all the recitals, most of the field trials, and quite a few of the tennis matches until Allie started losing and the fun went out of it.

As Allie grew up, John Chase's political career thrived and the demands of the young congressman's time increased, especially when he made the giant step to Senator. Likewise, the politician's wife made her obeisance to the Junior League and the torturous committees of Washington wives who devoted their afternoons and evenings to worthy causes such as saving other people's children.

Nothing was too good for Allie, however, so off she went to the very best schools, first to day schools in D.C., and later to those New England boarding schools whose role it is to prepare young women for the next generation of committees. And as Allie had learned young that she had to perform to get attention, perform she did—badly. Because while nothing was too good for Allie, Allie was never good enough for Mom and Dad. Not the tentative jeté, the imperfect seat, the lazy backhand that sliced out, certainly not the grades that started with *B*'s and made a steady slide to *F*'s as desperate but futile stabs at perfection gave way to sullen indifference and then determined screwups. If she could not be the perfect success, she would be the perfect failure. If she could not be the ideal princess, she would be the ideal dragon. She would turn her beauty around to be the beast. And nobody had intended that to happen: not Mom or Dad, not the coaches or the teachers—not even Allie.

What in most girls was adolescent rebellion settled into a protracted war: Allie against her folks, Allie against her teachers, Allie against the world, Allie against Allie. She had no real friends, just a series of temporary allies and co-conspirators. She did most of her talking to shrinks, then stopped talking to them altogether, unless to exercise her blossoming talent for sarcasm and disdain.

Allie discovered early on that the pretty bottles in the household bars and liquor cabinets gave her a powerful weapon in her war against life as she knew it. Surreptitious sips from guests' glasses soon became nighttime raids to snatch half-full bottles, bottles that gave her a breezy high to chase boredom away, smoothed the anxieties, and placed her parents at the far end of a telescope when looked in at the wrong end.

She met the challenge when Mom and Dad took to locking the liquor cabinets, as willing cohorts at school taught her that credit cards opened doors in more than the symbolic sense, and that your basic manicure tools, when handled with panache in a manner never described in *Seventeen,* will open most of the locks installed to prevent the servants from pilfering.

Later on, she discovered the potential hidden in Mom's medicine cabinet. How when you drop a Valium in a glass of scotch, your afternoon is pretty much taken care of. She drifted through entire days and nights without a hassle in sight or a care in the world except how to restock the chemical larder. An unusually cooperative shrink bought her story about anxiety attacks and prescribed the stuff for her, in nifty five and ten mils, and Allie became known in the hallways of academia as a girl who could actually give pharmaceutical change. Then Allie went to another doctor and claimed to be really, really depressed, whereupon the good doctor referred to his *PDR* and discovered that the treatment for depression was an antidepressant and wrote scrip for it. So Allie had an unlimited and legally sanctioned supply of speed. Allie had her dawns and dusks, and could swap and trade with her friends.

Teenage boys, their hormones bouncing around like Ping-Pong balls in a vacuum, sniffed her out as an easy mark. Allie discovered sex, which wasn't so bad except she didn't discover birth control with it, and she got pregnant. Scared enough to confide in her mother, Allie then made the discreet visit to the discreet office. ("Dad is going to have you killed," she told the doctor and nurse, "to keep you from talking.") After that, teenage boys became too immature for Allie, who made the important transition from prey to predator and found any number of older men willing to be stalked and brought down.

And it was pathetically easy; boring, really. Allie had inherited her mother's hair, and from somewhere a pair of blue eyes that shone with life even in the photographs. The genetic sculptor had fashioned a classically chiseled face and a form that embodied the current American ideal. "How could a girl as pretty as you . . ." was a refrain that Allie heard over and over again after spectacular screwups or misbehavior. She was expected to be the prom queen and the sweetheart, and she responded to these expectations with an almost savage perversity. Sex was a weapon. Sex was revenge.

So by age seventeen, she had done it all: all the drinks, all the drugs, all the boys, and all the men. And she was so tired of it all. So one fine day, she looked out her window at the big ocean and decided that the other side might offer something new, and she whipped out the old credit card one more time to open the airplane door and flew to Paris. That was three months ago, and nobody had heard from her or seen her until three weeks ago, when some kid had spotted her in London.

The description of Allie's youth had taken some time, and a working lunch had been served by a staff quite used to serving working lunches. Chicken sandwiches, fruit salad, wheat crackers, and cheeses had been laid out quietly and consumed with no great enthusiasm. Allie's story had a way of sapping an appetite—except Neal's. He ate it and enjoyed. Surveillance work had taught him that whenever food appeared, you ate and appreciated it.

"Why did you wait three weeks to tell anyone that Allie had been spotted?" The more interesting question, Neal thought, was why they had waited three months to do anything at all, but he knew better than to ask. That was a question for later, if at all.

"We didn't. Scott did," Chase said eagerly, finding something for which he couldn't possibly be blamed. "Teenage loyalty, whatever. He came to us just five days ago. We went to Kitteredge."

"Who did Scott call? You or Mrs. Chase?"

"Me," said Liz Chase.

"Was he a boyfriend?"

"Just a friend."

Neal picked a stem of grapes from the plate and popped one in his mouth. Something was screwy here. "And he just happened to run into Allie in London? Why was he there?"

"A trip with his school."

Nice school, thought Neal, whose own class trip had been to Ossining.

"Anything unusual happen just before Allie took off?" Neal asked, feeling stupid. It was a stupid, pat question, and usually the kind of information parents volunteered.

Nobody answered. Neal chewed on another grape to kill time.

Two grapes later, he said, "Shall I take that to mean that nothing unusual happened, or that something unusual did happen and we don't want to talk about it?"

"Allie was home for the weekend," Liz said. "She just hung around, really."

"No, Mrs. Chase, she didn't just hang around, really. She flew to Paris. You see, in most runaways, there is what we like to call a 'precipitating factor.' A fight with the parents, a fight *between* the parents . . . maybe the kid had been grounded, forbidden to see a boyfriend . . . had her allowance cut—"

"Nothing like that," said Chase. He sounded really sure about it.

"Too bad. It helps if there was. If you know what a kid is running from, you have a jump on what she's running to. But just business as usual?"

More grapes.

"When did you last see Allie?" Another stupid, pat question.

"Saturday night I went to a party, a fund-raiser," Liz Chase said. "John was in Washington. He got home . . . when, darling?"

"Ten, I suppose."

"I didn't get in till late. I imagine it was after one. I looked in on Allie in her room. She was asleep."

"Asleep or passed out?"

Chase said, "I don't particularly care for your attitude."

"Neither do I," Neal answered, "but we're both stuck with it."

Liz jumped in. "When we got up Sunday . . . late . . . Allie was gone. She'd told Marie-Christine—"

"Who?"

"One of the staff. Allie told her that she was going for a walk."

"Which she did."

"Which she did."

For a second, Neal felt that he should stand up and pace around the room. One of those "nobody leaves until" numbers. Instead, he sank back into the sofa and said, "All right, so after you have your coffee and omelets and read the Sunday *Times,* you notice that Allie hasn't come home yet. Then what?"

"I drove around looking for her," Liz said.

The Senator didn't say anything.

"And you didn't find her."

"But I did find the car, parked downtown by the bus station, so right away I thought . . ."

She let her thought drop off as if she was trying to think up a new ending. From the looks on everyone's faces in the ensuing silence, Neal thought this one could be a four- or five-graper. He couldn't take it.

"You thought that Allie had taken off again."

Liz nodded. She hit him with those brown eyes flecked with green and filled with sadness. *What are you trying to tell me, Mrs. Chase?* "How many times has Allie run away?" Neal asked. He flipped through the report. No mention of previous times. Swell.

"Four, maybe five times," said Lombardi, doing his job.

"Overseas?"

"No, no," Lombardi said quickly. "Twice to New York. Fort Lauderdale once. L.A."

"One time to her grandparents in Raleigh," Liz said. "That was when we were in Washington."

"Is Allie close to her grandparents?"

"Allie is not close to anybody, Mr. Carey," said Mrs. Chase.

The sun was calling it a day. Neal watched the ocean turning a slate gray.

"So then you called the cops and the FBI and the state patrol and the National Guard?"

"I called her school," Lombardi said as Chase turned a deep red, "and asked to speak to her—"

"Slick."

"And they said she hadn't come back from her weekend home."

"So *then* you called the cops and the FBI and the state patrol and the National Guard."

This was called "baiting the client" and was the kind of thing that got you canned. Or it could get the client jazzed up enough to drop his guard and tell you something juicy. Or it could do both.

"Or did you call the Gallup poll?"

Set the hook and yank the line. Chase came out of his chair like a trout out of a stream.

"Listen, you little bastard—"

Why is everyone calling me a little bastard today?

"Darling—"

"It's all our fault, right? All the parents' fault! We gave that kid everything! Now I'm supposed to destroy my future for her? She doesn't want to be here, fine!"

"Yeah, it's okay with me, too, Senator, but now you want her back in the picture."

"You don't work for me anymore!"

Neal stood up. "I don't work for you, period. I work for the bank. They tell me to go after your kid, I go after your kid. They tell me to forget it, I forget it."

Lombardi got up. Then Liz got up. "Find my daughter."

It wasn't a plea, it was a command. It was the kind of command that comes from a beautiful woman, the kind of command that comes from a mother. It was the kind of command that comes from a wife who doesn't need Hubby's okay. Neal heard it all three ways.

Good old Marie-Christine brought in coffee and they started again.

No, Allie had not used the AmEx card since buying the air ticket. Yes, she had trust funds from both sets of grandparents but no way of touching the funds without her parents' signatures. She had her own bank account as well, but she hadn't drawn anything from that, either. So she was on her own financially, which was very bad news. It meant that she could either beg, steal, or sell herself. Begging wasn't very lucrative, and you usually had to buy your begging spot from the local thug. Stealing takes considerable skill. Selling yourself doesn't.

And little Allie would need a lot of money, because drugs aren't cheap and the people who sell them are.

"If it was strictly up to me," Neal said, "I'd advise you to clean out Allie's closets, make yourself a nice album, and get on with the business of mourning. Because the girl you knew probably doesn't exist anymore."

Because sometimes it's just too late, folks. The streets take the child you know and turn that child into someone you don't even recognize. Neal flashed on the Halperin kid, on that goofy look he had on his face all the time, even after . . .

"May I see Allie's room now, please?" he asked.

LIZ AND LOMBARDI TOOK HIM THERE.

It looked like a hotel room: elegant, sleek, comfortable . . . but nobody lived there. No pictures, souvenirs, no posters of rock stars on the wall.

Walk-in closet, private bath, of course. Bay window, view of the ocean. "This is going to take a while," Neal said.

"If we're not in the way . . ." Liz answered.

Neal gestured to the bed. Liz and Lombardi sat down and put their hands in their laps.

Neal searched the room. It was a relief to be doing something practical, something quiet, something he was good at. He went through the drawers and the closets carefully, slowly.

"Are you in the habit of searching Allie's room, Mrs. Chase?"

"Wouldn't you be, Mr. Carey?"

"But you haven't removed anything."

"No."

Neal opened the top drawer of Allie's dresser and ran his hand along the inside top. He felt the edge of the tape and gently pulled it off. He smelled the two joints.

"Emergency stash," he said. "Expensive stuff, too."

"Money is not Allie's particular problem in life," Liz said.

Didn't used to be, Mrs. C.

Searching the contents of the drawer, Neal asked, "Did you used to take away drugs you found here?"

Liz nodded. "We fought about it."

"What about the prescription stuff?"

"Same thing, once we caught on."

Neal finished with the drawers and moved to the closet. Allie had a few clothes. Neal flipped through the dozen or so jackets before he found another strip of medical tape stuck to the inside lapel of a nice little denim job.

He removed the three joints from the tape and flipped them to Lombardi. "Hawaii Four-oh."

He didn't find anything else until he got to the portable Sony TV. He twisted the fine-tune dial off and found the Valium that had been glued to the inside rim.

"Not to worry," he said. "They use the same kind of paste you used to make in kindergarten. You can eat a quart of it and you won't get sick."

"I never dreamed . . ." Liz Chase was shaking her head.

"You're not a pro, Mrs. Chase."

Neal moved into Allie's bathroom. The medicine cabinet alone took almost half an hour and yielded nothing very interesting. Likewise, the underside of the bathtub rim. Neal emptied the sink cabinet and crawled underneath. He found Allie's major stash in a small plastic trash bag taped to the bottom of the sink.

"Jackpot!" he called out.

Liz Chase stood in the doorway. "What?"

Neal sat on the floor, rooting through the bag. "Well, we have your uppers, and your downers, and some grass and hash, and a little coke."

"My god."

"It's not all bad news. No needles."

Neal handed her the bag and smiled. "May I take a look at Allie's car, please?"

"It's in the garage."

It had a lot of company. There were seven cars in the garage. Allie's was a modest Datsun Z. The others were all sleek little sports jobs that Neal didn't recognize. That wasn't too hard, though. Neal didn't know too many cars that weren't on the IRT.

"John was very interested in cars for a while," Liz explained. "As a matter of fact, so was Allie. It gave then something they could share, I think."

"Everybody needs a hobby."

Neal started with the glove compartment, just in case there was a note in there nobody had noticed. Maybe a note that read "I'm in such and such a place and here's my address and phone number." He didn't find it. He found the usual glove compartment crap. A couple of road maps, a service manual, an open package of cherry Life Savers, lipstick, an emergency pack of cigarettes, a comb, a brush, a pint bottle of Johnnie Walker Black.

He felt around between the seats for "she went thataway" clues and didn't find any of those, either. He also didn't find any dope of any kind, which sort of surprised him. It was dark by the time he finished.

NEAL SANK BACK INTO THE BATHTUB that came along with the guest room. He had filled it with steaming hot water to try to ease the ache in his body and his soul. The first sip of scotch spread a soothing warmth through his insides, and after a few minutes he was able to pick up his paperback copy of *The Adventures of Peregrine Pickle* and lose himself in the eighteenth century. Which was his life's goal, anyway.

He relished the quiet. Chase and Jiminy Cricket had headed back to Washington for one of those crucial votes. The missus was preparing herself for yet another fund-raiser for an undoubtedly good cause. What had Dickens called it? "Telescopic Philanthropy"? Although Neal had to admit that given a choice between Mrs. Jellyby and Liz Chase, there was no contest. Anyway, she'd hoped that he "wouldn't mind dining alone." He didn't. The cook laid on, with hopefully unintentional irony, a London broil, rice and asparagus, and followed it up with a raspberry tart. Neal washed it all down with the appropriate wine, and was about half-bagged when he hit the tub. After a chapter of *Pickle,* he laid the book down and thought things over.

Allie hadn't planned to take off. No good doper leaves a

stash like that behind if she's thought about it. No, Allie was upset when she left. She'd made the decision in a hurry, impulsively, sometime Saturday night or Sunday morning. She'd given it a little more thought in the car and taken whatever stuff she had with her. But she hadn't gone back to the house to collect anything else, which meant she was a piss-poor druggie, or she really didn't want to go home.

Also, she wanted to stay gone. Most *casual* runaways, who are fed up with the discipline, or bored at home, or want attention, want to be found. Consciously or unconsciously, they leave clues all over the place. They also find that life out there is a lot worse than life at home, and they come back. Unless life out there is better than life at home. Or life at school, which was something he'd better look into, except he didn't think he'd be allowed to. The Chases had simply withdrawn Allie *in absentia* as it were, to avoid a scandal. So forget that. But it impressed him that spoiled little Allie hadn't reached for the plastic, or wired for money. She was gutting it out, and this was a girl who wasn't used to gutting it out. So why?

He fiddled the hot-water tap with his foot. He didn't feel like sitting up to reach it and it left his hand free to fiddle with the scotch. He wished he'd taped the afternoon's interview, because there was something back there that was bugging him, really bugging him, and it was rattling around in the dimmer corners of his mind, just out of reach.

Neal checked his watch when he heard the knock on the bedroom door. It was a few minutes past two in the goddamn morning. He said "Come in," anyway.

Liz Chase shut the door behind her. Neal wondered why she was wearing black silk to sleep alone in, but that was her business. The black turned her blond hair gold. She sat on the edge of the bed, pulled her legs up underneath just as she had that afternoon, and tugged the hem of the nightgown down around her knees. Then she just sat there looking at him.

Neal had read about this kind of thing in detective novels, but it never had happened to him. He didn't think it was happening to him now, either, but his throat tightened up and he swallowed hard nevertheless.

"Yeah?"

"This is not easy for me."

She bit her lip and nodded her head several times, as if she was trying to make up her mind.

"Allie has been with a number of men," she said.

"There are worse things, Mrs. Chase."

"Apparently . . . the Senator is one of them."

Whoa.

Allie had left a note—in the car, where she knew her mother would find it, because she knew dear old Dad wouldn't come looking.

It had been going on for years, since she was "old enough," like ten, and it had started with fondling and extra-special hugs and bonus kisses. It hadn't been all the time, just every once in a while, and she had been scared to tell. She had tried to tell Grandpa and Grandma that one time, but she couldn't, she was so ashamed. "Please, Mom, don't be angry, don't hate me," she wrote. And they had never done . . . you know . . . gone all the way, until last night and Daddy just wouldn't stop, just wouldn't stop, just wouldn't . . . and she didn't know what to do. She just couldn't face them, just couldn't face her mother, and so she was taking off for good.

So let's take another look at little Allie, who was never good enough, but good enough for Dad. Allie, who drowned the memories and numbed the feelings, and who went out looking for sex instead of love because she didn't know the difference, and who maybe had it buried real deep in the past until Daddy took her again, except this time she was old enough that she'd never forget, and old enough to know what it meant. And you thought you knew this kid, Neal. You thought you had her pegged. You never learn, do you?

"Where's the note?" Neal asked when Liz was finished.

"Is it important?"

"It will be when I take it to the cops, and if you destroyed it, Mrs. Chase, it makes you guilty of a half dozen crimes I can think of."

"You're going to the police?"

"Soon as I get dressed. You want to come with me?"

"My husband—"

"Fuck him."

She held up for another second or so and then she lost it. Suddenly. As if she'd been stabbed in the heart and the pain had just hit her. It seemed like the beautiful face aged ten years in the seconds that she held back the tears, and then they came out in wracking sobs.

"My baby. My poor little baby. She needs so much help. She needs me and I don't know where she is! I have to tell her! I have to tell her!"

"Tell her what?" Neal asked, and if she said something like "That I love her," he was about ready to smack her in the mouth.

"On top of everything else, what she must be thinking! I have to tell her, at least that."

"Tell her *what,* Mrs. Chase?"

She settled herself down, he had to give her credit for that. She drew herself back from the edge of hysteria and settled down to help her daughter. She caught her breath and spoke quietly—slowly.

"He's not her father."

Whoa and double whoa.

SHE HAD TURNED AROUND WHILE Neal put his clothes on, and she sat patiently while he poured himself a drink and tossed down half of it. If he smoked, he would have lit one up.

"Does the Senator know that Allie isn't his?"

She nodded.

"Since when?"

"I suppose Allie was eight or nine. We had a terrible fight. I threw it at him."

"But you never told Allie."

"I'd been meaning to."

"Where's the note, Mrs. Chase?"

"In a safe-deposit box—my own."

Smart lady.

"Does anyone else know about it?"

"No."

"So the Senator doesn't know that you know that—"

She shook her head. "I haven't said anything to him about it. If I did, I'd have to leave him, and if I left him, I wouldn't get the help I need to find Allie, would I?"

No, lady, you probably wouldn't.

"Are you going to the police?" she asked.

"No."

Because you're right, Mrs. Chase. If I take this to the cops, it's all over. I'm off the case, the Senator is out of office, Friends loses interest, and Allie gets to read about it in the foreign edition of *Newsweek* and will bury herself even deeper than she already has. No winners.

So the basic rules apply. John Chase is a wealthy member of the U.S. Senate, and he might be President someday, and he has money in the bank. So he gets to rape his stepdaughter and get away with it and also get someone like me to clean it all up. Neal Carey, Janitor to the Rich and Powerful.

And that son of a bitch is counting on Allie's shame to shut her up while she's posing for "The Waltons Go to Washington" pictures, and then he'll stick her away in some really faraway school someplace, maybe one of those Swiss jobs. And I'm going to help him do it. Because it's better than having that kid out there thinking she's had sex with her own father and quite possibly dying over it. And because I want to finish college one of these days.

"There's something else to think about, Mrs. Chase. If Allie needs drugs, and food and shelter and all that, and she doesn't have money . . . she'll do anything to get it."

"What do you mean?"

"You know what I mean."

"Allie would never do that."

"Yes, she would. You're doing it. I'm doing it."

And we ain't even haggling over the price.

NEAL LAY AWAKE FOR MOST of what was left of the night. He hadn't had dreams about the Halperin kid for months, and he didn't want to start again. But when he closed his eyes, he saw the kid again, and thought about the "ifs." If they had only let the kid be what he was—an amiable, not overly bright gay teenager. If they had treated the case as more than a ground ball and sent two guys instead of just Neal. If only room service hadn't been closed that night.

He gave up trying to sleep around five, took a wake-up shower, said a quick goodbye to Elizabeth Chase, and asked for a ride downtown. The driver let him off at an Avis counter. Neal got lost about fifteen times before he found Scott Mackensen's school in Connecticut.

5

Scott Mackensen was running to lacrosse practice.

"Coach will kill me if I'm late again," he said to Neal Carey, who thought the boy was a little too eager to get going.

Neal looked behind him to the beautifully tended green fields where several boys tossed the ball among them in studied insouciance.

"It'll only take a minute," Neal lied.

"That's worth five minutes of stadium steps," Scott answered. He was tall, muscular, clear-eyed Jack Armstrong and all that shit, but Neal saw that those clear eyes looked scared. He knew then that there was no hurry.

"Later, maybe?" he asked.

Scott waged a brief skirmish with his conscience. Neal had seen it a few hundred times. Duty versus self-interest. Scott was just young enough that duty had a shot at winning, and Neal didn't want to push a quick decision. He waited.

"There's a coffee shop in the village—The Copper Donkey. Give me two hours." Scott backed away as he talked.

"You got it," Neal said as Scott turned and ran toward the practice field.

Maybe I should have let The Man send me to boarding school, Neal thought as he walked back to his rented car. The Barker School looked pretty nice. "Nestled in the rolling hills of northwest Connecticut," the brochure had doubtless proclaimed, and indeed, the Berkshire foothills framed the sprawling campus.

Neal slipped into the rented Nova, put it in drive thinking it was reverse, and smacked the front bumper into a white post placed there precisely for such ineptitude. He hated to drive and had done so only because he couldn't screw Graham into making the trip.

"Connecticut?" Graham had said in dismissal. "They got bees in Connecticut."

Neal found The Copper Donkey without major mishap, but he took ten minutes to parallel park on the narrow village street. (Twenty bucks had gotten him past that part on the driver's test.) The village, Old Farmstead, was bona fide New England quaint. Colonial and Victorian houses, all beautifully kept, competed for the oohs and aahs of tourists. Neal didn't ooh or aah. He had his fill of quaint from the plumbing in his building.

The Copper Donkey catered to the private-school crowd. The boys came over from Barker, and the girls from nearby Miss Clifton's, which Neal thought sounded like an instant muffin mix, but which had been one of Allie's pit stops on her race through the academic elite. He figured that even the patient folk at the Donkey wouldn't appreciate him nursing a cup of coffee for an hour and a half, so he wandered off in search of a bookstore. He found Bookes, which surprised him by having the good sense to stock John MacDonald's latest. He found a quaint sidewalk bench and settled down to commiserate with Travis McGee.

He and Travis got through a quick hour with no trouble. (Well, none for Neal. Lots for Travis.) Neal went into the Donkey and got a booth at the back.

Scott arrived almost on time. He had showered and changed, and looked fresh and even younger in a white sweater, stone-washed jeans, and brown loafers. He looked around for a moment, spotted Neal, then looked around again to see who else was there. Nobody was.

Sitting down, he started right in. "I don't know, maybe I should never have said anything. First Mr. Chase, then the other guy, now you. I don't want to get involved with the police. I just got accepted to Brown."

"I'm not a cop."

"Then I don't have to talk to you."

"No. Which other guy?"

"A big guy. Kind of young. Older than you, though."

"Tall, heavyset, curly black hair? Pushy?"

Scott nodded. "Real pushy."

I'll kill Levine, Neal thought.

"Do you want something?" Neal asked, gesturing at the menu.

"I'll have some coffee. I have an exam tomorrow."

Neal signaled the waitress, pointing at his own cup and Scott. She brought the coffee over quickly.

"I just want to check a few details," Neal said.

"Like what?"

"Like your whole story is bullshit."

Scott set his cup down. "What do you mean?"

"I've been looking at your yearbook, Scott. Track, football, lacrosse, basketball. You say you saw Allie in Hyde Park and 'gave chase,' no pun intended. 'Gave chase'? Nobody talks like that. That's the sort of thing cops say when they lie on the witness stand."

"She didn't beat me, exactly. She ran into the subway."

The kid was lying. Person looks up and to the right when they're telling you something, they're making it up as they go along.

"The subway? In Hyde Park?"

"Hyde Park Corner. There's a station there."

A hint of that wonderful teenage defensive whine had snuck into his voice. Neal didn't answer him.

"I didn't have a token," Scott continued.

"You mean a ticket."

"Yeah, okay, a ticket."

Neal played with the salt and pepper shakers on the table, moving them in lazy figure-eight patterns.

"I'm not a cop," he said. "If you tell me that's the story, we finish our coffee and it's over. But we'll both know you're holding back."

Scott took a deep breath and let it out in a long sigh. "You won't tell anyone?"

"The dean of admissions will never hear it from me."

"If this ever got out—"

"It won't."

"A friend and I—he doesn't go to this school—stayed over a few days after the school trip. We got kidding around one night . . ."

"Go ahead."

"We called one of those services. You know, they have phone numbers in the paper? We called one of them."

Neal's heart bounced. "And they sent a couple of ladies over," he said.

"Yeah."

"And did you . . ."

"Yeah."

"And was one of them Allie Chase?"

Scott looked shocked. "No! No way! Really!"

"Okay, okay. I believe you."

"After we . . . we got talking a little, and we asked these girls if they knew where we could get some hash." This last tidbit came out in a rush and Neal could see the kid relax.

"Hey, Scott, I'll bet they knew, huh?"

"Yeah." He sort of chuckled. "They called this guy who said to come meet him."

"*And you went?*"

"I know it sounds dumb, but it was right out in public. Right by this movie theater in Leicester Square. We even knew the place, because we'd seen the new Bond movie there."

"Where does Allie come in?"

"She was with him."

"With who? The dealer?"

"Him and two others. A guy and a girl."

"Did you talk to Allie?"

"No. When she walked up with this guy, she was laughing and all, but then she saw me and she turned away real quick, behind the other girl, and they backed off into the alley."

"Scott, are you sure it was her?"

Scott nodded. "Real sure."

"How come?"

"Allie and I . . . you know . . . we'd partied."

"Then what happened?"

"We bought the hash and took off."

"Did you try to approach Allie?"

Scott blushed. "Her friends were pretty punk-looking. I didn't want to push it."

"You were right. You did the right thing."

"Anyway, when I got back, I thought I should tell Mrs. Chase, but I didn't want to—"

"Tell everything. Sure."

"So I made up the story about seeing Allie in the park."

"How did Allie look? Okay?"

"Yeah, I guess so. A little ratty maybe. Sweatshirt and jeans."

"Was she stoned?"

"Yeah, maybe. She was laughing a lot."

"What about the dealer? What did he look like?"

"Cool. Very cool." Scott smiled.

Some detectives can deal with "civilians," others can't. They get impatient and scream things like "'Cool. Very cool.' What the hell does that mean?" Such detectives love to get clothing-store robberies, because the witnesses are perfect. ("This forty-two long in a cheap maroon blazer, gray polyester slacks, and Buster Browns comes in and . . .")

"What was cool about him?"

"He had real short hair and was wearing a double-breasted suit with a T-shirt! He was real slick with the money and the dope, like it was all a big joke, like he was selling hot dogs, or something."

"Big guy? Little?"

"About your size. Bigger-boned."

"If he plays football, what position is he?"

"Halfback, maybe a small tight end."

"Did he have a name?"

"Not that I heard."

"Anything else?"

"Yeah, he had three safety pins stuck through his ear."

I'm glad you brought that up, Scott. That might just help identify him. "Three safety pins?"

"Yeah," answered Scott with unmixed admiration.

"What about the girls? You remember their names?"

"Ginger and Yvonne."

Swell.

"The name of the service you called?"

"Sorry."

"C'mon. You do this a lot?"

"No! We were drunk! You know."

"How about the hotel?"

"The Piccadilly Hotel."

Never ask a witness more than two questions in a row he can't answer. Make sure you pitch him a watermelon every once in a while. Builds his confidence. The Gospel According to St. Joseph. Graham.

"Did the two hookers seem to know Allie? They say hi or anything?"

"I don't think so."

"Did the dealer say anything to her?"

"No. Not a word."

"Anything else you remember or you want to tell me?"

"It was kind of a blur. You know?"

Neal nodded. He knew.

"Thanks, Scott," he said, going through the ritual. "You've been a big help."

"Can I go?"

"Hey, you have an exam tomorrow."

Scott started to slide out of the booth.

"One more thing," Neal said, realizing he was doing a Columbo imitation. "The hash, how was it?"

Jack Armstrong All-American Boy grinned. "Primo."

NEAL'S MOTEL ROOM WAS NOTHING SPECIAL, but it had the essentials—a bed with a rationally placed reading light, a phone within easy reach, and a color TV that brought in the Yankees game. It also had clean glasses. Neal was feeling semicivilized, so he used one of them to belt down three slugs of scotch before dialing the phone.

Ed Levine answered after seven rings. He said hello with the voice of a man who doesn't like being called at home.

"Ed?"

"Yeah?"

"Keep your fat fingers off my fucking case."

Neal hung up the phone and sat back in bed as Guidry smoked another Angel. Maybe, he thought, maybe he could find the aptly named Alison Chase if she was still with this dealer.

The dealer was a pro, no question. He had good technique and some connections. He screened his first-time customers coming in and did small-time courtesy deals for business connections. And if he had turned Allie on, he hadn't turned her over—yet. Definitely a yet, because a businessman doesn't waste a commodity as valuable as a beautiful young girl. Unless he really loves her; then it will take a little longer.

So there was a place to start. Find the dealer and you have a shot at finding Allie. A long shot, indeed, but you've seen them hit before.

Just to encourage him, Guidry threw a curve that didn't, which the batter pulled right and put over the fence as the base runner trotted contemptuously home.

Neal consoled himself with Chapter Seven of *The Making of the English Working Class* and another scotch.

NEAL SPENT A VERY BORING day and a half waiting for the FedEx package from Graham to arrive. He killed time with chapters eight through fifteen, Travis McGee, and *Mr. Ed* reruns. The desk rang him when the package came.

In it were three Xeroxed pages from a rag called the London *Daily Leveller*: the classified ads for May 7, the night that Scott

Mackensen and his friend had let their fingers do the walking. Most of the ads were of the "for a good time, call" variety, but there were a number of specialty acts: mother/daughter teams, B&D mistresses ("Imelda knows you've been a bad boy"), a wide world of ethnic specialties (Neal wondered what a "full treatment Bulgarian hour" could possibly entail). There were bad little girls who wanted to be spanked first, some who wanted to be spanked afterward. Many had cute names. There were three Bambis, but to Neal's intense relief, no Thumpers. A goodly number had French names, and not a few had threatening ones. Neal thought that any man dumb enough to call up a woman named Stiletto and invite her into his room deserved whatever he got.

There were also a lot of agency listings. Most used sophisticated names like Erotica and Exotica, and Neal yearned for an agency of frigid hookers called Antarctica. His personal favorite, though, was Around The World In Eighty Minutes. Of course, there was no listing for "Ginger and Yvonne: Sex, Drugs, and Rock and Roll," because nobody ever got that lucky.

"You said last time was it," Scott Mackensen protested over the phone.

"I know. I'm sorry."

"Will this really help Allie?"

"Could."

There ensued one of those long, irritating silences Neal was getting used to on this gig. And not a grape in sight. He settled for a bite of his Hershey bar—the healthy kind, the one with almonds.

"I have a test tomorrow," Scott said.

I know the feeling, kid. "On what?"

"Macbeth." He sounded mournful.

"I'll help you with it. I've taken a few exams on *Macbeth* myself."

"Really?"

"Yeah. The witches did it."

SCOTT STARED AT THE ADS laid out on the counter in Neal's motel room. He moved his index finger slowly down the page, then shook his head.

"Sorry," he said.

"Try again."

"I can't remember!"

"Jesus Christ! *How many call girls have you been with?*"

"I *was* drunk!"

Attaboy, Neal, he told himself, browbeat a witness who's really trying. That'll help.

"I'm sorry," he said. "We're both tired. Try it this way. In your hotel room in London, where was the phone?"

Scott pointed to a spot on the counter. Neal moved the phone there and put a chair in front of it.

"Okay," he said. "Sit down. Where was the paper? Okay. Which hand do you dial with? Good. Now look at the paper. Don't think. Just point."

"Somewhere around here," Scott said, pointing toward the lower third of the first page.

"Good. Now was it the name of an agency, or just a couple of girls?"

"Just *girls.*"

"Good."

Good, not great. But it was progress. Something to work from.

Scott sank back in his chair and let out a long sigh. He was an exhausted kid. He looked at Neal and smiled.

"We have to stop meeting like this," he said.

Neal went for the brass ring.

"Hey, Scott. Did you take any pictures of these girls?"

Neal watched the kid's spine stiffen.

"You mean dirty pictures?"

"No, I mean you tell your friends what you did and they say 'Bullshit,' and you whip out a couple of Polaroids of the girls."

Scott looked him right in the eye and told him the God's honest truth.

"No way."

"Just a thought. When's your test?"

"First period."

Neal whipped through a few of the big themes in the old Scottish play, discoursed on how many times the word *man* was used, and for extra credit threw in a few notes on the uses of color in the imagery. Then he sent Scott on his way and phoned Joe Graham.

NEAL WAS AT SCOTT'S SCHOOL bright and early, first period. The kid's dorm-room door was a breeze, one of those spring-bolt locks that yodel "Come on in, pardner."

The room was your typical boys' school hovel with a sort of dirty laundry Cristo effect. Neal found Scott's desk and went straight to the top right drawer, the locked one. It was a little less friendly than the door lock, but opened up after a little persuasion.

The usual collection of bullshit was in there. A bunch of letters from a girl named Marsha, another bunch from a Debbie. Lots of pictures: Marsha or Debbie with Scott on a beach; Marsha or Debbie with Scott at a dance; just Marsha or Debbie on a boat; just Scott on the boat, taken by Marsha or Debbie; Marsha or Debbie posed romantically under a willow tree. Neal didn't see any of Marsha and Debbie pounding the crap out of Scott. He leafed through a couple of *Penthouse* magazines, a passport, and a brochure on Brown University before he came to a thin packet of pictures secured by a rubber band. Bingo. Scott and a friend with arms around two girls who were neither Marsha nor Debbie—in a hotel room. Hello, Ginger. Greetings, Yvonne.

Neal took the best picture and slipped it into his jacket pocket. He locked the desk drawer and walked out of the room, whistling a happy tune, wondering how Scott was doing in class.

Joe Graham, listening from the stairway, heard the whistling and left by a side door.

THEY MET IN THE PARKING LOT of the post office. Neal slid into the passenger seat of Graham's car.

"So what do you have so important I have to come to Connecticut to hold your hand for?"

"I have Allie hooked up to a dealer, name unknown, naturally, who has friends in the 'love for rent' business. I have two working girls, names unknown, naturally, but narrowed down to about twelve phone numbers, who know the aforementioned dealer. I have shit."

"You're doing okay."

"Yeah, right. Do you want to lay the odds on our finding Allie Chase in London?"

"About the same as Jackie O peeling my banana at Lincoln Center."

Neal laid the photo on the dashboard.

"Visual aids, very nice," Graham said.

"I've been thinking about something."

"Hard to believe."

"Allie Chase ran before."

"So?"

"Twice to New York."

Graham pretended to study the picture.

"If I'd have picked her up, I would have told you about it," he said.

"So you didn't, and I didn't, and—"

"There's nothing about it in the file."

"At least not in the file we've seen."

Graham perused the picture some more. "Nice-looking girls."

"What's going on, Dad?"

"Son, I don't know."

I hope you don't, Dad. Goddamn, I hope you don't.

6

A FEW WEEKS AND A FEW JOBS after Neal had started working for
Graham, he answered a knock on the door, to find the gremlin
standing there, his arms full of packages and a brand-new mop
and broom clutched in one hand.

"What's this?" Neal asked.

"I'm fine, thank you. How are you? Your mother home?"

"Not lately."

Graham brushed him aside and stepped in.

"You live in a toilet. A toilet."

"It's the maid's year off."

Graham swept off some garbage from the kitchen counter
and set the packages down. "We're going to fix that."

"You buy me this stuff?"

"No, you bought you this stuff. I took it out of your pay
for the last job."

"You better be kidding me, man."

"This," said Graham with an appropriate flourish, "is a mop.
You use it to clean floors."

"Just give me the money."

"This is a broom. You also use it to clean floors," Graham said, looking around, "although maybe I should have brought some dynamite."

That morning, Neal discovered that Graham was a first-class neatnik, a psychopathic cleaner of the highest order. Out of the bags came sponges, dishrags, dish towels, Brillo pads, bug spray, disinfectant, lemon oil, Windex, paper towels, detergent, Comet cleanser ("The best, don't let anybody kid you."), toilet-bowl cleaner, and a package of bright yellow rubber gloves.

"I like things to be neat and clean," Graham explained, "at work, and at home."

They cleaned. They crammed months of accumulated trash into plastic garbage bags and carried it downstairs. Then they swept—like your mother never did. ("The broom's not going to get everything, you see, so you have to get down on your hands and knees with this brush, and use the dustpan.") Then they mopped, with Graham showing Neal not only the correct ratio of cleanser to water but also the proper way to swing the mop "so you're not just shoving the dirt around." This was followed by scrubbing, waxing, polishing, disinfecting, and scraping until Neal Carey was tired, irritable, aching, sore, and living in an immaculate apartment.

"And how long you think it's gonna stay this way once my mother gets home?" Neal demanded.

"You keep it this way. Another thing, you eat like shit."

"I eat okay."

"Candy bars, Sugar Pops—"

"I like candy bars and Sugar Pops."

"There's another bag in the hall. Get it."

"Yes, sir."

Neal returned with the bag and asked, "What is all this stuff?"

Graham removed the contents. "A frying pan, a pot, a pot

holder, two plates, two forks, two spoons, two knives, one can opener—"

"I got a can opener."

"A spatula, eggs, bread, butter, Dinty Moore beef stew, a jar of peanut butter, a jar of grape jelly, some spaghetti . . . these things are called vegetables, you will learn to like them—"

"No way."

"Or I will break your face. I will bring more next week. Every Thursday, we are going to have a cooking lesson."

"You're talking 'we,' you better bring a friend."

"Or you're fired. You think you're the only underage, under-sized sneak thief in New York?"

"Not the only, just the best."

"Then you had better get yourself some pride, kid. Because you live like an animal. Your mother doesn't take care of you, so you'd better learn to take care of yourself. Or you can't work for me."

HE WORKED. AND LEARNED. Easy stuff at first, like tailing some-one from a distance; how to keep an eye on the guy without looking as if he was looking.

"First thing you look at are the shoes, Neal, the shoes," Graham told him during one of the many sidewalk lectures. "Two reasons. One, you can always spot him in a crowd. Two, the guy turns around and spots you, you're looking down, not right into his baby blues."

They practiced that for a week, Neal following Graham down Broadway, on the subway, on the bus, down crowded streets, down nearly empty ones. One day tailing Graham east on Fifty-seventh, Neal was concentrating so hard on Graham's shoes, he bumped right into his back.

"Now, why did that happen?" Graham asked him.

"I dunno."

"Good answer. Exactly. You don't know. The pace, Neal, you have to watch the pace. Everybody has a different stride—long, short, slow, fast . . . I shortened my steps. I kept walking just as fast, but I shortened my stride. I took smaller steps. I made you bump into me. The first block or so you're tailing, measure the guy's step against the cracks in the sidewalk. What is it? Step, step and a half to each crack? Count it off. Is it slow or fast? It's like music, so sing to yourself if you have to. Keep time.

"Another good reason to match his step is he can't hear you so easy. A guy who knows how to shake a tail is going to listen as well as look. He'll hear the difference in walking sounds, and if he hears one sound too long, he'll know he's pulling a caboose. So it's like you imagine he's got paint on his shoes, and you walk in his footprints."

So they spent a week with Neal following Graham and matching his pace and his stride. Graham would take the kid along crowded streets and then suddenly down empty ones, where the boy's every footfall would echo in his own ears.

"You're tailing an amateur, it doesn't matter, Neal. Save your energy and just stay out of sight. But a pro, it's like it's a habit with him, to mix up his walk slow and fast and slow again . . . . He's going to play Simon Says: Take one giant step, one baby step." They went at it again. A solid month of tailing. After the first week, Graham knew that Neal was the most talented prospect he had ever seen—fast, canny, and the lucky owner of a set of looks that was quite literally unremarkable. Graham worked him hard, leading him on chases down the shopper's paradise of Fifth Avenue, where every store window offered a reflection, onto subway trains, into coffee shops, movie theaters, and men's rooms, through the parks and the alleys. At first, the kid was always easy to detect or to shake, but after a short time, Graham found himself working hard to lose the little bastard, and then hard even to see him.

"Find the blind spot," Graham told the kid, "and stay in it for as long as you can."

"What's the blind spot?"

"The blind spot . . . the alley . . . the slipstream; a spot behind the guy where he just doesn't see you. Usually, it's behind him, slightly to his left side, about fifteen feet back. But it depends, you know, on his height and build. That's why it's good you're a little shit, because it gives you a bigger blind spot to stay in."

"Yeah, I know what you mean. Like when you're following somebody, and you get into the rhythm, and then you feel like you're invisible, like the guy can't see you."

So they practiced finding that spot, picking a stranger at random out of a crowd and following him. Neal got good at it, real good, and Graham marveled at the kid's ability to fade back into a crowd, to disappear momentarily, and then reappear instantly back on the track. And a shadow made more noise than Neal Carey.

"Use the crowd," Graham lectured. "Horizontal, too, not just vertical, because you can get beside your guy if you use the crowd right. Like try to find a woman with real big ones, and get beside her. Then when your guy turns around, he's not even going to see you, he's too busy checking out her Daisy Maes."

Soon Neal graduated to trickier stuff.

"Today," Graham announced one time, "you're going to follow me from the front."

"That doesn't make any sense."

"That's why it's so beautiful. No one is going to be looking for a tail in front of him." Graham showed him, crossing the street and then crossing back in front of a guy they picked at random. Graham used store windows and the mirrors of parked cars to follow his man, not missing a beat when the man turned into a bookstore off Fifty-seventh.

Neal tried and failed miserably, losing his mark after five minutes.

"Because you didn't listen, Neal. Remember what I told you: Every step is different. Do the soles of his shoes slap the side-walk? Do they click? If it's a woman wearing high heels, that's a different sound. Maybe the mark's wearing sneakers."

Back at it. Until "Front Following" became automatic. Then they moved on to "The East Side–West Side," where the tail stays on the opposite side of the street. ("Why does the chicken cross the road?" Graham asked. "So the chicken he's following doesn't make him.")

Then they went to the two-man stuff: relays, pass-offs, front and back doors, peekaboos ("Peekaboo. I see you. You see me. But you don't see him."), and the ever-tricky "Fake Burn," in which you let the mark give you his best move and "lose" you, while your unseen partner stays on the mark's relaxed ass.

Neal loved the "Fake Burn," loved it with an intensity that inspired him to create his own variation: "The Solo Fake Burn," known in the Carey household as "Neal's Very Own Special Fake Burn."

"You can't have a one-man 'Fake Burn,'" Graham replied with disgust when Neal announced his invention. "The whole point is that you have two men."

"Not necessarily," replied Neal with a degree of preado-lescent satisfaction that might have aggravated a man more sensitive than Graham.

"Okay," Graham said, "I'm going to walk out this door and be back in two hours, and I want you to tell me where I've been and what I've been doing."

Graham polished off his beer and headed out into the street. He made Neal about twelve seconds later, because the dumb little bastard was wearing red socks that could have given Ray Charles a headache. Graham made a mental note to correct the kid on that, and settled into the not unpleasant task of teaching him a lesson. He crossed Broadway against the light but stopped in the island, noticing with pride that Neal hadn't jumped after him. Then he crossed the rest of the street and ducked down the IRT entrance on the uptown side of Seventy-ninth, bought a token, and walked back up the downtown side. Sure enough, Ol' Red Socks was still with him. So he stopped at a newsstand, looked at a paper, reached into his pocket for a coin, changed his mind, and headed straight back at Neal, forcing him to front follow for a good fifteen minutes.

Now I've got him worn down, Graham thought, I'll finish him off, and he checked to see the red socks back in a crowd at the cross-town bus stop. He got into the line to board the bus, and used the bus's side mirror to see the red socks get into line about five old ladies back. When it came his turn to get on board, he stepped past the door and leaned against the front of the bus until he saw the red socks go up the steps.

Bye-bye, Neal, thought Graham as he stepped out across the street. See you later.

Graham ambled along the sidewalk, looking back to see whether maybe, just maybe, the kid had hung tough. But no red socks, no Neal, lesson administered. "The Solo Fake Burn" indeed.

An hour and a half later, Neal entered McKeegan's to find Graham occupying his usual spot at the bar.

"You got your hair cut and had a BLT at The American. The bread was soggy. Next time, tell 'em take it easy on the mayo."

Graham reached down and pulled up the boy's pant leg. Plain old white socks.

"Reversible," said Neal. "The key to 'The Solo Fake Burn' is to make one man into two men. The first man had red socks. The second man didn't. The rear doors of buses also help."

"Neal Carey could follow you into the can and hand you the toilet paper," a proud Graham told Ed Levine, "and you wouldn't know he was there."

OTHER SUBJECTS EMERGED, such as Photography 101. ("It is very hard," Graham lectured, "to get the guy's face and pecker in the same shot. But try, because if you just get the pecker, the guy will deny it's his. Unless it's humongous.") Or Dirty Fighting. ("The basics of hand-to-hand combat, Neal, are simple. Forget this karate shit, like Levine goes in for. Just pick up something hard and heavy that's not your pecker and hit the guy with it. And don't always try to break his jaw, like on *Rawhide*. There's time for that when he's unconscious. Hit him in the knee, or across the shins. The elbow is always nice.")

And thus the education of Neal Carey continued.

NEAL'S MOTHER WAS HOME.

She looked like shit. Her eyes resembled blue marbles after a hard day's play on the sidewalk. Greasy brown hair hung uncombed over her face, and her skin had the life and luster of chalk. She looked just like herself.

She was happy to see Neal. "Baby," she said. "Baby, you look good. Mama's missed you."

"So where you been?" asked Neal, crossing over to the couch, where she sat slumped, to give her a peck on the cheek.

"Around and about, around and around."

Neal heard soft sounds behind the closed bathroom door.

"Your pimp here?"

"He's not my pimp, baby," she said. "He's my manager. Momma's a little sick, baby, but she's gonna be better soon."

"Why don't you stay this time? Get off that shit. I'll help you."

"Now isn't that a touching scene?"

Neal turned toward the voice, to see Marco come through the door. The pimp wore a white linen suit and a sky blue shirt open at the collar. A single gold chain hung from his neck. His full black hair was greased and combed straight back. He was solid without seeming heavy. He held a syringe in his right hand.

"You're Neal, right? Johnny, say hello to Neal."

"Hello, Neal."

Johnny was huge. He had both fat and muscle. You could land planes on his flattop. Make pancakes on his open palms.

Neal didn't answer. He watched as his mother stretched out her arm. Johnny took off his belt and wrapped it around the woman's arm until a vein stood out clearly. Marco squeezed the syringe until the tiniest drop glistened on the edge of the needle.

"Don't do that," Neal said.

"Quiet, Neal. The doctor is working."

"I said don't do that."

"Yeah, and we all heard you. Now shut up."

Neal slipped his hand into his right back pocket and pulled out a metal shoehorn. He slid the curl over his index finger and felt the cool metal settle firmly into his palm, the wide edge sticking out.

He waited for Marco to bend over to his mother's arms and then he burst across the room. Lifting his arm over his head, he slammed the hard metal edge down right between the pimp's eyes. Marco dropped to his knees as the blood pumped from his shattered nose onto the formerly white suit.

"Jesus! I can't see! I can't see!" Marco screamed as Johnny grabbed Neal and Neal's mother grabbed the syringe. Marco pulled himself up on the arm of the couch, felt for the silk handkerchief in his breast pocket, and wiped the blood from his eyes. His legs trembled as he made his way over to Neal and backhanded him once and then twice across the mouth.

"You think you're a man, little shit?"

Neal's mother watched from inside a fluffy cloud as the men stripped her son and held him down on the couch. Marco had gone at him with the belt for what seemed like a long time when she heard the boy's first cry and thought she should go to him. But he was so far away.

Ed Levine got quiet when he got angry. Graham was straining to hear him.

"Is this dink connected?"

"By a thread. An uncle in numbers. Nobody heavy."

Graham had forced the story out of Neal, who had finally showed up for work two days late and barely able to walk. He had gently cleaned the boy off, medicating the cuts that threatened to become infected. He had seen some beatings as a kid, but he had never seen anything like this. Neal's back and legs were a red and purple contour of welts and bruises where the pimp had lashed him with the buckle end of the belt.

"Nobody beats on one of my people," Levine said.

"Phone call to Mulberry Street takes care of him. They owe us a couple."

"No. This is personal. I want him for myself. Set it up."

"C'mon, Ed—"

Levine's glare ended the discussion.

Joe Graham didn't like it.

Levine had told him to set the guy up and he had set the guy up, but he wasn't happy about it. Standing in a dark alley with a vicious dope-pushing pimp and his gigantic thug, Graham just hoped that Ed Levine knew what he was doing. Ed Levine was a big guy, but this ox with Marco was a whole lot bigger.

"Where's your friend?" Marco asked him. The pimp, still decked out in his trademark white suit, was nervous.

"He's coming."

"He better be. I don't like standin' around when I'm holdin'."

"I don't like standing around, period."

"I hear that."

Come on, Ed, thought Graham. I hope you're not slopping down that Chinese food somewhere and forgot about our little appointment.

Marco said, "You don't mind my friend pats you down. Not that I don't trust you . . ."

"Hey, it's business, right?" answered Graham.

Graham lifted his arms as Johnny carefully and gently checked him for weapons. The guy is a pro, thought Graham, feeling a little more scared and wishing more than ever that Levine had just let the old Italian guys on Mulberry take care of this.

"He's okay," Johnny reported, smiling pleasantly at Graham.

"What happened to your arm?" Marco asked.

"I stuck it someplace it didn't belong."

"Hope she was worth it!" Marco laughed.

Graham chuckled politely and made a note to add this to Marco's tab.

"Good evening, gentlemen."

Graham turned with relief at the sound of Ed's voice and then regretted it. Levine was dressed in a three-piece gray pinstriped suit. What, Ed, are you going to rumble or sell them term life?

"How ya doin'?" asked Marco, sizing him up. This did not look like a guy who would want to buy dope.

"I'm doing fine," Levine answered. "It's you I'm worried about."

"You got no worries about me, my friend. I'm legit."

"Your health, I mean. I'm worried about your health."

There it was. In the air where everyone could feel it. Somebody was going to get hurt.

"Who are you?" asked Marco. He wanted to get right to it.

"I'm the guy who's going to bust you up bad," Ed answered in a conversational tone.

Before Graham could move or shout a warning, Johnny came at Levine from the blind left side with a swooping right hook designed to cave in Ed's jaw. Graham watched amazed as Levine leaned away from the fist and grabbed the wrist with his own left hand, switched his weight to his right foot, and kicked low and hard with his left.

The sole of his foot caught Johnny hard on the side of his planted left knee, and the sickening sound of bone and cartilage giving way as the giant crumpled to the ground with a scream made Graham want to lose his dinner.

Marco began to sweat but forced a smile. "You're in big trouble, sport. My Uncle Sal—"

"Thinks you're a sniveling little scumbucket. At least that's what he said to me at the social club. He doesn't like guys who beat up little boys, either."

Graham should have known the punk had a gun. Didn't they all? He cursed himself for not having checked him in the endless second it took for the pimp to reach inside his jacket to his shoulder holster.

Levine waited until he saw the muscles in Marco's wrist tense as he grabbed the handle of the revolver. He waited for the exact moment when the forearm lay flat and tight against the chest. Then he stepped back on his left foot, brought his right foot up level with his own chest, and then straightened his leg with a lightning kick that hit Marco's wrist like a hammer on an anvil. Marco's wrist snapped like a dead branch.

Marco stood, shocked and stupid, his right arm graciously numb and his hand caught inside his lapel. At least he understood now what was going on, although he couldn't believe this guy was so pissed off about some stupid hooker's little kid. Credibility came quickly with a sharp kick that cracked two ribs and doubled him over in pain. He was trying to hit the deck when three fists banged into his face with jackhammer speed, breaking his nose and left cheekbone. He felt only relief when his knees crashed onto the concrete. The alley in front of him spun in fiery red and sickly yellow as he heard the little one-armed guy ask, *"Where did you learn that stuff?"*

Levine was just reaching his stride, his breathing even and the slightest sheen of sweat beginning on his forehead. Chiding himself for getting out of shape, he did a reverse spinning dropkick that hit Marco flush in the side of the head and sent him flying into an unconscious heap.

"Is he dead?" Graham asked.

"I don't think so," Levine answered. He squatted down beside Marco and grabbed him by the broken wrist, squeezing hard. The sharp pain woke the pimp up. "Are you listening to me, asshole? Your career in New York is *over*. You got that?"

Marco listened numbly. An end to physical pain was the height of his worldly ambitions.

Graham had walked out into the street to fetch a cop who had been guarding the alley for them. He was a young patrolman, two years on the force and eager for a good arrest.

"He's yours and he's holding," Graham told him. "Easy felony. Do us a favor, though, and just drop the big guy off in an E Room and lose him, okay? You take care of that other thing?"

"The kid's mother. Yeah, we sent her out on a bus couple hours ago—one-way ticket."

"The kid?"

"Wasn't around."

"Okay, good job. Go pick up your prize."

They went into the alley, where the cop surveyed the scene. One mob-type gorilla lay whimpering against the wall, and a very duded-up wise guy, with a face that now looked like pie from the Automat, was kneeling and clutching a hand that was pointed uptown.

"Jesus Christ," the cop said, all kinds of alarms going off in his head, "are you sure this guy isn't connected?"

"He got *dis*connected," Levine said.

The patrolman none too gently hauled Marco out of the alley.

Graham stopped them on the way out. "Hey," he said to the pimp, "what happened to your arm?" Then he went over to Johnny, leaned down, and whispered in his ear, "We're turning you out for one reason. You spread the word. Nobody, but nobody, lays a hand on Neal Carey. Ever."

"Not while I'm around, mister."

"Good. Because he's a friend of the family."

7

One afternoon when Neal was thirteen, Graham arrived at his place with two packs of football cards, a roll of medical tape, and a pair of small scissors.

He set all this on the kitchen counter and then stood on his toes and inspected the top of the refrigerator.

"You have to clean up here," he said.

"You're the only one who ever looks."

"I brought you presents."

Neal checked out the items on the counter and said, "I'd rather have *Playboy*."

Graham unwrapped the football cards and set aside the two rectangles of flat, powdered bubble gum. He dealt five of the cards out, facedown, like a poker hand, and then handed the five to Neal.

"Look at them," he said.

"I'm too old for football cards, Graham."

"You too old to get paid?"

Neal examined the cards.

"Now hand them back."

Neal shrugged and gave him the cards. Graham merged them back into the rest of the pack, played with them for a minute, dealt out five cards, and handed them to Neal.

Neal looked at them and asked, "So?"

Graham opened the refrigerator. "You got no milk in here, no eggs, no orange juice. So, one of the cards was in the first *and* the second bunch. Which? Don't look."

"I'm gonna go shopping this afternoon. I think maybe Roosevelt Grier."

"You 'think maybe Roosevelt Grier'?"

"It was Roosevelt Grier."

"Roosevelt Grier is correct. Let's play again."

"Why?"

Graham didn't answer, but he shuffled the cards, selected five, and handed them to Neal. Neal had looked at them for maybe five seconds before Graham snatched them out of his hand, regrouped the cards, and handed them back.

"John Brodie?"

Graham shook his head.

"Matt Snell."

"Three more guesses, you might get it."

"I don't know."

"Right answer, but not good enough. It was Doug Atkins."

Neal grabbed a small spiral pad and pretended to carefully write out a shopping list.

"Okay," he said, "it was Doug Atkins. What difference does it make? What's the point?"

"The point is, in our business, you see somebody more than once, you better know it. Point is, in our business, you better develop an eye for detail. Quick and accurate. The point is—"

"In our business—"

"You need a memory."

Graham resumed his inspection of the kitchen. "I'll do the shopping. You stay here and memorize these cards."

"What do you mean, 'memorize'?"

"Gimme your shopping money."

Neal went into the bedroom and came out with five dollars.

"Where's the rest of it?" Graham asked.

"What rest? The cost of living here—"

"Soda, candy bars, magazines . . . What happened to that budget we made up?"

"It's *my* money."

"Give."

Neal came back with another seven dollars and slapped them into Graham's hand.

"I'll be back," Graham said.

"Yippee."

GRAHAM SET THE TWO LARGE GROCERY BAGS down on the counter, put the perishable items in the refrigerator, took the cards from Neal, and sat down. He opened the roll of medical tape, cut ten small strips, and taped them across the names of the players on the front of the cards. Then he held up a card in front of Neal.

"John Brodie."

Graham held up the next one.

"Alex Sandusky."

Another one.

"Jon Arnett."

He got all ten, first try, no mistakes.

"Not bad," Graham said.

"Not bad?"

"Take another look at them," Graham said, and he gave Neal a couple of minutes before taking them back. Then he taped over everything but the eyes. He held up a card to Neal.

"George Blanda?"

"'George Blanda?'" Graham mimicked.

"Alex Sandusky?"

"It's George Blanda."

"Tricky."

"Your first guess is usually right."

They went on this way most of the day. Graham would place the cards in various groups, flash them, and have Neal recite them in order; or show him five different groupings and then ask in which group a particular card had been. On and on, backward, forward, and sideways—until Neal could answer correctly. Every time.

Next Saturday. Neal's place.

"Jimmy Orr," said Graham.

Neal closed his eyes. "Five eleven, one eighty-five, eighth year, Georgia."

"Gino Cappelletti."

"Six flat, one ninety, sixth year, Minnesota."

"In the picture on the card, was he wearing home or away?"

"Home."

"You sure?"

"Home."

"Home is right."

"Yeah, I know. Look, Graham, I don't want to hurt your feelings, but football cards are getting boring."

"Yeah?"

"Yeah."

"Right."

Next Saturday. Graham's place.

"Miss April."

"Thirty-six, twenty-four, thirty-seven. Brown hair, green

eyes. Likes sunbathing, swimming, and water polo. Wants to be an actress. Turnoffs: tan lines and narrow-minded people."

"Miss October."

"Thirty-eight, twenty-five, thirty-eight. Blond, and blue. Five foot five. Hails from Texas. Likes horses, mellow music, and picnics. Wants to be an actress. Turnoffs: pollution, world hunger, and narrow-minded people."

Graham got the tape out. "Who's this?"

"Janice Crowley. Miss . . . some winter month . . ."

"Which winter month?"

"February."

"You guessed."

"But I guessed right."

"How did you recognize her?"

"Modesty forbids."

A FEW SATURDAYS LATER. NEAL'S PLACE.

"I have a new one," Neal said to Graham as he came through the door.

"A new what?"

"Memory game." Neal held up the Saturday *New York Times*. "The crossword puzzle."

Graham looked at it. There was nothing written in the squares.

"So what, you're going to do the puzzle?"

"I already did."

"Cute, Neal. Now let's get to work."

"It was tough."

Graham plunked himself down in the decrepit easy chair. "You asked for it, kid. Okay, twelve down."

"Apse."

"Where are the answers?"

"Tomorrow's paper."

"Thirty-one across."

"Kipling."

And so on and so forth, Graham wrote the answers in and checked the papers the next day. They were all right. Graham told Ed Levine about it, and he told Ethan Kitteredge. Ethan Kitteredge phoned a friend at Princeton, who came up to New York with a bunch of tests. Neal didn't want to take them until Graham held up three hundred baseball cards and offered the alternative. Neal took the tests and did pretty well.

8

NEAL AND GRAHAM HAD FINISHED a particularly easy job one night, an over-and-out surveillance on a visiting toy salesman who had found his own Barbie doll in the Roosevelt and who should never have ordered room service.

"When his old lady hears these tapes . . ." Neal said as they strolled up Broadway.

Graham shook his head. "No, we'll just file the report and use the tapes as backup."

"You're no fun."

Graham slowed his pace, tipping Neal off that he had something on his mind. He wasn't long getting it off.

"Neal, remember those tests you took?"

"That you made me take? Yeah."

"You did good."

"Swell."

Graham made a point not to look at him as he said, "So you're going to start Trinity School in the fall."

Neal froze. "Bullshit, I am."

Graham shrugged.

Neal turned to face him. "Who says? Who says I start Trinity in the fall?"

"The Man says. Levine says . . . I say."

"Yeah? Well, I say no way."

"Nobody's asking you."

Neal was angry. "It's a prep school! Kids wear jackets and ties! Rich kids go there! Forget it!"

He started to turn away, but Graham grabbed him by the wrist and held him still.

"This is a great opportunity for you."

"To be a fag. And leggo of me."

Graham released his wrist. "You're thirteen years old, Neal. You have to start thinking about your future."

Neal stared at the sidewalk. "I think about it."

"Yeah, you want to be me."

Graham saw the tears begin to form. He pushed on, anyway.

"You want to be me, son. But you can't be."

"You do okay."

"I do fine, but you can do better."

"I don't want to be better than you!"

"Listen, Neal. Listen. You're smart. You have brains. You don't want to spend your whole life sniffing people's sheets, peeking through windows—"

"We do other things. The time we found that old lady who inherited the money . . . the lawyer we caught ripping off that guy . . . that kid that ran away we found—"

"I'm not saying you can't work with me anymore. I'll always want you to work with me. But you have to go to school!"

"I go to school."

Graham laughed. "When you feel like it."

"Okay, I'll go to school, I will. But not that school!"

"The Man wanted to send you to one of those boarding schools in New England. I talked him out of it."

"Talk him out of this!"

"I don't want to."

Neal spun around and walked away—fast. Let Mr. Wizard follow me if he can, he thought. Ain't going to any rich little snobby fag school.

Graham let him go. Let him hide out for a while and think it over. He pointed his own nose to McKeegan's for a cold one and a shot.

NEAL SHOWED UP THERE TWO DAYS LATER. He found Graham sitting on his customary stool. Neal sat down at the other end of the bar.

"Those schools cost a lot of money," he said.

"A lot," Graham agreed.

"Time you add in books, fucking uniforms, all that shit."

"Very expensive."

McKeegan brought Graham his pastrami on rye, fries, and a fresh beer. "The kid want anything?" he asked Graham.

"The kid doesn't work for me anymore."

"*The kid* has money of his own," Neal said. "Give me a Coke." He would have ordered a beer, but knew that failure would be a disaster.

"Diamond Jim will have a Coke," McKeegan responded.

"So these books and stuff," Neal continued, "where would I get the money? You won't let me steal."

"The Man will pick up your tab. Plus your usual pay for jobs. Also something he called 'a modest allowance.' You steal, I break your wrists."

"Here's your Coke," McKeegan said. "Shall I keep the change?"

"Gimme."

"You've been associating with Graham too much."

"Tell me about it."

Graham took a break from his pastrami. He knew he should have had the corned beef. "The Man said something about 'grooming you for better things,' whatever that means. At first, I thought he was talking about a horse."

"Maybe he was."

"Maybe."

Neal sipped his Coke and set it down—an expansive gesture. He was pleased. "Tell you what. I'll come back. Same pay. No school."

"McKeegan, isn't this kid underage?"

"You'll never get anyone as good as I am."

"Probably not, son."

"So?"

"So, it comes to this." Graham turned on his stool to face the boy. "You go to this school or you go your own way."

Neal threw the Coke back as he'd seen the men do with the real stuff. "See you around," he said, and headed for the door.

"You know what I think?" Graham asked as he inspected the pastrami for fat. "I think you want to go to this school but you're afraid, because you think the other kids are better than you are."

PROBLEM WAS, THE OTHER KIDS thought so, too. Neal felt stupid enough anyhow, wearing the blue blazer, khaki slacks, and cordovans. With the white button-down shirt and brand-new old school tie. White fucking socks.

Then there was that assignment in Mr. Danforth's English class about your life at home. Neal had scribbled something straight out of *Leave It to Beaver* and the class had laughed its collective head off at him and Danforth got pissed at him.

What am I supposed to write? Neal thought. That my hophead hooker of a mother has split, and the nearest thing I got to a father is a one-armed dwarf whose idea of a father-son outing is breaking into somebody's office and lifting files? So don't ask me for real life, Mr. Danforth, because I don't think you can handle reading it any better than I can take writing it. Settle for June Cleaver and be happy.

Or how about the usual jokes? Your mother's like a doorknob. Everybody gets a turn. Your mother is like the Union Pacific. She got laid across the country. When these made the rounds, Neal was the only kid in school who knew for a fact they were true.

And when the talk turned to family vacations, Christmas presents, brothers and sisters and crazy aunts, Neal had nothing, flat-ass nothing, to say, and was too proud and too smart to make things up. Nor could he invite other kids over to his place, because it literally was his place—no mom-and-pop combo, cookies on the table—and his place was a one-room slum.

Neal was a lonely, miserable kid. Then that son of a bitch Danforth made him read Dickens.

Oliver Twist. Neal devoured it in two all-night sessions. Then he read it again, and when it came time to write about it . . . Boy, Mr. Danforth, can I write about it. Your other students may *think* they know what Oliver feels, but I *know* what he feels.

"This is excellent," Danforth said, handing him back his paper. "Why don't you talk in class?"

Neal shrugged.

"You liked Dickens," said Danforth.

Neal nodded.

Danforth went to his bookcase and handed Neal a copy of *Great Expectations.*

"Thank you," Neal said.

Neal went straight back to the neighborhood, bought himself a jar of Nescafé and a half-gallon of chocolate ice cream, and dug in to spend the weekend with Pip.

The reading was great. The reading was wonderful. He was never lonely when he was reading—never cold, never afraid, never alone in the apartment.

He returned *Great Expectations* with a small essay he'd written, and received *David Copperfield* in exchange.

"DID YOU LIKE IT?" DANFORTH ASKED.

"Yeah, I liked it . . . a lot."

"Why?"

"I don't know. It made me feel . . ." He couldn't find the word.

"I know what you mean." Danforth smiled at him. "You're okay, Carey, you know that?"

Parents' night was hell. Neal dreaded it with a near-tangible fear: exposure. He could hear the taunts that would follow him around the hallways the next day and ever after: bastard.

That night, he sat in the back of homeroom as the parents drifted in, smiled their dull smiles, shook their wooden handshakes, feigning interest in their daughters' dumb pastels and sons' stupid poems.

He looked impatiently at his watch every few seconds and frowned a "Where the hell are they?" frown for the benefit of anybody who might be watching, awash in the adolescent conviction that everyone was watching. He was slumped so low in his chair that he didn't see her come in, but he sure as hell heard her. Her rich voice dripped class.

"Hello, I'm Mrs. Carey, Neal's mother. How nice to meet you."

She was beautiful. She made Mrs. Cleaver look like a

carhop. Her auburn hair was perfectly coiffed. Her gray dress was letter-perfect for the occasion. Brown eyes sparkled at the teacher, and as she held her hand out, the poor man almost kissed rather than shook it.

She strode to the back of the room, displaying a warm maternal smile as she kissed Neal on both cheeks and subtly hauled him from his seat. "Show me everything," she said.

They walked the school together, pretending fascination with the various displays. She oohed proudly over his prize essay on Dickens's London. She charmed teachers and parents, sipped punch, and nibbled cookies. She apologized for having to leave so early and swept, yea verily *swept,* out the door.

Neal found Graham at McKeegan's later on. "Where did you get her?" he asked. "She was perfect."

Graham nodded.

For two hundred bucks, he thought, she'd better be perfect.

"You're Faginesque, you know that?" Neal asked Graham. They were in a dark staircase in Neal's building.

"What do you mean? I like women. Don't tiptoe. You don't make noise stepping *on* the stair; you make it stepping off."

"That's what I mean. Fagin was a character in *Oliver Twist* who taught boys how to steal and stuff."

"I don't teach you how to steal." Graham didn't have much patience at the moment for this Fagin shit. He was trying to teach the kid something important. "You plant your foot— not heavy, but firmly. You step off lightly, like you don't weigh anything."

"Yeah, okay, not steal. But stuff like this."

Neal planted his foot on the edge of the step. The result was an awful screech.

"You want to wake the whole building?" Graham asked.

"Always, always step to the butt end of the stair. That's where it's the most solid, least likely to squeak. Also you can feel your way. You can feel where the next step is. 'Faginesque.' I'll give you 'Faginesque.' Get to work."

Work this evening was learning how to climb stairs without making any noise. Work was doing it with your eyes closed. Work was realizing that you make more noise going downstairs than going up, so, generally speaking, you sneak up but run down.

"Christmastime," Graham said as Neal practiced his step technique, "I run out and buy presents for those people who put carpet on their stairs."

"Nice people," Neal agreed.

Going downstairs was a genuine bitch, mostly because you can't find the butt end of the step with your toe and you're afraid of pitching forward and breaking your neck. So observed Neal to his tutor about the fortieth time he'd fucked up the maneuver.

"Worse comes to worst," Graham said, "and it will, you get down on your belly and swim downstairs."

"Swim?"

"Try it. Don't be afraid. Lie down, headfirst, and do the dog paddle."

"I can't swim and I don't have a dog."

Neal felt stupid as shit lying down dangling over the stairs.

"You've seen Lassie, haven't you?" asked Graham. "Do like Lassie does, when she has to save that little bastard from drowning."

"Timmy."

"Right. Whatever. Quit stalling."

Graham put his foot on Neal's ass and pushed.

It wasn't so bad when you got used to it, Neal thought, doing like Lassie does, et cetera. He made his way to the bottom of the stairs.

He asked Graham, "How do you do this with one arm?"

"You don't. You hire some stupid kid to do it for you."

He walked over Neal's back and out the door.

A COUPLE OF MONTHS LATER, Neal tried to climb through a window and talk at the same time. He had something on his mind.

"If I gave you the money, would you buy me something?"

Graham stood on the fire escape. "What? Beer? Cigarettes? Rubbers?"

"A book."

Neal was backing through the window, his feet already in the kitchen sink.

"A book? You really want to go through a window like that? So you can't see what's in the room awaiting your arrival with a Louisville Slugger? What book, Neal? *Swedish Sex Slaves? Ruby and the Firemen?* Like that?"

Neal climbed out. "*Tom Jones.*"

He started back through the window, headfirst this time.

"*Tom Jones?* Is it dirty?"

"Dirty enough, they won't let me buy it."

"Are you really this stupid, Neal, or are we just having an off day? Going into an apartment window head in the air like a hanging curveball? You go in like that, you come out on a stretcher, anyone's home."

Neal eased his way out. "So will you?"

"What's so important about this book?"

"David Copperfield read it when he was a kid. You know David Copperfield?"

"Yes, I know David Copperfield. I saw it twice. Freddie Bartholomew and W. C. Fields."

"Really? W. C. Fields? Who'd he play?"

"I don't know. Guy who was always broke, owed money."

"Mr. Micawber."

"Yeah, okay. Now will Mr. Carey please show me the correct way to enter a domicile via a window, if this literary discussion is over? Or shall I pour tea?"

"I don't know."

"What don't you know?"

"The correct way to enter a domicile via a window."

"Why didn't you ask?"

FEETFIRST, FACING THE WINDOW, and swing through. Like you're on the monkey bars. Then walk purposefully through the kitchen and down the hallway and into the bedroom, which will be on your right. Don't tiptoe. Tiptoes are for ballerinas and guys who go to jail for B&E. Which you are neither. First thing, grab something that looks pawnable and put it in your pocket. If someone is there and you can't get out, don't fight. Let him grab you and call the cops. Levine will be right there to arrest you.

So you're in the bedroom and the guy is asleep. You put his watch in your pocket and place this nice little mike under the side table. Put the watch back. I said put the watch back. Now go out the way you came in.

Easier than Maloney's sister. Your old Dad taught you well. Home now for a Swanson's TV dinner and a book.

Thus, Neal Carey grew up and learned a useful trade.

9

"Today," said Joe Graham with his brightest nasty smile, "we are going to play a game."

"Swell," said sixteen-year-old Neal, who possessed that finely tuned sixteen-year-old sense of sarcasm.

They were sitting in Graham's apartment on Twenty-sixth Street between Second and Third. The place looked like an operating room, only smaller. The countertop of the efficiency kitchen glistened and the sink and tap handles shone as brightly as the soul of a seven- year-old Catholic girl leaving confession. Neal could not figure out how a one-armed man could make a bed with hospital corners you could cut yourself on. The bathroom contained a toilet that begged sunglasses, a similarly shimmering sink, and a shower—no bath. ("I don't like lying around in dirty water.") Graham had moved in ten years ago because it was an upwardly mobile Irish neighborhood. He had failed to discern that all the upwardly mobile Irish were moving to Queens. They came back to the neighborhood only on Saturday nights to sit in a local tavern and listen to songs about killing Englishmen, sanguinary concerts punctuated by maudlin renditions of the dreaded "Danny Boy."

On this particular Saturday, an unseasonably warm autumn afternoon, the neighborhood was noisy with the sounds of playing children, old couples returning from their weekly grocery shopping, and neighbors hanging out on the sidewalk enjoying the sun.

Neal would rather have been enjoying the sun, especially in the company of one Carol Metzger, with whom he had planned a stroll in Riverside Park and maybe a movie. Instead, he was cooped up in Graham's stuffy shrine to Brillo, about to play a game.

"The game is called Hide-and-Go-Fuck-Yourself," Graham announced, "and the rules are simple. I hide something and you go fuck yourself."

"You win. Can I go now?"

"No. Now, let us say I have lost my earring—"

"Your *earring*?"

"Just play the game. I have lost my earring. It is somewhere in this apartment. Find it."

"What are *you* going to do?"

"I'm going to have a beer."

"Can I have a beer?"

"No. You can look for the earring."

Graham went to the fridge and got a cold one. Then he sat down on a stool by the kitchen counter and turned to the sports section of the *Daily News*.

Neal began to search the apartment. If he could nail this stupid thing early, maybe Graham would let him out of here and he could still catch up with Carol Metzger. The way her brown hair fell on her shoulders made his stomach hurt.

If I were an earring, where would I be? he thought. This

seemed like the most logical way to go about this. He looked under the cushions of the small sofa in Graham's "sitting area."

"Good idea," Graham said.

There was no earring in the sofa. There was no earring under the sofa. There wasn't even any dust under the sofa; no pennies, rubber bands, paper clips, or toothpicks, either. Neal looked in the seam between the seat cushion and back of Graham's Naugahyde easy chair. No earring.

"The Giants are eight-point dogs tomorrow," Graham noted. "At home against the Colts. You want in?"

Neal didn't bother to answer. He knew this bit. Graham was just trying to distract him, disrupt his concentration.

Graham continued: "Eight points. Tempting. You can give a touch and still make. Of course, the stupid bastards would find a way to give up a safety in the last twelve seconds and bust your balls."

"*Where's the goddamn earring?*"

"Go fuck yourself," Graham said pleasantly. There were far worse ways to kill a Saturday afternoon than torturing Neal: watching college football, for example.

An ugly suspicion hit Neal. "Is this earring on, as they say, your person?"

"That would be, as they say, devious." "Because if it's in your underwear, I'm not looking for it."

Graham was tempted to say something about this Carol girl but thought better of it, sixteen-year-old love being a sensitive sort of thing. "So if I tell you to search my drawers, you wouldn't take it the wrong way?"

Neal rifled through Graham's chest of drawers. This wasn't too hard. The socks were neatly balled and organized by color. The underwear was folded. There were little plastic containers for formerly loose change. Neal got a quick surge of hope when he found the little tray containing cuff links and tie tacks, but there was no earring. Nor was it under the laundered shirts, stiff in cardboard and tissue paper, nor under the sweaters.

"You told me to search the drawers!"

"So?"

"So it's not there."

"Gee."

Neal tried the closet next: coat pockets, shelves, the works. In a moment of inspiration, he searched the vacuum-cleaner bag. Nothing. While he was zipping it back up, Graham slid off his stool and came over.

"You're going about this all wrong, son."

"Figures."

"The key to finding an object is not to look for it."

"I can do that."

Graham ignored the remark. "Don't search for the object; search the space. Don't run around looking where you think the object might be; look at what is. Got it?"

Neal shook his head.

"Okay," Graham said, "you got the room, right? That's what *is*. In the room, there is supposed to be an earring, right? That's what *might* be. What are you going to look at, what *is* or what *might* be?"

"What is."

Graham was getting excited. "Right! So you search the room!"

"That's what I was doing!"

"No, you were searching around the room."

Neal sat down in the easy chair. "I'm sorry, I don't get it."

Graham went to the fridge and got out a beer and a Coke. He handed Neal the Coke. "Okay, you like to read, right?"

"Yeah."

Graham was thinking real hard. "So when you read, do you skip all over the page? Read a word here, a word there?"

"No."

"Why not?"

"Wouldn't make any sense."

"So what do you do?"

"Well . . . you read paragraphs . . . and sentences."

"Okay! So break the room up into paragraphs! Read the room!"

Now Neal was getting excited. He didn't quite have it, but the connection was almost there. "Yeah, but how do you break a room up into paragraphs?"

"Divide it up into cubes."

"Cubes?"

"Sure. It would be squares, except squares are only two dimensions, and rooms are three dimensions. Then you search a square at a time. Search the whole square. Don't look for the object; search the cube. If the object is there, you'll find it. If not, *move* on to the next cube."

"That makes sense."

"How about that? Now find the earring while I finish my beer and look for investment opportunities," Graham said. He returned to his stool and perused the point spreads.

Neal found it in the fifth cube, beneath the radiator.

He held the earring up in triumph.

Graham nodded. "The cube system is good, of course, when you are looking for some specific object, but it's even better when you are just searching for something."

"What do you mean?"

Graham sighed in mock exasperation. "Sometimes, Neal, you're sent into an apartment, or an office, or a house just to see if there's anything peculiar, out of the ordinary; with the cube system, you're unlikely to miss anything, like maybe a twelve-inch mahogany dildo carved like Mount Rushmore or something."

"Because you're just looking, not looking for something, and therefore you're not narrowing your vision with preconceptions."

"If you say so, son. We'll pick this up next week. Now get out so I can watch Ohio State massacre Wisconsin in peace."

"We're done?" Neal asked, visions of Carol Metzger dancing in his head.

"For today."

Neal scrambled for the door.

"Neal!"

Neal stopped in the doorway. He knew it was too good to be true. Graham was probably going to send him out to look for something, like a gum wrapper he had initialed and left in Times Square.

"Yeah?"

"You got money for the movie?"

How did he know? "Yeah . . ."

Graham extended a ten-dollar bill. "You'll want to take her somewhere decent afterward, get a bite to eat."

Neal shook his head. "Thanks, Graham, but I don't want—"

"Take it. You're a working man; you deserve a little walking-around money. Take her someplace they have napkins."

Neal took the money. "Thanks, Graham."

"Get out; I wanna see the pregame show."

Neal split. Graham went back to his paper, but his mind was more on Eileen O'Malley, who had been sixteen when he was sixteen, and who had blue eyes that could stop your heart.

10

"You give good search, Neal," Joe Graham said one Saturday morning during one of their weekly training sessions.

"Thanks."

"You read a room really very well." This was true. Neal had just finished searching Graham's apartment for an M&M, a brown one, the regular kind, not the peanut. He had found it in less than ten minutes, taped in the water tank of the toilet.

"But," Graham said as Neal winced, "Helen Keller could come in here, know the place was tossed."

"Isn't she dead?"

"Doesn't matter. She could still tell." This week, Neal actually had a Saturday-night date, a real date, with Carol Metzger, so he was in a particular hurry. Nevertheless, he was annoyed that Graham was never happy. What did he want?

"Go search my top drawer."

That's what he wanted.

Neal went to the drawer and visually divided it into cubes. He lifted up the plastic tray full of change, saw nothing very interesting, and was about to set it down when Graham told him to freeze.

"Look at the way you picked it up," Graham said. He waited for an answer.

Neal didn't have one. He had just picked the damn thing up, that's all. He shrugged.

Graham continued, "You picked it up diagonally, at an angle."

"I should be shot." What the hell difference did it make?

"You have to lift this straight up. Straight. Why?"

"Oh yeah, so you can set it down in exactly the same place."

"You're not as stupid as you look. Of course, that would be impossible. Now practice."

"Practice?"

"It's not as easy as it seems, lifting things straight up, setting them down. I'm going to practice on a cold bottle of Knickerbocker."

So Neal spent an hour and a half lifting things up and setting them down, and it wasn't as easy as it seemed. He found the best technique was to stand at a little less than arm's reach, with his elbow slightly bent and wrist cocked downward.

"What about fingerprints?" he asked Graham. Have you ever thought of that, wise guy?

"Yeah, well, if you're tossing an FBI agent, you might want to bring gloves along, but if you do it right, your average homeowner isn't gonna know you've been there, never mind think about fingerprints."

The next thing they worked on were window treatments. "That's what interior decorators call curtains and venetian blinds and that stuff," Graham said.

"What do you know about interior decorators?"

"There's one lives in this building whose interior I'd like to decorate."

"God."

"So look behind the curtain there."

"I looked already."

"Yeah, you looked bad, now I want you to look good."

Neal reached for the curtain.

"Stop."

"I haven't even touched it!"

"You were about to pull it *back*. Don't pull it *back*, pull it *out*, and no smart remarks."

Neal pulled the curtain out.

"Now let go of it."

Neal did.

"And?" Graham asked.

"And it fell back in the same place."

"Doesn't matter so much if it's a guy's place, but women notice these things. Woman comes home and there's a corpse lying on the floor; she calls the cops and says, 'There's a body lying in a pool of blood over by the curtain, which is out of place.' Now raise the blinds."

"You're going to stop me before I touch the cord, aren't you?"

"Yes. First lick your finger."

"Then do I spin around three times and say, 'There's no place like home'?"

Graham made a lewd gesture. "Spin on this," he said. "But first lick your finger, then—"

"Which—"

"Any finger. Just do it. Now . . . using the spittle—"

"*Spittle?*"

"Mark the windowsill and match it up with the bottom edge of one of the thingies on the blinds."

Neal did, raised the blinds, and then lowered them to the exact spot.

"And you thought your Uncle Joey was crazy."

"Same thing with windows up and down, right?"

"Bright boy."

Neal went to the fridge and grabbed a Coke. "So probably the next thing you're going to show me is how to do closet doors, medicine cabinets, that sort of thing?"

"I'm looking at you with new respect, Neal. Now usually this is the stuff that only professionals, women, and advanced paranoids notice, but there's no harm in being careful, right?"

"I like careful."

So they went to work on the closet door in Graham's bedroom. First came a lecture from Graham, which Neal didn't mind, as it gave him a chance to sit down and finish his Coke. Graham told him that if the closet was shut, it was no issue. But sometimes suspicious people will leave a closet door ajar deliberately, and then you had to be careful to leave it exactly the same way. There were two good ways to accomplish this.

"You can mark the opening along the side of your shoe, or you can do what the subject probably did, which is to line the edge of the door up with something else in the room, usually something on the wall, and usually something very obvious.

"Hinged doors like this one are trickier than sliding doors. Why?"

"Because you have to check both the inside and outside edges of the door against possible marks on the wall, and also because it's harder to match the exact perspective that the subject used to make the mark."

"You're sharp today. This is why I prefer to make measurement from the doorsill to the door, because there's no perspective to worry about. If it's two inches, it's two inches, as you know from bitter personal experience."

"You have to be careful about closed doors, too, don't

you? Don't people sometimes leave tape or hair or something stretched across the door?"

"They do in books and movies a lot, yeah. And sometimes in real life, but yes, son, you're right. It doesn't hurt to check."

"You said that already."

"I'll say it about fifty thousand times."

They practiced being careful for a couple of hours, leaving marks on doorsills, medicine cabinets, windows, bedspreads, pillows, even flower arrangements. It was exacting work that demanded precision. Neal was bushed when they finished.

"So," Graham asked, "who's your date with tonight?"

"Nice try."

"You should tell your old Dad these things."

"You'll never know."

"Why not?"

"Because you'd never shut up about it. You'd want to know everything."

"Is she one of those rich Trinity babes?"

"I dunno."

"You 'dunno'? Have you met this girl?"

"I don't know if she's rich."

SHE WAS. OR HER PARENTS WERE, ANYWAY. Their apartment occupied half a floor on Central Park West.

Neal was nervous. This was the first time he had gone to Carol's home, the first time he was to meet her parents. She'd been after him to do it for weeks.

"You *have* to meet them," she'd said, "if we're going to go on a real date. You know, at night. Or they won't let me."

Going to her home, meeting her parents, Saturday-night date: It was fraught with peril on several levels. It elevated their relationship from the safe status of friends just hanging out on weekend afternoons to boyfriend and girlfriend, and the news would be out all over school before classes started Monday morning. Neal wasn't sure how he felt about that. Scary stuff on the one hand, but on the other it was great. Then there was the parent thing. Neal didn't have a lot of experience with parents, his own or anybody else's. He knew from *Leave It to Beaver* that parents tended to ask a bunch of questions, the answers to which would probably propel them to throw him out and lock Carol in her room—with armed guards.

"CAROL'S NOT QUITE READY YET," her father would say, lighting his pipe as he looked Neal over from head to toe. "Have a seat, young man. Take that chair there, the electric one."

Her mother would hover about nervously, smiling tightly while she contemplated changing the locks on all the doors.

"What does your father do?" Carol's father would ask, raising thick eyebrows.

"He's in travel, sir."

"And does your mother work?" Mrs. Metzger would ask.

"Uh . . . yes, ma'am."

"What does she do?"

"Public relations . . . sales."

"We'd like to meet your parents sometime," Mr. Metzger would say.

"So would I, sir."

This was going to be a disaster.

"WHAT FLOOR?"

"Huh?"

"What floor do you want?" the doorman asked.

"The Metzgers'?"

"That's the penthouse."

"Swell."

"Are they expecting you?" the doorman asked.

"I'm afraid so."

The doorman gave him an ugly look and pointed to the elevator. The operator settled for a smirk as he took him up. Neal took a deep breath in the foyer and rang the bell. Here we go.

Carol opened the door right away.

"Hi!" she said. She looked flushed, nervous, and glad to see him. "Meet my parents."

Her parents were on their hands and knees on the floor.

Mrs. Metzger looked up at him. Neal saw where Carol got her looks. Mrs. M. was wearing a sequined black evening gown and a lot of jewelry. "It's a pleasure to meet you, Neal, but don't come in any farther, please."

Mr. Metzger, clad in a dinner jacket, said, "Likewise, Neal."

"Aren't you all supposed to be facing East?" Neal asked.

Oh God, why do I say these things?

"Mrs. Metzger's contact lens," Carol's father said.

"And we're already late," Mrs. Metzger said.

Carol looked at him and shrugged.

"I can find it," Neal said.

"How's that?" Mr. Metzger asked, his hand gently sweeping the thick gray carpet.

"I can find it. If you'll all stay still."

Carol looked at him strangely.

Less than two minutes later, Neal held the lens gently on his index finger. He had found it on Mr. Metzger's pant cuff.

"Neal," said Mrs. M., "thank you! How did you do that?"

"Practice."

Carol's mother looked at her and said, "I *like* this one."

"Hope to see you again, Neal. We have to go, Joan."

"MY PARENTS LIKE YOU," Carol said much later as they were walking back from a Chinese dinner after the movie. "They have good taste, my parents."

The elevator ride lasted about eighty thousand years. Her parents weren't home yet, and Carol and Neal sat down on the sofa next to each other. Her kisses were delicious and kisses were enough, more than enough, for this night. They were sitting at a proper distance when her parents discreetly rattled their keys at the door.

11

"I REALLY DON'T WANT TO BE DOING THIS," Neal said to Graham. Neal was seventeen and there were a whole lot of things he really didn't want to be doing. Lacing on boxing gloves in a stinking old gym off Times Square headed the list at the moment, however.

"I don't blame you," Graham answered, "but it's either this or that kung fooey crap Levine does."

The gym was on the second floor of a decrepit building off Forty-fourth Street and smelled like the inside of a jockstrap that had been left in the laundry bag about a month. Neal took another look around the room, where a dozen or so honest-to-God boxers banged on speed bags, heavy bags, and each other. Another guy was jumping rope, an activity that looked a little more appealing.

"Why," Neal asked, "do I have to learn to fight at all?"

"Company rule."

"It's stupid."

The guy lacing up his gloves looked as if he had stepped out of a casting call for *Darby O'Gill and the Little People.* He kneeled in front of Neal's stool and blew cigarette smoke in the kid's face.

"It's the manly art," Mick croaked, pulling the laces a little tighter for emphasis.

"I never been in a fight yet they stopped to put gloves on," Graham responded.

"You hang around a scummy class of people. Okay, kid, on your feet."

Neal stood up. He banged his gloves together as he'd seen them do on television. The hollow *thwump* was reassuring.

"Take a poke," Mick offered.

"You don't have gloves on."

This amused Mick. He snorted and it sounded like an old steam engine going to its last reward. "You ain't gonna hit me."

"He's probably right," Graham said.

Neal launched a tentative right that looked like it had all the lethal menace of a kitten swatting at a Christmas-tree bulb.

Mick leaned away from the punch and shot a center-right jab that ended a quarter inch from Neal's nose. "Keep your left up," he said with a measure of disgust. "Ain't you never fought nobody?"

"I run away."

"Yeah, I knew fighters like that. But the old squared circle gets smaller in the late rounds."

"Squared circle?"

"Can't stay on the bicycle all night."

"That's why I take the subway," Neal said.

"We're gonna have to start from scratch." Mick sighed.

So they started from scratch. Three times a week, after school, Neal reported to the gym to study boxing under the tutelage of Mick, pugilist. He learned to keep his left up, to pop his jab, to counter hooks with straight rights, and to keep his mouth shut and his chin tucked in. He learned to do push-ups, sit-ups, and pull-ups. He hated all of it.

After three months of this, Mick decided he was ready to spar with a live boxer.

The great event took place on a Saturday morning and Joe Graham and Ed Levine came to watch. Levine wanted to check on Neal's progress. Graham averred that anytime there was a chance of Neal getting punched, he was going to be there to enjoy it.

The sparring partner was a young man named Terry McCorkandale. He was from Oklahoma, had a red crew cut, and looked like his mother had conceived him with her first cousin. He was a sparring partner of another pro, who was a sparring partner of a ranked contender.

This record gave Neal some comfort. True, the guy was a pro, but just barely, judging by his record. Besides which, Neal was feeling pretty good about his training. He was no boxer, he knew, but he could hold his own. He stepped into the ring, shook hands with McCorkandale, and flashed a quick smile at Levine and Graham. Then he assumed his defensive stance and shot out a crisp left jab.

He woke up hearing McCorkandale pleading defensively, "I just tapped him. Honest."

"Glass jaw?" Mick asked Graham.

"Glass brain," Graham answered.

"What day is it?" Mick asked Neal.

"January."

"Close enough," Levine said. "Let's try it again."

Neal was on his feet but not quite sure how he had gotten there. He knew he had been humiliated, but he didn't mind that as much as he did the physical pain. McCorkandale was smiling at him apologetically.

Mick whispered in his ear, "Lucky punch, kid. Go get him."

Neal had an album of the *1812* Overture at home, and the

next three minutes were like living inside the drum section. The Tulsa Terror rattled on him like a snare drum, beat a few timpani shots, and thumped a couple of bass drumbeats before Neal could move his hands. He could not have been more helpless if he had been tied up in telephone wire. He was only grateful this guy wasn't really trying.

"Interesting strategy," Levine observed to Graham, "wearing the guy out like that."

"That Neal's a terror."

Neal the Terror did what he could. He started to laugh. It was funny to him now that every time he attempted a punch or a parry, he got hit with three shots, so he covered up the best he could and got pounded on. And giggled.

"I gotta stop this," Mick said.

"He's not hurting him," Ed said.

"This kid's gotta fight tonight. He won't be able to lift his arms."

"So?" Levine asked Mick while Neal was in the shower.

"He's hopeless," Mick wheezed. "The worst I ever seen."

"Yeah, okay. No more lessons."

"Aw, thank God, Ed. I ain't got the heart. What that kid does to the Sweet Science shouldn't be done."

"You want a milk shake?"

"I can eat solid food. I want a cheeseburger."

Neal and Graham were at the Burger Joint, of course, after the big match. Neal's jaw was a little puffy and he had a black eye.

"That was fun, Neal. I enjoyed that. Thanks for the afternoon."

"That makes it all worth it, Graham."

"You did pretty good. I think your ribs bruised his hand once."

"I had him right where I wanted him. Another ten minutes, he would have dropped," Neal checked his face in the mirror on the side wall. "Carol's not going to like this."

"Are you kidding? Women love that stuff. If you had a broken nose, she'd propose to you."

"I need an iced coffee."

"For your face?"

"It does kind of hurt."

Neal took small bites of his burger. The iced coffee came and Neal alternately sipped at it and held it against his jaw. He felt really tired all of a sudden.

"Forget about it. Guy was a pro."

Neal shook his head. "That's not it. I don't know what to tell Carol. Her parents."

"She doesn't know what you do?"

"Get real."

"We're not the what-do-you-call-it, the CIA, son. You can tell her."

"If I tell *what* I do, I'd have to tell her how I got doing what I do."

"So?"

"So she'll split. And if she doesn't, her parents will make her split."

"You got quite a problem there, son—"

"Tell me about it."

"With your head."

Graham tossed a five on the table, chucked Neal under the chin, and left. Neal sat there for a while and then went home to get ready for his date.

So a couple of dates later, Neal told Carol all about himself. About never knowing who his father was, about his junkie mom and what she did for a living. About how she'd disappeared and he lived on his own. And he told her he did some work on the side for sort of a detective agency, but how that wasn't what he wanted to do with his life. He wanted to be a professor.

And she hugged him and kissed him and he took her back to his place and they made love and it was all wonderful and they talked about going to college together and always being there for each other.

A week later, Carol's dad took him aside when he went to pick her up. Mr. Metzger led him into the study. Carol had told them about Neal's life and both he and Carol's mother didn't think that she was ready for quite such an exposure to the real world just yet. Certainly Neal could understand, and they could still be friends in school.

Neal and Carol snuck around for a while. She would tell her parents lies and get a friend to cover for her, and sometimes she would even spend the night at Neal's. At first, it was exciting and romantic, but then it got to be just tiring and sad, and Neal figured that he did enough sneaking around in his life. He should be able to love in the open. So after a while, they became just friends, and then not even that.

One night over a late dinner, Neal told Graham the story and capped it off with his mature judgment.

"You can't trust anyone, Dad."

"That's not true, son. You can trust me."

12

NEAL CAME BACK FROM CONNECTICUT to an empty apartment. It didn't surprise him, even though Diane had been sleeping there more nights than not lately.

They'd had one of those quick but wicked fights the morning he'd left to meet Graham at the train. She couldn't understand that anything could be so urgent that he had to miss an exam, or that anything could be so confidential that he couldn't tell her where he was going or what he was doing. He wanted to tell her that he didn't understand it, either, but the rules told him to keep his mouth shut.

"Am I allowed to know how long you'll be gone?" she'd asked.

"I'd tell you if I knew."

"Gee, thanks."

"How's the studying going?"

"Great."

He didn't doubt it. He knew Diane was smarter than he was and worked harder to boot. She was the star of every class and seminar, and so insecure, she was the only one who didn't see that.

They'd met in Boskin's Eighteenth-Century Comparative Lit

seminar just a few weeks after the Halperin job. He'd been reading and drinking, more drinking than reading, when they managed to contrive a conversation in the hall. He took her to coffee and she took him to bed, explaining somewhere in there that she had time for a relationship but not for a courtship. He found that the page-boy cut of her dark brown hair and the hats and vests and baggy clothes she wore disguised a quite feminine body. She made love like she studied, with a fierce concentration and attention to detail, and she slept right through the nightmares he was having in those days.

So now, he called her room at Barnard. She answered on the fourth ring.

"Yeah?"

"Hi."

"You missed a hell of an exam."

Might as well get this over with.

"I have to go away for a while."

He could feel her anger over the phone. "More secret guy-type stuff?"

"Yeah."

"I sleep with you, you know?"

"I know."

"So when do I get to know you? When do I see the other half? What's so bad? What's so special about *your* secrets?" she asked, then added with a small chuckle, "Hey, Neal, you show me yours, I'll show you mine."

His chest felt tight. It hurt. "If I show you that stuff, you'll leave me."

"If you *don't* show me that stuff, I'll leave you."

It hurt a lot more. He didn't have anything to say.

"Besides," said Diane, "I'm not leaving you, you're leaving me."

"Can I come over?"

"All of you or part of you?"

Part of me, and fuck you.

"I guess I'll see you when I get back," he said.

"Maybe."

She hung up.

Good going, Neal, he thought. Well, probably for the best, anyway. You've raised self-pity to an art form; this will give you a chance to create another masterpiece.

He checked the clock. It was 11:30. He dialed Levine at home.

"Hi. I hope I woke you up."

"Not exactly."

"And you answered the phone? How *is* the little woman? On top of things?"

"What do you want?"

"I'll need a safe house."

"What's wrong with a hotel?"

"It has other guests. I'll need a safe house."

Neal could hear Janet's voice in the background. A fine whine that had improved with age.

"I'll work on it," Ed said. "What else?"

"Cash."

"Keep accounts."

"When Allie ran away before, did *you* pick her up?"

The pause was just a shade too long. "What the fuck are you talking about?"

Nice try, you lying sack of shit.

"Nothing. Listen, go back to what you were doing."

Levine slammed the receiver down.

How come everyone's hanging up on me tonight?

He dialed Graham.

"Dad!"

"Son . . ."

"Find anything?"

"Not a thing."

"How about in Ed's desk?"

"Zip. If we ever dealt with Allie Chase, there's nothing there to show it."

"Well . . . thanks for the effort."

"Always a pleasure. When do you take off?"

"Tomorrow. Next day. I'm waiting on some stuff from Ed."

"Mind if I go back to bed?"

"Sweet dreams." He hung up quickly, just to break the pattern.

Neal rooted around the refrigerator until he found a beer hiding in the back. He popped it open and drained about half of it in the first swallow. Maybe if he just showed up at Diane's, displayed his sweet, sad face, she'd take him in. Probably not. He finished his beer and went to bed.

The phone woke him early.

"Wake up, fuckhead," Levine said.

"What do you want?"

"Nothing," Ed said. Then he hung up.

The doorbell rang about noon. Neal was making coffee, strong, black hangover coffee. The kind of coffee meant to bring life back to your fingertips. He wasn't thrilled to hear the doorbell. Maybe it was Diane, but probably it wasn't. He thought about ignoring it, until it went off again, machine-gun-style, as if somebody was leaning on the button.

Joe Graham was leaning on the button.

"Wakey, wakey," he said when Neal opened the door. He didn't wait to be asked in, but walked past Neal, sniffed the coffee, and grabbed a cup out of the cupboard. He examined it carefully. "Is this clean?"

"I washed it personally."

"I'll take a chance."

He poured himself a cup, found milk and sugar, and poured a healthy measure in of each. Then he poured another cup—black, no sugar—and set it down on the counter. He lifted his own cup in a toast. "Bon voyage."

"You know something I don't?"

Neal took a sip of the coffee and believed once again in the possibility of a supreme, merciful God.

"I know a lot you don't know, son, about everything, but I also know that you're leaving tonight at eight o'clock," Graham said. He took a ticket packet from his jacket pocket and tossed it to Neal. "I know that some guy named Simon Keyes—are you ready for this? he's a safari guide—will meet you at the airport. He's going to be gone most of the summer. You can use his apartment to detox the kid."

"*A safari guide?* This is getting bizarre, Graham."

Neal started on his second cup.

"He safari guided The Man once. Friend of the family, so to speak. Guess what else I know."

"Decency doesn't allow—"

"You're supposed to have the kid back by August first."

"Any particular time?"

"Seriously."

"Seriously."

Graham ground his rubber hand into his natural one, the way he always did when he was worried. "This coffee isn't too horrible. I'm surprised. They also don't want her back much *before* August first."

"Children should be seen and not heard?"

"Something like that."

Yeah, something like that, Neal thought. John Chase is walking a narrow line, and he thinks he's the only one who knows it. He wants Allie back just long enough to play her role in "The Waltons Go to Washington," not long enough to sing

"Daddy's Little Girl." He must want to be Veep pretty badly to take that kind of risk.

"Today is what, May twenty-eighth?"

"Twenty-ninth."

"Twenty-ninth. That gives me something like nine weeks to find her, get hold of her, fix her up, and persuade her to come back, and these people want it brought in on the button? Gee, what if I can't?"

The rubber hand was really busy now, rubbing away. Graham didn't like this thing, either.

"If you can't bring her in on the date . . . forget it," he said.

"Forget it?"

Graham shrugged. It was an eloquent gesture, the answer to a Zen koan.

"Yeah, okay," Neal said. "I get it."

Allie is useful for a few days if it's the right few days. Otherwise, leave her where she is.

"Smells, right?" Graham said, rubbing a sheen onto the rubber hand.

"Like a garbage strike in July."

"Right?"

Graham poured another cup. Neal saw he wasn't finished with the news.

"What else do you know?" Neal asked.

"Your graduass-school thing. You can pick it up again." Graham stirred the sugar in with great care. "Next fall."

Could be worse, Neal thought. They could have just tossed me out. But the rubber hand was turning again. There was more, and he knew what it was.

"*If I* bring Allie back by August first."

Graham frowned and nodded.

The sound of one hand clapping.

| PART TWO |

THE MAIN DRAG

13

Foggy London Town was sunny and hot, really hot. Summer had taken an early jump on spring. Neal stepped out of Heathrow's struggling air conditioning into an outdoor sauna.

"A bit on the warm side, I'm afraid," said Simon. "We're on to having a drought, actually. Everything is turning sort of monochromatic brown."

"I thought it rained all the time here," Neal said.

"I'm glad I'm off to Africa, where it's cooler," Simon answered.

Neal laughed politely at the joke, until Simon's puzzled expression told him he wasn't joking.

"It is, actually, cooler there. Have you ever been?"

"No, I'm afraid not."

Simon was an eccentric. Neal guessed his age at late fifties, but knew he could be ten years off in either direction. He was tall and angular, with an Adam's apple that belonged to a different species, and he walked with that particularly British purposefulness that people find so endearing or annoying. With the temperature tilting toward eighty, it tended toward the latter.

Simon was wearing a pink striped shirt, leaf green trousers, paisley ascot, blue argyle socks, and shoes that looked like moccasins but laced up. All this was topped off by a gray head with the odd lock of brown, shiny blue eyes, and a nose that should have been on Mount Rushmore, except it's a small mountain.

He was a friend of Kitteredge, had taken Ethan and wife on safari, and based himself out of London. He found very little in the civilized world of much interest, and *therefore* could *be* trusted never to reveal the story of Allie Chase. He was to *be* Neal's London host.

"I'm off in a week, actually, but that should give us *time.* I gather I'm to *be* your local expert. You're *some* sort of man hunter, or *some* such thing."

"Girl hunter, actually."

Simon laughed. "Oh *yes.* Well done."

He led them through the *maze* of parking lots as if they were *late* for lunch with the Queen. He stopped on locating a small silver sports car, a convertible with the top down.

"This," he announced with a flourish, "is a Gordon-Keble."

"It's nice," Neal said, self-consciously inane. The extent of his knowledge about cars was that they had a steering wheel and four tires—unless left overnight in his neighborhood.

"There were only thirteen ever made," Simon continued with shy pride. "I own three of them."

"That's great."

"One of my vices," Simon confided in a tone more appropriate to a confession of sexual relations with twelve-year-old Chinese girls dressed up as nuns.

"What are the others?"

"Other cars?"

"Other vices."

"You'll *see,*" Simon answered seriously. "Shall *we* take the *Keble* to town?"

Simon tossed Neal's single bag into a small space behind the seats as Neal settled into the car. Neal sank back in the bucket *seat* and felt at least two inches off the ground.

Simon turned the key in the ignition and the little car came to life with demonic energy. Neal had the scary impression that the car had been waiting for this moment; it throbbed with predatory vibrations that reached from the soles of Neal's feet to the top of his hair. It hummed like a wolf at the edge of a flock of sheep, like the worst boy on the block let out of his room.

"Quite a feeling, isn't it?" Simon asked proudly.

"*Yes.*" Terror.

Simon drove as if he knew something about physics that Einstein hadn't thought of and God never intended. If nature abhorred a vacuum, Simon positively loathed one, and rushed to fill in the tiniest gap in the heavy flow of speeding traffic. He passed on the right, left, center, and all variations in between, and the Keble responded as if involved in some kind of blood compact with its human master.

Neal sat as low in his seat as possible and kept his eyes closed as much as pride would allow.

"Why only thirteen?" he shouted over the rushing wind in an attempt to stave off vomiting by conversing.

"After Gordon was killed, Keble just lost the heart for it!"

"How was Gordon killed?" Neal asked, hating himself, knowing the answer would make him even more miserable.

"Swerved to avoid a grouse and jumped a stone wall! Landed in a church graveyard! Convenient, that!"

Simon crossed three lanes of traffic, oblivious to a chorus of blaring horns and curses, to take advantage of a two-foot gap created by an exiting car. He accelerated up a wicked outside curve, dove down the ensuing hill, braking just in time to avoid sodomizing a dairy truck, slid into the passing lane, and floored the accelerator. The gearbox sounded like a Chinese opera.

"I've had three bad smashups myself!" Simon shouted by way of reassurance. "One in Madagascar! Laid up for months! Broke several major bones!"

As the slightly thinning traffic allowed the driver to exercise his full gifts and the car's fiendish potential, Neal prayed that Simon's skull wasn't among those major bones. Pale and sickened, Neal was plastered to the seat by what he knew could be only G forces, and he no longer hoped for survival, only a quick and merciful immolation. As anxiety perspiration joined the flow of heat-induced sweat, and the silver demon sped farther and faster toward a fiery death, Neal silently composed a postcard to Joe Graham: "Dear Dad, having a wonderful time. Wish you were here."

14

Simon's flat was a second-floor walk-up on Regent's Park Road, a quiet street not far from the London Zoo: a good neighborhood for a safe house. Simon owned the entire house but rented the ground floor to a respectably married gay couple.

After all, Simon explained as they climbed the narrow staircase to his flat, "I spend most of my time in Africa, so it seemed a bit impractical to keep the whole thing."

The flat was small. A sitting room faced the street and ran the whole width of the apartment. A small kitchen ran off this room, and the bed and bath ran off the kitchen.

Two floor-to-ceiling windows highlighted the sitting room, and a daybed flanked one of the windows. Simon set Neal's bag down beside this bed. "Here you are, at least until I leave next week. I hope you'll be comfortable."

"It's great," Neal said, then he noticed the walls. His jaw dropped.

Simon noticed.

"My other vice," he said. "I like books."

No kidding. The entire room was lined with bookshelves,

all of which were jammed with first editions. A card table in the center of the room struggled against the weight of heavy book catalogues. Stacks of books sat in every corner and unoccupied nook. Neal stepped to the nearest wall and stared at the book spines on the shelves. A lot of them were nineteenth-century explorers' memoirs—Burton, Speke, Stanley—all first editions. Then Neal saw the volumes of Fielding and Smollett.

"Simon, this is fantastic."

Simon visibly brightened. "You read?"

Neal nodded as he stared at the volumes.

"What do you read?" Simon asked.

"This," Neal answered, pointing at the shelves. "I read this. In paperback."

"You can touch them."

"No, that's all right."

"They won't crumble in your hands."

Neal was actually afraid that they would—books that precious, that old. He thought he could spend his whole life quite happily in this room.

"Do you collect?" Simon asked.

"I'm a starving student."

"I thought you were a private eye."

Neal smiled. "That, too."

And I don't make much money at that, either, he thought.

"What do you study?"

"Eighteenth-century lit."

"Odd combination, detective and academic."

A number of wry and ironic responses occurred to Neal, but he settled for "Well, they both involve research."

"Indeed."

A crowbar couldn't have pried Neal's eyes from the bookshelf.

"Who's your favorite?" Simon asked.

"I'm doing my thesis on Smollett."

"Aah."

That's what everybody says, Neal thought. What they mean is, Aah, how boring.

Simon stepped to the bookcase and took out four volumes. He handed one of them to Neal and stood expectantly as Neal perused it.

It was a rare first edition, first volume, of Smollett's *The Adventures of Peregrine Pickle.*

Neal had never expected even to see one of these, and now he was holding one.

"Simon, this is a first edition."

Simon grinned. "The 1751 unexpurgated version. But it's better than that." He gestured with his chin for Neal to examine the book.

"Handwritten marginal notes . . ." Neal looked at the notes more closely. He couldn't quite believe what he was seeing, but it sure looked like old Smollett's scrawl. He looked up from the book to Simon and raised his eyebrows.

Simon nodded enthusiastically. "From Smollett himself. Great stuff. Nasty remarks about the real people he was satirizing, little asides, that sort of thing."

Neal's hand started to shake. "Simon, is this . . ."

"The *Pickle.*"

"There have only been rumors that this existed."

Simon giggled. "I know."

"This must be worth—"

"I paid ten for it."

"Thousand?"

"Yes."

"Pounds?"

"Yes."

Neal swallowed hard. The notes in these four volumes could make his thesis. Hell, it could make his career . . . He handed the book back to Simon.

"Mind you, I could sell it for twenty or more. I should do, really. I'm not all that keen on Smollett, no offense."

"None taken."

Only a handful of people were keen on Smollett, Professor Leslie Boskin at Columbia University being one of them.

Simon took the volumes and laid them on Neal's bed. "I know one collector, Arthur bloody Kendrick . . . Sir Arthur bloody Kendrick, who suspects that I have these. He'd pay a king's ransom, mind you."

"Why not let him?"

"The swine doesn't love books, he loves possessing them. He sees books as commodities, investments. He doesn't deserve books." Simon's face flushed with indignation. "Actually, you are one of the few people who know that I have these. One of the few people who know these volumes even exist."

"I'm honored."

"You love books. I can see that. I do hope you'll have an opportunity to browse through these volumes while you're here."

I do hope I will, too, Neal thought.

"Actually," said Neal, realizing that he'd actually just said *actually,* "I have to be going. I'm going to check into my hotel tonight."

Simon's face showed his disappointment. "Oh. I was hoping we'd have a chance to talk about books. I'm heading to my cottage in the country first thing tomorrow. Just for two or three days before I head to Africa. Are you sure you wouldn't rather come up with me? Surely you can't be in that great a rush."

"I'm afraid I am."

"Pity. The cottage is in the Yorkshire moors. An old shepherd's cot, actually. Peaceful. A place you can hear your heartbeat. I'll leave directions should you change your mind."

"Thanks."

"At least stay to dinner. We can talk about books."

Dinner was a beefsteak tougher than a jockey's butt, vegetables with the taste boiled out of them, potatoes, tinned fruit, a red wine you could walk on, and conversation devoted entirely to books. Neal thought that, all in all, it was delightful. The only thing that might have made it better would have been the presence of Professor Leslie Boskin.

15

"Scholars have been talking about the *Pickle* for years, but I don't think it even exists," Professor Boskin said, waving his cigarette around. He smoked a lot when he was excited, and he was always excited when he was talking about Smollett.

Neal Carey sat there rapt. He was a senior at the time, an English major, and Boskin was an academic star. Neal had chosen Columbia University for two reasons: instructions from Friends, and Professor Leslie Boskin, the country's foremost scholar of the eighteenth-century English novel. A famous authority at age thirty-seven, he had come out of a nowhere Pennsylvania steel town to win a scholarship to Harvard, which he parlayed into a Rhodes. His first book, *The Novel and the New Reading Public,* redefined the field. He was a true eighteenth-century gentleman: He paid his bills, shouted his share of the rounds, and believed first and foremost in the sanctity of friendship. One of those friends was Ethan Kitteredge, who on the deck of *Haridan* had told Boskin the truly picaresque life story of his promising young student Neal Carey. Not long after that, Boskin invited Neal to partake of a Chinese dinner. Every aspiring undergraduate in the English program knew what that meant: an invitation to become a graduate student under Boskin's wing. Two years of harassment, browbeating, nit-picking, and slow torture.

Neal was thrilled. It was all he had ever wanted. He dug into his Peking duck and listened. Boskin was on a roll. His black eyes glowed.

"You see, Smollett struggled for years just to get noticed. He had an inferiority complex like a mule at a donkey convention. He was Scottish, he was relatively uneducated . . . in those days surgeons were pretty low on the social scale. So when his first novel, *Roderick Random,* came out, he thought he'd finally be accepted by the London literati." Boskin paused to lay some strips of duck and some plum sauce onto the pancake and to take a sip of Tsingtao. "But he wasn't. Johnson, Garrick, all the boys still snubbed him. So then he writes *Pickle* and he lets them have it. Really vicious satire. Not to mention the Lady Vane memoirs he throws in for the hell of it. Imagine it, here is the supposed diary of a highborn lady all about fucking around; and people are wondering, where did Smollett get this shit? And *Pickle* is a smash! The public loves it! And he's picked up by London society. Johnson, Garrick, all the boys."

Neal watched Boskin shove a huge hunk of the pancake into his mouth, chew it quickly, and wash it down with a slug of beer. It was true, Neal thought, Boskin really would rather talk about Smollett than eat.

Boskin set the beer down and continued. "But now he's feeling badly about all the vicious shit he wrote in *Pickle,* so when he's asked to do a second edition, he takes most of it out. But he has one copy somewhere—*one copy* in which he puts all the notes: who's who, what the joke is, and the truth about Lady Vane. Was she his mistress? Is all the juicy stuff true?"

Boskin jabbed his chopsticks into his Dragon and Phoenix

and came up with a piece of shrimp. "So Smollett gets old. As do we all, so drink up. He goes to Europe for his health. Gets a tumor the size of a baseball on his hand. His daughter and only child dies. Life sucks the big one. Miserable, bankrupt . . . he finally croaks in Italy. But we know for a fact that he had a copy of every one of his books with him when he went for the deep drop. So what would the widow do? No money . . . no prospects . . . no piece of The Rock . . ."

"Sell them."

"Right! All she had to trade on was her late beloved's fame. So she sold his whole collection, one by one. And every other book has surfaced except his *Pickle*. The *Pickle*. Four volumes of literary treasures. That's how the rumor started. They say it's never surfaced because it has all these marginal notes with all the goods on Samuel Johnson, Garrick, Akenside, and, of course, the sporting Lady Vane.

"Any collector, any eighteenth-century scholar, would give his left testicle to have a look at those volumes. Except they don't exist. The rest of that duck is yours, by the way."

Except they did exist—in Simon Keyes's apartment. Neal had held them in his hands, books that could provide his future, his fortune, and his freedom. And he'd put them back on the shelf.

16

THE PICCADILLY HOTEL was as simple as its name. Not plain or unattractive, but simple in the sense that it knew what it was: a good solid place from which to do business, tour the city, go to the theater, and take in the sights of London. It offered large rooms, big beds, decent food, and room service. You could ring up for anything you wanted at the Piccadilly Hotel. The Piccadilly Hotel knew that people went to hotels to do things they didn't do at home.

The lobby was large, built in the days when people met socially in hotel lobbies. It featured a lounge with old wing-back chairs big enough to seat Peter Lorre *and* Sydney Greenstreet, and a decently dark, mahogany bar that was somehow always cool in hot weather and warm in cold weather. It was the kind of bar where the men always kept their ties knotted but felt relaxed, anyway; the kind of a lounge where the barkeep would never disturb you to ask whether you wanted another but was always there with your drink at the slightest glance.

The lobby ended at the registration desk. The Piccadilly Hotel had too much sense to make a new guest search for the bloody thing, and it was always staffed by at least half a dozen red-jacketed clerks who knew their business: See that the room was paid for, and get the guest to it. If you made a reservation at the Piccadilly Hotel, you always got a room. They didn't believe in overbooking; in fact, they always kept a couple of rooms saved for emergencies. You could stay for a night or a year at the Piccadilly Hotel. The rules were the same. You paid your bill, and kept your jacket on.

Neal shucked his off the moment he stepped into his room, a nice large one on the sixth floor, with a small window air conditioner that struggled bravely against the heat. He kicked his shoes off on the ubiquitous red carpet and surveyed the room with a consumer's eye. The blue wallpaper was the color of the sea after a storm, and was decorated with prints of heavily muscled, bare-chested, bare-knuckled boxers toeing the line. A manly room.

The bed had been built in an era when gentlemen kept their riding boots on for afternoon expressions of affection. Like the hotel, it was large and sturdy, and proclaimed itself the focal point of the room. A small bathroom led off from the right. It had a deep old tub, an adequate sink, and newly refurbished countertops and mirrors. One small window broke up the wall, and a double-jointed gymnast might have made out the view of Piccadilly Circus.

Neal gave the bellhop a grotesquely large tip and dismissed him with a "What's your name, in case I need anything?"

Then he carefully hung up his jackets—the all-purpose no-wrinkle blue polyester blazer and the striped seersucker—and his summer-weight trousers. He laid his folded shirts out in a bureau drawer, placed his cheap travel alarm clock on the bedside table, and put some paperback books on the lower shelf. He carefully laid out his toilet kit on the bathroom counter and took some manila folders out of his briefcase and laid them around the room, then placed the British editions of that month's *Playboy* and *Penthouse* on the floor in the bathroom.

After ringing room service for a bottle of scotch and a bucket of ice, Neal changed into a fresh blue shirt and red regimental tie. He knotted the tie, then undid the top button of his shirt and yanked the knot down. Next, he lit a cigar, puffed on it until it started to smoke, and left it burning in an ashtray to stink up the room.

He overtipped the room-service waiter, poured three fingers of the scotch down the bathroom drain, and made a weak one for himself. Then he sat down with his copy of the classified ads that had lured Scott Mackensen into the world of big-time sin, and started to dial numbers.

Team Number One showed up a half hour later. They were each rather pretty. The senior member sported flaming red hair, freckles, and wore a green dress and impossibly clichéd black mesh stockings. Her colleague was a pleasantly plump blond lady. Neither of them were the ones who had dated Scott and friend. Both of them tensed up when they saw only one man in the room.

"Relax," said Neal. "I just want to talk."

"Don't you like us, love?" asked the green dress, just about fed up with freaks.

Neal gave them their standard fee in cash, with his apologies and reassurance.

Team Number Two was made up of two black-haired, blue-eyed, black-dressed, severe types, who accepted Neal's apology and cash with a dry sneer of contempt.

Team Number Three consisted of two Irish girls, who were delighted with the money. Team Number Four was a pair of positively gorgeous black women, and Neal secretly felt abashed that his dismissal stuck in his throat for a long moment. Team Number Five claimed to be a mother and daughter team, and might have been for all Neal knew. It made him wonder what kind of man would go for a threesome with the older woman and a woman who was at least twenty-five dressed up as Alice in fucking Wonderland. Team Number Six arrived about one, and were smashing-looking, with a smashing fee, but still not the right ladies. Neal felt he was getting close, though, and showed them the Polaroid.

"Hard up, are you, darling?"

"You could say that."

"Sorry. Never seen them. If that's it, then, we'll just be tripping along. Are you a frustration freak, is that it?"

You don't know the half, lady.

Number Six offered to perform for him, if that's what he wanted. Number Seven were transvestites.

Number Eight was a cop.

An enormous cop. His wide shoulders sloped from years of stooping under small ceilings and through small doors. His large head was matched by a large nose. He had sad, cop eyes. Eyes that had seen it all and wished they hadn't. He was wearing a three-piece gabardine suit and refused to sweat. Neal put him in his late forties.

"May I come in?" he asked, entering.

"Sure."

Good cops take possession of a space, and this one was a good cop. Most rent-a-cops shove their ID at you, but this guy didn't bother. He sat down and invited Neal to do the same.

"My name is Hatcher," he said. "I'm from Vine Street Station. Do you know where that is?"

Neal sat down on the edge of his bed. "No."

"It's across Man-In-The-Moon Passage. Do you know where that is?"

"I don't know where anything is."

Hatcher nodded. "It's just outside the kitchen and the laundry. Do you know why I'm telling you this?"

Yeah, I do, Neal thought. You could tell me what you want to tell me straight out, but you're establishing a pattern of question and answer. "Not really."

"This hotel does not require a house detective, because I can be here on a moment's notice. I am not the house detective. I am a London police inspector."

"Would you like a drink? I have scotch, scotch and water, and scotch on the rocks."

"Scotch, thank you."

Neal poured three fingers into a glass and handed it to Hatcher. Then he sat down again on the bed and waited.

"The hotel staff cannot have helped but notice considerable traffic in and out of your room."

"I'm looking for a girl."

"Apparently."

"A particular girl."

"Rather particular indeed, Mr. Carey."

Neal shrugged and tried to look stupid. It wasn't tough. He hadn't figured on a cop stepping into this.

"And you have yet to find her?" Hatcher asked.

"Not yet."

Hatcher sipped at his drink. "But you intend to continue this search for . . . the Holy Grail."

"Yup."

Hatcher's sad eyes grew a little sadder. Then he stared at the floor before staring back at Neal. It was an old cop move and it didn't surprise Neal much. It did surprise him that it shook him up a little.

"Not in *this* hotel, lad."

Neal stood up and freshened his own drink. He held the bottle up in an invitation that Hatcher accepted.

"Why not?" Neal asked.

"We don't mind a little of the old in-and-out, man. But you have them trooping up here at a pace that would do credit to an Australian rabbit."

Neal took a chance on getting his ribs bashed in. "So? It's not illegal."

"It's unseemly."

"So you don't mind guests running whores up here, you just don't want to get a reputation for it."

Hatcher shook his head. "I don't mind guests 'running whores up here,' I just want to receive a piece of it."

Neal smiled.

"Understand, Mr. Carey," Hatcher said. "This telephone business tends to cut the lads out—the bellboys, the concierge, the local constabulary who are coming up on retirement and who aren't likely to get that promotion before the pension is set . . . . The referral fees are missed."

"What are you suggesting?"

Neal could see the cop was annoyed at having to spell it out.

"I am suggesting that you try to exercise a bit of control over your libido, and that when the need does arise, so to speak, you ring the bellboy."

And if I was looking to get laid, Neal thought, I wouldn't mind at all. But my only shot at Allie is over the phone. He stepped to the door and opened it. "Sorry."

Hatcher ignored the door. "You don't mind if I have a look-see?"

"It's your town."

"What brings you to London?" Hatcher asked from the bathroom.

"Business."

"You have been busy."

Neal knew what was coming.

"Oh dear," Hatcher said.

And here it comes.

Hatcher came back from the bathroom holding a plastic film canister.

"It's not mine," Neal said.

Hatcher reached into his jacket and took out a set of hand-cuffs. "Nevertheless."

Neal held his hands out in front of him to show his spirit of cooperation and said, "Why don't I tell you what I'm really doing here."

HATCHER WAS BACK IN HALF an hour with the hotel's telephone records. "Your Mackensen lad made only three calls from the room."

They checked the phone numbers against the classified sex ads. Number eleven matched. Neal reached for the phone.

"No longer in service, lad. I checked already."

"But the next number should be the dealer's."

"True, but it isn't much help. It's a phone box in Leicester Square."

THEY WERE THERE IN TEN MINUTES. Hatcher pointed to the phone box. It was unoccupied.

"Your dealer is a cute one," he said. "The girls knew to reach him there. Maybe he keeps regular hours. Different phone booths at different times.

"You haven't asked me for my advice, lad, but I'm giving it to you, nevertheless. Give it up. Go back to the States and tell your aunt and uncle to forget about their daughter. It's a fine thing you're trying to do, but . . . Even if you were to find her, you're more likely to get a knife in your innards than get your cousin back. You've no business being on the Main Drag."

"I have to try." He gave it a nice touch of nobility.

"Suit yourself."

"Thanks for your help."

Hatcher smiled. "Forget about it. Literally."

NEAL STRAIGHTENED UP THE ROOM. He picked up the magazines and newspapers and tossed them in the trash bin. He opened up a window to let the cigar stench out. He rinsed the glasses out in the bathroom sink and then fixed himself a fresh drink while he drew a bath.

It isn't so bad, he thought as *he* lay in the hot water. He didn't have an address but he did have this phone booth, or *box,* in the vernacular. And the location fits Mackensen's story. And tomorrow I'll check it out. And find the dealer. Who'll lead me to Allie.

Right.

17

EXCEPT HE WASN'T THERE. Like a road-show Shakespeare when Hamlet's missed the bus, the dealer wasn't onstage when the lights came up and the supporting cast was in place.

So Neal waited for him, which wouldn't have been so bad except for the bloody heat. Neal had learned to say "the bloody heat," because everybody around him was calling it that. In a country where air conditioning is considered decadent and they sell you an ice cube in your drink, temps in the nineties were a pain indeed.

Neal sweated through long afternoons in the square. He had picked a bench that gave him a nice view of the phone box and its surroundings. He also could check out most of the square's pubs, movie houses, and eateries. Now a bench in a public park is a jealously guarded commodity, so Neal was careful not to monopolize his spot and draw unwanted attention from any of the long-timer winos, senile pigeon aficionados, or schizoid bums for whom the square and its benches were something called home. Public parks and gardens, built by proud city patrons and matrons as a pleasant gathering spot for the upper middle class, had long since become one of the few surviving habitats of society's detritus, a crucial place to sit or lie down. So a regular in Leicester Square was more or less tolerated unless he caused trouble. Screaming above the city's natural decibel level, pushing the panhandling act too hard with a tourist, dealing dope too visibly, or whipping out a weapon to lay claim to a spot on a bench were but a few of the offenses that might disturb the sensibilities of the local gendarmerie. The serene London bobbies, those fabled paragons of patience and civility, might drag a repeat offender into a convenient alley or doorway and stomp the bejesus out of him. The judicious application of nightstick to shin discouraged recidivism. The occasional hard case might require a more thorough going-over, and the rawest copper soon discovered that a trip to hospital could keep a nuisance off the beat for weeks at a time. Neal wasn't surprised to discover that the London cops had their own version of New York's Finest's "Teacher, May I" technique, in which one officer raises the student's arm high above his head, stretching out the thin sheaf of muscle that covers the rib cage. Then his partner administers the lesson in one of two modes: If he just wants to get his point across, he jams the butt end of his nightstick into the student's ribs, inspiring an instant shortage of breath coupled with a few moments of searing, albeit temporary, pain. But if the teacher wants the pupil absent from class for a few days, he swings the nightstick like a Jimmy Connors forehand at Wimbledon, cracking the student's ribs. Class dismissed.

So Neal took pains not to attract attention, which was more or less his role in life anyway, and therefore came naturally. Anyone who tries too hard not to attract attention almost invariably does. This is particularly true on the street, where the denizens have antennae finely tuned to the least twitch of the unnatural gesture. The only way to be inconspicuous is to be so plainly obvious, people don't see you.

"This comes from our cavemen days," Joe Graham had explained during one of the interminable anthropology lectures he had delivered to young Neal, "when we operated under the theory that what isn't moving can't hurt you. This was a fallacy, of course, but that's what they thought, because they weren't that smart to start with. They had about as many brains as your average transit cop. Anyways, they thought, Until it moves, it's a rock. When it moves, it's a saber-toothed tiger or something else that can eat us. This is why, to this day, people see motion. Sitting still, they don't see. You show me a saber-toothed tiger that can sit still. I'll show you a fat tiger."

Also a bored tiger, Neal thought. Tedium is the detective's most steadfast companion. It never goes away for long and it always comes back. Neal used to chuckle at the detective shows he'd see on TV, which were twelve minutes of commercials and forty-eight minutes of action. He knew they should have had twelve minutes of commercials, forty minutes of stupefying monotony, seven minutes and fifty seconds of paperwork, and ten seconds of what you might call action, if you weren't too particular about your definition of action.

Not that boredom was necessarily bad. On those rare occasions when things got exciting—someone pulling a knife, or much worse, someone pulling a gun—boredom looked pretty good. You could do a lot worse than boredom. But it was hard for Neal to keep that perspective in June in Leicester Square in London during the hottest summer in recorded history. Waiting for somebody who didn't show up. Who might never show up. Someone who might have once spent an evening with Allie Chase and then booted her along her merry way. Somebody who was a missing link, as it were, in a very thin chain.

Waiting, while the clock ticked slowly but the calendar raced. Neal had managed to skip Einstein, but he already knew that time was relative. Minutes dragged, hours stood positively still, but days zipped past him like taxis in the rain. May was gone, June was already a week old, and Neal was no closer to finding Allie. And finding her was only the start. Grabbing her would take time, cleaning her up more time, and time was a funny thing: Every hour seemed to take a week, and every week seemed to take about an hour. He had time on his hands and he was running out of time. Back in the States, the Democrats were gearing up for their August party, Senator Chase was polishing the acceptance speech, Ed Levine was sending Neal telexes demanding news, and Neal was sitting on a bench, racing toward his "drop dead line" in slow motion. Eight weeks now, and counting.

The heat didn't help. Neal's shirt would be stuck to the back of the bench ten minutes after he sat down. The crotch of his jeans would cling tenaciously to his balls, and his armpits would smell like a Mississippi chain gang by noon.

There wasn't a breeze, not the slightest whisper of a cool breeze to break the still and sullen air.

Neal would force himself to get up and move. He would sit on his bench for two hours and then walk for one. Around and about Covent Garden, Piccadilly Circus, Soho, Chinatown. Some days, he'd walk down to the National Gallery and watch the crowds in Trafalgar Square: hundreds of teenagers; no Allie.

Mostly he sat, however, the tiger at work. He'd arrive on his bench around noon. (One nice thing about drug dealers are their hours. You want to talk to a dealer before noon, you'd better know where he lives.) He'd plop down on the bench, spread his arms out, and have a glance at the *International Herald Tribune* to check out the baseball standings. It took maybe five minutes for the little prickles of heat to start on his arms and back, followed shortly by the sweat that would become a trickle and then a stream. He had found a café by the tube station, and it sold a reasonable facsimile of a bagel. It became his habit to start his day with a Styrofoam cup of black coffee and a plain toasted bagel with butter. Satisfying himself that the Yankees still held first, he'd scan the headlines, then ball the bagel wrapper up inside the empty cup and toss it into the trash basket behind the bench. Then he'd settle in to watch the show. He began to know how movie ushers felt when the film had been running for three months. The sidewalk vendors already would be setting up their wares along the wrought-iron spiked fence that bordered the square. They sold the usual assortment of cheap souvenirs: cute little bobby dolls that never beat up raving psychos, T-shirts with Buckingham Palace silk-screened on the front, buttons that said LONDON UNDERGROUND—the usual crap. Neal's own favorite was a T-shirt emblazoned with a map of the Underground system. He resisted buying one. There were also the food and drink vendors who peddled warm, syrupy Cokes, soft ice cream that lasted an average of thirty-four seconds before melting down your wrist, thick Cadbury milk chocolate bars that melted even quicker and somehow always found their way onto your shirt, salted peanuts that only a far-gone lunatic would consume in this weather and that were always in hot demand. Neal craved . . . craved a real New York City street frank, one of the ones made from rat hairs, industrial waste, floor sweepings, and God knows what else, for which he cheerfully would have slaughtered the Queen. The closest he could come was a little stand run by some Pakistanis that sold a product the locals called the "Death Kabob." It wasn't bad, really, except for being the Main Drag's answer to Ex-Lax, but it couldn't touch a Columbus Circle dog with hot mustard and onions spread all over it.

After the vendors arrived, the tourists started in, which makes perfect sense if you think about it. There were a lot of Americans, but also great hordes of Italian teenagers, who always seemed to travel in groups of three thousand, and tidy little gaggles of Japanese photo freaks. Neal had never seen an ethnic cliché come to life before, but it was really true about the Japanese: They would take a picture of anything, and they all took the same pictures, as if they didn't know you could make more than one print from a negative. They drove Neal nuts. He had spent a lifetime avoiding having his picture taken, and now he was sure he was going to pop up in five hundred photo albums in greater metropolitan Kyoto. Not that it mattered. It was, as they say, the principle of the thing.

However, mostly the tourists were fellow Americans: "My fellow Americans," Neal thought once, flashing on Lyndon Johnson, and mostly they were that middle-aged type who want to travel but don't want to leave home. So they go to English-speaking countries. You can go to Canada only so many times, so here they were in London, and boy, were they surprised. London had changed considerably from those great Forties movies. In those great Forties movies, people didn't have foot-high purple hair or say "fuck" every fourth word. Also, it was always foggy and cool in those great Forties movies. Uh-huh.

And their travel agents had told them there was no crime in London. Crime was reserved for those vaguely greasy people like Italians and French, not to mention Africans, Indians, and Orientals—but not the English.

Neal sat and mused about crime in England one sultry day as he sat watching a pickpocket make his week's wages from a single tour group meandering through the square. Why is it, he wondered, that about half of all great popular English literature is about crime and yet everybody, English or foreign, will tell you there is no crime in England? The English popular tradition is obsessed with robbery and murder, starting with Robin Hood, moving up through Dickens, then to Sherlock Holmes, and on to Agatha Christie , who had single-handedly depopulated fictional aristocracy. Even staid historical works featured set-piece public whippings and hangings, and mass transportations to Australia and so forth, and yet England maintains the reputation for public order and civility. Maybe, Neal theorized, people figure that England ridded itself through the rope or the long-distance boat trip of its criminal class, so now everybody who was left in the country was genetically disposed toward being law-abiding. He considered his theory for a while, then dismissed it as he watched the pick maneuver toward his next victim.

Neal wondered about a bunch of things as he watched his countrymen absorb the culture of the Main Drag. He wondered how many of them, wary of visiting really foreign lands where people spoke a different language and did really strange things, realized that a good proportion of the Third World had migrated right here to good old civilized London; that many of the Empire's former subjects had taken the phrase *Commonwealth* at face value and decided to try to get a little bit of the common wealth in the heart of the imperial city. It was a cruel joke, really, considering the fact that these Africans, Asians, and West Indians had created a big chunk of that wealth back in the good old days in their native lands when they bought at inflated prices the cheap consumer goods cranked out in factories in Manchester and Birmingham, and marketed by London firms. Well, the good old days were long gone, blown away by the Marne trenches, and the Blitz, and the "winds of change" that had transformed the British Empire into the British Commonwealth, or as some wags would have it, the Commonpoor. Neal wondered how many of the tourists would get beyond the artificial Mary Poppins land of tourist London to go into the Brixton slums and Notting Hill Gate hovels, or onto the stretch of Bayswater Road that had become known as "Little Karachi," or how many would journey north from London to the vast rust belt of the industrial Midlands, where the factories had lost their markets, or up into the sooty coal towns that made their West Virginia cousins look like Opryland, USA. He wondered how a supposedly intelligent man in his fifties could be so stupid as to carry his wallet in his back pants pocket.

Another phenomenon that engaged Neal (what the hell, he had nothing else to do while on this fool's errand) was the propensity of American tourists to wear clothing extolling the virtues of hometowns they had just paid lots of money to escape. It seemed that half the people he observed wore T-shirts with slogans such as NO PLACE BUT ELKHART and I LUV ALBUQUERQUE, or baseball caps proclaiming loyalty to home teams, which under further consideration Neal realized he understood perfectly. After all, he was the one who checked the papers twice a day to get the baseball scores and root in absentia for Steinbrenner's team to win the Pennant, which even Neal acknowledged was like cheering for the Nazis to overrun Holland. He wondered why he was being so goddamn superior to the tourists and their expression of affection for their homes. Shit, he thought, he'd rather be home, too. He wondered why, though. He also wondered where the hell this dealer was. And where, oh where, has my little Allie gone? Seven weeks, now, and still counting.

Meanwhile, the hawkers and the gawkers were always well established by one or two o'clock, and by two-thirty or so the freaks, winos, druggies, and hard-core crazies moved on to their ordained places onstage, waiting with varying degrees of patience for the bit players to clear off.

Neal would get off his bench around this time and stroll over to the Dilly on the odd chance that Allie had opted out of the pro ranks to join the recalcitrant hippies and fake down-and-out young travel scene that gathered to sit like stoned vultures around the statue of Eros. These kids sat hunched over, checking out the other kids, watching the swirling traffic, passing the surreptitious joint, enormously self-satisfied with their mass nonconformity. Allie was never there, individual nonconformity being her particular taste and talent. Neal felt sorry, though, for poor Eros, doomed to watch over a mob of kids for whom sex had become so commonplace it was an absolute bore. And aren't you developing a fine and snooty sense of irony? he thought. He didn't like himself much these days.

The futile walk gave him an excuse to stretch his legs and shift the dried sweat around a little, and also work up a little fresh sweat. His route took him past, and all too often *into,* a Wimpy Bar, which brought up melancholy memories of Nick's. He learned to smother the piece of cardboard the Brits called a hamburger with mustard (extra charge), catsup (ditto), and salt (on the house) before choking it down along with the greasy chips, which is what the Brits called their poor facsimile of french fries.

After the first week, he had begun to vary his route. He would walk down St. Martin's Lane, past the perpetual demonstration outside the South Africa Embassy, over to Trafalgar Square. He'd check out the throngs of tourists and school groups milling around Nelson's column. Good old Lord Nelson, who in winning the great naval battle of Trafalgar saved England from Napoleon and assured the rights of all Englishmen to drive on the wrong bloody side of the road. Then Neal would cross over on to Whitehall Street and wend his way through the crowd on the narrow sidewalk, then through Horse Guards barracks, across Horse Guards Road, and into St. James's Park.

If there was any spot in London that Neal at his most xeno-phobic had to admit he loved, it was St. James's Park. Here was refuge. Built around a superbly designed man-made lake, the park was an oasis of gentility in its finest sense. The towers of Buckingham Palace peeked in the distance over the several hundred varieties of the park's trees. Neal would stroll, yes stroll, along the walkway to a large kiosk that sold tea, sandwiches, and pastries. He didn't even mind standing in line at the cafeteria there, but would purchase his cup of tea, a couple of sugary doughnuts or perhaps a ham sandwich, and then walk over to the lakeside. Here he would rent a chair for ten pence and throw bits of doughnut and bread to the ducks, of which there were a stunning variety. He was sure he would have noticed Allie Chase if she had been riding on the back of one of the humon-gous black swans that glided past him, but otherwise he forgot about the case altogether.

On a bandstand near the kiosk, a military band played show tunes and light classics to a crowd gathered in canvas chairs or picnicking on the grassy slope. Neal, who hated mili-tary bands, show tunes, and light classics, grew quite fond of the daily concert and was sorry when the IRA blew up the bandstand later that summer, putting an end to the music and killing two soldiers.

This was old England, Neal thought, or at least it was what he thought old England might have been or should have been. The tourists went mostly to Hyde Park, but St. James's Park was usually full of nannies wheeling prams or looking after toddlers, government workers from the nearby Whitehall ministries on lunch break, and retirees for whom a walk in this place was a daily routine.

After finishing his tea, Neal would sometimes walk north to the Mall, up Waterloo Place to lower Regent Street, and up to

Piccadilly. Or he would head south down Horse Guards Road to Great George Street, Bridge Street, nod to Big Ben, then take the long hike up Victoria Embankment.

This broad promenade along the bank of the Thames was a haunt for some vagrants and kids, but it never produced Allie Chase for him. Still, he made it a habit. He preferred active futility over passive futility, even if he was breaking Joe Graham's philosophy of the fat and happy tiger.

He'd get back to the square by 3:30 or 4:00, check out the scene, and then steel himself for the coming ordeal in the Underground. Each afternoon, he'd make the rounds of several tube stations during rush hour. Even amateur, unaffiliated panhandlers can make out okay in a big city during rush hour, if they have any smarts at all and a nice face. Allie had both, so Neal would launch himself on a two-hour journey from Leicester Square to Piccadilly, change to the Bakerloo Line and go to Charing Cross, check out the huge station there and then carry on to Embankment, change to the Circle Line, hit Victoria, Sloane Square, South Kensington, and Gloucester Road. There he would switch to the District Line for a quick swing to grimy Earl's Court and then carry on up to Notting Hill Gate, where he hoped he wouldn't find her, and on north to Paddington, where he would catch the Metropolitan Line, make a quick check of Baker Street, which always brought Sherlock Holmes to mind (maybe *he* could locate Allie), and over to King's Cross, where he'd take the long Underground hike through the suburban commuter crowds to get back on the Piccadilly Line, have a peek at the Covent Garden station, and then back to Leicester Square.

All this in the faint hope that young Allie was using some variation of the "I've lost my purse and need enough money to get home" scam that was a favorite of panhandlers worldwide.

This tends to work better at rush hour, when there are a lot more potential samaritans to bilk, and when one is not so obvious to the thugs who control the thriving begging trade. A quick panhandler can keep moving better through large crowds and make a fair bit of change even if she couldn't occupy one of the key choke points smack dab in the middle of the traffic flow.

Now there are a number of different strategies in this scam, and it really depends on how gutsy you are and how well you can afford to dress. If you're really down and out, you're better off just asking for subway fare—small change—to a nearby stop, because nobody's going to believe you live in the suburbs and need that much more money to get back. But if you can get your hands on some better threads, you might want to give the bigger-ticket items a try, especially if you've got the nerve to attempt the "I'm from out of town and need five or ten pounds to get home and here is my card with my name and address and I'll send you the money first thing" routine. The truly wonderful thing about the world is that there are people in it who will actually believe this and give the money. If you're a teenager and try this, pick on women who look like they might have a kid your age, because they don't want their own child stranded in the big bad city and they're afraid not to give you the money.

Or you can go for volume and stick with the tried-and-true "Buddy Can You Spare a Dime" routine, but you have to hit a bunch of buddies to make this one pay. Anyway, people would rather be conned, even if they suspect they're being conned, because they want you to work a little bit for the money. Or take a shot at making a really good cardboard sign: BROKE AND DESPERATE or HUNGRY AND ALONE. Always try to go for two bad conditions on the sign, though. It's that *and* that gives it the poignant quality.

Or maybe Allie wasn't begging. Maybe she was trying to

steal in the Underground. Neal hoped this wasn't the case, and really didn't expect it to be. Despite popular legend, subways are terrible places to pick pockets. Picks like a crowd all right, but they also like to be able to get away if something goes wrong. Subways are full of things such as turnstiles, gates, escalators, and narrow passageways that make running damn near impossible. Add to this the fact that crowds of commuters have been getting increasingly irritated with increasing delays. But it was the possibility that Allie was finding her daily bread in the Underground that sent Neal on his daily tour of purgatory. It brought to mind a sermon he'd once heard when the priest really got cooking on hell, about how it was a place where murderers, thieves, and lechers baked in perpetual, tortuous stench. At the time, that had sounded like the West Side Democratic Club's steam room when all the Ryan brothers were in it. But now, he knew differently. Neal, who had been raised on New York's subway, had never felt anything like London's Underground.

Steamy didn't quite describe it. Neither did *grimy* or any of the other dwarfs. It was killer heat. Godlike heat. All-pervasive heat that denied even the possibility of the existence of cool. Still and sullen heat. As if the air itself were heat. As if a cool breeze was just a memory of something that once was but would never be again.

Not that there was any room to breathe even if there had been something resembling oxygen. The horrific crowding on the cars began to break down even the fabled English stoicism. Stiff upper lips wilted. And that was when the train was moving. When it got stuck between stations, as it frequently did, and a polite announcement came over the PA system, the crowd responded with a single groan. People dropped their heads and stared at their feet and watched their sweat drip on their shoes. Then the train would jerk forward again, the movement providing no relief except the knowledge that the end of the ordeal was a bit closer.

Except for Neal, who wasn't riding to get anywhere, and who wasn't getting anywhere riding, either. Allie wasn't on the Underground. No cool breeze, no Allie. Six weeks left.

Like aging women, cities are prettier at night. The softer light shades the insults of aging. Darkness fades the lines and wrinkles that every good woman and every good city wear on their faces as signs that somebody has lived there.

If life in the city seems impossible in the daytime, at night it is irresistible. The night is for playing. For dining and dancing, for flirting and fucking. For making eyes and making love. The feet step a little lighter, and the blood flows a little faster, and the eyes race to the flash of neon blues and reds and ambers set off by the silky soft black of night.

People do things at night they wouldn't dream of by day. They see things differently. What was harsh becomes soft. Sordid becomes colorful. Whores become courtesans; hookers are ladies of the evening. Light reflects prettily off the broken bottles in the gutters. Everyone has a bit of the devil in them at night. There'll be time to deal with God in the morning.

The barkers stood in Soho doorways proclaiming the virtues of nude, absolutely nude, dancers inside. But not one of the dancers was Allie. And the bouncers guarded the gates to the flashy discos, beckoning the pretty and the well-dressed and the hip and turning away the rest. But none of the blessed or the cursed were Allie. And waiters served food and drink to the stylish after-theater couples and parties who mobbed the West End pubs and cafés after the curtains had rung down. But Allie was not to be found among the servers or the served.

Back on the square, Neal watched the phone box, and every once in a while he would ring the number to see who, if anybody, answered. But it was never Allie or her dealer. And Neal kept watching; only at night, he watched more carefully. He never sat still for long at night, when the scent of a solitary, sedentary stranger would waft its way to the delicate senses of the larger predators who prowled the night.

Neal knew that the night, like most pretty things, was dangerous. The money stakes were higher, for one thing, which brought the more serious players out. And too many of them were fueled by booze and drugs, which lent an ugly air of the unpredictable, and Neal hated the unpredictable.

So Neal patrolled the area, but he kept to the shadows, using corners and doorways, buying snacks at street-side windows, fading to the back of small knots of people as they checked out movie times, disco signs, and buskers. He used all the shading and masking and other subtle shit that Graham had taught him, and he didn't trust to the "cover of darkness." Darkness covered everybody.

"Everybody" was the hard core. The ponces checked their ladies and the dealers checked their turf. And the thugs worked the porn trade and the bodybuilders looked for poofters to roll. And the gangs were dangerous, looking for an excuse to fight. And the schizoids were worse, because they didn't need an excuse, just the ever-present jangle of the voices in their heads. And they were all out there.

Except Allie. Except her dealer. They were nowhere.

Five weeks.

That's how it went for a month. Neal was left with his slim lead and a bunch of maybes. Maybe the dealer had fucked up and was in the slammer. Maybe he hadn't paid his fees and was in the river. Maybe he'd decided on a career change and had taken up actuarial science. Maybe Allie had been with him that one night and that was it. Maybe all this was futile.

So Neal would sit in his room in the small hours of the morning and choke down his carton of Chinese take-away, wash it down with two warm room-service beers, and make his check-in call to Graham. Ask if he should call it quits and come home. Get told no. Bitch about it for a minute and hang up. Take a bath to try to wash off the day's accumulation of sweat and sleaze. Never quite manage it.

Then he'd think about calling Diane. Hell, he thought one night, you have two women in your life and you've lost them both. One you can't find, and the other can't find you. Brilliant.

And you're about out of time—with Diane as well as Allie. So call her. And say what? Tell her all about Friends and your fascinating line of work? Tell her that grad school is finished because you've fucked up the dirty job of finding an abused child and taking her back to her abusive father?

So he'd think better of it. Try to read. Give up and drink scotch.

Day after day, night after night. And the nights were bad. Worse as the days went by and he hadn't found the kid. Worse as images of the Halperin kid crept into his head when he tried to sleep, infecting his thoughts with images of death.

Face it, he thought. Allie could be anywhere. She could be sick and she could be hurt. She could be beat-up aching, or clapped-up aging, junked-up dying. Dead like the last kid they'd sent him after.

More and more, he went to sleep with the picture of Allie in his mind. And in his mind, she was dead.

18

SHE LOOKED GREAT.

He saw her reflection first as he was passing by one of the more expensive eateries that flanked the square. He happened to glance up, and her reflection caught his eye and jerked his head up and around. She was inches away. Behind a pane of glass. And she looked great.

Her blond hair glittered from the light of the lamp hanging above her, and even in the shadowy light of the restaurant, she looked healthy, alive. At this moment she was laughing. She wore a black sleeveless T-shirt tucked into black jeans tucked in to black ankle boots, sort of a demonic female Peter Pan. Her hair was cut short and uneven, above her ears, and her left ear sported a delicate silver chain that hung almost to her shoulder. She wore blood-red lipstick. She was drinking beer from a bottle. She was a beautiful girl having a wonderful time. And she was stoned out of her gourd.

For one awful second, Neal thought he might actually tap on the glass and yell, "Allie, come on. Time to go home." But he backed off quickly, found an eddy in the traffic flow, and watched. He was surprised to hear his own heart beating.

Allie was sitting with three other people. One was a young man of about Neal's build. His head was roughly shaved to a stubble, and he wore an impossibly filthy T-shirt that had been white in a time beyond memory. The shirt was torn in several places and the message FUCK THE WORLD had been crudely stenciled on the chest. He had a safety pin jammed through his right earlobe. He showed outrageously bad teeth when he grinned, which was often, as he was pointedly laughing at the witticism of the other man at the table, the dominant one. The laughter of the fawning ape. This one would be no problem.

A young woman sat beside him. She sported an orange, purple, and yellow crew cut, black eye shadow and lipstick, and had enormous boobs barely contained in a black leather jacket. She was chunky, her hips and butt jammed into leather pants, and Neal could barely imagine the rivulets of sweat that flowed underneath. She might have stretched toward attractive, but she was pretty enough for the laughing boy, who was all over her. She could be trouble, Neal thought, but not too much.

The other man was trouble. He was the A male, the leader of the pack. This was his table, his party, and his guests; his Allie.

He was of medium height, wide, stocky build—rugby type. He wore a pale khaki suit over a plain black T-shirt; no socks under soft brown loafers. A tiny stone that looked like an emerald adorned his left ear, and three fresh shallow cuts ran straight down from his left eye to his cheekbone. They had just scabbed over and Neal guessed they were self-inflicted. He was drinking something that looked like a tall gin, and he sipped at it as he looked over his glass at Allie and smiled. He was trouble: major league.

He uttered some fresh snippet of wit that sent Fuck the World into a new paroxysm of laughter. This was for Allie, and FTW probably didn't realize the joke was on him.

One very pissed-off waiter came to the table. Neal saw from

his look that the staff here would like nothing better than to throw this punk quartet out into the alley and maybe set fire to them if the chance arose and they had a spare match. But the punks had money and lots of it. The manager probably just wanted to get them fed and get them out before the regular customers got the idea that this was more than a fluke. The other customers were already getting nervous but looked too intimidated to complain.

The Suit ordered for all four.

Neal stepped back for a minute to think it over. He had a choice to make here: stand back and follow them or move in. Following was probably the safer choice. There was a small chance that the smart one could make him, but he doubted that. He could follow them through the night, get an address, and then make a nice slow move. But there was a chance, as there always was with a one-man tail, that he would lose them and he might never get another shot.

On the other hand, if he moved in unprepared, he might blow it for good.

He took a deep breath, edged his way through the crowd on the sidewalk, and entered the restaurant. The headwaiter greeted him with the wooden smile reserved for lone diners that says "I have to seat you but you ought to have gone to a counter, where you wouldn't take up a whole table, so please, at least run up a big liquor tab." That smile.

"Table for one, please."

"Yes, sir. Follow me please."

Neal pointed to an empty deuce across the aisle from Allie. "How about that one?"

"Really, sir?"

"Honest to goodness."

The man shrugged. "As you wish, sir."

He seated him at the table and handed him the menu. "Enjoy your meal."

Now what? Neal thought. Come on, genius, what next? You could reach over, tap her on the shoulder, and say "Gotcha." You could explain that you're on a scavenger hunt and you have to bring home a seventeen-year-old girl to a Vice Presidential candidate and get twenty thousand points, you could . . . actually smell her perfume, which was some wicked variety of musk. You could suddenly understand how some poor prep school teacher could . . .

Steady, lad. Let's take it easy. Let's wipe the sweat off your palms. Christ, you've only done about a thousand undercovers, and the basic rule is always the same: Get close, stay close, wait for an opening.

He studied the menu. Might as well get a good meal out of this. But there was nary a cheeseburger to be found. He decided on the lamb. "Waiter. Oh, waiter!" he heard the Suit say. So he was local East End. But he did a fine parody of an Oxbridge twit. The harried waiter came over.

"Where are our steaks?"

"Cooking, sir. Did you want them raw?"

"When I want any shit out of you, I'll squeeze your head." His eyes narrowed. He didn't like being fucked with.

"Kill 'im, Colin," laughing boy said.

A name. Colin. Thank you, baby Jesus. "If sir isn't satisfied . . ." said the waiter.

"Sir isn't leaving, if that's what you've got on your mind. Now get us our bloody food. Wimpy's have better service."

"Better food, too." Laughing boy was serious.

"Run along," Colin said.

Laughing boy chimed in dutifully, "Now!" The shout lifted every head in the place.

"Easy, Crisp," said Colin. "There's an art to this. Eat your salad."

"If you don't, I will. I'm starving." Oh, Allie, if you knew how long I've waited to hear you say that . . . or say anything.

Crisp pushed his plate to her. "You're always hungry. How come you don't get fat?"

"Yeah, Colin, how come?" she asked. It was a joke between them.

"Better living through chemistry, love," Colin said. "Better loving, too."

Oh boy.

"Have you decided, sir?"

The waiter startled him.

"I'll have the lamb, please."

"And the wine, sir?"

"You decide."

"Thank you, sir."

Colin was playing to a full house and loving it. He knew just how much he could bait the crowd of locals and tourists without forcing the manager to toss him. He had just the right edge, loud and sharp enough to disrupt the place. Putting it to the middle class he was, and no mistake.

"Well," Colin asked his mates, and anyone within earshot, "have you ever met a bloke from Oxford who wasn't a buggerboy?"

Crisp tried to keep up with him. "Have you ever meet a bloke from Oxford?"

"Not me. I hate buggerboys."

"Or do you just hate Oxford boys?" asked Allie.

"Oxford boys, Cambridge boys, Eton boys, Arundel boys . . . they're all buttjockeys. What they get up to between the sheets when the lights go out would make me mother weep."

"Your mother's dead."

"All the same."

"I need to hit the loo," Allie said.

"Again?"

"It's been a while."

Do I detect a slight tinge of the defensive? Neal asked himself.

"So go."

"Come with me."

"You're a big girl now. It's the one with the frock on the door."

"You know what I mean."

Their voices had dropped. This was private business. Neal saw that Colin didn't like his act interrupted.

"Later," Colin said.

"C'mon, Collie. Now."

Collie? As in Lassie, as in woof-woof, come quick, Timmy fell down the well?

"C'mon, please?"

Neal checked out her eyes. He could never remember whether the eyes were supposed to be the windows or the mirrors of the soul. Maybe both, like those one-way mirrors they use in precinct houses and your finer department stores.

Allie's eyes were tilting toward teary. Moist and soft, and Neal could swear they had been sharp and clear when he came in. A look like that on Seventy-second Street would draw the sales force for blocks around.

Colin took control. "Have another beer." Allie's fingers started doing a Buddy Rich imitation on the bottle. Her nostrils, as they say in the romance books, flared. Then she turned on the charm she'd learned from Mom and Dad.

"Maybe just a little something for my cold. Runny nose?"

Is it ever thus? Neal wondered. He had a friend at Columbia

who claimed that life was just a stack of record albums on an automatic drop. Problem was, they were all the same record.

Colin smiled back at her. A compromise had been reached. "Yeah, those summer colds are always the worst. Got a bit of a sniffle meself." He stood up. "Come on then, love. You two hold the table, eh? You can go when we get back."

The loos were in the basement at the end of a dark, narrow corridor. Allie leaned against the corridor wall as Colin screened her from view and held the spoon to her nose. She steadied it against one nostril and rested her finger against the other to keep it closed. She inhaled sharply and deeply and held her head back while Colin carefully dipped another spoonful from the vial in his hand. She snorted this one and shook her head gently back and forth.

Colin dipped into the vial again for a quick hit. Then he ran the little finger of his right hand around the rim of the vial, and with his left hand pushed Allie's shirt up and over her breasts. He gently rubbed a little coke around each nipple and bent over and licked it off. She bit down on the knuckle of her index finger and whimpered once, softly, as her right hand found his crotch and rubbed. He pulled her shirt back down. Her nipples stood out against the thin black fabric.

Colin smiled and removed her hand. "Very sexy, love. Very nice. Now be a good girl and pop back upstairs. I have to use the shitter."

She brushed past Neal on the stairway. His hand almost reached for her. Instead, he ignored her and followed Colin into the gents'.

To find that God had given it to him on a platter. Colin had draped his jacket over the stall door.

19

"Yes, sir?" the headwaiter asked as Neal stood at his station.

"Somebody lost a wallet. I wanted to turn it in."

"Oh dear. How good of you, sir." He looked through Colin's wallet and managed to mask the flood of what was welling up in his soul.

"Yes, sir. I shall just put it up here until someone claims it." Neal sat back down. Colin and company were happily devouring their steaks, conversation having given way to gluttony. They ate like pigs, though, so as not to let the side down.

Neal enjoyed his lamb. Dessert, coffee, and we'll see how this shakes out, he thought.

The headwaiter had obviously shared the happy news with the rest of the staff, who wasted no time in leading Colin down the primrose path of destruction. A good waiter can hurry or stretch a dinner with a few chosen words and inflections, and these guys were artists. They had now begun to treat Colin like the Duke of Topping-on-Snot, suggesting expensive extras in a tone that suggested that only lowlifes would refuse. Colin, swayed in equal parts by gin, beer, wine, cocaine, heady sex, and sheer hubris, put up a feeble resistance.

"Pudding, sir?"

"Perhaps some brandy, sir?"

"A liqueur for the coffee, sir?"

(A bill that equals the gross national product of Paraguay, sir?)

And finally: "Your check, sir."

"Thanks, guv."

The table was littered with the detritus of a glorious bacchanal that would have done Squire Weston and his ten hungry friends proud. Crisp punctuated the trencherman's orgy with a satisfied belch of Richterian tenor.

Colin wiped the last trace of his third chocolate mousse off his lips and reached in his jacket for his wallet. He reached again, then the other pocket; then his trouser pockets, side and rear. He stood up.

The waiter arched an amused eyebrow. That did it.

"Some fucking bastard stole my fucking purse!"

"Indeed, sir?"

The headwaiter came over and hovered ostentatiously, making dead sure that everybody in the place was watching. Everybody was.

"A problem, sir?" he asked.

"Some groveling whelp of a poxy tart stole my money!"

The headwaiter was nearly delirious with joy. "We will happily accept your personal check."

"I don't have any bloody personal check!"

"Oh dear."

Allie chuckled. A glance from Colin stopped her.

"Credit card, sir?"

"Right, he lifted me purse and handed me back me credit cards," Colin shouted.

Crisp got up from the table. "Let's just walk out. Come to a decent place and it's full of thieves."

The headwaiter was unperturbed. "How do you intend to settle your bill, sir?"

"I'll come back with the money."

"I'm afraid that won't do, sir."

"I'm quite capable of paying for it!"

"With what, is the issue."

"With the money in me fucking wallet!"

Now the headwaiter held center stage. With generations of music hall behind him, he gave a perfect delivery. "Oh, yes"—one, two, three—"your wallet." He rolled his eyes for the benefit of his audience.

Neal heard his cue. Enter, stage left. "Excuse me, maybe he's talking about the wallet I turned in."

The headwaiter turned scarlet and stared at Neal, his eyes accusing him of base treachery. He was trying to decide whether to bluff it out or not. There was a lot of money in the wallet. Neal turned up the heat.

"Yeah, the wallet I found in the men's room. I turned it in to you." He put a little extra New York street into his voice for Colin's benefit.

"*What*?" Colin stormed.

The headwaiter didn't take his eyes off Neal as he hissed, "Harry, did we have a purse turned in?"

"I'll go look."

"Thank you, Harry."

"I should mash your ugly face in, mate," Crisp said to the headwaiter.

"Shut up," said Colin. He studied the headwaiter's face,

memorizing details. The purple and orange crew cut was looking around the restaurant, making sure that everyone saw their
vindication. Allie smiled behind a napkin.

The waiter came back. "Is this it?" he asked. He wasn't as
good an actor as his boss.

"Yeah, that's it," said Colin, snatching it from him.

The headwaiter played it out. "Do you have some identi-
fication, sir?"

Colin flipped the wallet open to a picture of himself.
"Happy?"

"Overjoyed."

Colin flipped some bills on the table. "Keep the change. I
owe you one, guv." Then he addressed the crowd. "And to all
you happy couples out there, I hope you get fucked as good
tonight as you got in this place! C'mon, you lot." He led his
band out of the restaurant.

YEAH, OKAY, NOW WHAT? NEAL THOUGHT. You've made contact
so you have to follow up on it. Otherwise, if you try just to
follow them, and get spotted, you're screwed. You've walked
through the door, so it's time to smile and say hello.

He left a ten-quid note on the table and headed for the
door. The headwaiter stopped him.

"Thank you, sir, for returning the gentleman's purse," he said
with a smile as cold as his chilled salad forks. "I do hope we can
do something equally helpful for you someday."

"Like force-feed me pâté with a coal scoop?"

"Something along that line, sir, yes."

"Sounds like fun. Now get out of my way."

"Running off to join our new little friends, are we, sir?"

The waiter wasn't moving and Colin and friends were.
Neal also saw that the other much-abused waiter was standing

directly behind him. Attacked by a gang of vicious waiters, for Christ's sake?

Neal smiled pleasantly. "You know, usually, supercilious little fucks like you keep people like me *out* of the restaurant, not trapped in it."

"We just wanted to express our gratitude, sir."

Tick, tick, tick. Every second he stood there dealing with these assholes, Allie was getting farther away. Neal wondered whether the police were already on the way. Oh, well, what the fuck, he thought. He crossed his hands in front of his chest and grabbed the waiter's lapels. Then he straightened his hands with a snap, popping the waiter's stiff collar into his carotid artery. The world got all nice and woozy for the waiter, who pitched forward into Neal. Neal spun him and handed him to his startled assistant, and ran out the door.

Step one, he told himself, is to get lost in the crowd. You don't want the waiter doing any funny "He went thataway!" numbers for the local constabulary. Step two is to spot Colin and the Little Lost Kids before they fade back into a city of thirteen million other sweaty individuals. So pick it, kid, right or left out this door, and hope like hell you make the lucky choice. Neal would rather have licked every toilet bowl in greater Cleveland than explain to Graham and Levine how he could possibly have lost Allie Chase when she had been sitting right beside him in a restaurant. He made the choice to turn left outside the restaurant and plunged into the crowd of tourists who now thronged the street.

Now most people don't know how to get through a crowd, but most people didn't spend their entire adolescence chasing Joe Graham through Chinatown on market days and down Fifth Avenue at Christmastime. Neal silently blessed the malevolent leprechaun as he eased his way quickly through the traffic toward Leicester Square, his best guess and hope as to Colin's destination. He knew that angry people walk fast, and that they also tend to go to familiar places to cool off. Colin was sure as hell angry.

Neal thought he'd grabbed a glimpse of Crisp's head bobbing in the crowd about a half block ahead, but then he lost it. If Colin beat him to the square without Neal getting a look at where he was headed, it could be all over. Colin could head anywhere from the south side of the square, leaving Neal only a guess and a desperate search through the local pubs. He quickened his pace, finding every hole in the crowd and moving through it. He worked his way to the edge of the crowd, figuring he could race ahead and maybe even beat Colin to the square. That's when the cop grabbed him.

Neal stared up at the huge bobby, who had thrown an arm across his chest.

"Steady, lad," the cop intoned. "Do you want to get run over?"

Neal saw the edge of the sidewalk under his feet and realized that he had been about to step into the street, where even now taxis were rushing past. His heart slowed to a mere race as he forced a smile and said, "No, sir. Thank you."

He thought that he'd rather get creamed by the fucking cab than lose Colin and Allie, which was exactly what he was doing. They had to be in the square by now, and unless they were going there to hang out, he might have blown his last chance.

The signal changed and Neal ran across the street onto the broad sidewalk that made up the northwest corner of the square. No Colin, no Allie, no crew cut, no Crisp. Go fish. In fact, he couldn't see a goddamn thing with all the people out there. The unpleasant buzz of panic filled his ears for a second. Then he had a "just might work" idea. He crossed the north sidewalk, walking away from the square, and ran up a flight of stairs on the outside of the corner building. This was a second-floor restaurant, where a few tables looked out onto the square. He walked in. The place was packed and there was a line. Neal sidled his way up to the headwaiter. (He never suspected that his life would be so much in the hands of London's headwaiters.)

"Sir," said this one in a voice that told Neal that these guys must all go to school together, "perhaps you noticed the people in queue behind you?"

"I'm meeting friends," Neal said, "and I'm very late."

"And do your friends have names, sir?"

Tick, tick, tick. Maybe the old lapel trick . . .

"Lord and Lady Hectare," Neal said as he stood on tiptoes and waved to an old couple seated by the window. The puzzled old gentleman waved back feebly, just in time for the guard at the gate to see.

"Bring another chair, could you?" Neal said before the waiter had a chance to check his reservation list. Neal was gambling that the waiter wouldn't fuck around with any friend of the nobility anyway, and he headed straight for the table and stood over the couple, smiling his most ingratiating smile.

"Hello," Neal said as he peered out the window. "You don't know me from a hole in the manor wall, but I just need to stand here for a moment or so and look out the window." He scanned the square from left to right, farthest to nearest, and perhaps . . .

"Now see here," the old man was saying.

"Exactly," answered Neal. "I thought I saw a very rare Bumbailey's pigeon a moment ago land in a tree in the square. I just couldn't pass up a chance to spot it and add it to my list."

"A Bumbailey's pigeon!" the woman exclaimed. "I've never seen one, either!" She turned to look out the window.

"Balls," the old man said.

"I think it's a female, actually. Of course, I only got a brief look at it." There they were, headed down the west side of the square, not stopping for anything, presenting Neal with the perfect Hobson's choice. He could stand up here and watch them walk out of range, or he could run down into the square and lose sight of them.

"I have my opera glasses in my bag," the woman was saying. Neal wasn't listening. He was swallowing the bitter taste of fucking it up good. Bumbailey's pigeon, indeed. He was about to run for the stairs and give it a futile shot when he heard the sound of drums and cymbals, and saw Colin and his trio stop dead in their tracks and try to turn around. Too late. A crowd formed in back of them, and in front of them were the Hare Krishnas, fifty of them at least, snaking their way up the west edge of the square in perfect formation. As the lead members started to circle around Colin and Allie, Neal smiled a long smile. Maybe there is a God, he thought. Hare Krishna, Hare Hare.

"I think I see it!" the woman shouted. Other diners turned to stare at her. "A Bumbailey's pigeon," she explained patiently.

"I guess I'll be running along," Neal said. "Thanks." He made his way back to the foyer.

"Is something wrong, sir?" asked the headwaiter.

Neal looked at him with disgust. "*That* isn't Lord Hectare."

Then he went to join the parade.

THEY'RE PRETTY IMPRESSIVE, these Hare Krishnas, Neal thought as he joined the edge of the crowd of spectators. I mean, you always think of them as airheads, but they know how to throw a parade. And Colin certainly looks happy, trapped in the middle of their intricately weaving patterns and all red in the face and staring at the ground, while Allie laughs and sings along.

Neal worked his way around the chanting procession to put himself in Colin's path. He found himself standing beside Charlie

Chaplin's statue. Never one to disregard a prop, he casually leaned against the statue and faced front, watching the Hares jingle, bang, and chant with bemused detachment. Ultimate cool. This also gave him time to catch his breath and stop sweating in streams.

He was the first thing Colin saw as the figures finally cleared the way. Colin looked out past the last swirling Krishna to see Neal, one foot planted against the statue, grinning at him. Colin didn't believe in coincidence. In his business, as in Neal's, there is a word for people who do believe in coincidence: victims. He matched Neal's grin and walked carefully toward him. Neal didn't move, and the smile didn't fade, and Colin didn't like that one little effing bit. This was his turf.

Neal watched him coming, and also watched Crisp work his way around to Neal's left. A minor tactical error, Neal thought, as you should always play the odds that your adversary is right-handed and place yourself in position to grab that hand before it can do something nasty to your boss. Unless, of course, you're carrying something far nastier and don't mind using it. Neal pushed that ugly thought from his head and kept smiling as Colin came right up into his face.

Neal got off first. "I liked your Alex and his Droogs act in the restaurant."

"It's no act, rugger."

"No offense. Everybody has an act."

"What's yours?" He was still smiling, but Neal saw the edge behind it. He wanted to start crying and say it was all a mistake.

Instead he said, "I steal wallets."

Colin's eyes turned killer cold. The smile vanished into a frown. He shook his head slowly back and forth while Crisp waited for the order to bash Neal's head in. Neal could see Allie over Colin's shoulder, observing the scene with a petulant sneer. Neal knew he could duck Crisp's first shot. It was the second and third that had him worried, never mind what Colin might decide to contribute. Bright idea, he thought, trapping yourself against a statue. Very clever.

Colin finally spoke. "Now why did you have to tell me, sports fan? You had a nice thing going, the bit about returning my purse and all, and then you have to ball it up and fookin' tell me about it!"

Neal wasn't sure, but he thought the speech had the whiny tone produced by the last straw on a bad day. He sensed that Colin was more embarrassed than angry, and he almost started breathing again. On the other hand, he'd seen embarrassed people do some pretty wicked things.

"What am I supposed to do now, eh?" Colin continued. "You've put my balls to the mark and I *should* break your thieving fingers, eh? But I'm grateful for bailing me out back in the restaurant! Why do you want to put me in a position like this?"

"Just bored, I guess."

Colin looked him square in the eye. Either this bloke was crazy or he was the coolest character he'd seen since looking in the mirror that morning.

"Well, rugger," he started to say, then burst out laughing, "if it's excitement you're looking for . . ."

BEWARE THE HOSPITALITY OF THE SOCIOPATH. So thought Neal Carey as he leaned against the brick wall and threw up, which started his nose bleeding again.

It had started mildly enough with a few pints thrown back in a congenial Garrick Street pub. Colin played host and introduced Neal around, starting with his own retinue.

"Meet Crisp," he said. "We call 'im 'at because 'e's always eatin' the ruddy things. Known 'im 'arf me life, an' I don't think I know 'is real name."

"I play the guitar," Crisp said.

"Pleased to meet you."

Colin introduced the girl with purple hair. "This is 'is bird, Vanessa."

"I'm always eating Crisp," she said in a surprisingly middle-class accent.

"And this," Colin said proudly, clearly saving the best for last, "is Alice, your fellow Yank."

Alice? Neal thought. *Alice?* The finest schools America has to offer and that's the best you can come up with? He reached out to shake her hand. "Nice to meet you. Where are you from?"

She didn't take the hand and she didn't smile.

"Kansas," she said. Her blue eyes challenged him to call her a liar.

"Well, Dorothy, you're not in Kansas anymore."

"'Er name is Alice. She's from California."

Clever Alice, thought Neal. What better to hype the fantasy of a city-bound Brit than a golden California sunshine girl? "I've been out there. Where in California?"

She didn't pause a beat. "Stockton. A real shithole."

Neal smiled at her. You're not bad, Allie, not bad at all. "I haven't been to Stockton."

She still didn't smile back. Just looked at him flatly and said, "You ain't missed anything."

You ain't missed anything? Don't push it, kid.

"My shout," Neal said. The barkeep drew four Guinesses from the tap.

"What brings you to London Town, then, Neal?" Colin asked. "What wind blows you to our green and pleasant land?"

A pusher who quotes Blake? This is getting weirder and weirder. "Work."

"An' what would 'at be?"

"I'm a cop."

Maybe Colin didn't exactly choke on his beer, but it sure didn't go down the smooth way Lord Ivey intended when he brewed the stuff.

It was so much fun to watch, Neal said, "A private detective." No reaction at all from Allie, not a flinch.

"Get stuffed!" Colin shouted.

"Scout's honor. I'm over here guarding some executive stiff who's buying antiques, or something."

"An' you thought you might as well snatch a little nicker on the side."

"Why not?"

"An' when you saw me jacket 'anging over the shitter door, you thought it belonged to John Q. Tourist . . . ."

"But when I saw who it belonged to, I thought I better give it back."

Now let's see how big an ego you have, Neal thought. If you buy that one . . .

"It's a good job you did," Colin said.

. . . you think a lot of yourself.

"My pleasure," Neal said, looking just enough over Colin's shoulder to flash his most charming, sleazoid smile at Allie.

"Where are *you* from?" she asked. She wasn't making small talk.

"New York, New York. The town so nice, they named it twice," Neal answered. He knew that one mistake inexperienced undercovers often make is telling too big a whopper as a cover story. Keep it close to home, there's less chance of getting caught up in your own lies, especially when you're just feeling your way.

"The Big Apple," Colin said, flashing his cosmopolitan outlook.

Allie whispered something in Colin's ear. Neal didn't catch it.

"Later," Colin said.

She whispered again.

"I said later," Colin answered again. A trace of annoyance played across his face. He turned to Neal. "You want some excitement, then, rugger?"

"If you have any."

Colin's smile could best be described as mischievous. "Oh, we got some, all right. What kind would you like?"

He opened his palm to show the capsules of speed that appeared slick as Blackstone.

This, Neal thought, is the point in the TV episode when the canny private eye figures a way to say no, or cleverly palms the pills and fakes the effects. But this is mostly because Quaker Oats is sponsoring the show and wouldn't buy ads if the hero gets stoned for any reason whatsoever. Unless, of course, the villains hold him down and pour the stuff down his throat. Then the camera gets all blurry. But this was real life, which is even trickier than television—and often more blurry.

Neal took one of the capsules and knocked it back with a swallow of stout. Colin spread the rest around.

"Let's go to The Club," Allie said. "I wanna dance. And I *mean* dance!"

"Wha' about your engagement?" asked Colin.

"I have over two hours!"

"The Club it is, then."

THE CLUB WAS YOUR BASIC CAVE, only more primitive than Neal was used to in New York's SoHo. If New York was Cro-Magnon, this place was Neanderthal. It didn't really have a name.

"I dunno, rugger," Colin had explained when asked. "We just call it The Club."

Neal did feel he was being clubbed by the band, which had a name: Murdering Scum. They were an opening act for the night's headliners, The Queen and All His Family.

"What part of town are we in?" Neal shouted above the din.

"Earl's Court!" Colin answered. They had fought their way to the bar. Allie, Crisp, and Vanessa had joined the bobbing throng on the dance floor. The place smelled of beer and sweat.

Neal took a long sip of his beer, which accomplished two things: It gave him the closest acquaintance with horse urine he ever hoped to have, and it gave him time to think. This latter activity was becoming increasingly difficult. Sort of an imposition. The band was playing four hundred beats to the measure.

Colin was in better pharmacological shape than Neal, and less stoned, so the pause in conversation dragged, as things tend to do on Amphetamine Standard Time. But the ensuing two or three decades gave Neal a chance to observe Allie, which was the point of the exercise, after all. Good to keep your mind on that. Allie was dancing in a frenzied jerking motion that threatened to tear her head from her body. And she was having a very good time.

The Scum, as they were known to their friends, switched to a romantic ballad about "fucking till it's red and raw" and the lead guitarist seemed to be demonstrating the technique with pelvic thrusts that would have sent Elvis himself running to a revival meeting. The band reduced its harmonic structure to the sublime simplicity of a single chord, which made a certain kind of sense given the subject matter. The crowd was sure going for it in a big way, though. Of course, most of them had safety pins jammed through their ears or noses, which did indicate a tolerance for pain. They sweated inside their leather and denim.

Neal watched Vanessa and Crisp make Watusi leaps on the crowded floor. Every now and again, Crisp amused a fellow celebrant by spewing beer in his face, which seemed to be an acknowledged form of greeting. Neal looked around for Allie, and spotted her standing in front of the jerry-built platform that served as a stage. A sheen of sweat shone off her blond hair as she swung her head in a rhythm all her own.

Slow, one-beat-to-the-measure cadence somewhere in the frenzied rock and roll. Allie didn't want her love red and raw; she wanted it slow and soft.

"Beautiful, isn't she?" Colin asked. He saw Neal watching.

"Yeah."

"Off limits, Neal."

"No problem."

Not to worry, Colin, old sod, Neal thought. I'm only going to grab your beloved and carry her back over the big water. Whether she will or not.

Oh, well, time to play.

"Kind of hard to control, though, isn't she?" Neal asked.

"Alice? Not hard."

Neal gave him a little more of a prod in the psychic balls. "If you say so," he said, smiling.

He watched the little knots in Colin's jaw tighten. The pimp took a quick swallow of beer and set the bottle down hard on the bar. "Right," he said.

Colin worked his way through the crowd to where Allie was standing, her eyes closed and body gently weaving. He grabbed her by the shoulders, straightened her up, and gently lifted her chin with his left hand. She opened her eyes and smiled at him. He slapped her hard with his right hand. Her eyes widened and filled with tears.

Neal checked the impulse to head over there. Too early for the "white knight" bit, he thought. Also, Colin would beat the shit out of you and his friends would stomp on whatever was left.

Colin stroked the reddening splotch on Allie's cheek, then hauled back and hit her again, harder this time, snapping her head back.

Good going, Neal thought to himself. So far, you're doing a real good job for this kid.

He watched as Colin stood, hands at his side, and stared at Allie. She fought off her tears as her chin dropped to her chest and she stared at the floor. Without looking up, she held her arms straight out in front of her. After a couple of seconds that lasted about a week, Colin took her arms and pulled her to him. She burrowed her face into his chest and held him tightly. It was creepy, but Neal had witnessed worse at Westchester cocktail parties. What made this especially bad was that Colin looked over, found Neal with his eyes, and smiled. Alice hard to control? Right.

Now where have I seen this shit before? Neal asked himself. Oh, yeah, about half my life. A pimp is a pimp is a pimp. Come to Daddy. Oops, bad choice of words there.

He looked on as Colin and Allie started to dance. She made your basic miraculous recovery and began to move with the music. Like bad art imitating bad life, the band switched tunes, working into a hard-driving message song that the crowd seemed to know.

It was an anthem of sorts. Neal didn't catch the title, but the chorus went: "Burn it, wreck it, fuck it, tear it down." The crowd joined in with a passion that could spring only from deep feeling, and Neal found himself shamed at the condescension he'd felt all night. This was a song of the dispossessed, a screaming, angry *cri de coeur* born of a thousand years of a class-bound society. The dancers whirled in violent sweeps, bumping and bouncing against each other, surrogate objects for mutual rage. No harm meant you, bloke, but burn it, wreck it, fuck it, tear it down.

The inchoate fury swept around Neal, taking him along. He felt their anger, shared it. Anger at the hopelessness, at Da' and Granda' and you, all living off the dole in the same effin' project on the same effin' street with the same effin' neighbors in the same effin' heat. Anger at the toffs with their effin' BBC, and their effin' Oxbridge accents that keep out you and me. So let's burn it, wreck it, fuck it, tear it down. Fury at the useless effin' effort of it all, when every job's the same arsehole-lickin' beck and call, and who needs their Labour Party and their social-programs bull, so let's burn it, wreck it, fuck it, tear it down.

Neal shook his head to clear it, and then realized it was already clear. Who the hell expected the Murderous Scum to be eloquent, much less articulate? And didn't he feel the same sorts of things? Like real anger at the monied class whose messes he cleaned up for a living? Whose living rooms he occupied and whose scotch he drank when they were in trouble? And wasn't he their sheepdog? Go fetch my kid, Fido, good boy? And suddenly he felt like a traitor in this place, and the rage welled up inside him, and he wanted to beat the shit out of Senator John Chase, and tell him to go fuck himself, and take Ethan Kitteredge's little toy boat and crunch it in his hands and throw the pieces in his face and tell him what he could do with his private school education, and that was to burn it, wreck it, fuck it, tear it down, and he found himself joining in the dance and in the chorus, weaving, bobbing, bouncing, and slamming off the other dancers as the music throbbed through him and he was hearing the words about your great damn stinking family who will never understand, with their patriotic crap about this putrid, dying land, and the endless block of flats that make a prison you can't stand, and Christ, he understood! The sheer numbing, stupefying, fucking *boredom* of it! That you can never escape your class, so quit trying.

Then he was dancing with Allie—not dancing, really, but slamming. Shoulder off shoulder, laughing, singing, sweat flying from one to the other, and he knocked her down, off her feet, but she bounced up laughing and spun around, then put her shoulder into his chest and knocked him down, and burn it, wreck it, fuck it, tear it down. Tear it off, tear it away, tear it to shreds. Two thousand years of civilization, to produce what? Senator Chase for Veep? Then Allie picked him up and spun him around and pushed him off and then he was dancing with Colin. Hands locked, pushing forward and pushing back, chests slamming into each other, shouting at the top of their lungs the chorus that had now become a frenetic chant. Looking at Colin and seeing himself there, another country, another time. Tear it down, tear it down. One chord beating against the wails in a shriek of fury. Hare Krishna, Hare Hare. Tear it down. Then he and Colin fell down in a heap on the floor as the song ended in a crash of drums, and they lay on the floor together, laughing and laughing, and then laughing more as Allie fell face first on top of them, shaking her hair so that her sweat sprayed on their faces.

Neal listened to his heartbeat and felt himself breathing hard, and he made some decisions then and there about Colin, Allie, Kitteredge, and himself.

ALLIE WASHED UP IN THE WOMEN'S LOO. She slipped off her T-shirt and splashed water on herself, rolled on deodorant, and sprayed a touch of perfume between her breasts. She pulled a dark blue silk blouse out of her bag and put it on over her jeans, then went to work with the tiny makeup kit. She expertly penciled around her eyes, used just a trace of mascara, then a light blush; blood-red lipstick topped off the look, casual, expensive, a little dangerous.

"Killer," said Colin. He shouted out the door. "Neal, come in, lad, and have a spot of tea!"

Neal took a look at Allie and knew he'd seen this movie before. "What are you decked out for?"

"Not what. *Who.*"

"Oh."

Colin spooned out a generous dose of coke and held it up to Allie. She sighed. "Something more, babe?"

"Later."

"It's always later." She snorted the coke anyway, doing two spoons with practiced ease.

Colin took a hit and offered a spoon to Neal. He took it in, and tasted that funny metallic taste deep down in his throat. It wasn't very good coke.

Colin handed Allie a slip of paper. "You want me to send Crisp along?"

Allie shook her head. "It's an easy one. I've done it before. See you back at the flat."

She pecked him on the lips, waved a goodbye, and headed out the door. Neal didn't say anything; thought he'd let Colin bring it up if he wanted.

"It's just fucking, right?" Colin asked.

"Sure."

"I need a pint."

"I'm buying."

THE BAND WAS ON A BREAK. You could hear yourself talk. And think.

"You liked it?"

"Yeah."

"It's not so much bullshit. Most rock's become bullshit, you know. Like they forgot what it's about."

"It's physical."

"It's about living right now, and forget that other crap. There's no future anyway, so forget about it. Me, I wouldn't half mind if the IRA blew the whole city up, start with Fuckingham Palace."

"You want to kill the rich. I just want to take their money." Truer words, Neal, old pal, truer words.

"You take their money, you have to take their shit."

"Not if you do it right."

Colin looked at him differently. "Maybe we'll talk."

"Maybe."

They left The Club at about 2:00 A.M. Neal had a major buzz on from the speed, the coke, and God only knows how many pints. His head rang from the combined effects of drugs, alcohol, noise, and the nagging anxiety of not knowing where Allie was. *Maybe I should have split and followed her. Maybe she wants out and is just looking for her chance. Maybe I could have grabbed her at whatever hotel she's at and said "Here I am to save the day" and gone straight to Heathrow and caught the next flight out. Maybe. But more likely, I'd have blown the whole thing.*

So he hung with Colin, Crisp, and Vanessa.

"Come crash at my flat," Colin said.

"No thanks. I'll catch a cab back to the hotel."

"Not at this time of night down here. Come on, you can crash on the floor, go home in the morning."

"Streets aren't safe this time of the night," Crisp said. "Lots of punks wandering around." He grinned like an old horse headed for the stable.

"Yeah, okay."

They walked along the monotonous streets lined with blocks of flats, sweetshops, and news brokers. All the places were shut down for the night and few cars prowled the street. It was pretty dull. Until they came across the Pakis.

There were five of them and they were pissed. Pissed as in drunk. Pissed as in angry. Five larger than average Pakistani immigrants in loud pastel shirts, white jeans, and black loafers. They looked like a band at a cheap wedding. They blocked the sidewalk.

"Hello, Colin," said their leader. He impressed Neal as a muscular type.

"Your name wouldn't be Ali, would it?" Colin inquired pleasantly. "In fact, would all your names be Ali?"

Ali's name was, in fact, Ali. And he wasn't amused. "Where's your gang, Colin?"

"Fucking your mother, I should think."

For good measure, Crisp chimed in, "Why don't you stinking wogs go back to Pakistaniland where you belong?"

Ali smiled and said, "Colin thinks he's a big man now because he has some protection down on the Main Drag. But, Colin, this is not the Main Drag and you don't have any protection here."

"You see, Neal," Colin said, "you've gone and stumbled on what the BBC calls racial tension here. We don't like the Pakis. We don't like them taking our jobs, our flats, our shops, and our parks. We don't like them crowding up our city with endless brats and their ugly wives. We don't like their dingy color, their smelly food, their greasy hair, their bad breath, or their ugly, stupid faces. The only thing they're good for is providing poor blokes like us with a bit of a hobby. Our version of bird shooting—Paki bashing."

"Yes, Neal," Ali said in a voice that let him know he was in for it, "but one of the great features of Paki bashing is that the white fellows need to be twice our number."

He pulled a very nasty-looking leather sap from his jeans pocket.

Neal Carey hated fighting. He hated fighting for several reasons. One, he thought it was stupid. Two, it was scary and people got hurt. Three, he was bad at it and was usually one of the people who got hurt.

"Another time, then," said Neal, and he began to move around Ali. This might have worked, except that Colin had a question to ask.

"Tell me, is it your father, or mother, or both that take it up the arse in the loo at King's Cross?"

The sap flicked out and would have done considerable damage to Colin's brains, except he wasn't there. He had ducked beneath it and opened a deep cut from Ali's hip to knee with a single swipe of his blade. Ali dropped to his knees and let out a scream, which Colin quickly silenced with the toe of his shoe delivered soccer-style to the mouth.

In the meantime, Crisp reacted somewhat negatively to a vicious kick in the balls by straightening up with the beer bottle in his hand and smashing it on his assailant's chin. Undaunted, the young Pakistani punched Crisp in the side of the head and broke two knuckles, so he was a bit distracted when Vanessa laced him across the throat with a chain.

Neal was feeling considerable gratitude that his opponent seemed to be bearing no weapon and was prepared to duke it out in honorable, manly fashion. Neal assumed *the position*: right hand held in by his chest, ready to strike; left hand held high to block opponent's right. Block and then counterpunch. Except this guy was left-handed and launched a straight one that caught Neal flush on the nose. And hurt. And hurt even more when he did it again.

Neal wanted to fall down, which had always worked in the gym, but he figured that hitting the deck here would just invite a boot on the neck or a nice kick in the face, so he stayed on his feet and waited for the kid to push his luck with a third shot, which he did. Blessing his attacker's lack of imagination, Neal stepped to his own left and dodged the punch and drove a hard left hook into the kid's stomach. Son of a bitch if it didn't work. The kid doubled over and Neal took advantage of this to fall on top of him, knock him over, and lie on him.

Colin was beating the uncouth piss out of the last Pakistani when Vanessa spotted the police car turning the corner.

"Peelers!" she yelled.

Colin broke off his engagement and grabbed Neal by the back of the collar.

"Run like a bastard!"

Neal wasn't sure exactly how a bastard ran, but he assumed Colin was following his own advice, so he followed him. They ran several blocks before ducking into the proverbial alley, where he leaned against the wall, gasped for air, threw up, and started bleeding again.

COLIN'S FLAT WAS A SURPRISE.

It shouldn't have been, Neal thought. Dope dealers and pimps always make money, even young comers like Colin. The flat was by no means luxurious, but it was in a not-so-bad part of shabby Earl's Court. It was a second-floor walk-up, but spacious and surprisingly well kept. The sitting room was large and French windows led to a small balcony. The kitchen was not small, but certainly underused. A coffeepot and a tea kettle sat on a stove, along with jars of Nescafé and sugar.

Colin's bedroom was large and dark. A blackout shade hung even at night. Neal expected the water bed and the Che Guevara poster. He expected the five locks that secured the main door. He didn't expect the expensive television in the sitting room, nor the pricey stereo equipment, nor, especially, the brick-and-board bookcases lined with paperback volumes of poetry: Coleridge, Blake, and Byron. Colin was doing all right for himself.

Colin disappeared into the bedroom and came out with a bowl of hash. "Here. This will help cool you out."

He went into the kitchen and came out with ice wrapped in a paper towel. He handed it to Neal.

Neal placed the cold cloth on his face. It felt great. His nose had started to throb. He felt around it again and decided it really wasn't broken.

He loved undercover work.

Colin lit the pipe, took a long drag, and handed it to Neal. Neal shook his head. More than enough is more than enough.

"It's mild, Neal. Bopper dope."

Neal accepted the pipe and drew the hash into his lungs. He held it for a long moment, then exhaled. It beat the shit out of Ovaltine.

Carnal sounds came from the small bedroom. "Violence turns Vanessa on," Colin explained."

"Is it worth it?"

"For Crisp, it is."

"What's his real name?"

Colin shrugged and took another drag. He offered the pipe to Neal. Neal declined. More than enough is enough.

"I'm going to get some kip. I'll get you a blanket."

Daddy Colin.

Neal had just dropped off when Allie came in. He heard her long sigh, and heard her put the kettle on the boil. She stood impatiently until it whistled. He listened as she stirred in milk and sugar and then tiptoed to the bedroom door. He heard it open and shut again, and was surprised to hear her tiptoe back into the sitting room. She finished her tea while looking out the window. Then he heard her shuck off her shoes and her jeans and felt her lie down beside him.

"Push over and give me some of the blanket."

"If Colin comes out here—"

"I just want to sleep."

"Does he know that?"

Another sigh from Allie. "He's not alone."

"He came home alone."

"So?"

"Oh."

"Bright guy."

Neal gave it a shot. "You like living like this?"

"Yes. Now you want to shut up and let me get some sleep?"

Dear Dad, having a wonderful time. Wish you were here. By the way, tonight I'm sleeping with Allie Chase.

He woke up hurting. His nose felt like someone had driven a fist into it, and the rest of his body ached with righteous indignation. He was hangover thirsty and went into the bathroom to get some water.

Allie was sitting on the stool, her knees tucked up under her chin. She bent over with poignant grace, the needle poised over the small vein between her toes. She was concentrating hard, and noticed Neal only after she gently squeezed the plunger. She looked up at him as the heroin hit her. A small pop, but there it was.

"Well," Neal said, "they do say that breakfast is the most important meal of the day."

"Don't tell Colin."

"It's none of my business."

"That's right."

"He doesn't know you shoot up?"

"What happened to none of your business?"

"That shit's bad for you."

"But so good to me."

She got up, carefully put the gear back into her bag, and walked past him into the sitting room, where she lay back down on the floor and stared at the ceiling.

He followed her in and lay down beside her. "How long have you been using a wake-up?"

"My, aren't we hip. A couple of weeks. I don't know."

"Expensive habit."

"I pay for it."

"I bet you do."

"I'm not an addict."

"I didn't say you were an addict."

She rolled over on her side, away from him. "He knows I shoot up. He doesn't know how much."

She drifted off.

NEAL PROPPED HIS FEET UP ON THE BALCONY railing and gently leaned his chair back. The last of the afternoon sun felt good on his face. He had showered and shaved, borrowed a clean T-shirt from Colin, and was now sipping a cup of bitter Nescafé, on his way to feeling at least remotely human. Allie was safely tucked in and sound asleep. Crisp and Vanessa had gone out in search of food, and Neal and Colin had settled onto the balcony.

Colin was dressed for leisure. He was shirtless and wore denim jeans and biker boots. Reflective sunglasses shielded his eyes from the harsh glare of day.

"Sunday's a hassle, so I leave it alone," he was saying. "Too many citizens on the street and the coppers don't want to see you there. Sunday night's all right, though."

"I should get going," Neal said, yawning.

"What for?"

"The job."

Colin stretched like a cat. "Talk about the fox in the friggin' 'en coop."

"I don't screw around with it."

"Pity."

"Do you rip off *your* customers?"

"Never."

They sat quietly for a while. Neal thought about what he was up to, then tried not to think about it. Made him feel like shit.

"So are you a heavy dealer, Colin?"

"Not 'eavy enough. Bit of hash, bit of coke . . ."

"Heroin?"

"No. Wouldn't harf mind, but the nicker, lad, the nicker . . ." He rubbed his thumb over his fingertips, the universal sign language for cash. "Takes a 'eap of the filthy lucre to get into smack in any serious way."

"And the ladies?"

"Wha' is this? The BBC?"

"Just making conversation."

"I have a few lady friends who'd rather get paid for it. I take a finder's fee."

Yeah, I get a finder's fee, too, Neal thought. So to speak.

Colin set his head back to catch the rays better. "I was a little bugger during the 'ole 'ippie thing. Love and peace an' all 'at shit. The bloody Beatles and their wog guru. Fucking sitars . . ."

"You got that right."

"This punk thing. It *says* the world is shit. Get pissed, get stoned, get your rocks off. All there is."

These are a few of my favorite things.

"We just got back from a 'oliday in France," Colin said. "Got pissed, got stoned, got our rocks off in a different place."

You did? *You did?* It didn't take long for it to sink in. You working-class heroes were on some beach in France while I was sweating my balls off on the Main Drag looking for you!

"Colin, you aspire to the middle class."

"I aspire to a 'eap of filthy lucre."

"Yeah?"

"Not 'arf."

"Maybe I know where you could get it."

There followed what could be called a significant silence.

"Where's 'at?"

Neal set the chair back on the floor, put his cup on the railing, and stood up. He stretched and yawned. "We'll talk."

He patted Colin on the head and walked out.

Always leave 'em wanting more, he thought.

20

THE NEXT MORNING, NEAL was in a doctor's office, wincing bravely, fighting back the pain.

"Did that hurt?" Dr. Ferguson asked him. He bent Neal's leg back again.

"A little," Neal answered, lifting his head up from the examining table.

"You have a nasty strain here, I believe. You can get dressed."

Neal slowly brought himself into a sitting position and struggled back into his shirt. "Thanks for seeing me at such short notice."

Ferguson didn't look up from his prescription pad. "Any friend of Simon's, as the saying goes . . ."

Ferguson tended toward chubby, and seemed quite content with it. He had an owlish face and a full head of brown hair. He lived in the same St. John's Wood house that held his office. Not that he needed to. He had considerable private income in addition to his practice. He confessed a public passion for cricket, a private passion for his wife, and a secret passion for first-edition books, hence the Simon

Keyes connection. Neal had found his number in Simon's address book.

"I feel really silly, falling down the stairs," Neal said.

"Yes, well, those stairs of Simon's . . ." Ferguson answered. He handed Neal the scrip. "This will help you sleep. Also ease what we physicians like to call discomfort."

"I just can't find a comfortable position."

"'As the actress said to the bishop.' Yes, back injuries are inconvenient that way. Next time, you really should consider hurting your ankle. Simon tells me you're interested in books."

Neal tossed in another small wince as he lowered himself from the table. "You talked with him?"

"I was motoring up north and popped in at the cottage unannounced. He was quite gracious about it. He tells me you're a Smollett scholar."

"Hardly a scholar."

"And you're here looking at his collection."

Thank you, Simon, Neal thought.

"It's incredible."

"Does he still have the *Pickle*?"

Neal gave him his best Mona Lisa, inscrutable smile.

"I see that he does," Ferguson said. "Right. Try to stay off your feet. Lie flat, no sitting. If it's still giving you trouble in a week, come back and we'll have another look."

"Thanks again."

"Don't thank me. Just filch his *Pickle* and bring it over in the dark of night."

Ferguson chuckled at his joke.

Neal chuckled. Then he winced. Then he chuckled again.

There was still a good hour or so before the shops would open, so Neal treated himself to a long walk through Regent's Park. He went down Park Road through Hanover Gate and found a footpath that took him across the lake past the boat house. By the time he reached the south gate of the zoo, his shirt was soaked but he felt good sweating the weekend's poisons out of his system.

He stopped in at a grocers on Regent's Park Road and bought ten bottles of Coca-Cola, ten bottles of Pepsi, twenty Aero chocolate bars, three packages of sugar-coated tea biscuits, a pound of white sugar, two jars of honey, a dozen eggs, bread, butter, and jam.

He found a linen shop and bought two sets of sheets, three bath towels, and a dozen hand towels. At a small athletic shop, he bought four pairs of gym socks. An expensive little stationer's shop provided him with an expensive little attaché case with combination locks. His last stop was at the chemist, where he exchanged Ferguson's prescription for a large plastic vial of sleeping pills.

Simon's flat was brutally hot and stuffy, so the first thing Neal did was open the windows. Then he laid his groceries out in the kitchen and put the soda in the refrigerator. He tore the sheets up into thin strips and left them in the bedroom, then taped the towels to the sharp corners of the dresser and bedside table. He tied knots into each of the gym socks. Then he removed the bright white bulbs from the ceiling light and the bedside lamp and replaced them with low-wattage frosted bulbs. He took half of the sleeping pills and left them in the bathroom cabinet and put the rest back in his pocket.

Back in the sitting room, he removed the four volumes of Smollett's *Peregrine Pickle* and placed them in the new attaché case. He memorized the combination and locked it up.

By the time he was finished, it was noon, and already steamy hot out on the street. He bought a *Times* and grabbed an outdoor table under an umbrella at a sidewalk café. He had an espresso and a truly goopy Italian pastry as he scanned the paper. It didn't take him long to find what he was looking for: the London Philharmonic at Albert Hall. Thursday night. Proceeds to go to the World Wildlife Fund. Prince Philip to make opening remarks. Public welcome. And a large SOLD OUT notice bannered across the ad. Buy early next time, public.

He downed another espresso and grabbed a taxi back to the hotel.

An already harried concierge looked up from his list of problems. The house was jam-packed with tourists. "Yes, sir?"

"Yes. Would you have any tickets available for the Philharmonic on Thursday evening? July second?"

"Let me check, sir." He looked into a thick book. "No, sir. Terribly sorry. All booked."

"I've already booked. Name is Carey."

The concierge sighed through his smile. "That is different, sir. Let me find you." He went back to the book. "Sorry again, Mr. Carey. I don't seem to find you here."

Neal could hear impatient shuffling starting behind him.

"Maybe it's under another name. I'm with a party."

He let the silence hang.

The concierge gave in first. "Which party might that be, sir?"

"The Henderson party."

Back to the book.

"At this hotel, sir?"

"Wouldn't use any other."

"Thank you, sir." The concierge looked over Neal's shoulder at the next guest and gave a quick smile indicating his tolerance. Then he perused the book again. "No. Sorry, sir."

"Oh dear. Maybe she's using her married name."

The concierge could not resist a two-beat comic pause before he intoned, "And if we knew what that name was, sir, we might be able to find it."

"Zacharias. *Z* as in zebra, *a* as in appropriate, *c* as in choreography, *h* as in—"

"I think I can take it from there, sir."

No luck.

"Sorry once again, Mr. Carey. Are you quite certain—"

"Well, maybe Susan didn't make the arrangements, maybe Nell did. Could you look under Taglianetti?"

"Mr. Carey, we are just a bit busy at the moment. Would it be terribly rude of me to ask if you would be so kind as to look yourself and then inform me of your progress?"

"No, not at all."

"Here you are, then."

He handed Neal the book. Neal scanned it, looking for the names of married women who were going to the affair alone. He found five, their room numbers inked in beside them. He ran a chant several times through his head: Harris, 518; Goldman, 712; Ulrich, 823; Myers, 665; Renaldi, 422. Then he hurried to his room and wrote them down.

Now for the tedious part, he thought.

Ulrich 823 turned out to be German, so that was no good. Neal hung up as soon as he heard the "Ja?" on the phone. He tried Harris 518. "May I speak to Joe Harris, please?"

The voice was an old woman's. "I'm sorry, dear, you have the wrong party. Ask at the desk."

Okeydoke. Let's give Goldman 712 a spin.

"Hello, may I speak to Mr. Goldman, please?"

"Speaking." A man's voice. American. East Coast. Sounds about the right age.

"Mr. Goldman, this is Mr. Panto of Consolidated Limited ringing to confirm our appointment tomorrow morning."

"I think you have the wrong number."

"I'm terribly sorry. Is this Mr. Alan Goldman of Schreff and Sons?"

"No, this is Dave Goldman of just plain Goldman. I'm an attorney."

"I am sorry."

"That's okay. Have a good one." Dave Goldman hung up.

So, Neal thought, I know a few things about Goldman 712. He's a lawyer, here with his wife, and she isn't dragging him to any damn philharmonic Thursday night, he doesn't give a shit who's going to make opening remarks. Maybe I've found my couple. Better take a look at them to make sure.

NICE-LOOKING COUPLE, HE THOUGHT, which they better be after keeping me waiting an hour and a half in the hallway. Mid-forties, stylish, the wife an uptight brunette who puts in some time at the spa. He's well built. Black hair just beginning to show a little silver. What used to be called a snappy dresser. Amazingly white teeth. Full range of plastic: AmEx, Diners Club. Good tipper.

He didn't follow them out of the restaurant, but finished his own meal—an excuse for a hamburger that would have made the boys at Nick's weep—and read the *International Herald Tribune.* The Yankees were in first place.

THE PHONE WOKE HIM from a pleasant nap. It was only five o'clock and he hadn't planned to head out until seven or so.

"You haven't called in for three days," Ed said.

"No news."

"Then call and say 'no news,'" Levine answered. "*No progress at all?*"

"I'm doing the best I can."

"Do better. You have four weeks."

"Jesus Christ, Ed. You and I both know this is a fool's errand."

"Then you're just the man for the job. Call in."

Neal got out of bed and stepped into the shower. The cold water woke him up. Four weeks, he thought. A lot can happen in four weeks, Ed.

ED LEVINE SET THE PHONE DOWN.

"Nothing, huh?" asked Rich Lombardi.

"Not yet."

Lombardi set the case notes back on Levine's desk. "Might have been too much to ask for, anyway."

"It was always a long shot."

Lombardi left the Friends office and went to the nearest phone booth. He had a lot of calls to make. The convention was just around the corner, the Senator was on the short list, and there was so much to make sure of. Title this story *The Man Behind the Man*.

21

ALLIE WAS STONED OUT OF HER GOURD.

When Neal made it over to the Earl's Court flat around eight o'clock, he found her pacing the floor, muttering a semi-coherent diatribe against television game shows, particularly British ones where the contestants didn't win any money worth mentioning.

"No Frigidaires, either. No dinette sets, no living room combinations, washer-dryers. No Toyotas. No trips to Honolulu!"

"C'mon in," Vanessa said to Neal. "Colin's not here, though."

Neal knew that already. He had already placed Colin back in Leicester Square. "Where is he?"

"Taking care of business."

Spotting Neal, Allie switched gears and launched into an assault on American men, particularly the ones from New York who think they know everything about screwing, but don't.

"They're pigs. Pigs! New York boys just want to get into your pants, and then they don't know what to do there. I hate that!"

Vanessa disappeared into the bathroom.

"And ice cream," Allie muttered. "You can't get any decent ice cream in this lousy country. They give you some shit called ice cream, but it isn't. Neal, did you bring any real ice cream with you?"

"No. Sorry."

She stepped over to him and looked him in the eyes. "You're no good, Neal. You know that? No damn good at all."

She said it with such utter sincerity and then gave him a smile so dazzling that he couldn't quite believe she was strung out. He couldn't help liking her. It was almost as if she was aware of herself, making fun of the American bitch for everyone's entertainment.

"And the weather," she continued, "it's too fucking hot. We sang that in school glee club once. 'It's too fucking hot, it's too fucking hot . . .'"

"'It's too *darn* hot.'"

"Yeah, it's too darn fucking hot. It's supposed to be foggy and rainy. In all the movies, it's foggy and rainy. You ever see Sherlock Holmes with a *tan*? But I haven't seen any fog or any rain since I got here and that's weeks and weeks and weeks and weeks and *what* is Nessa doing to her hair?"

"Shaving half of it off," Vanessa answered.

Neal looked into the bathroom. Sure as shit, she was shaving half of it off—the left half.

Fascinated, Allie floated into the bathroom. "Why?"

"Bored."

"May I watch?"

"Sure, love, but you can't help. You'd slice me to ribbons."

Allie lay down on the tile floor and played with Vanessa's falling locks. Neal stood in the doorway.

"Alice," he asked, "do you have any dates tonight?"

"Do I have any *dates* tonight? Yes, Troy Donahue is coming

over and we're going to the malt shop. No. Frankie Avalon and I are going to a beach party. He broke up with that bitch with the boobs. Because he loves me. No . . . Wally Cleaver and I are going to the drive-in and I'm going to teach him how to make a girl happy, except I think he really loves Lumpy Rutherford.

"Do I have any dates tonight? You think you're Colin's administrative assistant now? Vice pimp? Vice pimp, that's pretty good. No, I don't have any dates tonight."

"It's okay with me."

"Oh, goody. Neal, go get us some real ice cream, okay? Some real, real ice cream. Chocolate ice cream. Yummy."

"I have to talk to Colin."

"*You* have to talk with Colin?"

"How does this look?" Vanessa asked them. The left side of her head was bald. The right half was a cascade of magenta locks.

"I like it," Neal said. "A lot."

He turned to leave.

Allie followed him. "I just remembered another song we sang in good old glee club. Wanna hear it?"

You could take her right now, Neal thought. Whisk her off on some excuse and be gone before Vanessa ever thought to ring the phone box . . . . He hurried down the stairs, and could still hear her singing.

"'A precious gem is what you are, You're Daddy's bright and shining star . . .'"

HE CAUGHT THE DISTRICT LINE TRAIN at Earl's Court, changed to the Piccadilly Line at South Kensington, and rode it to Leicester Square. The long wooden escalator carried him to the street level. He found Colin in the square, standing under the statue of the Earl of Leicester. The inscription on the base read: THERE IS NO DARKNESS BUT IGNORANCE.

"Hello, rugger," Colin said. Crisp sat on the ground beside him in his faithful-dog pose.

"How's business?"

"Buggers are tying up the phone," Colin answered, pointing to a queue outside the phone box.

"Shout you a pint?"

Colin looked around for a second, then said, "Why not. Crisp, mind the shop, there's a good lad."

They walked to a small pub on Floral Street. Neal found a table by the window and brought two pints over.

"I looked for you over at your place earlier," he said.

"Office hours."

"Alice is wrecked."

Colin shrugged. "'At's 'er business, isn't it?"

"Could affect your business. High rollers don't like junkies."

Colin stared out the window. "Well, rugger, 'er business or my business, it's none of your business."

Neal glanced out the window. "Might be."

"'Ow's 'at?"

"I need a girl."

Colin laughed. "Not Alice. I'll set you up with someone else."

"I need a girl for a job."

Colin took a long draw on his pint before he said, "My da was on the dole 'is 'ole fookin' life. He was always tellin' me, 'Son, ge' a union job. Ge' a union job an' you can fook off your 'ole life.' That was my da's great ambition.

"Is this a union job, Neal?"

"No."

"We're interested."

"It's a one-shot deal, Colin. Lots of money but very tricky. No mistakes. My ass is on the line."

"How much money?"

"Enough you won't have to send Alice out on any more dates."

Either a trace of shame passed across Colin's face or he was even a better actor than Neal thought.

"I love 'er, Neal."

"Right."

"What's the job?"

Neal shook his head. "I'll tell you tomorrow. The Serpentine. One o'clock."

Because you can't make it too simple, Neal thought. And you have to get him into a pattern of following instructions. Turn the relationship around. Otherwise, the whole thing will screw up.

"Why all the bother?" Colin asked.

"Yes or no?"

"Yes, rugger."

THE TAIL HAD PICKED NEAL UP in the square and followed him to the pub. He waited across the street and then stayed with him back to the hotel. He stayed a long way back and was real careful. The kid was supposed to be a pro.

LEVINE ANSWERED THE PHONE.

"I'm calling in," Neal said.

"Good boy."

"Take your fucking tail off me."

"What?"

"Next time, send someone knows what he's doing."

"Hey, Neal—"

"Take him off." Neal hung up.

Levine looked at Graham and Lombardi. "That Neal is some piece of work. Little shit thinks I put a tail on him. Asshole."

Graham's rubber hand ground into his real one. He had trained Neal better than to see tails that weren't there.

"Back off."

"The kid's on to something, I can smell it."

The phone connection from London was bad, so he had to repeat himself. "He *made* you. Back off."

"He didn't make me."

"Who's paying you? Off!"

"You got it."

The guy hung up the phone. He was pissed off. The kid was a pro. A real cute one.

Two scotches and a hot bath didn't settle Neal down much. That fucking Levine, he thought. That fucking Levine is going to blow this whole thing. If I as much as smell that guy again . . .

22

TUESDAY MORNING NEAL DECIDED to have a whopping big breakfast. He picked a table in the dining room that gave him an easy view of the door and dug into his *Times,* along with two fried eggs, hot cereal, toast, bacon, sausage, and a pot of coffee. He took his sweet time about it, but nobody joined him.

Then he went for a walk. The day was a scorcher, a real bitch, but if they wanted to play games, he'd play games. Nobody picked him up at the hotel door, certainly not the guy from last night, but it would be just like Friends to show him one tail so they could pin a different one on him. And he just wasn't ready for company on this thing—not yet.

He took a right down Piccadilly and set a torrid pace to Green Park tube station. He bought a 20p ticket from the machine and headed down the stairs, changed his mind, and walked back out on the street. He strolled down Queen's Lane, nice and slow, stopped at a cart and bought an ice cream, thought about Allie, and turned around and went back to the tube station. But now he picked up the pace, fast and hard, so if anyone was following him, it would cost them a hell of a sweat. He took the train to Leicester Square, rode the escalator to street level, rode the escalator back down to the trains, and took a Northern Line train to Tottenham Court Road, where he got off the train, switched to the Central Line, and continued on to Bond Street, where he switched to the Jubilee Line and rode it back to Green Park.

By this time, he was convinced that Levine had called his boy off, and he was soaked with sweat and covered with grime, but he felt good, as if he was working again, as if he was in first-class gumshoe shape. He was psyching himself up; talking himself into it; going undercover, deep undercover.

He could see the boat-hire dock on the Serpentine from the deck of the restaurant. He sipped an iced coffee and waited. He had a good hour before Colin was supposed to show up. Time enough to check out the terrain, time enough to be ready if anyone was setting him up. Neal Carey wasn't taking any chances.

"I can't swim, rugger," Colin warned as he gently lowered himself into the little squat paddleboat.

"I'll save you," Neal answered. He watched Allie, Crisp, and Vanessa getting into another boat. Neal was having a good time, and taking a little spin around the man-made lake in the center of Hyde Park wasn't a bad way to kill a sweaty afternoon. And he enjoyed Colin's discomfiture.

They paddled out toward the middle of the Serpentine and then just let the boat drift. Neal placed his jacket on the bottom of the boat and lay down on top of it. It felt gloriously cool down there. He left Colin sitting up in the heat. In the distance, he could hear Crisp and Vanessa singing at the top of their lungs—some song he didn't recognize but guessed was a butchery of Gilbert and Sullivan.

"So what is it, rugger?"

Careful, Neal lad, he thought to himself. This is it.

"My client is over here buying a book."

"I hope you're 'avin' me on."

"The book is worth twenty thousand pounds."

That got your attention, didn't it, Colin?

"What book is worth twenty thousand quid?" Colin asked suspiciously.

"The *Pickle*."

He went through the whole thing. About Smollett, the first and second editions, Lady Vane, the trip to Italy, the missing volumes.

When he had finished, Colin said, "So?"

"So our client, the guy I'm doing security for, just bought it for ten thousand pounds."

"Ten in't twenty, lad."

"And I know someone who'll buy it for twenty, Colin baby."

And I have you hooked, Neal thought. Colin was only a silhouette at the moment, but the silhouette was leaning way forward, listening hard.

"You can get 'old of this book?"

"With your help."

"I'm all ears."

"Jesus Christ!"

The boat rocked suddenly. Neal saw a head bobbing in the water. Then the head came over the side of the boat.

"Alice, for bleeding Jesus's sake . . ."

"I felt like a swim."

She hauled herself into their boat. "I was lonely," she said. "I missed you. Besides, look what those assholes are doing over there."

Those assholes Crisp and Vanessa were ramming their paddleboat into any other boat they could catch. They were at this moment in hot pursuit of a pair of Japanese tourists. Security guards at the dock were climbing into a rowboat.

"Jump back in, love. Me and Neal are 'aving a business discussion."

"Let her stay. It's about her."

"What about me?"

"I want you to ball a guy."

"How much?"

"Five thousand pounds."

"What, is he really gross or something?"

THEY BARELY OUTPADDLED THE WATER COPS, who had picked Crisp and Vanessa up and wanted the whole gang. The Japanese couple had abandoned ship, however, necessitating a rather complicated bilingual rescue effort, which gave Neal and his crew time to paddle to shore, dump the boat in some bushes, and run out to Rotten Row. They hailed a cab at Alexandra Gate.

"Westminster Bridge," Neal told the cabbie.

"I'm not balling anybody on Westminster Bridge," said Allie.

"Ten thousand," Colin said.

"Five, and there's more to it."

"I'm not balling anybody on Westminster Bridge."

"Ten or forget it."

"Forget what?"

"Where on Westminster Bridge?" the driver asked.

"No place," said Allie.

"Just on the Embankment is fine."

Neal paid the cabbie and started across the pedestrian walkway on the bridge. The view up and down the Thames was one of his favorites. It might be the best spot to see London, he thought, and he stopped about halfway across to take it in. Off to his right was a postcard view of the tower of Big Ben and the Houses of Parliament. To his right stretched Victoria Embankment. Right in front of him was Colin.

"Seven, then."

Neal turned his back and leaned over the railing on the downriver side. "Thursday night, Goldman's wife is going to a concert at Albert Hall. Goldman doesn't want to go, says he hates that stuff and he's going to the latest James Bond flick at the Odeon. But what he really wants is to get laid. I mean *laid*. He wants me to set him up. So I told him okay, I've worked it out. He's going to go to my room to do it, in case the old lady gets bored, comes back early."

"What—"

"Shut up and listen. He keeps the books in a locked briefcase in his room. While he's making happy in my room, I'm going to be in his . . . guarding the briefcase."

"They're goin' to figure out it was you."

"No shit. The agency will send people. In fact, I know just the guy they'll send. Guy named Levine. Very big, very tough. I'm going to need to disappear for a while. Can you handle that?"

"Sure."

"If things get rough?"

"I'll get rougher."

Neal leaned farther over the railing, pretending to think it over. Let Colin see thousands of quid slipping away. "I don't know, Colin. I'm taking a big risk here . . ."

"Take it."

Neal turned around and rested his back against the railing. He took his time checking out the boats and barges in the river below him. He studied Waterloo Bridge as if he was thinking of buying it. He looked from Colin to Allie to Colin to Allie and back again. Allie could not care less.

Colin would sell Alice to the gypsies for a shot at five thousand pounds. Neal knew a few things about scams. One thing was that you never talk anybody into a scam; you let them talk you into it. He ran his reluctant-virgin act for just a few more seconds.

"All right," he said. "But it's going to take some preparation."

"One more time," Neal said.

A collective sigh filled Colin's flat. They'd already been at it for three hours and gone through it several dozen times, and fucking Neal had banned all alcohol, hash, pills, and smack from the planning session.

"Come on," he repeated.

Crisp recited, "Colin and me wait outside the 'otel—"

"And—"

"An' I try to dress like a human being. Neal points out missus goin' as she comes ou' the door. Colin and me follow 'er an' stick to 'er like glue."

"Good. Why?"

"Ya didn't ask *why* before," Crisp whined.

"Tell me why, you can have a pint."

Four people instantly volunteered the answer. Neal hushed them and looked at Crisp. "Yes?"

"Because, if the missus gets bored a' the concert—which personally I can't imagine—she might decide to come 'ome an' that would fuck up the 'ole thing."

"Correct." Neal heard echoes of Joe Graham telling him to always fill his lies with lots of details. You have to keep Crisp and Colin out of the way for a while, so give them a mission and make them concentrate on it.

Neal took a bottle from his bag and dangled it in front of Crisp. "Then what would you do?"

"Get to a phone box and ring you."

"Where?"

"Goldman's room."

"When?"

Crisp grinned proudly. "Right away."

Neal tossed him the bottle and looked at Colin.

"I stay with the missus and find a way to stall 'er."

"But . . ."

"I don't 'urt 'er."

Neal raised his eyebrows.

"At all."

Neal looked at Allie, who was making a very successful effort to look indifferent. Colin snatched the book out of her hand, opened the window, and threw the book into the street. Allie rolled her eyes.

"I get all dressed up," she said, staring pointedly at Neal, "*like a little lady* . . . and I wait in the bar."

"Where . . ."

"Where I have one drink, that's all, and I wait for Neal to come get me. Neal introduces me to Mr. Wonderful and leaves. I ball his brains out and I take my time about it. I make it last. Then I take my money and come straight back here."

"What else—"

"I take it easy on the smack."

"How easy?"

"One pop."

He offered her a beer. She offered him her middle finger.

"Colin?" he asked.

"We wait for an hour outside Albert 'all. If she doesn't come out, we go to the tube station at Covent Garden. We watch for you. If you have your jacket off, then it's fucked and we make an 'asty exit. Jacket on, we follow you into the street. We get into the cab behind you. Follow you to the buyer's 'ouse. Wait outside. You come out—an' you better come out—with two bags. One wi' our money, one wi' yours. You give us ours and get back in your cab. We sit in the cab for five minutes so we don't know where you're takin' your nicker, you mistrustful bastard. You meet us 'ere, later. We hide you till it's safe."

"Vanessa."

"I wait here by the phone to take messages. Sexist and boring."

"Questions?"

There weren't any. They'd been over it so many times the past two nights that they didn't want to take a chance that he'd make them do it again.

"All right." Neal stood up and stretched. The rest of them hustled for their drug of choice. Colin opened two pints and handed Neal one of them. Vanessa and Crisp lit a bowl of hash and flipped on the telly. Allie slipped into the bathroom.

"She's a junkie," Neal said.

"She's not."

"How many times a day now?"

"Two or three. Just little pops, rugger."

"Not in her arms, I hope. Goldman sees needle tracks, might turn him off."

"This little piggie went to market, this little piggie stayed 'ome. This little piggie went wee-wee-wee . . ."

"Doesn't it bother you? You love her, right?"

"She'll get off it."

"Yeah."

Neal stepped out on the balcony. Colin followed him.

"Five now," he said. "A thousand a month for two months, assuming I'm still in one piece."

"Done."

Oh, Colin, Neal thought. You agreed to that one awfully fast. What are you up to?

"I'll take Alice shopping tomorrow," Neal said. "Get her something killer."

"You do that, Neal lad."

Yeah, Neal, Colin thought, you go shopping. I'll go shopping.

23

COLIN HATED TEA. Hated the smell, the taste, even the feel of it as it slithered down his throat. He had sworn when he split the home scene that he'd never choke down another cup of the omnipresent shit the rest of his natural life.

Nevertheless, he sipped it graciously as he sat in a booth in the back room of the Hunan Garden across the table from a smiling Dickie Huan.

Dickie Huan was a middle-aged Chinese who had several restaurants, an unshakable faith in free enterprise, and a great tailor. On this particular afternoon, he sported a dark gray three-piece pinstripe, a silk salmon shirt, and a blood-red tie. Aware of Dickie's sartorial sensibilities, Colin had done his best to dress for the meeting. He was aware that his all-white suit looked a bit gamy compared to Dickie's conservatism, but it was the best he could do for the occasion.

"How is tea?"

"Super."

Dickie Huan also hated tea, but believed in tradition. He

smiled gently over his raised cup. "What brings me the pleasure of your visit?"

Colin swallowed hard. This bit needed great balls. "I'm looking to expand my market."

Dickie Huan said nothing. This was obvious. Everybody was looking to expand his market.

Colin continued: "I want to enlarge the scope of my operation."

Again, Dickie didn't respond—just for fun.

Colin spit it out. "I want to buy heroin from you."

"Everyone does."

Colin tugged at his collar. The tie felt like a noose around his neck. "I understand you're expecting a shipment."

Dickie raised an eyebrow and smiled, although he was very pissed off that this round-eye freak with pins through his ear knew this much about his business. "So?"

"I want to buy a piece of it."

"Where will you get this kind of money, Colin?"

"I'll 'ave it. Saturday." Give myself a day to take care of Neal, he thought.

"Saturday is not today."

What are you, a fortune cookie? Colin thought. But he said, "I'll buy up to twenty thousand pounds' worth."

Dickie took a long time to answer. He wanted to phrase the insult just right. "I usually don't sell such small allotments."

"Then you must have a small amount to spare."

Not bad, Dickie thought. Not bad at all. "Sorry, Colin. I have promised another party every little bit."

Colin took a big chance. He thought for a moment about his fingers becoming Moo Goo Gai Colin, and then said, "I can put you into markets that John Chen can't touch."

Dickie's burst of Cantonese obscenities brought three waiters trotting to the table. One carried a double Beefeater with a twist. The other two hastily cleared the teacups as their boss regained his composure. "How you know so much?" Dickie asked as he knocked back his drink.

Colin felt a sweet surge of confidence. "I keep me ear to the ground. Now, Dickie, this bit is just the first. I can put you in markets all over the city. Places Chinese can't go." Dickie Huan needed no reminder of the unsubtle racism of Britain's punks. He colored slightly at the insult but decided to ignore it for the time being. After all, he wouldn't mind expanding his own markets.

"Why you come to me, Colin?"

Colin smiled his most engaging smile and told the truth. "You're the only one who might give me credit, Dickie."

So the punk comes to the chink, Dickie thought. Outsider to outsider. He liked the symmetry of it.

"Come on, Dickie. I've never let you down on the hash deals, have I?"

"That is child's play, Colin. Heroin is real business."

"Then think about real business. Think about where I'll be selling your heroin. Twenty thousand is just the start."

Dickie Huan thought about it. He had indeed told John Chen he could have the whole shipment. But he could give Chen twenty thousand back, tell him that the shipment was smaller than he'd thought. A chance to break into the round-eye neighborhoods didn't come every day.

"Come back into the kitchen, Colin," Dickie said. He saw Colin turn pale. "You see too many films. Come on."

Colin followed him back into a little steamy kitchen, where a half dozen sweating cooks were getting ready for the dinner crowd. Dickie leaned against a big, squat wooden chopping block. "Colin, you know if I save a piece for you, I cannot offer it back to the other party."

"You'll never miss him."

Dickie nodded and said something in Cantonese to one of the cooks. The cook handed him a meat cleaver and stepped aside as Dickie grabbed a large piece of pork and slapped it onto the chopping block. Dickie was the son of a Nathan Road butcher and knew what he was doing. With rapid strokes, he chopped the piece of meat into slices and then whirled the cleaver again and chopped the slices into little squares. The whole demonstration took ten seconds, then he swept the cubes of meat into a pan. He hadn't as much as touched the sleeves of his three-hundred-pound suit. He looked up at Colin and smiled. "Twenty thousand pounds. Saturday night. Don't disappoint me, Colin."

Colin left the restaurant whistling. Meeting Neal had been luck, he knew, but a lot of blokes would have settled for the twenty thousand. Colin had the balls to go for the big time.

ALLIE PIROUETTED PRETTILY. The changing-room attendant beamed at her and then at Neal. They were such a cute couple.

"Do you approve?" Allie asked him.

"I approve."

She tilted her head in a parody of fashion-magazine models. She looked drop-dead gorgeous. The new dress was a simple black sheath, off the shoulders and cut just low enough to hint at the pleasures of intimacy. A gold necklace highlighted the dress, her hair, and her eyes. The makeup was subtle.

"Will there be anything else?"

Neal looked to Allie.

"It's your movie," she said.

"That will be all, thanks."

"Come on then, dearie, we'll get it all wrapped up."

As soon as the saleslady turned around, Allie stuck her

fingers in her mouth, pulled her lips apart, and stuck her tongue out at Neal. Then she went to change.

Out on Oxford Street, he asked her to lunch.

"I didn't know crooks went to lunch," she said.

"Don't do me any favors."

"I'm hungry. Where do you want to go?"

"New York."

"For a burger, right? I know what you mean."

"They have good burgers in Stockton?"

"They have McDonald's."

They found a funky little French place that didn't care he wasn't wearing a tie or she was wearing jeans.

She knew her way around the menu, he noticed with amusement. Stockton is famous for its continental cuisine. She ordered the vichyssoise, a fillet, tarragon chicken, and apricot mousse. She also suggested the wines. He had what she had.

Maybe there was still time to do this the easy way, he thought.

"Ever think about going home?"

"What for?" she said through a mouthful of potato soup.

"Burgers."

She shook her head.

"Family?"

"That's what I ran away from."

"Maybe it would be different."

"It wouldn't be." She took a sip of the white wine and sat back in her chair. "Anyway, what about Colin?"

"I dunno. What about Colin?"

She gave him a cold smile, a practiced, ambiguous gesture meant to indicate simultaneous interest and indifference. A poker player calling but not raising the pot.

"Are you coming on to me?" she asked.

"No."

"Good."

She went back to her soup.

"How come you don't like me ?" he asked. "What did I do?"

"I like you. Let's just say I haven't had a real good experience with men, okay? Nothing personal."

"Okay."

"Okay."

During the chicken, she said, "I'm in love with him."

"With him or with his dope?"

"What's the difference?"

None.

It was a great lunch and the bill said so. He paid it and left a generous tip.

"Thank you for lunch," she said when they got outside.

"What did you say?"

"I said thank you. It was nice of you. Not part of the bargain."

"You're welcome. Thanks for the company. You want to take a walk in the park?"

She looked at him hard and smiled. "You *are* coming on to me."

"I'm just saying you have options."

"Yeah? What kind of options?"

"You can take a walk . . . in the park."

"If I told Colin you came on to me, he'd kill you."

"He'd try. You're a valuable piece of property."

"He loves me."

"Sure, why shouldn't he?"

"It's not just for the money I make."

"Yeah? What's your share of this job? What is he cutting you in for? Five thousand? Three? Two? We're running out of numbers here, Alice."

She blushed. "Colin handles all the money. He takes care of me."

Neal laughed at her. "*He* takes care of *you*?"

"He says I won't have to do that anymore after tonight. He promised . . . no more dates."

"Until he needs money again . . . then he'll turn you back out, and he *will* need money. You'll shoot it all up your arm."

He saw her wince and watched her think.

"*Which* park?"

"There's another option right there."

She signaled a cab. "St. James's Park," she said. "By Horse Guards Road."

He let her lead him to the tea kiosk there, where she bought two huge sweet rolls.

"After that lunch?" he asked.

"Not for us, idiot. Come on." She walked him over to the lake, where the ducks drifted off the shore, waiting for silly people with huge sweet rolls to feed them. She handed Neal one of the rolls and said, quite seriously, "Now, you break it up into little bits and toss it to the ducks. And try to spread the wealth around, so they all get a little."

He watched her feed the ducks. She gave it all her attention, as if she was the only person there and that was all she had to do in the world. Her smile lost its angry edge for the ten minutes or so that the roll lasted.

"You do this a lot?" he asked her.

"No."

She trembled a little. "We better get going," she said.

"Why?"

"Big night tonight."

"Are you cold? It's a hundred and ten out."

"I need to go home."

"Because the smack is there."

"I need to get ready, Neal."

"Just breathe deep."

"Fuck you."

"It'll get worse, Alice."

She sat down on a bench. He sat beside her. "So, tonight's my last date, huh?"

"If you want."

She nodded her head a few times. The color was starting to leave her face. "Yeah, sounds good to me."

"Then it's your last date."

She chortled. "Oh, you'll protect me, right? Get me off the smack? Keep me off the street?"

"That's right."

"Okay, white knight," she said, standing up. "Get me into a cab. I have to get home."

He dropped her at her flat, kept the cab, and went back to the hotel. He didn't feel like watching her shoot up, and he had stuff to do. As the lady said, big night tonight.

24

NEAL SAT IN ONE of the overstuffed wing chairs in the lobby of the hotel. He had chosen a seat where he could see both the elevators and the revolving door that led to the street. He tried hard to look composed and relaxed, but his stomach was jumping and his heart beating about eight trillion times a minute.

Please, Mrs. Goldman, get going. You don't want to be late for the concert. Please come out of the next elevator. She didn't.

He glanced out into the street, where he knew Colin and Crisp were waiting. Patience was not Colin's long suit. Come on, Mrs. Goldman. Another elevator. Two well-dressed American ladies, neither of them Mrs. G. Who's that? Another woman, not Mrs. Goldman.

He wondered about Allie, waiting in the hotel bar. At least he hoped she was waiting in the hotel bar, not shooting up in the ladies' loo, or worse yet, out on the street looking for a connection. Time was not on his side in this thing, so, Mrs. Goldman, any haste would be appreciated. The elevator bell rang again. He had followed her to her room a bare two hours ago and held the surveillance, so he knew she was in there performing the complicated ablutions and ritual that go with a big night out. Let's slip the frock on now, Mrs. G., and haul it down here. She wasn't in the elevator.

COLIN SHIFTED HIS WEIGHT from one foot to the other again and gave Crisp a dirty look. Not that it was Crisp's fault, he knew, but because Crisp was the only one there, and didn't mind, anyway. That was what he was there for.

"Tardy, tardy," Crisp said through a mouthful.

"Something's wrong."

"She's late, that's all. Maybe she's giving the old man a quick one."

Colin shot him an especially filthy look. "That would be just lovely, now, wouldn't it?"

ALLIE WAS TRYING TO HOLD IT TOGETHER. Her hand shook a little as she reached into her bag for a handkerchief. Goddamn Colin, anyway, she thought, and double goddamn that bastard Neal Carey. If they had let her have one little shot, just one little shot, she'd be all right. She'd be perfect. She'd be fan-fucking-tastic. Colin had even subjected her—no doubt at that prick Neal's urging—to a search. The fact that'd turned up a little envelope of powder didn't make it all right. She'd get even with him later.

Now she just wanted to get this over with. Do this john, pick up that triple motherfucker Neal, and get home for the promised fix. She didn't even care that this was her last trick, ever; that Colin had told her this was her farewell performance, her retirement party, her swan song. Fine and dandy, Collie baby, but I need a little taste. And if Neal doesn't hurry up and get in here, I'm going to go out and find one. One thing she'd learned in her short career as a lady of the evening: Every place has a back door.

MRS. GOLDMAN LOOKED GOOD. Almost worth the wait, Neal thought as he watched her stride through the lobby and out the revolving door. He gave her a few paces and then picked her up. She asked the doorman to get her a cab, and as he stood blowing his whistle, Colin and Crisp walked to the corner, where they had a cab waiting. Neal watched Mrs. G. climb into her taxi, and watched the car carrying Colin pull into traffic behind her. Colin looked out the window, saw Neal, and gave him a quick thumbs-up sign. Let's hope so, Colin, let's hope so.

HE FOUND ALLIE IN THE BAR working on her third gin. He walked up in back of her and leaned over her shoulder. She jumped when he whispered, "Give it five minutes, then come up."

She whipped her head around and glared at him. "Where the hell have you been?"

"Easy. Steady. You look great."

"Fuck you."

"Five minutes."

NEAL WENT UP TO HIS ROOM and fixed a tall gin and tonic and a scotch. He dropped four muscle relaxers into the G&T, sat down on the bed, and waited. A few minutes later, a soft knock came on the door.

"Come in. It's not locked."

She made an entrance. Slinky black dress, bright smile, her long strand of pearls held in one hand. Sexy, young, willing. It was a great act.

Her smile dropped as she saw Neal and her eyebrows arched in question.

"He just called. He's on his way. Nervous, I guess. Sit down. I made you a drink. Your favorite."

She plopped down on the bed. "Just how nervous is he?" she asked, raising the ugly specter of potential impotence.

"Pretty nervous."

"Great."

"Cheers."

She took a gulp of the drink and then they sat there looking at each other. A good two minutes passed while she sipped on her gin before she said, "Is this supposed to be a long concert?"

"Aren't they all?"

Another couple of minutes, and then: "Look, why don't I just go to his room, whip my clothes off, and—"

"That would kind of defeat the purpose."

"Oh, yeah."

Three minutes passed before she spoke again. "Maybe he's killed himself, couldn't stand the precoital guilt." Two minutes later, she passed out cold.

Neal picked up the phone, rang the front desk, and asked for Hatcher. Five minutes later, the detective called him back.

"I have a problem," Neal said.

"Why does this fail to surprise me? I'll be up." Hatcher suppressed a sneer with some effort when he saw the young lady passed out on Neal's bed. "A bit too much of the old persuasion, son?"

"She arrived this way."

Hatcher sniffed the near-empty glass of gin. "And she brought this with her, I suppose."

Neal shrugged. "I could never deny a lady a drink."

"I rather think you can never deny a lady at all. In any case, what is the problem?"

234 | DON WINSLOW

"I have to get her out of here."

"That is your problem. What is mine?"

"Hatcher, do you really want me to drag her through the lobby with all those people down there? How will it look?"

"With all respect to your privacy, why can't the young lady sleep it off right here?"

Neal did his best to work up a decent blush. What with the nerves and the fear and all, it wasn't tough. "Because the young lady is quite young. Hacker, I just want to take her home. Help me get her out quietly and into a cab, please?"

"This is a bit much."

"Okay. You're right. I'll just drag her through the lobby." He started to lift Allie off the bed.

"Is this the niece?" Hatcher asked.

Neal nodded.

"I don't believe you actually found her. *And* managed to bag her."

I'm not sure I believe it, either, Neal thought. "She's not in the bag yet."

"I'll ring a cab. We'll use the service entrance."

"HE'S GOT HER."

The overseas connection wasn't the greatest. The phone crackled and popped like a Rice Krispies commercial.

"Who's got her?"

"Carey's got the kid. She went up to his room with him, then they left out the back."

"Shit. You know where they went?"

The guy was enjoying this. "You said not to follow him."

There was a long silence. "*I* know where he went."

"What now, boss?"

"Can you do it?"

"I don't do that kind of work. But I know who will. Local talent named Colin. He's her pimp, and you know pimps."

A lot of snaps, crackles, and pops went by before he got his answer. "Okay. Make it happen. Here's the address. Phone number if you want it."

"Might come in handy."

"Hey, just get it done."

COLIN WAS IN A MAJOR-LEAGUE SWEAT. He'd been standing in the fooking Covent Garden tube station for close to an hour. No Neal. He grabbed Crisp by the shirt when he came back from the phone.

"Alice isn't back and no word from Neal. We've been fucked, Colin."

"Not yet, we haven't."

They hopped the train and rode it to Piccadilly. He breezed past the young doorman and got into the lift. Outside Neal's room, he felt for the knife in his jacket pocket and got ready to use it. He motioned Crisp to the other side of the door and then rang the bell. And waited. Waited a good five minutes before stationing Crisp at the lift and going to work on the door lock.

Inside the room, everything was gone: luggage, clothes, Neal, Alice, and the books.

Two minutes later, he was at the registration desk. "Mr. Carey's room, please."

"Mr. Carey has checked out, sir."

Triple poxy whoredog asswipe. "Did he leave a forwardin' address?"

"Let me see, sir."

Hurry, mate. Hurry, hurry, hurry, hurry.

"No, sir, sorry."

Colin slammed his fist on the counter. Then he headed for the door.

The doorman knew his lines. "Did you lose something, mate?"

"Did you find somethin'?"

Moments later, Colin and Crisp were in a taxi. Colin was thinking about bloody murder.

The doorman found the gentleman in the bar, just where he said he would be. "I did what you said."

The gentleman slipped him a tenner. "Good job."

The gentleman went to a phone and waited for the overseas connection to go through. "It's over."

"Hey, you sure?"

"He's a duster."

"What about her?"

"You kidding? A junkie and a pimp? It's the perfect relationship. Forget about her."

"Okay, get lost. Very lost."

ALLIE STARTED TO COME TO as Neal plopped her on Simon's bed. He was out of breath from lugging her dead weight up the stairs and maneuvering her into the bedroom. He was tying her wrists to the torn sheets when she woke up enough to speak.

"Are you kinky or something?" she asked, looking at the restraints but not necessarily objecting.

"I haven't had the chance to find out." He tightened the bonds just enough to hold her. It seemed to wake her up a little.

"Neal, what's going on?"

"Nothing. I want you to get some rest."

"Why are you tying me up?"

Neal sat down on the bed. He took her chin in his hand and lifted her face so that they were looking at each other.

"Alice, listen. No more smack. That's over with." He saw a fine edge of panic creep into her eyes. "I'm going to give you something to cool you out. It'll be okay, but no more heroin for you." She was still too woozy to really take in what he was saying, and he figured that was probably a blessing for them both. He broke a Valium in half and gave it to her with a swallow of Coke. The sugar would help. She fought him a little at first, but her body wanted sleep and her mind wanted refuge, so after a few seconds she took the pill. Neal sat with her for the few minutes it took her to go to sleep. Then he shut the door, went into the kitchen, and fixed himself a cup of coffee.

Seventy-two hours. He needed seventy-two hours and that should get them through the worst of it. She wasn't too badly hooked and there was no question of her dying of withdrawal. He knew he could nurse her through it, knew he could get her off smack and get hooked on Neal, because that's what it took. Three days of this and she'd belong to him as if he bought her at an auction. More than that, because she'd want it, too. That's the way junkies are, and it takes a long time before they get to a place where they can stand up by themselves. So he'd wean her off the dope, and tell her he loved her, that he'd be her new man and take care of her, that they'd take the money and split and live happily ever after. Then he would whip her on an airplane and take her back and hand her over and that would be that. And it's a shitty world, but there would be plenty of time to reflect on what a dark hole the universe is when this particularly shitty job was over. And he wasn't letting her out of his sight, because she wasn't going to be any Halperin kid. All he needed was seventy-two hours . . . seventy-two mean, sweaty hours— especially for Allie.

The ringing of the phone cut right through him. Made his heart jump a little before he reasoned that it was probably a friend of Simon's who didn't know his schedule. He went into the sitting room and lifted the receiver. "Hello."

"Hello, rugger."

Neal edged to the window and inched the curtain aside. Colin probably didn't have a gun, much less a rifle, but there was no sense taking chances.

Colin waved to him from the phone box—a cheery little wave accompanied by a wide grin. Vanessa was with him. He couldn't see Crisp, which meant that he was out back—along with God knows how many others. Neal closed the curtain and stepped back into the middle of the room.

"Hello, Colin."

"You're dead. She with you?"

"No."

"Lying bastard. She's dead, too."

"Come on up. We'll talk."

"I'll be up, all right, rugger. Not to worry. When I'm ready."

He rang off. Neal's mind raced. Come on, think. Cut through the fear and think. You weren't followed; you're sure of that. Sure or just arrogant? No, sure. Okay, who knew about this place? Simon. He's out. Kitteredge, Levine, and Graham. Couldn't be Kitteredge; makes no sense. Levine and Graham. Say it ain't so, Joe. And how would they hook up with Colin? Unless they knew about him all along. Unless I was sent to make Liz Chase happy, while the Senator and everyone else wanted Allie to stay lost. So when I find her . . . I'm written off. I should have seen it. No files on the kid. Fed the Mackensen bullshit story like it's gospel. No backup. No partner. Check in every day, let us know how you're doing . . . Well, I'm doing pretty shitty right now, Ed.

It's 11:15, give or take. Colin is waiting for the small hours, when screams can be written off as nightmares. When the streets are quiet. No passersby. Then he's got you.

The fear hit him again. The slash of the knife across his face. There was no way he could take Colin, no way.

Knock it off, Neal. Think. Run it through. You could call the cops. And tell them what? That you've kidnapped a girl? Fed her drugs? She's tied up in the other room? Not a good choice. Okay, deal. You have the books. Trade him the books for Allie. Why should he? He can have it all. But he needs the name of the buyer for it to do him any good. Bargain there. No, he can get that out of you. You'll talk. Colin holds a knife to Allie's face. Shit, babe, be honest. If he holds a knife to your face, you'll tell him.

And where would you go? Even if you got out of here, where would you go? You could make a break for it. Throw her over your shoulder and run for the tube. It's closed, moron, and you'd never make it five steps. A cab? Same. That leaves the car. Down the back stairs and into the garage. Assuming you make it, where could you take her? Fuck her. Maybe you can handle Crisp on the back stairs and make it to the car, but not with her. Dump her, babe.

Right, he thought. Then you'll have another face to add to the Halperin collection. So work backward. Go from the solution to the method. Where would you like to be? What's the ideal? Safe, quiet, isolated. A place the office doesn't know about. Think, think, think . . . a place you can hear your own heartbeat. How about a cottage in the Yorkshire moors?

Where did Simon say it was? Get to work, Neal.

He started to search the apartment.

NEAL FOUND WHAT HE WAS LOOKING FOR almost immediately. Maybe his luck was changing. It was a road map of Britain, with the route to Simon's Yorkshire cottage marked in bright orange, and notes on how to proceed on the unmarked roads. Neal went to the phone and dialed. It rang a long time.

"Dad?"

"Where are you?"

"Just listen, because I don't have much time. There's some stuff you have to know . . . ."

NEAL SAT DOWN ON THE EDGE OF THE BED. Allie was still sound asleep. Her face and hair were damp with sweat. He stroked her cheek with the back of his hand.

"I'm sorry, kid. I screwed it up. I tried to help you out and ended up getting you in more trouble. I'm really sorry."

He figured he still had an hour or so before show time. He didn't feel like sitting around letting the fear eat him out. He thought some more about Joe Graham and then did a very Joe Graham thing.

He cleaned. The place was a mess anyway, and that was hardly the way to repay Simon's hospitality. He found a broom and a mop, some powdered cleanser and floor wax, and set to work. He vacuumed and dusted, polished furniture and scrubbed and waxed the kitchen floor until the sucker gleamed like ice.

When he was done, he felt much better. Then he sat down with a book to wait it out.

The footsteps woke him. He could hear Colin trying to sneak up the front stairs. He checked his watch and was surprised that it was quarter to four.

The steps paused on the landing. He heard fumbling. He saw the thin piece of metal slip the lock. The door opened just a crack. Apparently, Colin didn't fancy getting whacked in the face with something hard and heavy. Too bad. Neal felt the sickening bile of fear rise. He fought to hold it down as Colin's foot pushed open the door. Colin stood in the doorway, both hands tucked inside his leather jacket. Which hand has the knife? Neal wondered. He remembered playing that game with the old Italian men in the neighborhood. Which hand has the candy? He'd never been very good at it then, either.

Colin said, "You've been trying to ring but the line was engaged, right?"

What if I give up, Colin? What if I throw up my hands and say you can take the book, take Allie? Instead, he said, "You should have come with an army, Colin."

Colin stepped in and locked the door shut behind him. "For you, rugger? Mind, I've seen you fight."

"You want a cup of tea? A beer?"

"We can start with a book."

"Start and finish."

Colin shook his head.

"Where are we, Neal? Whose place is this?"

Neal saw Colin's left wrist tighten. So it'll come from that side if it comes. When it comes.

"A friend's."

"Are you ripping him off, too?"

As a matter of fact . . .

"I'll give you the book. You leave Alice."

"True love, is it? The book'll do me no good without the name of the buyer."

"Okay, I'll toss that in, too."

Colin took a tentative step toward him. Neal backed away.

Colin said, "You're not in much of a position to toss anything, are you, Neal lad? I think I'll take the book *and* the girl. *And* you'll give me the name." The knife flashed out of his left pocket. He held it, blade turned flat, level with Neal's eyes, no more than a foot away.

The point sparkled and danced in front of Neal's eyes. He felt the thud in his stomach and the tightness of breath in his chest. He'd seen people get cut.

He let the terror come up, thought about his face sliced open, the sickening flap of flesh dangling, the scar he would wear for life . . . . Tears filled his eyes.

"She's dead, Colin. She must have OD'd."

Colin's hand dropped, not much, but just enough—enough for Neal to turn and run. He ran through the sitting room and flung himself through the sharp left into the kitchen. He had just enough lead to jump onto the counter.

Colin was half a second behind Neal. When he hit the waxed kitchen floor at full speed, his slick leather loafers went out from under him. He landed hard on his back, but not before his head took a nice bounce off the squeaky-clean linoleum. Neal raised the mop high above his head and jammed the butt end down into Colin's crotch as if he was planting the flag on Mount Everest. This gave Colin a new relationship with the concept of pain, and he rolled on the floor in a fetal position, groaning.

Neal picked the knife up from the floor and put it into his pocket. Then he stepped over to the refrigerator and pulled out the pan he had placed in the freezer. It was now packed with solid ice. "Crisp," he yelled in his best imitation of Colin, "get your arse in here!"

Crisp crashed through the flimsy back door and saw Colin rolling on the floor. He never saw Neal swing the pan of ice like Jimmy Connors smashing a high backhand. The heavy pan hit him square on the bridge of the nose, crushing bone and cartilage. Crisp was out before he hit the floor, which was probably a blessing, as he fell right on his shattered nose.

"You whore's bastard," hissed Colin with unintended

accuracy. He tried to struggle to his feet, but nauseating waves of pain held him to the floor.

Neal went into the bedroom, lifted Allie in a fireman's carry, and hefted her down the back stairs. He was breathing hard and heavy from excitement, fear, and the exertion of beating up Colin and Crisp, so it took him a little longer than he wanted to get down to the garage. He didn't have a great deal of time before Colin would suck it up enough to come after him. Knife or no knife, Colin would wipe him out in a fair fight, so Neal was hurrying to make sure there wouldn't be one. He leaned Allie against the garage wall while he fumbled in his pants pocket for the key. He noticed his hands were shaking. Just to make things better, Allie was starting to wake up.

He got the door open, pulled her over to the dreaded Keble, opened the passenger door, and worked her into the seat. This maneuver felt as if it took about an hour and a half, and he expected Colin to come through the garage door any moment. He finally got her and himself settled in the driver's seat.

Allie came to life. "Wazzup?" she asked sleepily.

"We're going for a ride."

"Thas nice," she said happily, and fell back to sleep.

Yeah, thas nice, Neal thought, if I can get this thing started and get us out of here. He put the key in the ignition—the trunk key. It didn't fit. Neither did the door key, no matter which way he tried.

COLIN WAS FUMBLING WITH HIS OWN EQUIPMENT, which seemed to be all there, even though that Yank bitch's whelp had tried to geld him. His nether parts ached, though, no mistake, and his head hurt like Sunday morning. He got to his feet and stood over Crisp, who lay as stiff and still as a girl fresh out of the convent.

"C'mon, mate, get up," Colin said, prodding Crisp with his toe. Crisp didn't move.

THE IGNITION KEY FIT as if it had been made for the purpose. Neal turned it, stepped on the gas pedal, and waited for the demonic car to throb with malevolent life. Instead, it whined a dry, rhythmic hack. He tried it again. Same thing. Neal said some words your mother never taught you, and tried again.

CRISP WOULDN'T MOVE. COLIN SHOOK HIM A FEW TIMES.

He came to. "My nose! What happened to me?"

"That beggar Neal smashed it. Let's go get him."

"You go get him" Crisp moaned, sinking back to the floor. "I've had enough of him."

Colin gave him a boot in the groin for good measure and headed down the back stairs. The motion joggled his throbbing balls, and he decided he might take two or three days to kill Neal when he found him. Then he heard the distinctive sound of an engine not starting coming from the garage at the bottom of the stairs. If there isn't a God, he thought, there bloody well certainly is a devil.

THE KEBLE WOULDN'T START, even though Neal was about standing on the gas pedal. All it would do was hack and spit, and Neal, who hated cars anyway, hated this car more than he had ever hated anything.

"PULLONA CHOKE," ALLIE SAID DREAMILY.

"What?"

"Pullona choke. Fucking Gordon-Keble won't start 'less you pullona fucking choke." She leaned over his lap and pulled the choke knob out about halfway. The engine roared to life.

"How did you know that?" he asked, but she was asleep again.

COLIN HEARD THE ENGINE. Too late, Neal bugger, he thought as he tried to turn the knob to the garage door. The fucker was locked from the inside. He raised his leg to kick it in, but the sheer agony that bolted through his right testicle changed his mind. He limped around to the front of the garage, stopping on his way to pick up a convenient two-by-two left over from the construction. He posted himself outside the sliding door. When you come to open this, Neal, arms all nice and raised and all . . .

NEAL PRESSED DOWN on what he figured to be the clutch and eased the car into first gear. Keeping a foot on the brake pedal, he raced the engine a couple of times, pleased with the resounding result. This isn't so bad, he thought. He let off the brake.

COLIN WAITED PATIENTLY FOR THE DOOR TO LIFT. He held the two-by-two up around his shoulders, ready to decapitate Neal. The delicious tingle of impending revenge eased the dull throb from his recent drubbing. C'mon, Neal lad . . . .

FIRST AND THIRD ARE A LONG WAY APART on a baseball diamond. But on a gearbox, they are barely distinguishable, especially to a mechanical moron like Neal Carey. He punched down on the accelerator and let off on the brake. The car flew backward. That's when Neal remembered that he'd forgotten to open the door.

Except that Colin had done it for him. The impatience of rage had gotten the better of him, and, suspecting some trick, he had leaned down to open the door and go in and get that bastard when the little sports car plowed straight into him. Colin took a short ride on the hood before rolling off to the right, avoiding the crush of wheels by inches.

Neal had swerved to avoid him, hit the brakes, and, in doing so, killed the engine. "Fuck!" he yelled, turning the ignition key. He could see Colin in the rearview mirror. Colin was on all fours in the street, shaking his head as if to clear it. The Keble coughed again.

Allie leaned against the door, lost in a happy dream, just aware enough of her surroundings to mumble, "Choke, you gotta pullona—"

"Choke, I know, I know," Neal snapped, a little too busy to reflect on the fact that a girl whose bloodstream contained enough drugs to sedate a small town could drive better than he could. He pulled the fucking choke, the car started, and Neal once again put it into first.

COLIN STUMBLED TO HIS FEET and realized he'd been run over by a car. He saw his assailant in front of him, dead in the water. He picked up his stick and was about to attack when the car started to back up, slowly at first, and then faster—straight at him.

NEAL WASN'T SUCH A TERRIFIC DRIVER going forward. Backward, he was a complete disaster. He tried to stop when he saw Colin, he really did. But when you step on the foot feed instead of the brake, you go faster.

COLIN DID WHAT ANY SMART, tough cookie would do: He ran. And not in a straight line, either. He zigged, he zagged, he ran as fast as a man who's been smashed to the floor, bashed in the balls, and crashed with a car could run. But the little auto kept coming after him as if he had a magnet strapped to his arse.

Neal was trying to do just the opposite, but that was the problem. Lacking any facility for thinking in reverse, he made the precise opposite happen of what he intended. Each time he tried to steer away from the madly fleeing Colin, he headed right for him. It was all pretty confusing, especially at that speed.

COLIN'S SCREAM WOKE UP VANESSA, who had been dozing in the phone box. She made a quick assessment of the scene and acted with dispatch.

"Stop!" she yelled as she chased the car down the street. "Stop! You're going to kill him! Stop!"

NEAL STOPPED. HIS SCRAMBLING FEET and hands finally found the right combination, and the high-performance vehicle screeched to a sudden halt, slamming Neal and Allie into the dashboard and then flinging them back into their seats as it lunged forward.

WHICH SURPRISED VANESSA, who never really thought you could get anybody to actually stop just by yelling "Stop." She was quite pleased with herself until she realized the little auto was now heading toward her, and she was about to turn and run when a shout from the window distracted her.

"He broke my nose, Vanessa!" Crisp bellowed as he hung out the window. "He broke my fucking nose!"

THERE WERE TWO THINGS ABOUT VANESSA that became important at this crucial point. The first was that, of all the players in the game, she was the freshest. That is to say, she wasn't

stoned into the Enchanted Forest and she hadn't been wres-
tling with a demonic triumph of automotive engineering.
Nor had she smashed her head on the floor, had rough sex
with a mop handle, or had her face smashed by a pan full of
ice. The second factor was that Vanessa was relatively unattractive. She had never had a horde of suitors fighting over
her, and she was bound and determined to hold on to the one
she had, a man who found her witty, sexy, and desirable. A
man who now stood in the window, bleeding and disfigured,
crying for justice.

So as the car bore down on her, Vanessa stood her ground.
Neal saw her standing in the middle of the street, Katie-Bar-the-
Door. He was on the verge of gaining a semblance of control
over this vehicular virago and even managed to slow down as
he steered around her. Mistake.

YOU'VE HEARD ALL THOSE STORIES about mothers lifting
Mack trucks off their children. Something about a chemical
combination of maternal instincts and adrenaline? Vanessa
had plenty of both going for her as she grabbed the driver's
door handle and jumped onto the narrow running board.
"You hurt my baby!" she screamed as she landed a nifty
right hand through the open window onto Neal's jaw. He
hit the brake, forgetting that damn thing about the clutch,
and the car shuddered to a stop. As Neal struggled to find
the ignition key, Vanessa smacked him again in the side of
the head.

"You hurt my baby!"

Neal tried to push her off with his left hand, but she had
a death grip on the inside of the window. Neal glanced at the
rearview mirror and saw Colin hobbling toward him, a stick in
his hand and blood in his eye.

CRISP FELT ASHAMED AS HE LOOKED out the window. Here was the love of his life and his best friend doing desperate battle in the street. And here he was, two stories above the fray, snug and safe. "I'll save you, Vanessa!" he yelled, and went looking for a way to make that good.

"NESSA, OFFA CAR," ALLIE SAID SWEETLY but firmly from her less than commanding position in Neal's lap. "Jes' goin' for a ride."

Vanessa was trying her best to pull the driver's door open and vent her full fury on her love's attacker, but Neal was at the same time holding the door shut and trying to start the car and was doing a pretty remarkable job of it, considering the bashing he was taking. But it wasn't working. So Neal let go of the gearshift to get leverage, leaned back, and popped Vanessa square in the chops with an overhand right. This girl can really take a punch, he thought. He had to give her that.

COLIN REACHED FOR THE PASSENGER DOOR to get his hands on that bitch Alice before he beat her new boyfriend into bread pudding. He had the door half open . . .

"OKAY, NESSA, HAVE IT YOUR WAY," Allie said, her patience exhausted. She wanted to go for a ride. Squeezing herself onto Neal's lap, she shoved her left foot down on the clutch, yanked the shift into first gear, and stepped down hard on the accelerator. This Keble did just what Daddy's Keble always did. It took off like a rabbit on Dexedrine.

Neal was surprised when Vanessa suddenly dropped from sight as glass shattered all over the roof of the car. He didn't have time to think about it, though. He just had time to grab the wheel as the Keble suddenly surged forward.

WHICH ACTION PRESENTED Colin with a clear choice: let go, or lose his arm. He took the latter course, and only rolled fifteen or sixteen times before coming to rest in the street.

"SORRY, VANESSA! SHOUTED Crisp, whose aim with the gin bottle had been off by *that* much. He threw another one at the fleeing car.

THE KEBLE ZOOMED OFF INTO THE NIGHT with its two fugitives. Neal gripped the wheel and played with the gearshift. Allie slept soundly against the door.

Then the damnedest thing happened. It started to rain.

THE SKY HAD BEEN SAVING UP all summer for this one and now it really let go. It didn't take Neal more than four or five minutes of frantic fumbling to figure out the windshield wipers and another minute or so to roll up the windows, by which time he was soaked down to his shoulders. He pulled the car over to the side of Camden High Street to check the map. The route had seemed simple when he'd memorized it earlier, but everything looked different on the ground, especially when you had a split lip, a blossoming shiner, and couldn't see a thing through sheets of rain in the dark.

He decided to take the Seven Sisters Road to the A406 and the A406 to the M-11, the major thoroughfare north.

He didn't even notice that he didn't have any trouble slipping into first gear and easing out onto the street.

COLIN HISSED WITH PAIN as he straddled his motorbike. Rain? he thought. *Bloody rain?* It hasn't rained in three months and now it has to come down in great awful buckets? There is a God, he thought, and he's a ball-stamper. Well, there was nothing to do but head off after them and see whether his luck was changing. He turned up the throttle.

THE KID AT THE GAS STATION was thrilled to death to see Neal pull up.

"I need gas. Fill it up," Neal said.

The kid spit a mouthful of water out and answered, "If it's gas you want, go to the States. We have petrol here."

"Whatever it is that makes this car run."

"Cars are on a train, mate. Over here we call it an auto."

"You want to stand there getting soaked or you want to hold a comparative linguistics seminar?"

"Money first. Then the petrol for your auto."

Neal handed him a ten-pound note.

"How do I get on the A406?" he asked when the attendant had finished pumping.

"Roundabout straight on. Second right."

"Thanks."

"Don't mention it."

The kid was even more thrilled when some moron on a motorbike roared in.

"Little sports car pass by?" the biker shouted above the din of the rain.

"Didn't pass by. Stopped for petrol."

"Where was he going?"

"I don't know where he was going, but he was using the A406 to get there."

"How—"

"Roundabout straight on. Second right."

"Thanks."

"Don't mention it."

NEAL TOOK IT NICE AND SLOW IN THE RAIN. Allie was peacefully sleeping and he was in no particular hurry—until he saw a single headlight in the rearview mirror, coming on fast.

Neal slowed down. If it was Colin, he might as well find out now instead of letting him follow them and blow another safe house.

He was going about forty when Colin pulled up along the driver's side.

"Pull over!" Colin shouted.

Neal tapped the gas pedal and the Keble shot ahead.

Colin kept up with them.

"Pull over!" he shouted. He was soaked, flushed, and furious. His white suit clung to him.

Neal tapped the accelerator again, forcing Colin to speed up. Neal knew the bike was no match for the Keble.

Trouble was, he was afraid to go too fast in this rain. Colin could probably win a game of chicken. Oh well, he thought, what the hell.

He stepped on the pedal again, getting a good head of steam and bringing Colin speeding up beside him. Then he hit the brakes.

The back wheels skidded and turned out and the car sped sideways for a good hundred feet. Colin sped right past it, twisted the brake handle, and flipped the little bike over the top of himself.

Neal remembered that old driving-school bit about turning in the direction of the skid, but didn't remember what it meant, so he just kept spinning the steering wheel back and forth until the car pointed ahead again and came to a stop. He looked in the mirror and saw Colin disentangling himself from the bike—very slowly. He fought off an insincere urge to go back and see whether he was all right. Then he put his foot on the gas and took the Keble for a ride as fast as he dared.

All this action actually woke Allie up for a second.

"We there yet?" she asked.

"Just looking for a place to park."

COLIN WATCHED THE TAILLIGHTS of the little car disappear over the hill. It had been a very bad night. He had lost the book, the money, the dope, Alice, Neal, his bike, and about a pint of blood. He was well and truly fucked.

NEAL EASED OFF ON THE PEDAL UNTIL the Keble slowed to something less than the speed of sound. Now that he didn't have to shift, he felt okay driving the thing, his heart was settling back into his chest, and he was headed for a place he could actually hear it beat.

| PART THREE |

A PLACE YOU CAN
HEAR YOUR HEARTBEAT

25

Simon's cottage was made of stone.

Neal felt stupid when he thought about the third little pig who was safe when the big bad wolf came huffing and puffing, but figured he was glad to be thinking at all, tired as he was. Allie was asleep as he pulled the car slowly up the dirt trail that led through the moor and up to the cottage. Far below and behind, the chimneys of the small village peeked above the last line of trees. They had driven north out of the rain, and the ground beneath the wheels was hard and firm, so he had no trouble pulling up to the cottage.

Leaving Allie in the Keble, he got out, stretched his sore legs and back, and looked around him. He'd never been anyplace like this. The view commanded miles of the barren moor. The cottage sat on a plateau beneath a sharp, rocky slope. The moor ran fairly level to both his left and right, and in front of him, the hill ran down to a small stream and a copse of trees, and a mile or so beyond that, the village. Faint purple heather, scrub grass, and rock covered the ground. It was windy up here, and the cool breeze that dried the stale sweat on his face felt wonderful.

His eyes ached from fatigue, and as he took a deep breath of the fresh air, he knew he wanted sleep . . . needed sleep.

He looked back to make sure Allie was still asleep, and then walked up to the cottage. It was a two-story affair, gray stone built around thick wooden beams. He found the old skeleton key under a rock, right where Simon had said it would be, and let himself in. The first floor was low-ceilinged, and he stooped even though he really didn't have to. A large fireplace dominated the front room, which had a stone floor, an old wooden table, and two old overstuffed chairs. A small bedroom ran off to the left. It was filled with books, no surprise there, and a small bed covered with old quilts and a thick army blanket. A kitchen of sorts ran off to the back. It had creaky wooden counters and a few shelves and cupboards, and a wood-burning stove. There was a basin but no tap. A narrow wooden door opened onto the slope of the hill and a stone retaining wall. Someone had made a weak attempt at gardening out back, and a sad rose trellis marked the effort. A narrow staircase led from the kitchen up to the second floor, which contained three bedrooms. Each was furnished with quilted beds and cane chairs.

The whole place had that comfortable discomfort of the beloved getaway. Old framed photos of Simon and family and friends decorated the walls and bedside tables. Cheap paperbacks and slightly moldy hardcovers lay scattered about. Neal went back downstairs and out front. He found the generator shack, read the carefully printed directions thumbtacked to the wall, and started it up. He might as well, he thought, have such comforts as electricity. An outhouse stood near the generator shack, and a cottage. He solved the mystery of water when he noticed the well about thirty yards in front of the cottage. He cranked the handle and, sure enough, a bucket of water came up, just like in the old movies when the city slicker goes to the country and learns real values. He took a sip of the water: It was clean and cold and tasted great. He hoped he wouldn't die from it. A true New Yorker, he believed that water should come out of faucets.

Hmm, well water, outhouses, a bathtub set in the open air. He could get used to this, he thought. And the quiet. He noticed it just then. The complete and utter absence of mechanical or human sound. He listened. Way off in the distance, perhaps over the hill, he could hear the faint sounds of what might have been sheep. He could hear the soft gurgling of the brook below him. That was all. That was it. He could hear his heartbeat. This was all new stuff to Neal Carey, who thought he had seen it all.

Remembering why he was up here, he walked back to the car and opened the passenger door. Allie was curled up, her head resting on the top of the seat. She was sticky with dried sweat and her face was puffy and pale. The next few hours would be bad, Neal thought. But he had to get it started. No more candy for baby Allie.

"Hey, wake up," he said, shaking her. She mumbled a few dark threats and cuddled up into a ball.

"Alice, c'mon, up."

"Donwanna."

"I don't give a shit what you wanna," said Neal, who was damned if he was going to carry her anymore. He still hurt from last night.

He pulled her out of the seat and let go. She tumbled out onto the ground.

"Hey!" she said, with more indignation than wit. She sat on the ground looking up at him, and then looking around. It took her only a minute to realize they weren't in downtown London.

"Where the *fuck* are we?"

Which reminded Neal of an old joke about pygmies that he didn't bother relating.

"We're 'on the lam,'" he said. He watched her search her memory. He watched real carefully. How much did Allie remember?

"Where's Colin?"

"I don't know."

She got up from the ground and brushed herself off. "I want to go back to London."

"No."

"Right now."

"Forget it."

She brushed past him and headed for the driver's door.

I didn't want to do this, Neal thought. He grabbed her by the elbow, stuck his foot behind hers, and threw her down. She got over her surprise in about half a second and started to get up, but he lifted her up by the shoulders and tossed her down on her back. She landed hard but got up and headed back toward the car. He stood in her way and she took a swing at him, a clumsy, looping swing that he caught easily, turning her wrist and bending her arm in back of her. He grabbed her hair with his other hand and forced her to her knees. He bent her over until her face grazed the ground.

It shocked him that he wasn't sorry, that this felt good, and he wondered whom he was so goddamned angry at, and he wondered where his mother was and whether she was even alive, and he wondered whether Allie was the only fucked-up person on this barren, beautiful hill, and why he had taken this job in the first place.

He lifted her up and turned her around so that they were face-to-face. It didn't help. He wanted to hit her. Hard. In the face. He wanted to tell himself that he would do it to settle her down, to get her in the house, part of the job and all, but he knew it wasn't true. He wanted to hit her because she was a woman and a junkie and a whore, just like the girl who hadn't married dear old Dad. That knowledge sickened him, tired him out more than everything he'd been through. He let go of her shoulders.

She knew, though. He saw in her eyes that she had seen it in his: the rage, the violence. She had flinched and braced herself for the slap she knew was coming. He saw that to her he was just another man who beat up women.

The slap didn't come. They stood on the windy hill staring at each other. Neal could hear his heartbeat all right; it pounded along with his lungs reaching for breath. Finally, he said, "I ripped Colin off. He thinks you helped me. I let him think that—"

"Jesus . . . you asshole . . . who told you to—"

"Because I don't want you to be with him anymore. I don't want you shooting smack anymore." The words came out between gulps of air, and it was as close to telling the truth as he could go right then. He walked past her into the cottage.

Allie caught her breath for a moment and then walked to the car.

Neal was trying to build a fire when she came back in. The afternoon had turned suddenly cold. He wasn't having much luck and thought that maybe he should have joined the Boy Scouts instead of Friends of the fucking Family, when she came through the door.

"Where are my drugs?" she demanded.

"Somewhere on the M-11."

"You sleazy cocksucker!"

"'People who live in glass houses . . .'" He touched the match to the old newspaper and it caught flame. He blew gently on it, as he'd seen in the movies, and had a modest success. "Don't you think it's cold in here?"

"It's fucking freezing!"

"That's because you're starting into withdrawal. It'll get worse. There are some wool sweaters upstairs in a wardrobe. I suggest you get a couple."

"I suggest you get me some dope, or I'm driving right back to London."

"Good idea. Call Colin when you get in. I'm sure he'd love to see you."

He let her draw her own conclusions. "Thanks for fucking up my life!"

"You're welcome."

"You at least owe me some dope!"

Neal added a small piece of wood to the fire and almost smothered it. He shifted things around with the poker and the fire came to life. He was concentrating hard on making the fire. It settled him down.

Then he took his shot. Carefully, because he knew that she wouldn't be lucid much longer.

"What I owe you," he said, "is ten thousand pounds. I figure that's more than fair, seeing as you didn't do a goddamn thing to earn it. But that's not your fault. What I owe you is a chance to get off the junk and stay off, because that was also part of our deal. No more junk, no more dates."

"What deal? We didn't make any deal."

"Yeah we did. Feeding the ducks. There are all kinds of ways to make a deal, Alice. Sometimes it's on paper, sometimes it's in words, and sometimes it's just understood. We had an understanding, and you know it."

"You're crazy!"

"Okay. How crazy am I? I have the books and I have you. I cool out here for a while, then go back to the States. I call the buyer, he gets on the next plane, and I get twenty thousand pounds. Crazy? Okay."

He poked the wood around a little more, as he'd seen in the movies. He could feel Allie thinking behind him.

"Now let's ask how crazy *you* are," he said. "I'll give you . . . *give* you . . . half the money . . . ten thousand pounds. All you have to do is get off the stuff, come to the States with me, and still be clean when I make the sale."

Her hands were starting to shake. Soon her whole body would start in.

"Why?" she asked. "Why would you do that for me?"

She wasn't grateful, she was suspicious. That was okay with Neal; suspicion was easier to deal with.

"I'm not doing it for you, I'm doing it for me."

"I don't get it."

"What a surprise. Listen, you didn't think I was going to trust Colin to hide me out and keep me safe, did you? Why would Colin take half when he could get it all? He'd stab me in the back—literally—the second I turned it on him. I was *always* planning to screw him, just like he was always planning to screw me.

"I didn't plan on . . . liking . . . you. I didn't want to leave you behind to be on the street for Colin until he used you up and booted you out. So I took you. We can say it was against your will if that'll make you feel better, but we both know the truth."

"Maybe *you* think—"

"Shut up and listen. So now that I've got you, what do I do with you? We have some time to spend together up here, and I don't want to have to tie you up and all that shit, I don't want to have to worry about you running off to the cops screaming that you've been kidnapped, and I especially don't want you deciding that heroin and hooking are your true lifestyle and getting to a phone and taking your chances with old Colin."

"Yeah, so . . .?"

"Yeah, so I'm making you my partner. I want you to have a rooting interest in my survival. There are going to be a lot of angry people looking for me over the next few months, and I don't want you standing there, pointing and saying 'He went thataway.'"

"I wouldn't do that."

"Let's just say I'm giving you a little motivation."

She tried to come up with her best spoiled-brat smile, the same one he'd seen her use with Colin. "Motivate me with some smack."

"No."

"Why not?"

"Because I need to trust you, and I won't trust a junkie. Junkies will do anything. You get the money if and when you're off the stuff."

She was starting to shake but she was also listening. It took an effort. "So you think you can buy me."

"Sure. Ten thousand pounds. Current exchange rate . . . about sixteen thousand dollars. You could be a very comfortable runaway for a long time on sixteen large, if you don't have a habit to support. It's called a fresh start, and they don't come around too often. Not this easily, anyway. I'd take it if I were you."

Her eyes were starting to tear up. Pretty soon, her knees would start to rattle and her ears would hum, and it would be no good talking to her. The smack would do all the talking, and she would listen. It was starting already.

"What if I don't take your 'deal'? What if *I* say no?"

"You won't. I'm only doing what you told me you wanted. Keep you off the smack and off the street."

She put her hands over her ears and shook her head. Thinking was hard—her junkie body was telling her brain to get out of the way. "I can't get off the junk, Neal. I can't. I thought I wanted to, but I can't!"

"I'll help you."

"What do you mean, help me?"

He turned away from the fire to look at her. "I mean help you. Couple of hours, things are going to get bad for you. You're going to get pretty sick. I'll help you get through it."

She looked scared. It surprised him. He'd never seen her look scared before. She said, "Who are you, Marcus Welby?"

"I know a little bit about this stuff."

"You were a junkie?"

"No, I wasn't a junkie. I just know about it."

Yeah, okay, Diane. More secrets, more holding back. More not trusting. Fuck you. Why is every woman in my life coming to visit just now?

Allie started to pace around the room. She ran her hands over the stone walls. "You bastard. You prick. You got me into this! Why couldn't you just leave me alone?"

Good goddamn question.

"I don't want to quit!" she continued. Her pacing picked up. Neal saw she was starting to panic. "I can, I just don't want to! I like it, all right? Who the *fuck* are you to do this to me?"

Another good goddamn question.

Neal stirred his coffee. Allie sat on the floor. She wrapped her arms around her knees and hung her head on her hands. She started to rock, slowly at first, then faster and harder, back and forth. Neal barely heard her crying, and when he looked over, he had to look hard to see the tears wetting her face. The pain in his chest felt like his heart breaking.

He fought it. It was like his body was wrapped in barbed wire and he couldn't move. It was like being ten years old and watching his mother fight it and lose, and walk out of the apartment and come back stoned. It was the rage he felt, and the hatred and the contempt, and the heartbreak, and it wrapped him up so tightly, he wanted to scream. He remembered stroking his mother's head with a wet cloth, and holding her hand and telling her it was all right, she could do it. But she couldn't. Not for him, not for her, and he hated her for it. For leaving him. For loving it more than him. For what she did to get it. He heard Allie's quiet, choking sobs, and saw her hugging herself, holding on to herself, and he couldn't move. Damn it, why couldn't he move? Grief and anger kept him pressed into the chair, and he couldn't breathe, and he wanted to scream, to yell, to shout out his fury, and he couldn't. Instead, he got up, and went over to her, and sat down beside her, and held her while she rocked. She grabbed his wrist and he rocked her then, back and forth, saying "I know, I know."

He left her a little while later to build a fire in the oven to heat water for tea. He couldn't find any sugar, but there was a large jar of honey in the cupboard. He spooned a large dollop into the tea, and held the cup while she sipped at it. Then he rocked her some more.

26

COLIN WAS IN TROUBLE.

He knew it as soon as he wheeled his bike down the old home street and saw two Chinese hanging around the corner. They were Dickie Huan's boys, and no mistake, and Colin flashed on the meat cleaver doing its bit on his fingers, and he turned the bike around. The two lazy effin' bastards hadn't seen him, and he headed toward East London and the old neighborhood, hoping Crisp would have the sense to do the same thing.

HE DIDN'T, OF COURSE. His first instinct was to find Colin, so he trudged dutifully back to the flat. Some good hash and a pint had helped to soothe his pains, and as he turned the corner to home, he was even thinking that the new facial arrangement might make him more interesting-looking.

"He won't be here," Vanessa said, pouting. Her head hurt, her man looked as if he'd been at a football game, and she figured that Colin had fucked everything up, anyway.

"We'll wait."

They didn't notice the leather-clad Chinese kids on the

corner. Chinese usually just fought Chinese and stayed in their own neighborhoods, so Crisp had no problem with them. He just wanted to quaff a couple more pints, toss some dollers, and go to bed. It just wasn't his night.

They were good, these Chinese kids. They gave the two *kweilo,* the shitty-looking boy and his strange girlfriend, enough of a head start and then followed them into the building and up the stairs, timing it so they arrived at the door just as Crisp was opening it.

The larger one jumped Crisp from behind, hauled him through the door, and landed on his back. He drew the knife out and stuck it in Crisp's neck, just enough to bring a trickle of blood. The other one put a revolver to Vanessa's head and pulled the hammer back. She kept her mouth shut.

"Where's Colin?" the big one asked, edging up the pressure of the blade.

The day had really gone to shit, Crisp thought, it really had. "Dunno."

"He owes money."

"I dunno where he is."

"He owes money."

"I'll get some. Let me up."

"You know where he is." It wasn't a question.

"No, I don't."

The Chinese kid stuck the point of the stiletto into Crisp's ear, just short of the eardrum.

Crisp wondered whether the incredible thump of his own heart pounding was the last thing he'd hear.

"You know where Colin is."

"He's on a bike chasing some Americans who stole his money!"

The sound of Vanessa shouting this surprised Crisp, who

was trying to lie absolutely, perfectly still. He breathed a little, then he felt the blade slip out of his ear.

What might be described as a heavy silence ensued. Finally, the aural surgeon asked, "Colin doesn't have the money?"

He didn't sound real pleased.

COLIN WASN'T EXACTLY FILLED with delight to be skulking back to the old neighborhood, either. But he could go under here, get lost and stay lost, at least until he could figure out a way of finding Neal and getting his money. Because, if he didn't, he was finished in London.

IT ISN'T EASY TO TRAIL SOMEONE WHO KNOWS YOU, especially when your mark also knows you're a detective, and especially when you're working on the same case. It makes for a long day.

However, Joe Graham didn't care how long the days were, or the nights. He did care that the last time he had heard from Neal Carey, the boy was trapped and about to get it but good. And he also cared . . . cared a whole lot . . . about what Neal had told him on the phone. That he'd been set up—by their old buddy Ed Levine.

From some angles, it made sense. There were no files in the office on Allie's previous adventures and there should have been. So maybe Ed had destroyed them. And Ed was working real closely with John Chase, and Ed was ambitious. And Senator Chase had been diddling his stepdaughter, which didn't make good campaign material. So maybe it was possible that Ed had sent Neal to London not to make sure that Allie came home but to make sure she didn't. And Ed hated Neal. So maybe it was possible that old Ed was cleaning a bunch of troubles off his desk, and settling an old score. Maybe.

But then from other angles, it just didn't fit. He'd worked

with Ed for over ten years, and in ten years you get to know a guy. And Ed had a good career going already; why fuck it up to go with a prick like Chase? And Ed wasn't the sort of guy who stands for somebody abusing a kid . . . he had proved that in an alley years ago. Which was another thing—Ed liked to settle his scores in person. If he wanted a piece of Neal, he'd take it himself.

No. Neal was wrong. It wasn't Ed.

Unless Ed was following orders. From Kitteredge, who got them from Chase. No, that wasn't possible. The Man wouldn't do that, not for a crummy Vice-Presidential candidate, not for the Prez himself. It couldn't be Kitteredge, either.

So who else? Who had access to information? Keyes's address?

The answer was where it always was: on the street.

And it wasn't easy staying on the street with a guy who knows who you are, but now they were dealing with me, Joe Graham thought, and I'm the best there is. I taught Neal Carey everything he knows.

27

"How did you find me?" Neal asked Graham. Neal was nineteen then, and disgusted. Graham had given him the simple assignment to get lost. In a city of some 13 million people, Graham had found him—in two days.

Graham smiled his filthy smile and looked around the small third-floor apartment on Waverly Place. "Easy. I told you to get lost, and you didn't. So you got found."

Neal wasn't in the mood for this bullshit. Spring break was too short and he had a paper on the Romantic poets to write. He had seen this stupid training exercise as an opportunity to get some work done. "Are you going to be cryptic, or are you going to tell me?" he asked.

"What's 'cryptic'? Does it mean smart? Smarter than a stupid nineteen-year-old who picks a classmate's apartment to get lost in? Are you going to get me a coffee or anything?"

"I'll have to grind some."

"Oh, yeah, this is the Village, I forgot." He pointed to his crotch. "Grind this. Just make some coffee. You know, if you were the Fugitive, that series would have been over after the first episode. You're easier to find than rice on Mott Street."

Neal took some expensive mocha blend out of the refrigerator. He had bought it specially to help him work on the paper. The coffee shop around the corner was his favorite in the city.

"Are you going to lecture me, or just sit there?" he asked Graham. There were days, many of them, when he hated Graham.

"I'm going to lecture you. I'm just dragging it out because I'm enjoying it so much.

"You see, Neal, when you want to get lost, the first thing you got to lose is yourself. You got to become a different person, otherwise you bring all your habits, and likes and dislikes, and all your connections with you. Anybody who knows you has a good shot at finding you. And I know you, son."

"Yes, you do, Dad."

"I know you got this spring vacation. I even know you got a thing to write. I know you want peace and quiet.

"I also know you're too cheap to rent a hotel room, even though Friends would have picked up the bill, and I know you haven't got your driver's license, so you didn't drive out into the country, where you probably should have gone."

Neal carefully poured the ground coffee into the filter and measured out the water in the carafe.

"I hate the country."

"So where is Neal going to find a place? From a classmate who lives off campus but is going away on a nice little student vacation. So your Dad gives you this assignment and then does some asking around. Now I know Neal isn't going out to Queens or Brooklyn, because he wants to enjoy himself. And I know he's not staying on the Upper West Side, because he doesn't want to bump into his Dad on the street, but he also doesn't have the discipline to stay inside and really hide like he should. And I know he's not going to the East Side, because it's all rich people and he's prejudiced against them. And I remember how many times Neal has told me that if he ever left the West Side, he would move to the Village. So it became a simple matter of elimination and a little legwork. How many of Neal's classmates live in the Village and are going to Florida for spring break?"

"One." Neal *was* disgusted.

"I only waited the two days so you could get some work done on your paper so you don't flunk out and embarrass me."

Neal looked at him with true awe. "That's amazing. That really is. That's like Sherlock Holmes!"

"Right. Also you wrote down the address on your phone pad."

"You broke into my apartment?"

"I have a key."

Neal was confused. "Yeah, but I took the note with me. I remember ripping it off the pad and putting it in my pocket!"

"Are we going to drink the coffee or admire its delicate aroma?"

"It's not done yet, and tell me."

"You tell me."

Neal thought for a minute, then he knew. He was so goddamned angry at himself, he wanted to scream. "I wrote the note with a ballpoint pen and it left an impression on the next page."

"That's right. You're an idiot."

"I am."

"But you're a live idiot." Graham stood up, walked over to Neal, and took him by the collar with his one real hand. "Listen, son, anytime you have to disappear, it's serious. You disappear because you have to. Now your fuckup with the notepad made it easy, but I would have found you anyway, for all the reasons I told you. When you disappear, you don't leave anything behind except yourself. You become somebody else. Or you'll get found. And the next time you get found, it might not be me, but someone who wants to kill you. You got that, son?"

"Yes, Dad."

Graham let go of him. "Good. Now get lost. I'll drink the coffee."

Neal walked down the stairs and onto the street. Two days later, he was unhappily ensconced in a sleeping bag in a state park in Rhode Island. He hated every minute of it.

Graham didn't find him, however.

28

GETTING OFF HEROIN WON'T KILL YOU. Problem is, you wish it would.

The body is a vindictive fucker. It wants what it wants, and when it can't get it, it starts dreaming up ways to motivate you: runny nose, runny eyes, aching joints, aching muscles. It makes your skin crawl and your nerves jump. It makes you shake, rattle, and roll. You get cold, freezing cold, and then you get colder, and you think you're going to shake apart, actually shake to bits. You start to breathe in short, nasal snorts and exhale in long sighs and groans. Sometimes the floor starts pitching like the deck of a small ship in a big storm, and then you just want to lie there and hold on to your knees, because they hurt so much. And if you could just get warm . . .

Neal wrapped Allie in blankets. She shivered anyway as she stalked the bedroom, trying to walk away the ache and the cold.

"'She can't take much more, Captain,'" she said.

"Huh?"

"Didn't you ever watch *Star Trek*? When Captain Kirk would make Scotty take it up to Warp Eight and the *Enterprise* would start shaking and Scotty would get on the intercom and say, 'She can't take much more, Captain'?"

"And then they'd all tilt from one side to the other."

"Yeah. Right. But then it would be okay."

"Until the next week."

"Give me something."

"I don't have any."

"Please . . ."

"I threw it all away."

He was sitting on the bed. She dropped to her knees in front of him.

"I'll blow you," she said.

"Alice . . ."

"I will. I'm good."

"C'mon," he said, lifting her up. "Walk. I'll help you."

He put his arm around her shoulder as they paced the room.

"Neal, I'm not going to make it through the night."

"Yeah you will."

"I'll die."

"No you won't."

Yeah you will? No you won't? Brilliant stuff, Neal thought. Maybe you can open up an office, charge forty bucks an hour, and say, "Yeah you will." "No you won't." He almost wished he hadn't thrown the smack away. This girl was hurting bad. And his record at getting women off heroin wasn't so great.

"I'm scared," she said.

"Me, too."

"Wrong answer, you asshole! *You're* scared? *Now* you fucking tell me? This whole thing was your goddamn idea!"

She started to laugh. "*You're* scared."

She was laughing as she started pounding on his chest and his arms with her fists. Her laughter quickly turned to tears.

THE CRAMPS STARTED LATER. She tried to throw up but couldn't, and her retching dry heaves hurt as much as the cramps. Neal held her from behind—one hand on her neck, and the other pressed into her lower stomach muscles. Between heaves, he draped her head with a cool cloth and talked to her, telling her she'd get past it, she'd be okay, that she wouldn't die. He sang her songs, whatever lullabies he could remember from his mother's snatches of maternal cogency. He summarized the plots of *Star Trek* episodes, playing all the parts and making the noises of phasers and communicators. They played games: Name a rock group for every letter of the alphabet (The Angry Aardvarks, The Zany Zebras), sing the theme music from old TV shows. (They got *The Brady Bunch* but couldn't recall *The Partridge Family*.)

Morning came at last.

Neal thought it had probably been the toughest night of his life.

He knew it had been the hardest of Allie's. She had sweated it out, hung tough, all those good clichés. Now she was finally asleep. With the dawn had come a little peace.

He needed it. It had been a night spent with a tortured Allie, and a night spent with his own ghosts: a girl that he could help, a mother he couldn't. A thousand memories of that woman in pain and need, and a little boy unable to do a thing who hated her for it, hating himself for it. But on this night, in the here and now, he had helped. And they got through it together.

As he slumped in his chair, watching Allie sleep, getting rested for the next paroxysm of need that would hit her, he realized that his rage was gone. The sorrow would always be there, he knew, but the rage was gone. Maybe there is a God, he thought, and he sent me Allie Chase.

ALLIE DIDN'T KNOW WHERE SHE WAS when she woke up a while later. She sat up with a start, then noticed Neal and managed a weak smile. Then she leaned over and threw up into the bucket Neal had put there for the purpose.

"I love morning, don't you?" Neal asked, receiving a muttered obscenity in reply. He tossed her a damp cloth to wipe her face.

She tried to get out of bed, but her legs were wobbly. Neal grabbed her elbow and helped her up. They made a shaky trip down the stairs and he plunked her down in a chair in front of the fireplace. It took him a couple of minutes to get the fire started, and then he carried a smoldering stick into the kitchen and lit the wood-burning stove. He put the water on for tea, and spooned a large dollop of honey into Allie's cup. "You okay in there?" he yelled.

"Terrific." He took the sarcastic tone as a good sign.

"Be right in."

"Yip yip."

He looked out the window while he waited for the water to boil. Up the hill to his left, he could just make out a small dog hustling a herd of sheep along the crest. He wondered where the shepherd was and how far away he lived. Surely he'd notice the smoke from Simon's chimney and maybe stop by for a cup and a chat. Neal started to work on some lies to tell in that eventuality. Lost in mendacity, he was startled by the shrill whistle of the kettle.

He dumped what he figured was a couple of teaspoons of smoky, black tea into the bottom of the pot and poured the boiling water over it. Then he swished the pot gently a few times and let it set. He found the strainer and a tray and took everything over by the fire, where he poured Allie the first cup.

"Drink," he ordered. "Yummy."

"I'll throw it up," she warned.

"Jesus Christ, we wouldn't want you to throw up!"

She took the cup and sipped. "Sweet enough."

"Bitch, bitch, bitch."

"That's what I am."

Neal shook his head.

"What? I'm not a bitch?"

"Yeah, you are. But I think it's more of a habit than a permanent condition."

"I like being a bitch."

"Are you hungry?"

Her look of total disdain answered his question.

"I am," he said.

"Then eat."

He found some oatmeal cookies in a cupboard and took them back in.

"Is today going to be as bad as yesterday?" She looked like a scared child. It reminded Neal how young she really was.

"No. You won't get as violently sick. You'll be real jittery, though, and you'll get the aches again. But not as bad."

"How come you know so much about this?"

"I read a lot."

"Can I have a cookie?"

He handed her the bag. "Knock yourself out."

They sat quietly for a few minutes. Then she said, "I don't suppose there's like a radio in this hole."

"There's like not."

"Sure, make fun."

She got out of the chair. Slowly. It looked as if it hurt. She walked over to the front window and looked out. "Pretty."

"Yeah." More brilliant repartee, Neal thought.

"I stink."

"Don't get so down on yourself."

"No, I mean I smell. Like bad."

So much for Dr. Carey and positive reinforcement. "Do you want to take a bath?"

"Like yes." She smiled back at him. If you can make fun of me, she was telling him, so can I.

"Like okay."

"Where's the bathroom? I don't remember . . ."

"Outside."

"Get real."

"That's as real as it gets."

She looked at him real hard. "Next time, I pick the hotel."

Next time?

"C'mon. I'll show you where it is." It took them a good five minutes to walk the hundred feet to the tub. She was like an old lady. They stopped twice while she bent over to ease the soreness in her lower back. He hadn't planned to heat water for her, but then he figured it would make her feel better.

"I'll get a chair, you can sit outside for a while. Air'll do you good."

"What are you going to do?"

"Heat the goddamn water."

"How come you're being so nice?"

"I'm a jerk."

"Then can I have more tea?"

He took the cup from her and strode back into the cottage. Student, private eye, butler. May I help you?

It took forever to heat enough water for even a shallow bath. He'd check on her every few minutes, look out to see that she was still in her chair and not gimping in the direction of the village to get the next bus back to London and the needle. Never trust a junkie, he thought. But she stayed in her chair, dozing off from time to time, or watching the sheepdog work his flock.

The awkward moment came when the water was ready. Neal poured it into the tub, saving a bucket to rinse off with, handed her a towel, and started to walk away to give her privacy. She got up, stared at the tub, stared at Neal, stared at the tub, and then back at Neal again.

"What?"

"I don't think I can get in." She tried lifting her left leg to demonstrate. She could barely lift her foot to knee level.

"You want me to help you?" he asked, without the trace of a leer.

"I'd have to get undressed," she objected. "In front of you."

A shy hooker? he thought. The proverbial new wrinkle.

"Alice, don't you get undressed in front of men all the time?"

"That's different. They're strangers." He appreciated the inverted logic that made what she said make sense.

"Okay. I'll turn my back. You get undressed. I'll help you into the tub as quickly as I can, then I'll go away. You call me, and we'll reverse the process."

"I don't know."

"The water's getting cold. If you're not getting in, I will." She thought about it for a second. Neal checked her out to see whether this was just a hooker game, a little hide-and-seek seduce-the-cop game. But she looked shy just then. She really did.

"Okay. But don't look where you don't have to."

"Think of me as your doctor."

"I could tell you stories . . ."

He turned around and heard her fumbling with her clothes. Her hands being none too steady, it took a couple of minutes. Then he heard a long sigh before she said, "Ready."

He tried to focus on her eyes, but you know what it's like when you try not to look at something. Her body was beautiful, and Neal quickly dismissed the sinking feeling in his gut.

"Come on, before the water gets cold," she said. She was blushing, and the gooseflesh must have come from the crisp morning air. She crossed her arms over her breasts and looked away from him. It might have been the sexiest gesture he had ever seen.

"Turn around," he said.

"What?"

"So I can lift you into the tub, idiot."

"You don't have to get mad."

"I'm not mad."

"You sound mad."

She turned around and Neal made a determined effort not to look at her as he held her around her waist and struggled her into the tub.

She let out an unholy shriek as she hit the water. "Getting *cold*? This is boiling!"

"It'll feel great in a minute."

"I thought you were going to go inside."

"On my way." He talked as he walked. "Now don't try to get out on your own! You could fall and hit your head!" He realized he sounded like somebody's mother.

I have to get out of this business, he thought. He went inside and drank two cups of tea and ate six oatmeal cookies.

"NEAL!"

"What?"

"I wanna get out!"

"Okay!"

She had spent a good half hour lying in the bath. He had

looked out every few minutes (well, she was in a tub, you couldn't see anything) to make sure she hadn't drowned or run away. When he came out of the cottage, she was sitting up, her hair full of suds.

"Rinse me?" she asked. "I can't bend over to get my head in the water."

He poured the bucketful over her head, and she shook her hair out like a wet dog.

She held her hand out and he turned her and lifted her out of the tub. Their bodies touched as he set her on her feet on the ground. He let go of her quickly and wrapped a towel around her.

"We'd better get inside," he said, and started walking her to the cottage. She did much better this time, and only needed a little support climbing the stairs. She got dressed in some old clothes he had found. They were too big for her, but the pants stayed up with a belt and the jersey was comfortably baggy. Neal was stoking the fire when she came downstairs, all on her own. She stepped gingerly into the sitting room.

"Neal?"

"Yeah?"

"I need some smack."

She came into his arms and cried for a long time.

29

COLIN HATED LIVING THIS WAY.

He had scrunched himself down in his grandda's flat, a dingy cellar in the Old East End. He had a mattress in the corner of the sitting room and he could see the street through the one tiny window. He tried hard not to watch every pair of feet that came by, but the thought that Dickie Huan was tracking him down made it tough.

The room was a pit, a real trash heap, and the old man smelled bad, what with the steady diet of cheap sausage and cheaper beer. Plus the filthy old codger watched telly every second that he wasn't down to the pub, and he liked those quiz shows where fat old bags in pink frocks won holidays to Brighton for knowing the Christian names of every Prime Minister since Christ was a road guard, or the titles of every ultraboring song they used to sing before they took a quick poke up the old canal and started breeding. If Colin had to sit through one more episode of *Poldark,* he thought he would just let Dickie Huan slice and dice him into pigeon feed. It might be less painful.

And the old one couldn't shut up, either, not for a moment.

He engaged in a never-ending monologue about the war, and then it was Gerry this and Gerry that until Colin would scream out that he wished Gerry had won the bleeding war, anyway, so that at the least the beer would be worth drinking.

Or the old boy would maintain a running dialogue with the quiz-show contestants, shouting out the answers, all of them wrong, and then heaping abuse on the stupid cows when they rejected his well-intentioned advice.

His other hobby was getting on Colin. He enjoyed the spectacle of his big-shot grandson creeping back to the old neighborhood to hide out, and he never let Colin forget that he owed his existence to the old man's sufferance. The dirty drunken bastard would deliver lengthy soliloquies about the evils of drugs and fancy ladies, about ponces and 'hores, and dope peddlers, and above all poofters and buggerboys. He was convinced, or pretended to be, that Colin fell into the last category, so he made sure to spice his anecdotes with references to "sodomites" and "bumjockeys" he had known in the Navy, replete with tales of dark and murky deeds done in hammocks.

"Ye're not such an effin' great deal now, are ye, Colin lad?" he'd ask while gumming a sausage. "Wi' yer toff suits of clothes and yer leather shoes all nice and shiny. Now yer content to have a cup of tea with yer old gentleman's gentleman, who ye haven't bothered to as much as send a pack of fags to, and a year gone past. No, you were too good, then, wi' yer 'hores and yer poofters and floggin' dope like a Chinaman."

Which brought up a touchy subject.

His grandda had tremendous stamina for such an old croaker, Colin thought as the coot launched into yet another diatribe against him. Colin's only solace was that his grandmother had died, so he didn't have to listen to this in stereo.

Colin tuned him out and reflected on his own misery. Not

only did he not have Alice, with her delicious body and the delicious things she did with it, neither did he have his ten thousand quid that bastard Neal had done him out of. Worse than that, his hard-won drug and prostitution business, which he had spent years building up, was going to skat because Colin didn't dare show his face aboveground, lest he be chopped into Tuesday's lunch special. Which brought him back to brooding about Neal, who had caused this whole mess. And here he was, living in a root cellar with a crazy old man who smelled like a dead goat, dribbled his breakfast egg down his one decent shirt, and talked to the telly.

Weren't you the one, Colin asked himself, who swore he'd get out of this neighborhood and never come back? Now look at you, Colin lad, with one shirt to your own back, and afraid to go home. He had to find Neal and Alice, and that was an end to it.

LIFE WAS NO HOLIDAY FOR CRISP these days, either, what with two Chinamen following him every step that he took.

They had let him up off the floor that night, pushed him around a little for emphasis, and told him they'd be watching him. He'd better lead them to Colin, they said, or they would hold him responsible for the money. The girl, too. And they gave their opinion that it would take this girl one long time to work off twenty thousand pounds.

So now they followed him, not even bothering to be subtle about it, confident that he was frightened enough to lead them straight to Colin. He would, too, if he could figure out where the bugger had got to. He wasn't anywhere on the Main Drag, or on King's Highway or at Paddington or Victoria or any of the clubs. He had buggered off, left his old china (no pun intended) holding the old bag. He was probably in France by now, soaking up the rays on the beach, but Crisp wasn't going to tell his twin shadows that. They might get upset and go back to work with the knife. So for the time being, he settled for the uneasy status quo, and wandered around London as if he was looking for someone.

Sod Colin, anyway. Sod and double sod him.

In his mind, Colin kept going back to the flat on Regent's Park Road. To be sure, it was a painful and humiliating memory, and he knew he had made mistakes there, but he knew it was his only starting point. As he lay on the filthy mattress, he went over it again and again, asking himself the same questions. Whose flat was it? Why had Neal gone there?

To sell a book, perhaps?

Or perhaps to take one home.

Colin knew only one way to find out.

30

MUCH TO HIS SURPRISE, Neal liked mornings best. He had always been a night person, but in the cool and quiet of the Yorkshire mornings, he found contentment of a sort. He got up long before Allie, who still had tough nights a week after her last fix. As she slept off her exhaustion, Neal would start the fire in the stove and fireplace and then haul water to the bathtub. He'd force himself into the cold water, even coming to the point where he found it refreshing. He'd wash his hair quickly, towel off, and trot back inside to stand by the fire. He'd put the water to the boil, make himself a strong pot of tea, generously heaping in milk and sugar. Then he'd make toast over the open fire and eat it outside with his second cup of tea. All he found missing was a newspaper, but after a few days, he hadn't even missed that. He didn't care about who was killing whom, or even how the Yankees were doing. It didn't seem to matter up here.

Sometimes in the early cool of morning, he thought about just disappearing and not dealing at all with the troubles he knew were waiting. He recognized it as a fantasy—Graham would track him down through Keyes; he would run out of money;

Allie would recover and want to move on with their deal—but he was surprised at its appeal. The quiet and seclusion were powerful drugs. He started to forget about Colin, about John Chase, even about Levine fucking him over. There'd be a time to deal with all of that.

Not necessarily this morning, however—or any particular morning.

So sometimes he'd read a book along with the second and third cup, and other times he'd just sit—something he never thought he'd do—and enjoy the morning as it brightened and warmed. He'd watch the mist clear over the wood in the valley, and watch the shepherd and his dog move their sheep over the crest of the ridge.

He'd have maybe an hour of this quiet before Allie would wake up. He would hear her pad down the creaky stairs, stop and look for him in the kitchen, and then come outside. She would bring her cup with her and pour the last tea out of the pot. She liked it sticky sweet, and would spread gobs of butter and jam on the toast he'd make for her.

They spoke little on these early mornings. Sometimes she would tell him about her dreams from the night before, but mostly they just sat and listened to the morning. Sometimes she would fall asleep in her chair for a few minutes, and he would know that her dreams had been bad and her sleep shaky. Other mornings, she would light one of her few remaining cigarettes and smoke it slowly with deep, long drags. She'd sit far back in her chair and stare at the sky, and Neal didn't have to ask or wonder about what she was thinking.

It was always Allie who broke their reverie, suddenly standing up and carrying the teapot and cups back into the cottage. She'd come back a few minutes later, dressed and her hair brushed, and gently kick the leg of his chair, where he would

290 | DON WINSLOW

be taking a catnap. He would get up and they would walk over the top of the hill. The first time they did this, three days into her withdrawal, they made slow progress, and she leaned on his arm for the few minutes that they walked. He knew it embarrassed her. He watched her determination take over as their morning walk became a symbol of her independence, her shift from passive victim to active participant, and he always let her set the pace. She was recovering quickly.

The crest of the hill was a revelation, as it sloped steeply on the other side to a deeply wooded valley, which lay in stark contrast to the bleak beauty of the moor. The first few times that they climbed to the crest, they were content to stay there and enjoy the view: the short tufts of stubby grass and heather giving way to the lush green meadow, a brook, and then the wood. But on the third morning, Allie wordlessly set off down the slope, leaving him to follow or not. He did, staying well behind her, letting her lead them to the side of the brook. He sat down beside her on a fallen log. She was puffing, fighting for air, and her face was flushed with the effort. She was smiling. They sat for a long time until she could catch her breath, and the climb back up to the cottage was hard for them both.

"You're going to owe me sixteen thousand dollars, mister," she said between gasps, "and I'll have earned every penny."

After that, they pushed their walk a little farther every day. They found some stones on which they could cross the brook without getting wet, and it led to a natural footpath through the thick green wood. It was cool in there, cool and dark. Birds they didn't recognize fled in short hops in front of them, scolding them for their intrusion. Sometimes Neal and Allie would sit in the dark of the wood and listen to the birds. Other times, they would walk straight through and come out the other side to a meadow bordered by a rail fence. The meadow was oval-shaped and at the far end was a narrow gate that opened onto a trail leading back up the slope to the open moor. Some mornings, they arrived to find the shepherd there. The old man would lean on the rails of the fence, smoking a pipe, a shotgun cradled in his arm as he directed the efforts of his dog.

The frenetic Border Collie would gather the sheep into a rough circle, and then the shepherd would shout "Gate!" and the dog would drive the sheep headlong through the gate and up the trail, barking and nipping at recalcitrant heels. Other times, the shepherd would walk well ahead, his mind on foxes and stouts, and Neal and Allie would hear his shout from a distance. The dog didn't care; he knew his job. The voice was good enough. This ritual became a favorite part of their day, and they tried to time the walk to the rhythms of the dog and the shepherd.

As Allie got stronger, she would push herself farther, leading them out of the meadow and up the hill on the other side. Much to their surprise and delight, they found a small, deep pond over the opposite hill and decided that one afternoon they would go back and swim.

The return walk was usually slow and leisurely, but they rarely spoke. It was as if they feared words would bring the real world back, and the real world was too full of memories, and pain, and problems.

And heroin. And Colin. And heroin.

The walk always made them hungry. After the first week Neal trusted her enough to leave her at the cottage while he hiked down into the village to replenish their stores. He didn't want to attract any more attention than he had to by bringing the Keble, London plates and all, into the tiny village.

For lunch, they would have bread, cheese, and fruit. Canned soup on colder days. Sometimes thick slices of ham with mustard. Allie's appetite improved by the day, and Neal always ate like a pregnant horse anyway, so lunch was a big occasion. They ate outside when the weather let them, on a table they had made from an old door and two sawhorses. They drank cold tea, syrupy lemonade, or plain water. Neal would have loved a beer, warm or no, but was afraid to let Allie have any, and equally reluctant to be selfish by drinking in front of her.

They napped after lunch. She would fall exhausted into her own bed in the large bedroom, while Neal would settle into his own bed in a guest room. At first, he didn't sleep—suspicious that this nap bit was a dodge for her to sneak off. But she was truly tired, especially if it had been a rough night, and the exercise and fresh air did her in. Him, too. He'd try to read but would fall asleep after a few minutes. One of those deep, heavy sleeps. One afternoon, they climbed the stairs together, arriving at their respective doors at the same time. They stood in the hall for a long moment before Neal turned and went into his room. He shut the door behind him and realized that he had never done that before. He opened it quickly, to see her standing there, looking hurt and scared, and they both laughed a nervous laugh. She reached out and took his hand, gave it a quick and gentle squeeze, and went into her room. She left the door open.

He went to his own bed and flopped down on it. Jesus, Neal, he thought. Just Jesus, that's all. He meant to brood on the whole thing for a long time but fell asleep instead. After that afternoon, it became another ritual. They would climb the stairs together, pause in the hallway, she would squeeze his hand, and they would go to their separate beds.

They would sleep for a couple of hours or so, rising in the late afternoon to start the preparations for their supper and her bath. She began to take over the chore of heating her own water, and after a couple of days could easily manage getting in and out of the tub, to Neal's simultaneous relief and regret. The late afternoons could get heavy, with doubts and fears sneaking in with the approaching dark. She would really start to feel the need again, and get jumpy and edgy—hostile.

It often rained in the late afternoon, the day brooding along with them, the dark sky mocking their darker thoughts: she of dope and parents and lover left behind, he of the reality that was coming fast as summer waned, of those same parents, and Friends of the Family, and nominations to high office, and decisions that could not be put off much longer. They thought about a truth she didn't want to know and he didn't want to tell.

So it was a tense silence that colored their late-afternoon teas. Forced inside by the weather, they would sit by the fire and sip their tea, pointedly reading old paperbacks, and the quiet was not something they shared but something that divided them.

THEY WERE IN THE COTTAGE for two weeks when the visitor came. Neal returned from a supply run in the village one afternoon, to find Allie pouring tea for the shepherd. The collie lay by the fire, savoring an oatmeal cookie. The shotgun was in the corner behind the door.

"Pardon the intrusion," the shepherd said, getting up. "My name is Hardin."

"I've seen you work the sheep," Neal said, looking at Allie, who gave him a warm, domestic smile.

Hardin continued: "The missus tells me you're here on honeymoon. Bit different, that."

Okay, Allie, Neal thought, if you want to play . . .

"Actually, I'm working on a book deal."

"Honey, I thought you wanted to keep it a secret. Neal is very shy, Mr. Hardin . . . it's his first big sale."

Yeah, she wanted to play, all right.

"Lot of money in books, is there?" Hardin asked. He had

a face like crinkly leather, etched by wind and sun. Gray eyes peeked shyly out from under heavy gray eyebrows, and his shy smile cracked the heavy bush of his gray beard. Long silver hairs flourished in his ears. He looked woolly, like an old ram.

"In this one, we're hoping—may I warm that up for you?" Allie asked. She was having fun, and Neal had not seen her have much fun before.

"Perhaps your mister would like some," Hardin said gently.

"I'm sorry, darling. I'll be right back."

Hardin stuck his hand out. "Just to make it proper, Ivor Hardin."

"Neal Carey."

"Ohh, your wife uses her maiden—"

"Yes, she does." Whatever it is. "What's the dog's name?"

"Jim."

"Good name."

"Good dog."

Allie returned with a mug of tea for Neal, then sat down. She had a couple of hundred questions for Hardin about being a shepherd, and he was totally charmed by the time he had taken three more cups of tea and five more oatmeal cookies. He lived alone, it turned out, and had for some years, and Jim was the only company he usually had. Mr. Keyes made it up only a few times a year anymore, so Hardin wasn't used to seeing folks in the cottage. Not folks as pretty as the missus, meaning no offense.

"Life on the moor is lonely, to be sure," he allowed, "but I wouldn't live anywhere else and the dog is used to it. It's as hard to find a good working dog these days as it is to find a good working man, and when Jim gives it up, I expect I will, too. Move to the village and become a nuisance to the widows."

"I can't imagine you as a nuisance," Allie said, and Neal believed she meant it.

"Kind of you, missus, me already having eaten half your biscuits. Next time I come calling, I'll shoot the rooks out of your garden to pay for my pudding."

He pointed his beard at the shotgun and winked.

"We don't have a garden," Allie said.

"I know," Hardin answered, springing his little joke. Everyone laughed except Jim, who'd probably heard it already.

Hardin finished off his tea, put an oatmeal cookie in his coat pocket—"For Jim"—and said his thank-yous and good-byes. Allie told him to stop in anytime.

And he did, usually around teatime.

It was after one of Hardin's visits, after an hour or so of playing house, that Allie lapsed into a sudden quiet. She fidgeted for about twenty minutes, then asked, "So when we get back to the States, and sell the book . . . split up the money . . . then what?"

He was ready with a clever response.

"What do you mean?"

"I go my way, you go yours?"

If I knew my way, Allie.

"I don't know."

"Oh."

She got up and went into the kitchen, and came back a minute later with a fresh cup of tea.

"I thought you kind of liked me," she said, standing behind him.

"I do."

"So why haven't you done anything about it?"

Neal had never really known what the word *nonplussed* meant. Now he thought he knew.

"Jesus Christ, I kidnapped you! What more *could* I do?"

Neal got up and took a walk in the rain.

HE WAS DRENCHED WHEN HE CAME BACK, and just as confused as when he had left. She met him at the door with a towel and a blanket, then hurried into the kitchen, returning with a hot cup of tea.

"You're crazy," she said as she rubbed his head with the towel.

"I won't argue with you."

"Like they say in the movies," she said in a mock scolding tone, "you'd better get out of those wet things before you catch your death of cold."

Neal climbed the stairs, wondering just what the hell was going on with him. It had started out to be a pretty straight-forward job and turned into something different. You're adrift, he thought, and drifting further away. Cut off from Friends, playing house with a teenage girl. And the only crazy thing you haven't done so far is go to bed with her. Did you just say "so far"? Jesus Christ. It was July 20, time was running out, and he didn't know what to do or how to do it.

Supper that night was a simple repast of boiled potatoes and cold sliced ham, and was quieter than usual.

THE CREAK OF THE BEDROOM DOOR WOKE NEAL.

Allie was standing there, clad in the plaid flannel shirt they'd found in one of the chests.

"You okay?" he asked.

"I need to talk to you."

Why do the Chase women always need to talk to me in the middle of the night? Neal wondered.

Allie sat down on the edge of the bed, inspiring in Neal a simultaneous anxiety and a faith in genetics.

She started deliberately and slowly, as if she'd rehearsed and worried over each word. "There are things you need to know about me."

That's funny, Allie, there are things you need to *not* know about me.

"If we're going to be partners," she continued.

"Go ahead," Neal said, feeling guilty. Allie, he thought, I already know.

"I . . . God, this is so hard . . . I didn't just run away. I mean, for just no reason. Same thing for the drugs. I mean, I know I'm screwed up . . ." She stopped and hung her head, staring down at the rough fabric of the army blanket.

"You don't have to tell me anything," Neal said. "We're partners, anyway."

"I want to. It's been on my mind."

Neal nodded.

"My father . . ."

I know, baby, I know.

Slow tears dropped on the blanket.

"He . . . he and I . . . no, *he* . . . used to . . ."

Neal forced himself to look at her, forced himself to lift her chin and look her in the eyes.

"I guess . . ." she said, "the word is *incest*."

He stroked her cheek. "I'm sorry. I am so sorry."

"The drugs helped me to forget . . . and the sex . . . I guess it helped me to get even. I don't know."

Neal felt her tears on his shoulder. You can take away her pain, he thought, not all of it, but a lot. If you had half her courage, you would tell her the truth. He's not your father, Allie. You have to live with a lot, but you don't have to live with that. He's not your father.

But if I tell you now, I might blow it all, and I don't have the guts to risk it. And I'm sorry.

So instead, he said, "It's all right. It's all right. It doesn't make a difference. It's behind you now. It's behind you."

"I'm never going back."

"You don't have to. You don't have to," he chanted softly until she fell asleep and he pulled her down beside him. "You don't have to."

Betrayal, he thought, is the only ending to any undercover.

31

"WHAT DO YOU THINK HE'S UP TO?" Levine asked Graham. They were sweating out a hot afternoon in the New York office. "He hasn't called in; he's checked out of the hotel; if he's at the safe house, he's not answering. He's disappeared. What's he up to?"

GRAHAM WISHED HE KNEW. Since the night of Neal's phone call, he had worried his head off. He had kept a close eye on the British papers and had seen nothing about an assault, never mind a murder. And he had called Keyes's apartment a hundred times if he'd called it once.

Neal had disappeared—gotten lost—just as he'd taught him. But why hadn't he checked back in? Because he still thought that Ed was dirty, that there was a leak in the organization? Then why hadn't he gotten in touch with his old Dad? Called him at McKeegan's? Does he think I'm dirty now? That I'm in on it? No, Neal couldn't think that.

A worse option came to mind. Maybe Neal hadn't escaped the trap. Maybe he was a prisoner somewhere, or worse. Graham didn't want to believe it, couldn't believe it. Neal Carey was too good. He'd have gotten out and taken the client out with him. But where?

Or had Neal decided that one double-cross deserved another? Taken the girl somewhere to cut a deal on his own. Or had the little fuckhead gone soft and fallen in love with her? Jesus Christ.

"We've got, what, ten days?" Levine asked.

"Eleven," Lombardi said. "You think you're going to hear from him? Maybe he has Allie and is working on some deal of his own."

"Maybe," said Graham.

Levine looked at him real strange: angry.

"Neal Carey is a snotty little bastard, but he's not a double-crosser. Not with us." Ed said it firmly and to both of them. Ed was pissed, thought Graham.

"Hey, you sent a head case to get a head case," Lombardi said. "They're probably shooting up together."

"Shoot this," said Graham with an appropriate gesture.

"Hey . . ."

"Are you boys finished?" Ed asked. "Because we have a problem to work out here."

Lombardi stood up. "No. *You* have a problem to work out here. *I* have a problem to work out in Newport. One very angry senator."

Graham handed Lombardi his seersucker sport coat.

"So go to Newport," he said. "Let us know if Allie's home. Have you looked under the bed?"

"That's enough," Levine said.

Lombardi gave Graham a look that was meant to be tough.

"Maybe when this is all over," he said, "you can get a job in a casino. People can put quarters in your mouth—"

"And pull my arm. Is that the best you can do?"

"Hey, you're the clown."

Lombardi picked up his briefcase and made his exit.

"I should have gone to law school," said Levine.

"It's not too late."

Ed plopped himself down on his desk and looked through the Chase file for the thousandth time. Or pretended to. Then he said, "What are you not telling me, Joe?"

"Nothing."

"Where's the kid?"

"Do I know?"

"Do you?"

"No!" Graham said with righteous indignation. "Hey, look out the window, would you?"

"What, Neal and Allie are out there?"

"No, see if that fuck Lombardi has left the building. Stupid shit forgot his wallet."

"Good."

"Come on."

Ed looked. "He must still be in the elevator."

"I'll catch him. Yell at him when he comes out."

"It's seven floors."

"You got lungs. Give him one of those kung-fooey yells."

"I'd like to," Ed muttered as Graham headed out the door.

Graham pressed the elevator button and went right to work when it came. A seven-floor ride was ample to memorize the credit-card numbers, but he wasn't as young as he used to be.

COLIN COULDN'T STOP SWEATING, and it wasn't the heat.

As he maneuvered his motorbike through the outskirts of the city, he could feel a hundred pairs of slanted eyes on him, his mind creating gruesome pictures of flashing knives and cleavers. It wasn't logical, he knew that. He had lost them when he'd gone under in the East End, but he was spooked nevertheless. So he made triply sure that nobody was hanging about Regent's Park Road at three in the morning as he pulled his bike up to the sidewalk.

He waited outside for half an hour to see whether any lights came on in the darkened flat, then decided that either heigh-ho nobody home or the inhabitants were asleep. He crept up the stairs, stealthy and silent as an ox, and paused in front of the door. Unpleasant memories of his humiliating defeat here checked him briefly, and then he let himself in.

He let his eyes get used to the darkness and then pulled the window shades down. He listened for the sound of breathing anywhere and then turned on a lamp. He noticed instantly what he hadn't observed on his last visit here: books, everywhere. The clue light was lit.

He wasn't sure what he was looking for, but he knew that this flat was his only link with Neal. He didn't dare go to the hotel, because Dickie Huan would hear about it twenty seconds later, cozy as he was with that whoreson house pig Hatcher. Besides, he wasn't all that interested in the spot Neal had run *from*; this is where he had run *to*, and hadn't planned on being found out, either.

It didn't take long for Colin to discern that the flat belonged to some bloke named Simon Keyes, and that Squire Keyes was positively honks about books. Could Keyes be the mystery buyer? The flat didn't look the home of a man who could plunk down twenty thousand quid for a book, though.

Or did it? Think about it, Colin. If you was buying stolen goods, would you have them delivered to your home? Say hello to the missus and set the hot stuff in the parlor, there's a good man? That might start a bit of a huff over brandy and cigars, eh? Not bloody likely. No, you'd have a little hidey-hole somewhere.

Like some gents have a piece of fluff stored away, this chappie's got himself a little library love nest. A place to come in the afternoon and cuddle up with his books, run his fingers through the pages, rub the rich leather covers. You've a filthy mind, Collie lad, but a brilliant one at that.

But that wasn't helping to find the soon-to-be-late Neal Carey. Where did you run to, Neal, with your fancy motor and my fancy lady? Let's just have a look-see.

He pried open Simon's desk drawer and looked around: letters mostly. Christ but this one liked to write letters. Looks like he had carbon copies of every letter he ever wrote. No mention of Neal, though, just lots of chatter about this writer and that publisher and please do come for the weekend sometime up to the moor, and didn't that sound like a lot of fun? He gave up on the desk drawer and started in on the card table. This was even more boring. Catalogue on catalogue of books and pictures, and bids put in writing to Sotheby's, and the bloke did shit a ton of nicker on his books, don't he, and hold on, Collie you idiot. Something flashed in his brain. Up to the moor? Up?

He dove back into the desk drawer and found the letter.

"Dear Larry," it started, and then lots of polite toff chatter, right, get to the good part. "Please do come up to the moor weekend next." Followed by a lot of crap about how nice it would be to have some time with you and some chippie named Mary and then: bingo, directions. Up the M-11 as far as . . . sound a bit familiar, does it, ring any bells? Ding-dong? Big Ben?

Maybe, Colin thought, I'll have to invite myself up to the moor for a little weekend party of my own. He grabbed the copy of the letter giving directions to the cottage and headed down the stairs and out the door. He was thinking that maybe life wasn't such a kick in the balls, after all, when a swift one right in the old yobs dropped him to his knees. Through watery eyes, he could make out the smiling face of one of Dickie Huan's boys, and, behind him, a rather relieved-looking Crisp.

"THANKS," COLIN MUTTERED TO CRISP, "a whole bloody lot, chum."

They dragged him into the backseat of a car. One of the Chinese drove and another held his revolver on the two prisoners.

"You might have mentioned something, Colin. Like, 'By the by, Crisp, old friend. If this thing goes down the crapper, Dickie Huan's boys might be looking for us.' You left me holding the bag. What was I supposed to do?"

"How did you find me?"

"Well it wasn't too fookin' clever, hiding at your granda's now, was it? You only have two fookin' relations."

"They didn't know that, though, did they? Only my dear chum Crisp knew that."

"I'd be bathing facedown in the river if I didn't know that."

"Next traffic signal, I'm jumping out."

"They speak English, you bloody moron."

"That's right, you bloody moron," said the one with the pistol, "so don't do anything stupid."

He shoved the gun in Colin's face for emphasis and fun. Trailing Colin had been ridiculously easy, much easier than following someone through the twisted maze of Kowloon.

The car weaved up through Soho and into the back streets of Chinatown. The driver hauled Colin out of the back and pushed him toward the back door of the restaurant. He gestured to Crisp. "You go."

"Go where?"

"You kidding me? Just go."

Crisp went. Colin watched him slump off toward the Main

Drag, faintly hoping he'd come back with reinforcements. Fat chance.

Dickie Huan was in his tiny office in back of the kitchen. Colin didn't see any cleaver. The thug pushed him into a small cane chair in front of the desk. Dickie Huan looked over at him like a strict headmaster in a cheap school.

"You disappointed me, Colin."

"I'm a bit down in the mouth about it myself. But go ahead and sell the heroin to Jackie Chen. Next time, maybe."

"Jackie Chen bought elsewhere."

Bad news, that.

"You lose face, huh?" Colin asked.

"Fuck 'face.' I lose twenty thousand quid."

Colin felt sort of warm and runny inside. This is no time to panic, lad, he told himself. "I'm *this* close to having the money, Dickie."

"You're this close to eating with your toes, too. Where are you getting the money?"

Colin leaned in over the desk and whispered. Good dramatic effect.

"I'm selling a book."

"I kill you right now, Colin." Dickie Huan didn't like being fucked with.

"No, really. A rare book. A rare stolen book."

The "stolen" bit was a good strategy on Colin's part. Your basic criminal always feels deep in his heart that theft increases the inherent value of an object.

"Stolen? From who? You got a buyer?"

Colin tasted the sweet air of life as the door to escape opened just a crack. "That's the problem, Dickie. You put your finger right on it."

Dickie Huan valued justice—which to him meant revenge.

But he didn't value it twenty thousand pounds' worth. He'd have Colin taken into the meat locker and kicked around just to make sure he was telling the truth and to teach him a lesson.

"ACCOUNTS," THE VOICE SAID with a practiced professional lilt.

"Yeah, I have some questions about my bill."

"Name and number, please."

"Lombardi, Richard," Graham said, then rattled off the number.

"Yes?"

"You have me down for a bunch of calls to London, England!" Graham said, as nastily as possible.

"Yes?"

"Well, I didn't make any damn calls to London!"

"Our records show—"

"I don't give a damn what your records show—"

"Our records show that you made five calls from a phone booth and charged them to your account."

"*From a phone booth*? Who are you trying to—" Joe Graham was having fun, particularly when the operator got huffy.

"Yes, sir, from area code two-one-two, number eight-five-five five-seven-two-eight."

"To *what* number in London?" he challenged.

"It's on your bill."

"I don't have my bill with me."

He listened to the long sigh, the one meant to let him know that people who called to complain about their bill certainly ought to have said bill in front of their noses.

"May I put you on hold?"

"Time is money, lady."

She returned a couple of minutes later and read off the number. Very slowly. He asked her to repeat it and then hung up. Then he dialed the overseas number. It rang seventeen times before someone picked it up.

"'ello?"

"May I speak to—"

"This is a phone box, mate. You 'ave the wrong—"

"A phone box. Where?"

"In the 'otel?"

"What hotel?"

"The Piccadilly. Got to run."

Graham hung around for a while, thinking things over, and then decided he could think better in McKeegan's. He had a beer and a hamburger, then another beer, and ambled back toward his apartment. The walk let him think, helped him make up his mind. When he did, he stopped in a phone booth on the corner and made a collect call to Providence, Rhode Island. He was surprised that The Man answered his own phone. He expected a butler or something like that.

He told The Man everything.

32

IN THE SUNNY DAYS OF LATE JULY, the lake became their playground. They would pack a picnic lunch of fruit and cold sliced meat and make the long hike over the moor and down through the sheep meadow to the wood, where they'd sit in the shade and watch the daily performance of Hardin and Jim. When the old man had shouted, "Gate!" and the collie had driven his charges from the meadow and along the lane, Neal and Allie would continue on, climbing the next hill to reach the lake.

The lake wasn't really a lake at all but the remnants of a quarry—a reminder of a turn-of-the-century effort to make the moor bear more than tufts of grass, to make its stony soil pay. The villagers below had dreamed of selling the native stone to the gentry to build fine houses. But the gentry found it cheaper to import Scandinavian wood than transport Yorkshire stone, and the quarry failed after eight years of back- and heartbreaking labor. It became a convenient spot for the local youth to meet and produce more local youth, who would in turn leave the village to make a living elsewhere.

However, Neal and Allie had no idea of the quarry's history, quickly dubbed it "The Lake," and went every afternoon to skinny-dip. Well, Allie did, anyway. Neal could bring himself only to peel down to a pair of boxer shorts he'd found in a chest of drawers. This shyness was not faked. Neal had no intention of baring himself to Allie, mostly because she bared herself now so freely to him. She would shuck her clothes as naturally as a young girl in love, and if Neal found it disconcerting, all the better. She was more than aware of its effect on him, and of the reason that he clung so stubbornly to the thin facade of the ridiculous boxer shorts, and why he stayed waist-deep in the water, even when she sunbathed on the long slab of rock that rose from the cold blue of the quarry. She would tease him about his modesty, at the same time enjoying it immensely. She thought about all the guys who could never wait to get into her pants, and here was one she couldn't talk into getting out of his.

She flirted with him, she played, she luxuriated in feeling attractive. She bathed in sunshine and his admiration. For Allie, sex had always been a commodity: something she traded for money or affection, attention or revenge. A quick exchange of need for need. Now she enjoyed the sweet leisure of courtship, the tantalizing slowness of discovery, the muted music of her body falling in love. After a quick, freezing swim, she would lie on the rock, letting the warm rays of the sun cover her—and it was him covering her, warming her, his heat filling her and warming her, him melting her and melting in her. And then she would open her eyes a slit, pretending to sleep but watching him shyly watching her, watching him swim determined laps, and thinking, That won't help you, Neal, that won't save you, but go ahead. She would laugh softly to herself and perhaps drift off into a sweet sleep, wake up and find him on the rock above her, reading a book and trying not to think about her, stare at her, gaze on her. And she would know, in that infallible, infuriating feminine wisdom that makes life possible, that he would eventually come to her, come in her, and she would enfold him and hold him inside her and they would feel the whole world in their joining. There was time for all of that, and now even the waiting was delicious, the gentle pangs of want. She loved him, and she was in no hurry.

For Neal, the lake became the symbol of his dilemma. There was the cold, refreshing reality of the water against the sunbaked dream of the glistening rock and the golden girl. The siren song of Allie. Naked, she would perch on the rock above him, Mythology 101 sprung to seductive life. Her skin alone, dappled in sunlight and shadow, made him dizzy. He was swimming in desire. He could feel the insistent tug, the hollow thump, the fierce quick stir in his groin, the pleasant ache. He hadn't felt it since Diane. Hell, he thought, he hadn't felt it *before* Diane.

It complicates things, he thought, and things are complicated enough. You can deal with it later. Now you have five days to make it work. Five days before the shit hits. There's a lot to do: make arrangements with Dr. Ferguson about the book . . . get on a plane with Allie . . . disappear. That would be the hardest of all, because Levine would come after him.

Joe Graham sat in Chase's hotel suite, listening to the tirade.

"I didn't want you to send that kid," Chase was yelling. "But you all said he was the best! The best *what*? Fuckup? Head case? Let's face it, gentlemen, he isn't coming back and he sure as hell isn't bringing my daughter with him!"

He was red in the face, Graham noticed, pure power-trip rage.

"I think we had better consider damage control now, gentlemen," Lombardi said.

I'll bet you do, Graham thought.

Levine hung tough. "We still have four days before your deadline expires. A lot can happen in four days."

Let's hope so, Ed, thought Graham. Let's hope so.

Lombardi laughed and said, "You haven't even heard from Carey in weeks, and will you stop doing that?"

"Doing what?" Graham asked.

"Rubbing your artificial hand into your palm. It's driving me nuts."

"I do it when I'm worried, and I'm worried about Neal."

"You'd better worry about him if I ever get my hands on him," Chase roared.

Fuck you, Graham thought. Fuck you all. Neal had Allie and now he's missing, and one of you pricks arranged it and I think I know who. If my kid is hurt . . . if my kid is dead . . .

He rubbed his rubber hand into his palm and stared at Lombardi.

IT WAS AFTER A PARTICULARLY COMPELLING afternoon at the lake, during which she was certain Neal was finally going to touch her. She could feel him sitting on the rock above her, could feel his glances and was sure that he was just on the verge of sliding down and laying his hands on her shoulders. She could feel herself stroking the backs of his hands, and pulling him tighter, and she knew he was just about to come to her, just about . . . when he stood up and jumped into the cold water. This time she was pissed off, and she was quiet the whole walk back to the cottage, and they ate their dinner in silence. She went up to bed without a word of good night and watched the doorknob for a long time, willing it to turn.

When it did, Neal stood in the doorway. *Just* stood in the doorway.

"We're leaving," he said. "Tomorrow after breakfast."

"I don't want to."

"I'm not asking. It's time."

"It's time for a lot of things."

He stood in the doorway for what seemed like an hour. Then he turned suddenly and shut the door behind him.

THE NIGHT WIND STUNG Colin's face but he didn't let up on the bike's throttle. The pain felt almost good—it focused his fury. Dickie Huan's lads had stomped him pretty good. Pretty cute they were with their little hands and feet, but he would meet them again sometime, on his turf and on his time, and then they would find out just how cute they were.

But that was for later. Now he was headed to settle with his old girl Alice and his old buddy Neal. It had taken some talking to convince Dickie to let him go alone. Dickie had wanted to send a fookin' army, but it was explained to him that Yorkshire villages aren't used to seeing a horde of Chinese and it might attract negative attention. And besides, the book might be business, but killing Neal was personal. And killing Alice would be a nice hobby. He might even get generous and let Dickie play.

He let his mind imagine Neal and Alice in bed. It helped him forget his cuts and bruises. "Sweet dreams, lovebirds!" he shouted into the wind. "Colin's on his way!"

33

NEAL GOT UP EARLY AND COLLECTED his few belongings. He put
the copy of the *Pickle* in his briefcase and locked it. He poured
himself a cold bath, washed up quickly, then heated water to
shave. He heard Allie get up. She came down the stairs and
brushed past him in the kitchen without a word. She put up
water on the stove for her own bath, staring out the window
while it heated.

"Good morning," Neal said.

She didn't answer.

"You're not talking to me?"

"How does it feel?"

Then she carried the bucket outside, poured it into the tub,
shucked her clothes, and stepped in. For once, the cold air didn't
seem to bother her, and she took her time bathing.

When she came back in, Neal was sitting at the table, reading some old paperback. Allie went into the kitchen, pulled
eggs and bread out of the pantry, and began to make breakfast.
When it was ready, she tossed Neal's plate of eggs and toast in
front of him, and said, "So we're leaving today."

"That's right."

"Don't I get a say? I thought I was a partner."

"A junior partner."

"A fifty-fifty partner."

He looked up from his plate. "Knock it off."

You're not getting off this easy, Neal, she thought. I didn't trade one Colin for another. You're not going to treat me like this.

"No, Neal," she said, "*you* knock it off! I want to know what's next. What happens when we get back to the States?"

"You get sixteen thousand dollars."

"I mean what happens between you and me?"

Oh, Allie, not now, he thought. Just give me a few more days to work things out. Just trust me.

"Let's just take it slow, okay?"

"*Slow*? Haven't we *been* taking it slow?"

"So let's keep taking it slow."

"Maybe I'll just take my money and split."

He looked up from his plate and met her eyes. "You can if you want to, Alice. You have to know that."

She ate a few bites of toast, then got right to the heart of things. "Why won't you make love to me?"

"Jesus, Alice" was the best he could manage at the moment.

"Why?"

"I don't—"

"You don't think I'm attractive."

"I think you're very attractive."

"Then what is it?"

He took his time. "How do I explain this . . ."

Then she got the idea, the wrong idea, but she got hold of it and it hurt her. "It's because of my father, isn't it? That's why!"

"Alice, that's not it!"

"I shouldn't have told you!"

"No, I'm glad you did."

Her face contorted in pain. She tried for the mocking laugh she used to have, but it didn't work, and she screamed at him, "I thought you *loved* me!"

"I—"

"But you can't love a junkie whore who fucked her own father!"

He started to explain, to try and tell her . . .

But she was already headed out the door.

Let her go, he thought. Let her blow off steam. She can't go far. Let her be alone for a while.

COLIN WAS LOST. All these dirt roads look alike, he thought, and there are no signs. He was consulting Simon's directions again when he saw a little dog running toward him, barking.

"Jim!"

Colin heard the voice before he saw the old man. The dog stopped in his tracks, sat down, and began to wag his tail.

That's better, Colin thought.

Until he saw the shotgun.

"Who would you be?" the old man asked him.

"Good morning," Colin said in his best toff accent, flashing his most charming smile. "I'm afraid I'm lost."

The old man didn't smile back. He's looking at the cuts and bruises on my face, Colin realized.

"Went off the road with the motorbike," he explained, adding a self-deprecatory chuckle. "Stupid."

Still no smile from the old coot, and the dog's tail had stopped wagging.

"I never liked those things," the old one said. "Now, who would you be?"

I'd be the Aga bloody Khan if I had the money, you ancient hairy bastard. "I'm a friend of Simon's."

"You don't look like a friend of Simon's."

Colin knew how to handle the yeoman class.

"Nevertheless," he intoned, and let the awkward silence do the rest.

"Simon's out of country," the shepherd said.

"That's all right, actually," Colin said. "I've come to see Neal and Alice. Would you know if they're in?"

"I would."

"And could you tell me where the cottage is?"

"I could."

Colin let the precise, polite grimace of impatience cross his face. "And . . .?"

The shepherd turned around to point downhill and took his bloody time about it—quite enough time for Colin to grab the wrench from his toolbag.

Leave her alone, for a while, Neal thought again a few minutes after Allie had left.

Like you let the Halperin kid alone. Poor, stupid little Jason Halperin, from Cincinnati, who you took from that gentle queen on Twenty-third Street. You took him to the Hilton and it was late. You were both hungry and room service was closed. And Jason Halperin was so docile, relieved almost, to be caught, and you figured you could leave him alone for ten minutes while you went across the street to grab a couple of sandwiches. He was engrossed in some stupid movie on television, and you told him that you were locking the door from the outside, which is impossible, and you'd be right back. And you didn't bother to cuff him, because why put the kid through any more shit, right? And service was so slow, it was a bit more like twenty minutes before you came back with the roast-beef sandwiches and the Cokes and the Twinkies, and there was fourteen-year-old Jason Halperin hanging from the clothes rod in the closet. Because you had left him alone and there were things he couldn't face alone and you should have known that.

The yapping of Hardin's dog woke him from the reverie and he took it as a signal. No, don't leave her alone for a while. Go find her—now.

Neal rushed out the door. The butt of the shotgun hit him square across the upper ribs and he dropped to his knees, sucking for air. He could barely raise his head to see Colin standing there, and Allie standing frozen beside him.

"'avin' a little spat, were we?" Colin asked. "Let's all go back inside and talk it over."

He ushered Allie inside with the barrel of the gun and sat her down on one of the kitchen chairs. Then he went back out and nudged the shotgun under Neal's chin. "Trouble gettin' up, rugger? Want some 'elp?"

Neal struggled to his feet, went in, and crumpled into the other chair. His ribs were burning and it was hard to breathe.

"First things first," Colin said. "I'll take the book now."

"In the bedroom," Neal said. His eyes began to focus. He recognized the gun as Hardin's.

"Yeah, 'at's right, Neal. I thought the other cottage was your little love nest at first. Alice luv, get the book, will you, dear? Before I blow Neal's 'ead off?"

She went upstairs.

"Neal, Neal, Neal," Colin said sadly. "You 'ad to make this difficult."

"Take the book. Leave Alice."

"No, I don't think so. Ah, 'ere's your beloved. Alice, open the case."

"Both dials to fifty-three," Neal said.

She opened the case and set it on the table. Colin leaned over to gaze at the book. "Better late than never, hey, rugger?"

He was getting comfortable now. He held the shotgun against his hip in the crook of one arm. His finger was on the trigger and he had the barrel pointed at Allie. "Neal lad, give us the name of the buyer."

"I'll trade you the name for Alice."

"Well that's quite generous of you, considerin' I 'ave the book, Alice, and this shotgun, and you 'ave fuck all."

"I have the name."

Colin lowered the barrel, dropping it down to Allie's knees. "It would be a shame, Neal, but I'd do it."

His finger tightened ever so slightly on the trigger. Allie turned dead white, her teeth sinking into her lower lip.

"Dr. John Ferguson, Eleven St. John's Wood."

The barrel swung to Neal's face. "Truth?"

Neal nodded.

"If I find it isn't, Neal, I'll take a knife to 'er pretty face, and . . ." He winced and shook his head.

"It's the truth."

"I believe you." He stepped back and leveled the gun back at Neal's face. "Well, lad, I've never shot anyone before—"

"Don't hurt him and I'll go with you," Allie said.

"You'll go with me anyway, Alice."

"I'll do anything you want. For as long as you want. Just don't hurt him."

Colin didn't take his eyes from Neal. He had made the mistake of underestimating him before. "How can I believe you, Alice?"

"I don't know! I swear!"

"I've got an idea." He fished out a set of works from his left pocket and dropped it on the table. He followed with a small glassine envelope. "Cook it up and shoot it, there's a good girl."

Allie grabbed it. He had brought it all. She had just lit the match under the spoon when Neal said, "Alice, don't."

Colin tightened his finger on the trigger. "Shut up."

A gun makes you see the world in a whole different way. All Neal wanted came in one single, fervent prayer: Don't let it go off. Please don't let it go off.

Allie tied the rubber hose around her arm and pulled tight. She chose a vein and lowered the needle to it. She was crying. "Promise me, Colin, you won't hurt him now."

"A deal's a deal."

Neal was trying to fight through the fear. If he lost her now, he lost her forever. She'd never fight her way back again. Not through the dope, and the selling herself. Not through what Colin was planning for her. Not through the ghosts that haunted her.

You've blown it, he thought. Blown it. You haven't done anything you started out to do.

And you haven't told her about her father.

"He's not your father," Neal said. He felt dizzy. He saw Colin's jaw tighten. Saw the barrel of the shotgun.

"What?" Allie asked. She froze with the syringe a millimeter from her arm.

"Shut up!" Colin yelled. Another ounce of pressure on the trigger and it would go off.

Neal felt as if he were swimming through fear, fighting to the surface. "John Chase is not your father. What he did to you was horrible, but he's not your father. Remember that."

"Who *are* you?"

Neal spat out the words as fast as he could, before the shotgun's roar could drown him out.

"They sent me to bring you back. Your mother wants you back, and John Chase is not your father."

"What are you fookin' on about?"

"All this time . . ." she said, staring at Neal.

"Shoot it or I shoot 'im. Now!"

She looked at Neal for a moment more, then touched the needle to her arm.

"Allie, don't!"

She pushed the plunger. It was a strong mix and took only a couple of seconds to hit. Her knees buckled but she caught herself on the table, then shook her head once. Twice. Peace flowed over her, into her.

Neal sank back in his chair.

"Right," said Colin. "Well, 'ere we go."

He grabbed the briefcase and shoved Allie toward the door.

"Cheers, rugger."

Allie's attack was feeble, heroin slow, but her raking nails hurt anyway and threw off his aim as he knocked her aside and turned to face Neal, who had sprung from the chair.

The blast caught Neal square in the chest and set him down in a bloody heap on the floor.

Colin hit Allie in the stomach with the butt of the gun, then crouched over Neal and felt his neck for a pulse. He didn't find one. He grabbed Allie by the elbow and shoved her outside toward his motorbike.

Neal had felt the first wicked shot of pain, and then a great sleepy, bloody weight pressing down on his eyes and his chest, and then blessed oblivion.

34

DR. FERGUSON ANSWERED THE TELEPHONE, only mildly surprised that someone would be ringing him at that time of the evening. He sometimes wished he had gone into specialized practice, with its nicely specified hours, but for the most part he was pleased with his work and with himself. Dr. Ferguson was a man content. He had a public passion for books, a private one for his wife of twenty-odd years, and an addiction to trout fishing that went beyond all reasonable bounds.

He lived modestly for a wealthy man, an heir. He preferred to put his money into important things such as rare books, an Argyll retreat, and a share in a trout stream in that same shire. So he set aside part of his house in London's St. John's Wood for an office, and saw most of his patients there or at the hospital. When the telephone rang on this particular evening, his nurse was long gone, so he answered it himself.

Rare was the caller who warned him not to interrupt, and Ferguson listened with rapt, if a tad annoyed, attention to the manic stream-of-consciousness verbal style of this lower-class

young man and allowed a good ten seconds of silence to pass
before he deigned to respond.

"Ah," he said, "may I speak now?"

Receiving an affirmative reply, he said, "First, may I inquire
how you came to be in possession of these volumes? . . . Actually,
it *is* my business, considering that you are asking me to purchase
them . . . . I see. I see . . . . No, tonight would not be convenient . . . . Yes, I'm quite sure. I don't do business at night, you
understand . . . regardless of what you have been led to believe.
I do, in fact, know a Mr. Carey, but he is a tobacconist and I
rather doubt that he would— The soonest I could possibly see
you would be at, let me think, tomorrow at half past one . . . .
Yes? And your name? . . . Well, I shall have to know— Yes, Mr.
Smythe, I shall look forward to meeting you at half past one
tomorrow. Good evening."

When the rather desperate young man rang off, Ferguson
sat down with two fingers of whiskey and searched his brain
for any trace of a Neal Carey who had some connections with
books. An hour or so later, he came up with an answer.

ALLIE'S WORLD HAD BECOME A CLOUDY MIX of grief and sleep.
Lying in the filthy Bayswater flat that was Colin's new retreat,
she would wake up from a drugged sleep and remember Neal
and the pain would start again. It wouldn't last for long, because
Vanessa would pop her a quick one again, a small shot of smack
that would send her back into reverie and sleep.

For a while, she thought she might have dreamed the long
ride to London, when she had clung to Colin's back and hung
on for life as he relentlessly sped back to the city. They had
stopped only three or four times—she couldn't remember—for
gas and for Colin to haul her behind some loo and shoot her
up. She knew she was a prisoner, but after a while she couldn't

remember why. She could remember only the sight of the shot-gun blast ripping open Neal's chest, and the blood, so much blood. She could remember fighting Colin during the first fix or two, but the next time she didn't fight, and after that, she rolled her sleeve up and held her arm out. And after that, she became impatient when Nessa was late with her shot.

She was in a tiny back bedroom of a small third-story flat. Either Crisp or Vanessa was always with her, and sometimes a young Oriental guy would come and check her out. She could sometimes hear Colin talking in the other room—a one-sided conversation that she realized must be over the phone. She didn't care. She wanted her shot. It let her sleep and gave her pretty dreams: dreams where the blood blossomed from Neal's heart and floated in the air and became a shiny bouquet of wet roses; in which she dove to the bottom of a deep, cold lake and found him there, smiling, pretending to be asleep; dreams of endless naps on warm, fluffy clouds that glided slowly over the city, and she could see everything and everybody.

Soon there was little difference between being asleep and being awake, and that was fine with Allie. She had tried real life and it had let her down badly.

CRISP AND VANESSA WERE PRISONERS, TOO. Prisoners of the stupid deal Colin had made with Dickie Huan.

"Not to worry," he told them. "One more small transaction and we'll be ass-deep in filthy lucre."

One more small transaction, Colin thought. He was nervous, and hated admitting it to himself. The idea of strik-ing a deal with an upper-class doctor scared him, and it was a blow to his pride. The son of a whore had sounded so bloody cool, so reserved. He had spoken to Colin with that same conde-scending tone he had heard from those bastards his whole life, and his dad before him. Well, never mind, taking the old fart's money was revenge enough.

And he'd need the money now, he thought—first to pay off Dickie and then to lay low someplace for a bit. Christ on the cross, he hadn't wanted to kill Neal, had he? Had he? Maybe he had. But he probably wouldn't have shot if Neal hadn't gone for him. Silly bastard, as if any tart was worth it, even a sweet piece like Alice. He had spewed up after shooting Neal. He'd given a few blokes the blade before, but never for the sweet by-and-by. It was sickening, it was. But then he remembered Dickie Huan's lads. Better Neal than me, he thought. And he did rip me off . . . all that nicker . . . and Alice.

Alice. What to do with Alice? She wouldn't keep her trap shut, would she? Mind you, no one would likely believe a junked-up mess like Alice, but still. Maybe Dickie would take her up. Sort of a bonus. No, no good. If she blabbed it to Dickie, that would be the end. Dickie would own him, charge him whatever price he wanted.

No, Amsterdam was the better answer. Go with Uncle Colin for a holiday. Let her peddle herself in the Damestrasse behind a window. She wouldn't last.

And it wasn't as if she didn't deserve it. Amsterdam's the spot. Take Dickie's bloody heroin and flog it on a higher market, anyway.

Right. But first to get rid of this fucking book. It was still only 10:30. Three bloody hours. Christ.

Such a balls-up could happen in three hours. He glanced over at Crisp, who was sitting on the floor munching on a bag of that obnoxious shit. He'd have to lose this one and no mistake. Little bloody good it would do to set himself up on the Continent with his new wealth, only to have this idiot and his ugly gash trailing along.

"I'll ring you up when it's all done, and you can get out of here. Bring Alice to the Dilly and I'll haul her up to her boyfriend."

"Neal seems to be taking this pretty easily," Crisp said. Colin noted that suspicion tainted his usual subservient whine.

"I took care of old Neal." Too true, he thought. "He just wants the trouble and strife in there back again. Sweet, isn't it?"

"I thought you were in love with her."

It's a good job he was shaking Crisp when he was. Bugger was beginning to get cheeky. "I was. Take a lesson from it."

Colin took a few extra minutes with the mirror to knot his tie, a maroon knit he fancied with the muslin jacket, pink shirt, and gray slacks he had chosen for the occasion. Then he slipped into the cordovan tasseled loafers and checked the shine on the toes. He'd show this Oxbridge shit what class was. He looked ridiculous.

"Well, kiss me, darling," he said. "I'm off to make our fortune."

"Have a nice day at the office, dearie," Crisp answered. He hoped like hell Colin didn't fuck this up.

Colin gave Huan's thug a playful slap on the shoulder. "Want to share a taxi, sports fan?"

RICH LOMBARDI WAS IN A BIG HURRY. The convention was about to start, and the Senator was in his suite waiting for the big meeting about what to do without little Allie.

It was a problem, all right, because little Allie wasn't going to show. Title her story *Little Girl Lost*. Oh well, he could figure out something to tell the press. He always had.

He tucked his shirt in, zipped up his fly, and smiled at the girl on the bed. She smiled back. She was young, blond, had incredible blue eyes, and wanted to be an intern in the Senator's office next summer when she graduated from high school. Well, that could probably be arranged.

Rich Lombardi loved his job.

"Gotta go," he said. "Meeting with the Senator. Gotta hurry."

He rushed out the door, past the little alcove with the Coke machine, past the little man with one arm who was crouched behind it.

Graham had no trouble letting himself into the room.

COLIN TOOK A LONG, DEEP BREATH and rang the bell.

Dr. Ferguson bugger took his own good time coming to the door. Colin tried to steady his heartbeat. This was it, mate: the breakout. Don't take any crap from the bloke, now, he thought. You have what he wants.

Ferguson was a smallish fellow, early fifties maybe, and dressed Savile Row.

"Mr. Smythe, is it?"

"Dr. Ferguson, I presume?" A little cheek to show the bastard I'm not afraid of him.

"Do come in."

Nice. Nice place. Antique furniture. Hunting prints on the walls. Books, of course.

"You brought the item with you, I hope."

Colin pointed at the attaché case clutched in his hand.

"May I see it?"

"May I see the money?"

Ferguson sat down and pointed Colin to a chair. "You are new at this, Mr. Smythe. The merchandise first, and if it's genuine, then we discuss the money."

Colin put the case on his lap and opened it. He handed the books to Ferguson.

The doctor opened up the first volume, checked out the cover, the spine, and the first few pages. Then he examined the other three volumes.

"These are from Simon Keyes's collection. I'm surprised he let it go."

"So is he."

"Ah, yes—"

Colin leaned over. "Let's cut the genteel bullshit. You had an arrangement with Neal Carey. I'm acting as, shall we say, his agent. Same terms."

"And how did you get this from Mr. Carey?"

"Do you care?"

"No."

Come on, come on, Colin thought. So close. Don't blow it now.

"Ten thousand, was it?" Ferguson was asking him.

Colin smiled. "Twenty, actually." Up yours, mate.

"Ah, yes."

Ah, yes, indeed. Twenty thousand sweet quid and Colin is set. I'll turn that twenty to fifty quick as your sister drops her knickers.

"You'll accept a check?"

Colin looked nonplussed.

Ferguson chuckled. "Sorry, a small joke."

I'll small-joke you, you smarmy twit. Twenty thousand quid may be play money to you; it's my fucking life.

"You do realize," Ferguson continued, "that I expected this delivery some weeks ago."

"There were problems."

"Apparently."

No. Christ, no! Don't let it go sour now.

The whoreson ballocks breaker spent about three hours

lighting his fucking pipe, then he said, "Fortunately for you, Mr. Smythe, truth be known, I would kill for these volumes."

Truth be known, Dr. Ferguson, I *did*.

"Then you won't mind giving me my money."

Ferguson gestured with his pipe to a closed door. "Shall we step into the library?"

"Yes, we bloody well shall, if that's where you keep the nicker." A small evil thought of hitting the bastard over the head and taking it all crept into Colin's mind, but he dismissed it. Mustn't be greedy.

"After you."

Colin stepped into the library.

"Hello, rugger."

COLIN BLINKED HARD. TWICE.

"Is something wrong, Mr. Smythe?" Ferguson asked. "You look like you've seen a ghost."

Colin recovered quickly. "Neal . . . glad you're all right, chappie."

And sweet bugger all if Neal wasn't sitting right there, not looking too good, but a damn sight better than he'd looked the last time Colin saw him. He was pale as a nun at an orgy, and the shirt that was draped over his shoulders revealed a bloody bandage that covered most of his chest. And he looked real tired, totally fagged, which wasn't bad, considering he had been dead and all.

"God's blood, Neal, that gun had a hair trigger, didn't it?" Neal didn't answer him. He didn't smile or laugh or nothing. Just sat and stared at him. Maybe he is dead, after all.

"When I was a lad," Ferguson intoned, and double sod him, "on my first bird-hunting jaunt, my father taught me to always, always check my load. Too heavy a shot, you ruin the bird. Too small a shot, you wound the bird. Of course, a load of rock salt . . . you lose the bird."

Colin whirled on him. "Yeah, well, you triple-sodomized poxy piece of ape dung, Dad never took me bird hunting, unless you count the time we boffed your grandmum in the gent's at Charing Cross, and *what* in the name of Lord Nelson's sausage is rock salt, while we're about it?"

"Steady, lad." This contribution came from a big bloke in the corner, and God's blood if it wasn't Hatcher, that half-honest peeler from Vine Street, who wouldn't even take a bribe from Dickie Huan. And he already had the irons out. This thing was turning to shit, quick like. Think, Colin lad, think.

"Where's Allie?"

Thank you, Neal. God bless you, rugger. I can always count on you.

"I dunnoo, Neal."

"Don't fuck with me, Colin. I'll take you out and shoot you." Colin wasn't thrilled that Hatcher was nodding.

"But maybe I could find out," Colin said.

Colin watched and sweated as Neal and the cop exchanged what could be called significant looks.

"Hatcher?" Neal asked.

Hatcher stroked his chin. He was thinking, Colin saw, which he knew was hard on cops.

"Not meaning to be difficult," Hatcher said, "but it leaves me, as it were, standing out in the cold looking through the window at the Christmas pudding. I understand what you're asking, you get your girl back safe . . . all well and good . . . and Mr. Keyes gets his books back, and the young punk goes scot-free. I get left in the same old dead-end job, putting the arm on ponces for the small money."

So much for half-honest, Colin thought. Must've left that half to home.

And it must have been a hell of a natter they had before I got here. Leave it to a greedy cop to queer a nice arrangement. Except it isn't so nice, is it? If I leave this room free as a bird, I still have Dickie to deal with . . . .

The cop continued: "If I may offer a suggestion. Why don't you leave me and the lad to have a chat alone, and I'll wager next month's take I'll have your girl for you quick as a Scotsman's funeral."

"Then what?"

Christ, Neal, don't encourage him!

"I'll charge our friend here with an assortment of major crimes against the Crown, and perhaps win a pat on the back from my grateful superiors."

Neal looked at Hatcher. "Enjoy," he said, and started out of his chair. He took it slow, and it still hurt.

"Hold on," Colin said. "Let's not be hasty." He gave Hatcher his most engaging hustler's smile. "How would you like to be a superstar?"

NEAL EASED HIMSELF DOWN ON THE BED in Ferguson's guest room. The doctor had insisted he rest, and Neal supposed it made sense. It would take a while for things to work out, anyway.

His chest throbbed. When the charge had first hit him, he'd thought he was dead. He was sure now that his heart had stopped for a second or so, either through pain, or shock, or fear, and the sheer force of the blow that had taken him off his feet had driven the air out of his lungs. He remembered hitting the floor, and that was about it before he'd passed out.

He'd come to when the collie started licking his face and sniffing him, and he saw Hardin leaning over him. The tough old shepherd got him to his feet and cleaned up the raw, rasping wound. He sterilized his knife with the flame of a match and used it to pick out the rock salt that was still embedded in the flesh. Then he asked Neal some hard questions.

When he heard the story, Hardin left Neal in the cottage and returned an hour later in an old Bedford lorry. First they went to the village, where they each had a whiskey and Neal placed his call to London. Ferguson had already heard from "Mr. Smythe," and had recalled Neal's name. He reasoned that Neal, for some bizarre reason, had betrayed his host by stealing his most valuable possession, and Ferguson was considering ringing the police. He agreed to wait until Neal could tell him the story in person, and then run him in if he wished.

The long ride to London was a torment in the bumpy old truck, and every jolt sent a burning stab through Neal's chest. When they arrived at Ferguson's in the small hours of the morning, Neal was in bad shape.

"Good God, man," Ferguson said as he helped Hardin carry Neal in. "What on earth has happened to you?"

They took Neal into the examining room and laid him out on the table. Ferguson went to work with real instruments, but not without remarking that Hardin had done a solid, if primitive, job, and then he asked Hardin about the nasty bump on his head. Hardin insisted it could wait. The doctor worked on Neal with tweezers, tongs, scalpel, and sutures, covered the whole bloody mess with sulfate ointment, and stuck a variety of needles into Neal, shooting him up with antibiotics and a tetanus vaccination for good measure. He tried to give Neal some sleeping pills, but he refused them. He desperately needed to tell the doctor about Allie.

Ferguson listened to Neal's tale with some skepticism. He was all for calling the police, even after he'd accepted Neal's

332 | DON WINSLOW

version of the events. It took all Neal's remaining energy to convince him that it would be the end of Alison Chase. Finally, they had compromised. Neal put a call in to the Piccadilly Hotel, and a few minutes later Hatcher rang back. He arrived at Ferguson's shortly thereafter.

Over whiskey in the doctor's study, it all seemed very civilized, almost like a game. Neal struggled to stay awake as they laid the plans for an ambush, a trap that—if it worked—would set Allie free.

"He won't have her with him," Neal said.

Ferguson agreed. "No, he's too wily for that."

"Well then, gentlemen," said Hatcher, "the only thing to do then is to get his nuts under the boot . . . and step on them."

HE HAD SAID GOODBYE TO HARDIN at the door and thanked him.

Hardin shook his hand and said, "You brought some excitement to the dog and me. We don't much care for excitement."

"Sorry."

"I don't suppose we'll be seeing you or the lady again."

"I don't suppose you will."

"I'm glad I had the gun loaded for crow, young man."

"So am I."

Hardin fumbled for a minute, then said, "That's a good young lady."

"Yes, she is."

"Hope you get her back safe."

"I will."

IT WAS NINE IN THE MORNING BEFORE Neal had laid down to try to sleep. Tired as he was, he couldn't drop off. He was thinking about Allie. The same thing happened this afternoon as he tried to rest. There was too much going on. Ferguson had made a few phone calls to the right people and arranged for twenty thousand pounds in cash. A very nervous young accountant arrived with the briefcase a couple of hours later.

"Rather irregular, this," he observed to Ferguson.

Colin stared longingly at the stacks of bills.

"It's a great shame, Neal," he moaned. "A bloody great shame."

"Get moving," Neal answered, "before I change my mind."

"Right, rugger."

Colin had left, followed at some distance by Hatcher. An hour later, the call came through.

"Hello, Neal," Colin said. "Four o'clock, Piccadilly Circus. They'll bring her. They're expecting me, though."

"Colin! *How is she?*"

There was a long silence. "Well, sport, you know junkies."

DICKIE DIDN'T BELIEVE IT, but there it was, twenty thousand pounds, neatly laid out in a briefcase, Colin's insipid face grinning at him behind it.

"I hope this is good stuff you're selling me, Dickie."

"Don't push your luck, Colin."

"Right you are."

The waiter brought over two small glasses of fiery Chinese wine. "All good deals begin with a toast," Dickie said. "Here's to our new relationship. *Gan bei,* bottoms up."

"Bottoms up," he said. "Let's go fetch my smack." Bottoms up, indeed, where you're headed, you fat fart.

VANESSA HAD A BIT OF TROUBLE GETTING Allie out of bed, and she finally had to hold out the promise of a fix if she'd be a big girl and come along. They walked down into the tube station and got her on the train with no more difficulty. They emerged at the Piccadilly station with Allie gentle as a lamb.

"She's a walking zombie," Crisp noted.

"That's Colin's problem," Vanessa said. She hoped there'd be no trouble getting their share of the money from Colin. She wanted to get Crisp well away from him.

The Dilly was crowded and noisy. Sirens blasted the afternoon air, and it seemed like every cop in London was pouring down into Soho. It made Vanessa edgy, anxious to find Colin, shake him, and quit this scene.

Except Colin wasn't there. Neal was.

The Circus was crowded with tourists and zoned-out kids. They didn't stand out or draw any attention.

"Where's Colin?" Vanessa asked. Crisp stood behind her. He didn't trust Neal a bit.

Neal made a point of listening to the sirens, figuring that Colin, with his twenty grand of Kitteredge money in nicely marked bills, must have made out all right. "In jail, probably."

Vanessa just nodded. Losing had become a way of life.

Allie stared at Neal. This dream was one of the best she'd had, and she was running on low. "Neal?" she asked. "That you?"

"In the flesh."

She took his face in her hands and looked into his eyes, real close. "Neal, I'm very glad to see you but I'm very fucked up."

"It's okay."

"It's like we're floating around the city, you know . . . all over. everything is going *whoosh, whoosh* like? Are you fucked up, too?"

"I think so."

She hugged him tight. "Oh good. Didn't want to be the only one. Didn't want to be alone. You don't think I remember stuff, but I remember. They sent you to get me. Good old Mom and Pop did, that's what you said. You gonna make me go home now? To good old Mom and Pop? You're not, huh, Neal?"

"I'm not."

"Promise?"

"Promise."

"Good, good good." Her face turned serious. "Can we go now?"

"Right now."

"Love you, Neal."

"Love you, Allie."

Neal started walking her to Oxford Street to hail a taxi. He wanted Ferguson to see her as soon as possible. He hadn't gone a block before he made them. Footsteps behind him—two pairs . . . not pros. He picked up the pace and listened. They were coming faster. Could he afford to pause, even if there was a cab handy? Would it be a knife, a sap, or another gun, maybe? The thought of the gun got to him and he fought off the fear. He slowed down a little but tightened his grasp around Allie's waist. The steps pulled closer, then alongside: Crisp on one side, Vanessa on the other.

Neal kept moving as they talked. "You want something?"

"We're in a bit of trouble," Vanessa said.

"I'm not in the mood."

Crisp grabbed him by the elbow. "Listen, mate—"

Neal straightened his elbow and grabbed Crisp by his belt. He lifted his arm as he moved. The motion hurt like crazy but it kept Crisp off balance and vulnerable. "I'm not your mate and if you give me any shit—any shit at all—I'll kill you right here."

Neal didn't think he would or could kill Crisp, but it sounded good.

"As I was saying. We're in a bit of trouble. What with Colin in the lockup and all."

"Your friends are your problem, not mine."

Vanessa was half-running to keep up with him. "That's not really true, you know."

She shoved something into his stomach. It was a magazine. "Have a look at this."

It was a *Newsweek,* opened to a page. On the page were the smiling faces of John Chase, wife Liz, and daughter Allie.

Neal tried to bluff. "So?"

Vanessa was much tougher, much smarter, than he ever gave her credit for. "Come off it," she said.

Neal dropped his head. He was so damn tired. He looked up again. "What do you want?"

"Out of here."

He thought about it for a few seconds. It was doable. "And then how do I know I can trust you?"

"You're a fine one to be talking about trust."

True enough.

"Okay, I'll think about it. Go back to the old flat. I'll ring you tonight."

She let go of his arm. "Midnight, Neal. Or I see if *Newsweek* wants to print my pictures of Allie."

Crisp tossed him a decent imitation of a confident smirk and the pair walked away. Neal flagged a taxi and gave the driver Ferguson's address.

"Where we going?" Allie asked.

"Someplace to get some sleep."

She narrowed her eyes like a bad actress doing suspicion. "You're not taking me home, Neal."

"No."

"Promise?"

"Promise."

Assured of that much, she fell asleep in the cab and was no problem putting to bed.

35

Lombardi handed Ed Levine the phone.

"It's for you."

Ed was grateful for a break from the sullen atmosphere of the hotel room, where John Chase sat in a near-catatonic state of anger.

"Levine," he said into the phone. He had made a habit of answering phones this way. It was professional, efficient, cool.

"So Ed," said the mocking voice on the phone, "where do you want her? Providence . . . New York . . . Newport?"

"Carey, you son of a bitch bastard. Where are you?"

"I'm with Allie Chase."

"You got her."

That got their attention in the room: heads lifted, ears perked.

"Of course I 'got her,' what did you think? They don't call me the best for nothing."

Levine held the mouthpiece to his chest. "He's got her," he said to Chase and Lombardi.

"What kind of shape is she in?" Lombardi asked quickly.

"What kind of shape is she in?"

"She'll take a nice picture. I don't think you'll want her to do *60 Minutes*, though."

Chase smiled. Lombardi went to pour himself a healthy G&T.

"You and me have a lot to talk about, Neal," Ed muttered.

"Oh, yeah, you bet your fat ass we do."

"Your mother—"

"Ed, you get a pencil, write this down. It's tricky. British Air, Flight One seventy-seven. Arrives Kennedy two P.M.—tomorrow. That's August first, by the way. Be there or be square."

"If you're screwing us around . . ."

Neal had hung up.

NEAL PUT DOWN THE PHONE and looked in on Allie. She was out cold. He reflected for a moment on the subject of betrayal. Graham had been right as usual, he thought as he looked down at the sleeping girl. Betrayal is the basic stuff of the undercover. It's in his bones. Then he went back to the phone.

AS A RULE, JOE GRAHAM liked other people's phone conversations better than his own. He was sitting in his apartment, four cans into a six-pack and seven innings into a ball game, when the phone rang three times and then stopped. By the time Hoyt had come out of his stretch and let loose a slow sinker, the phone jangled again. This time Graham picked it up.

"Dad!" came the cheerfully mocking voice on the other end of the line.

"Son, it's been a long time."

"Meet me."

NEAL THOUGHT IT OVER AGAIN and then dialed Colin's old number. Vanessa answered. "Yeah?"

"What are the names on your passports?"

He made her spell them out twice, gave her instructions about where and when to meet him, and then hung up. Ten minutes later, Miss Vanessa Brownlow and Mister Harold Griffin had two reservations on British Air from Heathrow to Boston. Then Neal phoned Hatcher.

HEATHROW AIRPORT ON A SUNDAY MORNING is the eighth circle of hell. Three-quarters of the world's population either are greeting or seeing off the remaining fourth, jamming old, cranky Terminal Three in a sweaty mass of emotional humanity. Give Mother Teresa a couple of hours in Terminal Three on a Sunday, she'll be shopping for a machete.

Neal Carey was delighted to see the place. Allie firmly in tow, holding his hand and a small dose of Thorazine, Neal edged to the BA sales counter, paid for his and Allie's tickets with plastic, and Crisp and Vanessa's by cash. Blackmail payments are not tax-deductible. He avoided the crowd at the escalator and took the back stairs up to the Departure floor.

Hatcher was pretty good, Neal noted. He stayed about fifty or sixty feet back and eased his bulk through the crowd without pushing or shoving. Neal recalled a Grahamism: A civilian sees the crowd; a street man sees his way through the crowd. Neal led Allie into the bookshop, picked up some magazines she seemed to like and a paperback copy of Peeble's *A Short History of Scotland* for himself. Hatcher peeled off at this point and checked out the mobbed coffee shop. He came back a few minutes later and nodded to Neal.

Crisp and Vanessa were in the coffee shop, and they were alone. For once, they hadn't screwed up. Neal hadn't really thought that even this dynamic duo would be dumb enough to try to snatch Allie back in the middle of Heathrow Airport, especially not during a terrorist campaign when about half the white males in the building were plainclothes cops. But he wasn't taking the chance.

They had somehow commandeered a booth, and seemed oblivious to the hostility of the sullen waitress and the stares of the various Pakistanis, Indians, and Africans who found them bizarre. Neal slipped into the booth across from them. Allie followed.

He slid the ticket packet across the table to Vanessa. She looked it over and asked, "Why Boston?"

"You think I want to see you in New York?"

"You don't trust us?"

"Maybe I don't want to get off the plane and be greeted by a photographer from *Newsweek*. This will make it just a little tougher for you to double-cross me."

Vanessa didn't like it. "How am I supposed to get to New York then?"

"I don't care. You see the big guy over there at the counter? Tea, toast, and sausage? He's a cop." Neal cut Crisp's protest off. "I just want to make sure this all goes smoothly. Have you ever taken an international flight before? Okay, you go back downstairs with your ticket and passports and check in. They'll take your bags there. Then you go through security. Passports and tickets again. Now, just to be sure everything is hunky-dory, meet me again in the coffee shop inside the security area. I'll give you your money there."

"You're a cautious bastard," Crisp said.

"I wonder why."

HE LET HATCHER TRAIL THEM DOWN to check-in, finished off his own coffee, and said to Allie, "We're going to get on the plane now."

"Where are we going?"

"I told you. L.A."

"Disneyland. I want to ride that elephant thing."

"Dumbo?"

"Uh-huh."

"Yeah, I like Dumbo."

I seen a horsefly, I seen a deerfly, I ain't never seen an elephant fly.

"You gonna get me clean in L.A.?"

The question took him aback. "If that's what you want."

"That's what I want."

"Then we'll do it. C'mon."

The lady at the British Air counter was like all ladies at the British Air counter, cool and polite.

"I have an aisle and a window for you, Mr. Carey."

"Terrific."

"Enjoy your flight."

The line at security was long and slow. Nobody was taking any chances. Neal didn't mind. He had left plenty of time to catch the plane, and he'd just as soon the plane he was on didn't blow up in midair, not after all this. When it came their turn, he let Allie go first, and turned to nod his goodbye to Hatcher. The cop should be having a good day. His drug bust had made the morning editions and they had all spelled his name right. He gave Neal the thumbs-up sign: Crisp and Vanessa were through security.

He found them right at the coffee shop.

He said to Vanessa, "Allie should go to the loo now."

"I'll take her."

"I'll have your money. You want pounds or dollars?"

"Aren't you the considerate one? Dollars, please."

Vanessa took Allie by the hand and walked off. Neal looked

at Crisp and smiled. "How about you, champ, you want to hit the WC?"

"Turning poofter on us, Neal?"

"Let's do it."

The security lounge was far less crowded. Only people with tickets were in there, so they made it to the gent's loo with ease. They walked to the last stall, the handicapped one with lots of room, took a quick glance, and locked themselves inside.

"You got everything through okay?"

"I'm not in bracelets, am I?"

"Vanessa, too?"

Crisp nodded. "You worry too much."

Crisp pulled the stuff out of a makeshift pocket sewn inside his jeans.

The alcohol felt nice and cool on Neal's skin. The needle stung like a bastard.

NEAL PICKED A GOOD SPOT TO SIT and watch them board their flight. He wanted to make damn good and sure they got on. He thought about Lombardi. Call this book *Trust Level Zero.*

They strolled through the gate as if they'd been doing this all their lives.

Now it was his turn. Why do I feel so jumpy? he wondered. This is the easy part. He gathered Allie up and they hit the line. Ten minutes later, they were at the last checkpoint, and Neal eyed the attendant nervously. Can he tell? he thought nervously. Can he tell? Neal handed him the ticket and passport. Was the man looking at him more closely than he had the others? Can he tell? Is it the guilt in my eyes? Smile, now. Just a little, not too much. He can tell. I'm screwed.

"Enjoy your flight, sir," the agent said with just the trace of a smirk. He passed Allie right through. The plane took off right on time.

Levine hung the phone up. "They're on board."

"How do you know?" Lombardi asked.

"I have a source at British at Kennedy. He checked the computer. I'll call the Senator."

"Tell him I want to come along to meet them."

"You and me both."

"This better be good, Lombardi," Chase said over the phone. "You hauled me out of a meeting with half the crackers in Dixie."

"They're headed in."

"Have the car meet me. Have you called Mrs. Chase yet?"

"I work for *you*, Senator."

"Call her. She can get a helicopter down and still make it."

"How's it going there?"

"We have a good shot at it. Do you think you can get born again?"

"I feel like a new man already, Senator."

Allie liked the movie. She didn't have the headset on, but she made up her own dialogue, which wasn't too bad, Neal thought. She ate both their lunches and only had to go to the lav once for a refresher course in sedation. She was in a pretty good mood for a young lady as sick as she was. When she wasn't putting words into De Niro's mouth, she talked about life after getting straight, and California sunshine, and getting them a little house around Malibu somewhere. She bet she could pry some cash out of the old trust fund, Dad or no Dad.

Neal nodded and made listening noises and drank heavily.

The first-place Yankees had a twilight doubleheader against the Sox and he could just make the second game if he hustled. He was sick of himself, and sick of his lies, and it would be real nice to get involved in a game where they had some rules.

36

U.S. SENATORS WITH CHAUFFEURS AND LIMOS and twenty-dollar bills park where they want to at Kennedy airport, even right beside signs saying UNLOADING ONLY. Chase and Lombardi sat in the backseat. Chase drummed his feet and looked at his watch. The plane was due any moment and Liz hadn't shown up yet. Hung up in traffic. How could a helicopter get hung up in traffic? Lombardi was on the phone to his people at the convention. The Senator was still hanging in there. That cracker bastard was taking his time, though. Probably praying about it.

Ed Levine was set. Standing at Arrivals outside the Customs gate, he checked his troops again. He had brought along four muscle types. They were spread out well. Little Neal wasn't getting by. Two would grab the kid and waltz her over to Daddy for the hugs and kisses. The other two would grab Neal and stick him in a car. They would drive to some lonely parking lot, where Ed would expound on his displeasure. He had reluctantly promised Graham he wouldn't break anything; after all, Neal had brought the girl back.

A few minutes later, the light flashed on BA 177. Ed stepped outside to the car. Lombardi rolled the window down.

"Yeah?"

"I don't want to bother you or anything, but they're down and headed into Customs."

Chase set the car phone down. "How long?"

"Depends." Fuck you.

Chase gave him a dirty look. Levine could care less. This thing was about over and then he wouldn't have to deal with the sleazy SOB anymore.

"We'll be there in a minute. You haven't seen my wife, have you?"

Ed knew thirty-eight good answers for that one but didn't use any of them. "One at a time, Senator. One at a time."

Chase stood with the flowers Lombardi had handed him—a nice touch, in case any snoopy reporters stumbled on the scene. He watched an endless throng of people come out of the gate, none of them Allie. Just like her, though, he thought.

Lombardi wished they'd hurry the hell up so he could get back to the convention. Christ only knows what they were up to back there without him to handle it.

Levine knew that Neal was holding back deliberately, letting most of the crowd come through—the less chance of a scene. He checked his guys one more time. They seemed to pick up on the tension. They were alert, on edge. Just the way he liked them.

"Daddy!"

The high-pitched squeal echoed through the hall.

Levine watched as some little schlump with short blond hair advanced toward Chase with her arms out.

"Daddy!" she screamed again, throwing her arms around him.

"You're not my daughter," Chase said, trying to disentangle himself from her more than fervent embrace.

"No fucking shit?" she whispered. "Flowers! For *me*? How sweet! I'm famished. You know airline food." She proceeded to eat them, one by one. She did hand one to an anemic-looking boy standing beside her. He popped a daisy in his mouth and swallowed it whole.

"I'm Crisp. Can I call you Dad?"

The security types started to move in. Ed beat them to it. He grabbed Vanessa and lifted her off her feet.

"Where are they?"

"You must be Ed. Get your greasy hands off me, Ed. Before I scream for a reporter. That's better.

"I have a message for all of you from Neal. First, you're to let us go immediately. Or I call the press. Second, you're not to try to find him or the girl. Third, he *told* you not to send him on this thing. Alrighty right? Now, where can I get a taxi?"

Chase started to grab her. "You bitch—"

"Let them go," Levine said. He was red with rage, but he knew Neal Carey. "Let them go, Senator."

His boys were slick. They moved the Senator as if it was his idea. They steered him back to the car, forming a wall that masked his furious face and muffled his yelling.

Rich Lombardi stood there for a moment, shaking his head. Then he looked up at Ed Levine. "Title this bit *You're Finished in This Business.*"

Ed Levine shoved him a big middle finger. "Title this."

But as Lombardi was hustling away to catch up with Chase, Ed was thinking: I'll kill him. I'll find Neal Carey and kill him. It's over for him—his job, his apartment, his education. Hosed. Let him try the world with no friends and no family.

THE GUY AT BOSTON'S LOGAN AIRPORT didn't want to let them in, but their papers were in order, this fucking guy with the shaved head and a safety pin through his ear, for Chrissakes, and his broad with the orange and purple crew cut.

So he hassled them a little, then said, "Welcome to Boston, Mr. Griffin, Miss Brownlow."

NEAL BLUSHED. THE NEEDLE THROUGH HIS EAR had stung, but not like this homecoming. He felt like a jerk. He looked like a jerk.

THE HEAVILY MUSCLED GUY IN THE BLACK POLO SHIRT grabbed Neal the second he stepped out onto the street. He was professional. His hand was like a soft vise around Neal's bicep, while his partner gently took Allie.

"Neal?" She wasn't nearly strong enough to put up a struggle, but she leaned away from the muscle toward Neal.

"It's okay, Allie. It's okay," he said as his guy pushed on his chest, blocking his way to the girl. "They're going to take good care of you. They're going to get you straight."

"Neal?" She started to cry and held on to him tighter.

"Allie, listen, I do love you. But sometimes the best thing you can do for someone you love is to leave." He pried her hand off his arm, then softly kissed the tips of her fingers. "Goodbye, Allie."

The muscle started moving her toward a limo parked on the street. Neal looked over the thug's shoulder and saw Liz Chase get out of the back.

She stood on the sidewalk, crying, her fingers touching her bottom lip.

THE THUG STARTED TO TURN NEAL AWAY.

Allie was looking back at Neal as they pushed her along toward her mother. She looked scared and hurt.

He didn't see her collapse in her mother's arms, didn't see their embrace. All he saw was a big chest and a big forearm hauling him away. Then he heard a voice say, "Hurt him and I'll cut your balls off."

The guy let him go. Neal saw Graham standing there, an evil smile that didn't cover up his worry spread across his face. Neal looked behind him and saw Allie's head through the rear window of the car. It was rested on her mother's shoulder. Ethan Kitteredge sat next to them.

Ash blond hair. Impossible blue eyes.

"Hello, son."

"She's *his* daughter, isn't she?"

"Yeah."

"That's news to me, Graham."

"News to me, too. News to Kitteredge. News to the kid, soon."

"How—"

"Long time. All these blue bloods know each other. When you called the other night . . . let me change that, when you *finally* called the other night, told me what kind of shape she was in, told me your demands—and thank you very much and, by the way, fuck you—I called the mother like you said. She must've gotten on the honker to The Man, because in less time than it takes Guidry to tank a three-run lead, the phone goes off again and guess who, Neal?"

"Kitteredge."

"Who says okay. Fuck Chase, and the kid goes to the best laughing academy money can buy. Along with Mom, by the way."

"And you kept all this from Ed?"

"Yeah."

"He set me up, Graham. He was working the other side."

"No, he didn't."

"How—"

"Trust me." He gave Neal that satanic grin, then put a fatherly arm around his shoulders. "By the way, kid, Levine thinks you deliberately fucked us over. So does Chase. They don't know anything about Allie being The Man's daughter or nothing. They're going to think you made an arrangement with Mrs. Chase for a cut of the divorce settlement, which should be wicked big."

"But you're going to set them straight, right?"

"No. The Senator is still useful to us."

"After what we know about him? The Man can say that knowing what he knows about the Senator and his daughter?"

"It's business, kid. Nothing personal."

"Ed's going to think it's personal."

Graham tightened his hold a little. "Yeah, well, that's why we want you to disappear for a while. Let things cool off, you know?"

So I get to take the fall, Neal thought. You do the right thing and you get nailed for it.

"Now," Graham continued, "I know you're worried about graduass school. Your professor says you're on leave of absence. To do research." He handed Neal an envelope.

Neal opened it. The note from Kitteredge read: "Thank you for my daughter. You are, indeed, a friend of the family. I hope this partially compensates you for any inconvenience we may have, or will have, caused you." There was a draft for ten thousand pounds sterling and an open return ticket to London.

He handed the bank draft back to Graham.

"Take half of it, and get it to Allie. Send me the change."

"Are you crazy? The kid's got more money than God."

"I owe it to her. It's hers."

"You're sick."

"Tell me about it. Did I get any mail?" he asked.

"Not from Diane."

How does he know these things? Neal wondered.

"You want me to track her down? Tell her where you'll be?" Graham asked.

Neal shook his head.

"You think she'll be okay?"

"Diane?"

"Allie."

"Yeah, she'll be okay. What, you got something for this kid?"

Neal snorted. "Just another job. You think I could chance going into town, catch a ball game, couple of hot dogs before I get back on a plane?"

Graham pulled two tickets out of his shirt pocket: Yankees versus Red Sox—box seats, Fenway Park.

"Your old Dad takes care of you, doesn't he?"

"*Box seats?*"

"Father and son night. Two for one."

"Figures."

They started walking to the cab stand. "Did I mention," Graham said, "that you look like shit, with your head shaved and a safety pin sticking through your ear? Doesn't that hurt, for Chrissakes?"

"Not as much as the needle that made the hole."

"Well take it out. I don't want people thinking you're a fag."

"I'm getting to kind of like it."

"Great. What's next? A simple strand of pearls?"

They stopped at the cab stand.

"You did good, son."

"Thanks, Dad."

37

RICH LOMBARDI SLIPPED INTO THE DRIVER'S SEAT of his Porsche. All in all, things hadn't worked out too badly. The Senator hadn't gotten the Veep, but that was okay. This cracker wouldn't last more than one term and then they'd have a crack at the number-one slot. And Allie was tucked away in a rubber room somewhere and couldn't shoot off her mouth. He leaned back into the seat and was about to start the engine when he heard that fucking sound again, that rubbing. But it was only for a split second, because something cold and sharp was pressing into his neck.

"You know what I read in the papers this morning?" Joe Graham said. "I read they're training monkeys to help out quadriplegics, you know, guys who can't move their arms or legs? Yeah, these monkeys run all around their apartment and bring them things. Books, food, beer . . . you want one of those monkeys, Richie? Because if I press just a little right here . . . you'll need a monkey to make your calls to London for you."

"Don't."

"You set my kid up, didn't you?"

"No, I—"

The knife pricked his flesh.

"Yes."

"What for?"

"Afraid she'd talk."

"About what?"

He hesitated. Then he felt a trickle of blood running down his neck.

"Things we did."

Was there anyone who wasn't tapping that kid? Graham thought.

"That was worth Neal getting killed?"

"I didn't think they'd kill him."

"Allie going down the tubes?"

"She was there already."

"You're scum, you know that?"

Lombardi was trembling so hard, Graham was afraid he'd cut him accidentally.

"Put both hands on the wheel. Lean forward. Close your eyes." Lombardi started to cry as he did what he was told. Graham slipped out the passenger door and came around to the driver's window.

"Take a message to your boss. From Kitteredge. From me. When this term is up, he packs it in. He quits. He also doesn't fight this divorce. Tell him. And then you resign. You got that, hotshot? We see you anywhere near a politician again, you're on a waiting list for one of those monkeys."

He stepped away from the Porsche and into the waiting car. "You still want a piece of him?" he asked Levine.

Ed shook his head in disgust. "Not worth it."

"Right."

"I can't believe Neal didn't trust me," Ed said as they were driving away. "Pisses me off."

"Neal doesn't trust a lot of people."

"You gonna call him? Tell him he can come home?"

"No. Let's leave him be for a while."

Levine pulled the car out onto the street.

I'll miss the little bastard, though, Graham thought.

JUST NEAL

The ringing startled Neal.

He set the *Pickle* down with a tinge of annoyance. He stepped outside and saw the postman walking his bicycle up the road, ringing the bell on the handlebars.

"I'd have come to the village, Bill. You didn't have to come all the way up."

Hadley handed him a big pile of mail wrapped in string. "From the States, looked important."

"Well, thanks for the trouble."

"No trouble."

"Can I offer you a cup of tea? Kettle's on. Take the chill out . . ."

"Wish I could, but I haven't the time. Next week."

"Well, ta, Bill."

"Ta, Neal."

He watched the postman peddle down the track and then he checked out the sky. It might snow before nightfall. Hardin would be bringing the sheep in early. He'd stop in for tea.

He went back into the cottage and looked at the mail. A postcard from Graham; another letter from Allie, who was getting out in a week and going to a halfway house. A journal on eighteenth-century lit. A letter from a don at Oxford extending permission to use the archives. *Sports Illustrated*. Ten of them, and bless you, Graham. An envelope with Diane's return address on it.

I told you not to do that, Graham, but thanks.

He set the letter down unopened and went back to his book. Maybe he'd open it later, when he had a scotch or two to help him. Maybe not.

He was lonely, but he was used to that. He had his books to read.